PRAISE FOR THE NOVELS OF
#1 *NEW YORK TIMES* BESTSELLING AUTHOR
NICHOLAS SPARKS

Two by Two

"Sparks invites readers to take a journey that stares risks and rewards directly in the face. Whether it's tenderness between a husband and wife or affection between a father and his daughter, Sparks has definitely mastered the art of love." —*The Washington Times*

"Nicholas Sparks creates magic once again with [this] latest emotionally powerful novel."

—*RT Book Reviews*

See Me

"Sparks takes readers on a roller-coaster ride of emotion, from the soft tone of a love story to the adrenaline rush of a thriller." —Associated Press

"*See Me* is not only a tender, engaging, and heartwarming story, but it displays the meshing of two different and opposite lives that come together to prove that love conquers all. Gripping and riveting suspense adds another layer of depth and interest." —*New York Journal of Books*

"Powerful proof that Nicholas Sparks is a masterful storyteller who remains at the top of his game."

—BookReporter.com

"This deeply emotional book once again proves that Sparks understands human nature and relationships as well as anyone writing today."

—BarnesandNoble.com

The Longest Ride

"Sparks is a poet...a master."

—*Philadelphia Inquirer*

"*The Longest Ride* is epic Sparks...[It] showcases the author's most accomplished work to date...There are moments of perfection...Reaching not only young and old, the novel is commingled with enough cowboy action, literary flavor, and a maturing gift for dialogue to reach across the sexes." —*Mountain Times* (NC)

The Best of Me

"A creative genius...his book is great for any love story enthusiast." —HubPages.com

"Unforgettable...Makes you settle in for another romantic date with this well-respected and talented storyteller."

—*Fredericksburg Free Lance-Star* (VA)

"I could not put it down...a classic Nicholas Sparks tragedy but with a twist of hope...If I can pick my favorites from him, *The Best of Me* will rank with *Message in a Bottle* and *The Notebook*—it was *that* good."

—BookReporter.com

Safe Haven

"A compelling love story...a gripping tale of love and survival...a riveting 'read all night' page-turner."

—BookReporter.com

"Sparks has written another wonderful love story that makes you see true love in its simplest form and believe in it...a fantastic book about relationships, love, trust, and friendships."

—BestsellersWorld.com

The Last Song

"Romance, betrayal, and youthful discovery...Fans of *The Notebook*, *Message in a Bottle*, etc., will gobble it up."

—*Entertainment Weekly*

"A very enjoyable read...a plot that allows his characters to learn and grow from their experiences...Sparks is at his best."

—*Greensboro News-Record* (NC)

"Raw emotion, young love, family angst, and—ultimately—sweet resolution."

—*BookPage*

The Lucky One

"A tale of redemption...holds readers in suspense until the final chapter...it will test readers' beliefs in the power of destiny and fate, and how they relate to choices one makes in life."

—*Chattanooga Times Free Press*

"In true Nicholas Sparks fashion, the reader is engaged from the first to last page. The characters are authentic and the plot is engrossing and emotionally charged."

—*BookLoons.com*

The Choice

"A tender and moving love story."

—*Publishers Weekly*

"A heartrending love story...will have you entranced. And if *The Notebook* left you teary-eyed, his latest will have the same effect."

—*Myrtle Beach Sun News*

Dear John

"Beautifully moving...Has tremendous emotional depth, revealing the true meaning of unconditional love."

—*RT Book Reviews*

"For Sparks, weighty matters of the day remain set pieces, furniture upon which to hang timeless tales of chaste longing and harsh fate."

—*Washington Post Book World*

"Sparks lives up to his reputation...a tribute to courageous and self-sacrificing soldiers."

—*Booklist*

At First Sight

"An ending that surprises."
—*New York Times Book Review*

"Nicholas Sparks is one of the best-known writers in America and overseas for good reason: He has written stories that reveal the yearning for our most prized possession: love."   —*Mobile Register* (AL)

True Believer

"Time for a date with Sparks...The slow dance to the couple's first kiss is a two-chapter guilty pleasure."
—*People*

"Another winner...a page-turner...has all the things we have come to expect from him: sweet romance and a strong sense of place."   —*Charlotte Observer*

The Wedding

"Sweet but packs a punch...There is a twist that pulls everything together and makes you glad you read this."
—*Charlotte Observer*

"Sparks tells his sweet story...[with] a gasp-inducing twist at the very end. Satisfied female readers will close the covers with a sigh."   —*Publishers Weekly*

The Guardian

"An involving love story...an edge-of-your-seat, unpredictable thriller."   *—Booklist*

"Nicholas Sparks is a top-notch writer. He has created a truly spine-tingling thriller exploring love and obsession with a kind of suspense never before experienced in his novels."   —RedBank.com

Nights in Rodanthe

"Bittersweet...romance blooms...You'll cry in spite of yourself."   *—People*

"Passionate and memorable...smooth, sensitive writing... This is a novel that can hold its own."
                                                —Associated Press

"Extremely hard to put down...a love story, and a good love story at that."   *—Boston Herald*

A Bend in the Road

"Sweet, accessible, uplifting."
                                          —Publishers Weekly

"A powerful tale of true love."

                                                —Booklist

"Deeply moving, beautifully written, and extremely romantic."

The Notebook

"Nicholas Sparks...will not let you go. His novel shines."

"Proves that good things come in small packages...a classic tale of love."

"The lyrical beauty of this touching love story...will captivate the heart of every reader and establish Nicholas Sparks as a gifted novelist."

Safe Haven

ALSO BY NICHOLAS SPARKS

Two by Two

See Me

The Longest Ride

The Best of Me

Safe Haven

The Last Song

The Lucky One

The Choice

Dear John

At First Sight

True Believer

Three Weeks with My Brother

The Wedding

The Guardian

Nights in Rodanthe

A Bend in the Road

The Rescue

A Walk to Remember

Message in a Bottle

The Notebook

NICHOLAS SPARKS

Safe Haven

GRAND CENTRAL
PUBLISHING

NEW YORK   BOSTON

Copyright © 2010 by Nicholas Sparks
Reading Group Guide Copyright © 2011 by Hachette Book Group
Excerpt from *Two by Two* copyright © 2016 by Nicholas Sparks

Grand Central Publishing
Hachette Book Group
1290 Avenue of the Americas, New York, NY 10104
grandcentralpublishing.com
twitter.com/grandcentralpub

Originally published in hardcover by Grand Central Publishing in September 2010
First mass market edition: June 2012
Reissued: December 2012, December 2017

Grand Central Publishing is a division of Hachette Book Group, Inc. The Grand Central Publishing name and logo is a trademark of Hachette Book Group, Inc.

The publisher is not responsible for websites (or their content) that are not owned by the publisher.

The Hachette Speakers Bureau provides a wide range of authors for speaking events. To find out more, go to hachettespeakersbureau.com or call (866) 376-6591.

ISBNs: 978-1-4789-4837-7 (mass market reissue), 978-1-4789-4836-0 (trade paperback reissue), 978-0-446-57424-2 (ebook)

Printed in the United States of America

OPM

10 9 8 7 6 5 4 3 2

In loving memory of
Paul and Adrienne Cote.

My wonderful family.
I miss you both already.

Safe Haven

Acknowledgments

———— 🌿 ————

At the completion of every novel, I always find myself reflecting on those people who've helped me along the way. As always, the list begins with my wife, Cathy, who not only has to put up with the creative moodiness that sometimes plagues me as a writer, but has lived through a very challenging year, one in which she lost both her parents. I love you and wish there were something I could have done to lessen the loss you feel. My heart is with you.

I'd also like to thank my children—Miles, Ryan, Landon, Lexie, and Savannah. Miles is off in college, my youngest are in the third grade, and watching all of them grow is always a source of joy.

My agent, Theresa Park, always deserves my thanks for all she does to help me write the best novel I possibly can. I'm lucky to work with you.

Ditto for Jamie Raab, my editor. She's taught me much about writing, and I'm thankful for her presence in my life.

Denise DiNovi, my Hollywood friend and producer of a number of my films, has been a source of joy and friendship over the years. Thank you for all you've done for me.

David Young, the CEO of Hachette Book Group, is both smart and terrific. Thanks for tolerating the fact that I'm endlessly late on delivering my manuscripts.

Howie Sanders and Keya Khayatian, my film agents, have worked with me for years, and I owe much of my success to their hard work.

Jennifer Romanello, my publicist at Grand Central Publishing, has worked with me on every novel I've written, and I consider myself lucky for all she does.

Edna Farley, my other publicist, is professional and diligent, and is fabulous at helping to make my tours run smoothly. Thank you.

Scott Schwimer, my entertainment attorney, is not only a friend, but also exceptional at negotiating the finer points of my contracts. I'm honored to work with you.

Abby Koons and Emily Sweet, a couple of cohorts at Park Literary Group, deserve my thanks for all they do with my foreign publishers, my website, and any contracts that come my way. You're the best.

Marty Bowen and Wyck Godfrey, who did a terrific job as the producers of *Dear John*, deserve my thanks for the work they did. I appreciate the care they showed the project.

Likewise Adam Shankman and Jennifer Gibgot, the producers of *The Last Song*, were terrific to work with. Thanks for all you did.

Courtenay Valenti, Ryan Kavanaugh, Tucker Tooley, Mark Johnson, Lynn Harris, and Lorenzo di Bonaventura all showed great passion for the films adapted from my novels, and I want to thank you all for everything you've done.

Thanks also to Sharon Krassney, Flag, and the team of copyeditors and proofreaders who had to work late evenings to get this novel ready to print.

Jeff Van Wie, my screenwriting partner on *The Last Song*, deserves my thanks for his passion and effort in crafting screenplays, along with his friendship.

1

---※---

As Katie wound her way among the tables, a breeze from the Atlantic rippled through her hair. Carrying three plates in her left hand and another in her right, she wore jeans and a T-shirt that read *Ivan's: Try Our Fish Just for the Halibut.* She brought the plates to four men wearing polo shirts; the one closest to her caught her eye and smiled. Though he tried to act as though he was just a friendly guy, she knew he was watching her as she walked away. Melody had mentioned the men had come from Wilmington and were scouting locations for a movie.

After retrieving a pitcher of sweet tea, she refilled their glasses before returning to the waitress station. She stole a glance at the view. It was late April, the temperature hovering just around perfect, and blue skies stretched to the horizon. Beyond her, the Intracoastal was calm despite the breeze and seemed to mirror the color of the sky. A dozen seagulls perched on the railing, waiting to dart beneath the tables if someone dropped a scrap of food.

Ivan Smith, the owner, hated them. He called them

rats-with-wings, and he'd already patrolled the railing twice wielding a wooden plunger, trying to scare them off. Melody had leaned toward Katie and confessed that she was more worried about where the plunger had been than she was about the seagulls. Katie said nothing.

She started another pot of sweet tea, wiping down the station. A moment later, she felt someone tap her on the shoulder. She turned to see Ivan's daughter, Eileen. A pretty, ponytailed nineteen-year-old, she was working part-time as the restaurant hostess.

"Katie—can you take another table?"

Katie scanned her tables, running the rhythm in her head. "Sure." She nodded.

Eileen walked down the stairs. From nearby tables Katie could hear snippets of conversations—people talking about friends or family, the weather or fishing. At a table in the corner, she saw two people close their menus. She hustled over and took the order, but didn't linger at the table trying to make small talk, like Melody did. She wasn't good at small talk, but she was efficient and polite and none of the customers seemed to mind.

She'd been working at the restaurant since early March. Ivan had hired her on a cold, sunny afternoon when the sky was the color of robins' eggs. When he'd said she could start work the following Monday, it took everything she had not to cry in front of him. She'd waited until she was walking home before breaking down. At the time, she was broke and hadn't eaten in two days.

She refilled waters and sweet teas and headed to the kitchen. Ricky, one of the cooks, winked at her as he always did. Two days ago he'd asked her out, but she'd told him that she didn't want to date anyone at the restaurant.

She had the feeling he would try again and hoped her instincts were wrong.

"I don't think it's going to slow down today," Ricky commented. He was blond and lanky, perhaps a year or two younger than her, and still lived with his parents. "Every time we think we're getting caught up, we get slammed again."

"It's a beautiful day."

"But why are people here? On a day like today, they should be at the beach or out fishing. Which is exactly what I'm doing when I finish up here."

"That sounds like a good idea."

"Can I drive you home later?"

He offered to drive her at least twice a week. "Thank you, no. I don't live that far."

"It's no problem," he persisted. "I'd be glad to do it."

"Walking's good for me."

She handed him her ticket and Ricky pinned it up on the wheel and then located one of her orders. She carried the order back to her section and dropped it off at a table.

Ivan's was a local institution, a restaurant that had been in business for almost thirty years. In the time she'd been working there, she'd come to recognize the regulars, and as she crossed the restaurant floor her eyes traveled over them to the people she hadn't seen before. Couples flirting, other couples ignoring each other. Families. No one seemed out of place and no one had come around asking for her, but there were still times when her hands began to shake, and even now she slept with a light on.

Her short hair was chestnut brown; she'd been dyeing it in the kitchen sink of the tiny cottage she rented. She wore no makeup and knew her face would pick up a bit of color, maybe too much. She reminded herself to buy sunscreen, but after paying rent and utilities on the cottage, there wasn't much left for luxuries. Even sunscreen was a stretch. Ivan's was a good job and she was glad to have it, but the food was inexpensive, which meant the tips weren't great. On her steady diet of rice and beans, pasta and oatmeal, she'd lost weight in the past four months. She could feel her ribs beneath her shirt, and until a few weeks ago, she'd had dark circles under her eyes that she thought would never go away.

"I think those guys are checking you out," Melody said, nodding toward the table with the four men from the movie studio. "Especially the brown-haired one. The cute one."

"Oh," Katie said. She started another pot of coffee. Anything she said to Melody was sure to get passed around, so Katie usually said very little to her.

"What? You don't think he's cute?"

"I didn't really notice."

"How can you not notice when a guy is cute?" Melody stared at her in disbelief.

"I don't know," Katie answered.

Like Ricky, Melody was a couple of years younger than Katie, maybe twenty-five or so. An auburn-haired, green-eyed minx, she dated a guy named Steve who made deliveries for the home improvement store on the other side of town. Like everyone else in the restaurant, she'd grown up in Southport, which she described as being a paradise for children, families, and the elderly, but the most dismal place on earth for single people. At least once a week, she told Katie that she was planning to move to Wilmington, which had bars and clubs and a lot more shopping. She seemed to know everything about everybody. Gossip, Katie sometimes thought, was Melody's real profession.

"I heard Ricky asked you out," she said, changing the subject, "but you said no."

"I don't like to date people at work." Katie pretended to be absorbed in organizing the silverware trays.

"We could double-date. Ricky and Steve go fishing together."

Katie wondered if Ricky had put her up to it or whether it was Melody's idea. Maybe both. In the evenings, after the restaurant closed, most of the staff stayed around for a while, visiting over a couple of beers. Aside from Katie, everyone had worked at Ivan's for years.

"I don't think that's a good idea," Katie demurred.

"Why not?"

"I had a bad experience once," Katie said. "Dating a guy from work, I mean. Since then, I've kind of made it a rule not to do it again."

Melody rolled her eyes before hurrying off to one of her tables. Katie dropped off two checks and cleared empty plates. She kept busy, as she always did, trying to be efficient and invisible. She kept her head down and made sure the waitress station was spotless. It made the day go by faster. She didn't flirt with the guy from the studio, and when he left he didn't look back.

Katie worked both the lunch and dinner shift. As day faded into night, she loved watching the sky turning from blue to gray to orange and yellow at the western rim of the world. At sunset, the water sparkled and sailboats heeled in the breeze. The needles on the pine trees seemed to shimmer. As soon as the sun dropped below the horizon, Ivan turned on the propane gas heaters and the coils began to glow like jack-o'-lanterns. Katie's face had gotten slightly sunburned, and the waves of radiant heat made her skin sting.

Abby and Big Dave replaced Melody and Ricky in the evening. Abby was a high school senior who giggled a lot, and Big Dave had been cooking dinners at Ivan's for nearly twenty years. He was married with two kids and had a tattoo of a scorpion on his right forearm. He weighed close to three hundred pounds and in the kitchen his face was always shiny. He had nicknames for everyone and called her Katie Kat.

The dinner rush lasted until nine. When it began to clear out, Katie cleaned and closed up the wait station. She helped the busboys carry plates to the dishwasher while her final tables finished up. At one of them was a young couple and she'd seen the rings on their fingers as they held hands across the table. They were attractive and happy, and she felt a sense of déjà vu. She had been like them once, a long time ago, for just a moment. Or so she thought, because she learned the moment was only an illusion. Katie turned away from the blissful couple, wishing that she could erase her memories forever and never have that feeling again.

2

───── ❦ ─────

The next morning, Katie stepped onto the porch with a cup of coffee, the floorboards creaking beneath her bare feet, and leaned against the railing. Lilies sprouted amid the wild grass in what once was a flower bed, and she raised the cup, savoring the aroma as she took a sip.

She liked it here. Southport was different from Boston or Philadelphia or Atlantic City, with their endless sounds of traffic and smells and people rushing along the sidewalks, and it was the first time in her life that she had a place to call her own. The cottage wasn't much, but it was hers and out of the way and that was enough. It was one of two identical structures located at the end of a gravel lane, former hunting cabins with wooden-plank walls, nestled against a grove of oak and pine trees at the edge of a forest that stretched to the coast. The living room and kitchen were small and the bedroom didn't have a closet, but the cottage was furnished, including rockers on the front porch, and the rent was a bargain. The place wasn't decaying, but it was dusty from years of neglect, and the landlord offered to buy the supplies if Katie was willing to spruce it up. Since she'd moved in, she'd spent much of her free time on all fours or standing on chairs, doing exactly that. She scrubbed the bathroom until it sparkled; she washed the ceiling with a damp cloth. She wiped the windows with vinegar and spent hours on her hands and knees, trying her best to remove the rust and grime from the linoleum in the kitchen. She'd filled holes in the walls with Spackle and then sanded the Spackle until it was smooth. She'd painted the walls in the kitchen a cheery yellow and put glossy white paint on the cabinets. Her bedroom was now a light blue, the living room was beige, and last week, she'd put a new slipcover on the couch, which made it look practically new again.

With most of the work now behind her, she liked to sit on the front porch in the afternoons and read books she'd checked out from the library. Aside from coffee, reading was her only indulgence. She didn't have a television, a radio, a cell phone, or a microwave or even a car, and she could pack all her belongings in a single bag. She was twenty-seven years old, a former long-haired blond with no real friends. She'd moved here with almost nothing, and months later she still had little. She saved half of her tips and every night she folded the money into a coffee can she kept hidden in the crawl space beneath the porch. She kept that money for emergencies and would rather go hungry than touch it. Simply the knowledge that it was there made her breathe easier because the past was always around her and might return at any time. It prowled the world searching for her, and she knew it was growing angrier at every passing day.

"Good morning," a voice called out, disrupting her thoughts. "You must be Katie."

Katie turned. On the sagging porch of the cottage next door, she saw a woman with long, unruly brown hair, waving at her. She looked to be in her mid-thirties and wore jeans and a button-up shirt she'd rolled to her elbows. A pair of sunglasses nested in tangled curls on her head. She was holding a small rug and she seemed to be debating whether or not to shake it before finally tossing it aside and starting toward Katie's. She moved with the energy and ease of someone who exercised regularly.

"Irv Benson told me we'd be neighbors."

The landlord, Katie thought. "I didn't realize anyone was moving in."

"I don't think he did, either. He about fell out of his chair when I said I'd take the place." By then, she'd reached Katie's porch and she held out her hand. "My friends call me Jo," she said.

"Hi," Katie said, taking it.

"Can you believe this weather? It's gorgeous, isn't it?"

"It's a beautiful morning," Katie agreed, shifting from one foot to the other. "When did you move in?"

"Yesterday afternoon. And then, joy of joys, I pretty much spent all night sneezing. I think Benson collected as much dust as he possibly could and stored it at my place. You wouldn't believe what it's like in there."

Katie nodded toward the door. "My place was the same way."

"It doesn't look like it. Sorry, I couldn't help sneaking a glance through your windows when I was standing in my kitchen. Your place is bright and cheery. I, on the other hand, have rented a dusty, spider-filled dungeon."

"Mr. Benson let me paint."

"I'll bet. As long as Mr. Benson doesn't have to do it,

I'll bet he lets me paint, too. He gets a nice, clean place, and I get to do the work." She gave a wry grin. "How long have you lived here?"

Katie crossed her arms, feeling the morning sun begin to warm her face. "Almost two months."

"I'm not sure I can make it that long. If I keep sneezing like I did last night, my head will probably fall off before then." She reached for her sunglasses and began wiping the lenses with her shirt. "How do you like Southport? It's a different world, don't you think?"

"What do you mean?"

"You don't sound like you're from around here. I'd guess somewhere up north?"

After a moment, Katie nodded.

"That's what I thought," Jo went on. "And Southport takes awhile to get used to. I mean, I've always loved it, but I'm partial to small towns."

"You're from here?"

"I grew up here, went away, and ended up coming back. The oldest story in the book, right? Besides, you can't find dusty places like this just anywhere."

Katie smiled, and for a moment neither said anything. Jo seemed content to stand in front of her, waiting for her to make the next move. Katie took a sip of coffee, gazing off into the woods, and then remembered her manners.

"Would you like a cup of coffee? I just brewed a pot."

Jo put the sunglasses back on her head, tucking them into her hair. "You know, I was hoping you'd say that. I'd *love* a cup of coffee. My entire kitchen is still in boxes and my car is in the shop. Do you have any idea what it's like to face the day without caffeine?"

"I have an idea."

"Well, just so you know, I'm a genuine coffee addict. Especially on any day that requires me to unpack. Did I mention I hate unpacking?"

"I don't think you did."

"It's pretty much the most miserable thing there is. Trying to figure out where to put everything, banging your knees as you bump around the clutter. Don't worry—I'm not the kind of neighbor who asks for that kind of help. But coffee, on the other hand . . ."

"Come on." Katie waved her in. "Just keep in mind that most of the furniture came with the place."

After crossing the kitchen, Katie pulled a cup from the cupboard and filled it to the brim. She handed it to Jo. "Sorry, I don't have any cream or sugar."

"Not necessary," Jo said, taking the cup. She blew on the coffee before taking a sip. "Okay, it's official," she said. "As of now, you're my best friend in the entire world. This is soooo good."

"You're welcome," she said.

"So Benson said you work at Ivan's?"

"I'm a waitress."

"Is Big Dave still working there?" When Katie nodded, Jo went on. "He's been there since before I was in high school. Does he still make up names for everyone?"

"Yes," she said.

"How about Melody? Is she still talking about how cute the customers are?"

"Every shift."

"And Ricky? Is he still hitting on new waitresses?"

When Katie nodded again, Jo laughed. "That place never changes."

"Did you work there?"

"No, but it's a small town and Ivan's is an institution. Besides, the longer you live here, the more you'll under-stand that there are no such things as secrets in this place. Everyone knows everyone's business, and some people, like, let's say...Melody...have raised gossip to an art form. It used to drive me crazy. Of course, half the people in Southport are the same way. There isn't much to do around here but gossip."

"But you came back."

Jo shrugged. "Yeah, well. What can I say? Maybe I like the crazy." She took another sip of her coffee and motioned out the window. "You know, as long as I'd lived here, I wasn't even aware these two places existed."

"The landlord said they were hunting cottages. They used to be part of the plantation before he turned them into rentals."

Jo shook her head. "I can't believe you moved out here."

"You did, too," Katie pointed out.

"Yes, but the only reason I considered it was because I knew I wouldn't be the only woman at the end of a gravel road in the middle of nowhere. It's kind of isolated."

Which is why I was more than happy to rent it, Katie thought to herself. "It's not so bad. I'm used to it by now."

"I hope I get used to it," she said. She blew on the cof-fee, cooling it off. "So what brought you to Southport? I'm sure it wasn't the exciting career potential at Ivan's. Do you have any family around here? Parents? Brothers or sisters?"

"No," Katie said. "Just me."

"Following a boyfriend?"

"No."

"So you just...moved here?"

"Yes."

"Why on earth would you do that?"

Katie didn't answer. They were the same questions that Ivan and Melody and Ricky had asked. She knew there were no ulterior motives behind the questions, it was just natural curiosity, but even so, she was never quite sure what to say, other than to state the truth.

"I just wanted a place where I could start over."

Jo took another sip of coffee, seemingly mulling over her answer, but surprising Katie, she asked no follow-up questions. Instead, she simply nodded.

"Makes sense to me. Sometimes starting over is exactly what a person needs. And I think it's admirable. A lot of people don't have the courage it takes to do something like that."

"You think so?"

"I know so," she said. "So, what's on your agenda today? While I'm whining and unpacking and cleaning until my hands are raw."

"I have to work later. But other than that, not much. I need to run to the store and pick up some things."

"Are you going to visit Fisher's or head into town?"

"I'm just going to Fisher's," she said.

"Have you met the owner there? The guy with gray hair?"

Katie nodded. "Once or twice."

Jo finished her coffee and put the cup in the sink before sighing. "All right," she said, sounding less than enthusiastic. "Enough procrastinating. If I don't start now, I'm never going to finish. Wish me luck."

"Good luck."

Jo gave a little wave. "It was nice meeting you, Katie."

*   *   *

From her kitchen window, Katie saw Jo shaking the rug she'd set aside earlier. She seemed friendly enough, but Katie wasn't sure whether she was ready to have a neighbor. Although it might be nice to have someone to visit with now and then, she'd gotten used to being alone.

Then again, she knew that living in a small town meant that her self-imposed isolation couldn't last forever. She had to work and shop and walk around town; some of the customers at the restaurant already recognized her. And besides, she had to admit she'd enjoyed chatting with Jo. For some reason, she felt that there was more to Jo than met the eye, something . . . trustworthy, even if she couldn't explain it. She was also a single woman, which was a definite plus. Katie didn't want to imagine how she would have reacted had a man moved in next door, and she wondered why she'd never even considered the possibility.

Over by the sink, she washed out the coffee cups then put them back into the cupboard. The act was so familiar—putting two cups away after coffee in the morning—and for an instant, she felt engulfed by the life she'd left behind. Her hands began to tremble, and pressing them together she took a few deep breaths until they finally stilled. Two months ago, she wouldn't have been able to do that; even two weeks ago, there had been little she could do to stop it. While she was glad that these bouts of anxiety no longer overwhelmed her, it also meant she was getting comfortable here, and that scared her. Because being comfortable meant she might lower her guard, and she could never let that happen.

Even so, she was grateful to have ended up in Southport. It was a small historic town of a few thousand people,

located at the mouth of the Cape Fear River, right where
it met the Intracoastal. It was a place with sidewalks and
shade trees and flowers that bloomed in the sandy soil.
Spanish moss hung from the tree branches, while kudzu
climbed the wizened trunks. She had watched kids riding their bikes and playing kick ball in the streets, and
had marveled at the number of churches, one on nearly
every corner. Crickets and frogs sounded in the evening,
and she thought again that this place had felt right, even
from the beginning. It felt *safe*, as if it had somehow been
beckoning to her all along, promising sanctuary.

Katie slipped on her only pair of shoes, a pair of
beat-up Converse sneakers. The chest of drawers stood
largely empty and there was almost no food in the kitchen,
but as she stepped out of the house and into the sunshine
and headed toward the store, she thought to herself, *This
is home*. Drawing in a deeply scented breath of hyacinth
and fresh-cut grass, she knew she hadn't been happier in
years.

3

His hair had turned gray when he was in his early twenties, prompting some good-natured ribbing from his friends. It hadn't been a slow change, either, a few hairs here and there gradually turning to silver. Rather, in January he'd had a head of black hair and by the following January, there was scarcely a single black hair left. His two older brothers had been spared, though in the last couple of years, they'd picked up some silver in their sideburns. Neither his mom nor his dad could explain it; as far as they knew, Alex Wheatley was an anomaly on both sides of the family.

Strangely, it hadn't bothered him. In the army, he sometimes suspected that it had aided in his advancement. He'd been with Criminal Investigation Division, or CID, stationed in Germany and Georgia, and had spent ten years investigating military crimes, everything from soldiers going AWOL, to burglary, domestic abuse, rape, and even murder. He'd been promoted regularly, finally retiring as a major at thirty-two.

After punching his ticket and ending his career with the military, he moved to Southport, his wife's hometown. He was newly married with his first child on the way, and though his immediate thought was that he would apply for a job in law enforcement, his father-in-law had offered to sell him the family business.

It was an old-fashioned country store, with white clapboard siding, blue shutters, a sloped porch roof, and a bench out front, the kind of store that enjoyed its heyday long ago and had mostly disappeared. The living quarters were on the second floor. A massive magnolia tree shaded one side of the building, and an oak tree stood out front. Only half of the parking lot was asphalt—the other half was gravel—but the lot was seldom empty. His father-in-law had started the business before Carly was born, when there wasn't much more than farmland surrounding him. But his father-in-law prided himself on understanding people, and he wanted to stock whatever they happened to need, all of which lent a cluttered organization to the place. Alex felt the same way and kept the store largely the same. Five or six aisles offered groceries and toiletries, refrigerator cases in the back overflowed with everything from soda and water to beer and wine, and as in every other convenience store, this one had racks of chips, candy, and the kind of junk food that people grabbed as they stood near the cash register. But that's where the similarity ended. There was also assorted fishing gear along the shelves, fresh bait, and a grill manned by Roger Thompson, who'd once worked on Wall Street and had moved to Southport in search of a simpler life. The grill offered burgers, sandwiches, and hot dogs as well as a place to sit. There were DVDs for rent, various kinds of ammunition, rain jackets and umbrellas, and a small offering of bestselling and classic novels. The store sold spark plugs, fan belts, and gas cans, and Alex was able to make duplicates of keys with a machine in the back room. He had three gasoline pumps, and another pump on the dock for any boats that needed to fill up, the only place to do so aside from the marina. Rows of dill pickles, boiled peanuts, and baskets of fresh vegetables sat near the counter.

Surprisingly, it wasn't hard to keep up with the inventory. Some items moved regularly, others didn't. Like his father-in-law, Alex had a pretty good sense of what people needed as soon as they walked in the store. He'd always noticed and remembered things that other people didn't, a trait that had helped him immeasurably in his years working CID. Nowadays he was endlessly tinkering with the items he stocked, in an attempt to keep up with the changing tastes of his customers.

Never in his life had he imagined doing something like this, but it had been a good decision, if only because it allowed him to keep an eye on the kids. Josh was in school, but Kristen wouldn't start until the fall, and she spent her days with him in the store. He'd set up a play area behind the register, where his bright and talkative daughter seemed most happy. Though only five, she knew how to work the register and make change, using a step stool to reach the buttons. Alex always enjoyed the expressions on strangers' faces when she started to ring them up.

Still, it wasn't an ideal childhood for her, even if she didn't know anything different. When he was honest with himself, he had to admit that taking care of kids and the store took all the energy he had. Sometimes, he felt as though he could barely keep up—making Josh's lunch and dropping him off at school, ordering from his suppliers, meeting with vendors, and serving the customers, all while keeping Kristen entertained. And that was just for starters. The evenings, he sometimes thought, were even busier. He tried his best to spend time doing kid things with them—going on bike rides, flying kites, and fishing with Josh, but Kristen liked to play with dolls and do arts and crafts, and he'd never been good at those things. Add in making dinner and cleaning the house, and half the time, it was all he could do to keep his head above water. Even when he finally got the kids in bed, he found it nearly impossible to relax because there was always something else to do. He wasn't sure if he even knew how to relax anymore.

After the kids went to bed, he spent the rest of his evenings alone. Though he seemed to know most everyone in town, he had few real friends. The couples that he and Carly sometimes visited for barbecues or dinners had slowly but surely drifted away. Part of that was his own fault—working at the store and raising his kids took most of his time—but sometimes he got the sense that he made them uncomfortable, as if reminding them that life was unpredictable and scary and that things could go bad in an instant.

It was a wearying and sometimes isolating lifestyle, but he remained focused on Josh and Kristen. Though less frequent than it once had been, both of them had been prone to nightmares with Carly gone. When they woke in the middle of the night, sobbing inconsolably, he would hold them in his arms and whisper that everything was going to be all right, until they were finally able to fall back asleep. Early on, all of them had seen a counselor; the kids had drawn pictures and talked about their feelings. It hadn't seemed to help as much as he'd hoped it would. Their nightmares continued for almost a year. Once in a while, when he colored with Kristen or fished with Josh, they'd grow quiet and he knew they were missing their mom. Kristen sometimes said as much in a babyish, trembling voice, while tears ran down her cheeks. When that happened, he was sure he could hear his heart breaking, because he knew there was nothing he could do or say to make things any better. The counselor had assured him that kids were resilient and that as long as they knew they were loved, the nightmares would eventually stop and the tears would become less frequent. Time proved the counselor right, but now Alex faced another form of loss, one that left him equally heartbroken. The kids were getting better, he knew, because their memories of their mom were slowly but surely fading away. They'd been so young when they'd lost her—four and three—and it meant that the day would come when their mother would become more an idea than a person to them. It was inevitable, of course, but somehow it didn't seem right to Alex that they would never remember the sound of Carly's laughter, or the tender way she'd held them as infants, or know how deeply she'd once loved them.

He'd never been much of a photographer. Carly had always been the one who reached for the camera, and consequently, there were dozens of photographs of him with the kids. There were only a few that included Carly, and though he made it a point to page through the album with Josh and Kristen while he told them about their mother, he suspected that the stories were becoming just that: stories.

The emotions attached to them were like sand castles in the tide, slowly washing out to sea. The same thing was happening with the portrait of Carly that hung in his bedroom. In their first year of marriage, he'd arranged to have her portrait taken, despite her protests. He was glad for that. In the photo, she looked beautiful and independent, the strong-willed woman who'd captured his heart, and at night, after the kids were in bed, he would sometimes stare at his wife's image, his emotions in turmoil. But Josh and Kristen barely noticed the photo at all.

He thought of her often, and he missed the companionship they'd once shared and the friendship that had been the bedrock of their marriage at its best. And when he was honest with himself, he knew he wanted those things again. He was lonely, even though it bothered him to admit it. For months after they lost her, he simply couldn't imagine ever being in another relationship, let alone consider the possibility of loving someone again. Even after a year, it was the kind of thought he would force from his mind. The pain was too fresh, the memory of the aftermath too raw. But a few months ago, he'd taken the kids to the aquarium and as they'd stood in front of the shark tank, he'd struck up a conversation with an attractive woman standing next to him. Like him, she'd brought her kids, and like him, she wore no ring on her finger. Her children were the same ages as Josh and Kristen, and while the four of them were off pointing at the fish, she'd laughed at something he'd said and he'd felt a spark of attraction, reminding him of what he had once had. The conversation eventually came to an end and they went their separate ways, but on the way out, he'd seen her once more. She'd waved at him and there'd been an instant when he

contemplated jogging over to her car and asking for her
phone number. But he didn't, and a moment later, she was
pulling out of the parking lot. He never saw her again.

That night, he waited for the wave of self-reproach
and regret to come, but strangely, it didn't. Nor did it feel
wrong. Instead, it felt... okay. Not affirming, not exhila-
rating, but okay, and he somehow knew it meant he was
finally beginning to heal. That didn't mean, of course,
that he was ready to rush headlong into the single life.
If it happened, it happened. And if it didn't? He figured
he'd cross that bridge when he came to it. He was willing
to wait until he met the right person, someone who not
only brought joy back into his life, but who loved his kids
as much as he did. He recognized, however, that in this
town, the odds of finding that person were tiny. Southport was too small. Nearly everyone he knew was either
married or retired or attending one of the local schools.
There weren't a lot of single women around, let alone
women who wanted a package deal, kids included. And
that, of course, was the deal breaker. He might be lonely,
he might want companionship, but he wasn't about to sacrifice his kids to get it. They'd been through enough and
would always be his first priority.

Still... there was one possibility, he supposed. Another
woman interested him, though he knew almost nothing
about her, aside from the fact that she was single. She'd
been coming to the store once or twice a week since early
March. The first time he'd seen her, she was pale and
gaunt, almost desperately thin. Ordinarily, he wouldn't
have given her a second glance. People passing through
town often stopped at the store for sodas or gasoline or
junk food; he seldom saw such people again. But she

wanted none of those things; instead, she kept her head down as she walked toward the grocery aisles, as if trying to remain unseen, a ghost in human form. Unfortunately for her, it wasn't working. She was too attractive to go unnoticed. She was in her late twenties, he guessed, with brown hair cut a little unevenly above her shoulder. She wore no makeup and her high cheekbones and round, wide-set eyes gave her an elegant if slightly fragile appearance.

At the register, he realized that up close she was even prettier than she'd been from a distance. Her eyes were a greenish-hazel color and flecked with gold, and her brief, distracted smile vanished as quickly as it had come. On the counter, she placed nothing but staples: coffee, rice, oatmeal, pasta, peanut butter, and toiletries. He sensed that conversation would make her uncomfortable so he began to ring her up in silence. As he did, he heard her voice for the first time.

"Do you have any dry beans?" she asked.

"I'm sorry," he'd answered. "I don't normally keep those in stock."

As he bagged her items after his answer, he noticed her staring out the window, absently chewing her lower lip. For some reason, he had the strange impression that she was about to cry.

He cleared his throat. "If it's something you're going to need regularly, I'd be happy to stock them. I just need to know what kind you want."

"I don't want to bother you." When she answered, her voice barely registered above a whisper.

She paid him in small bills, and after taking the bag, she left the store. Surprising him, she kept walking out of the lot, and it was only then he realized she hadn't driven, which only added to his curiosity.

The following week, there were dry beans in the store. He'd stocked three types: pinto, kidney, and lima, though only a single bag of each, and the next time she came in, he made a point of mentioning that they could be found on the bottom shelf in the corner, near the rice. Bringing all three bags to the register, she'd asked him if he happened to have an onion. He pointed to a small bag he kept in a bushel basket near the door, but she'd shaken her head. "I only need one," she murmured, her smile hesitant and apologetic. Her hands shook as she counted out her bills, and again, she left on foot.

Since then, the beans were always in stock, there was a single onion available, and in the weeks that followed her first two visits to the store, she'd become something of a regular. Though still quiet, she seemed less fragile, less nervous, as time had gone on. The dark circles under her eyes were gradually fading, and she'd picked up some color during the recent spate of good weather. She'd put on some weight—not much, but enough to soften her delicate features. Her voice was stronger, too, and though it didn't signal any interest in him, she could hold his gaze a little longer before finally turning away. They hadn't proceeded much beyond the *Did you find everything you needed?* followed by the *Yes, I did. Thank you* type of conversation, but instead of fleeing the store like a hunted deer, she sometimes wandered the aisles a bit, and had even begun to talk to Kristen when the two of them were alone. It was the first time he'd seen the woman's defenses drop. Her easy demeanor and open expression spoke of an affection for children, and his first thought was that he'd glimpsed the woman she once had been and could be again, given the right circumstances. Kristen, too, seemed to notice something different about the woman, because after she left, Kristen had told him that she'd made a new friend and that her name was Miss Katie.

That didn't mean, however, that Katie was comfortable with him. Last week, after she'd chatted easily with Kristen, he'd seen her reading the back covers of the novels he kept in stock. She didn't buy any of the titles, and when he offhandedly asked as she was checking out if she had a favorite author, he'd seen a flash of the old nervousness. He was struck by the notion that he shouldn't have let slip that he'd been watching her. "Never mind," he added quickly. "It's not important." On her way out the door, however, she'd paused for a moment, her bag tucked in the crook of her arm. She half-turned in his direction and mumbled, *I like Dickens.* With that, she opened the door and was gone, walking up the road.

He'd thought about her with greater frequency since then, but they were vague thoughts, edged with mystery and colored by the knowledge that he wanted to get to know her better. Not that he knew how to go about it. Aside from the year he courted Carly, he'd never been good at dating. In college, between swimming and his classes, he had little time to go out. In the military, he'd thrown himself into his career, working long hours and transferring from post to post with every promotion. While he'd gone out with a few women, they were fleeting romances that for the most part began and ended in the bedroom. Sometimes, when thinking back on his life, he barely recognized the man he used to be, and Carly, he knew, was responsible for those changes. Yes, it was sometimes hard, and yes, he was lonely. He missed his wife, and though he never told anyone, there were still moments when he could swear he felt her presence nearby, watching over him, trying to make sure he was going to be all right.

Because of the glorious weather, the store was busier than usual for a Sunday. By the time Alex unlocked the door at seven, there were already three boats tied at the dock waiting for the pump to be turned on. As was typical, while paying for the gas, the boat owners loaded up on snacks and drinks and bags of ice to stow in their boats. Roger—who was working the grill, as always—hadn't had a break since he'd put on his apron, and the tables were crowded with people eating sausage biscuits and cheeseburgers and asking for tips about the stock market.

Usually, Alex worked the register until noon, when he would hand over the reins to Joyce, who, like Roger, was the kind of employee who made running the store much less challenging than it could be. Joyce, who'd worked in the courthouse until her retirement, had "come with the business," so to speak. His father-in-law had hired her ten years ago and now, in her seventies, she hadn't showed any signs of slowing down. Her husband had died years earlier, her kids had moved away, and she viewed the customers as her de facto family. Joyce was as intrinsic to the store as the items on the shelves.

Even better, she understood that Alex needed to spend time with his children away from the store, and she didn't get bent out of shape by having to work on Sundays. As soon as she showed up, she'd slip behind the register and tell Alex he could go, sounding more like the boss than an employee. Joyce was also his babysitter, the only one he trusted to stay with the kids if he had to go out of town. That wasn't common—it had happened only twice in the past couple of years when he'd met up with an old army buddy in Raleigh—but he'd come to view Joyce as one of the best things in his life. When he'd needed her most, she'd always been there for him.

Waiting for Joyce's arrival, Alex walked through the store, checking the shelves. The computer system was great at tracking inventory, but he knew that rows of numbers didn't always tell the whole story. Sometimes, he felt he got a better sense by actually scanning the shelves to see what had sold the day before. A successful store required turning over the inventory as frequently as possible, and that meant that he sometimes had to offer items that no other stores offered. He carried homemade jams and jellies; powdered rubs from "secret recipes" that flavored beef and pork; and a selection of locally canned fruits and vegetables. Even people who regularly shopped at the Food Lion or Piggly Wiggly often dropped by on their way home from the store to pick up the local specialty items Alex made a point of stocking.

Even more important than an item's sales volume, he liked to know *when* it sold, a fact that didn't necessarily show up in the numbers. He'd learned, for instance, that hot dog buns sold especially well on the weekends but only rarely during the week; regular loaves of bread were just the opposite. Noting that, he'd been able to keep more of both in stock when they were needed, and sales rose. It wasn't much but it added up and enabled Alex to keep his small business afloat when the chain stores were putting most local shops out of business.

As he perused the shelves, he wondered idly what he

was going to do with the kids in the afternoon and decided to take them for a bike ride. Carly had loved nothing more than strapping them into the bike stroller and hauling them all over town. But a bike ride wasn't enough to fill the entire afternoon. Maybe they could ride their bikes to the park...they might enjoy that.

With a quick peek toward the front door to make sure no one was coming in, he hurried through the rear storeroom and poked his head out. Josh was fishing off the dock, which was far and away his favorite thing to do. Alex didn't like the fact that Josh was out there alone—he had no doubt that some people would regard him as a bad father for allowing it—but Josh always stayed within visual range of the video monitor behind the register. It was a rule, and Josh had always adhered to it. Kristen, as usual, was sitting at her table in the corner behind the register. She'd separated her American Girl doll clothing into different piles, and she seemed content to change her doll from one outfit to the next. Each time she finished, she would look up at him with a bright, innocent expression and ask her daddy how he thought her doll looked now, as if it were possible he would ever say he didn't like it.

Little girls. They could melt the toughest hearts.

Alex was straightening some of the condiments when he heard the bell on the front door jingle. Raising his head over the aisle, he saw Katie enter the store.

"Hi, Miss Katie," Kristen called out, popping up from behind the register. "How do you think my doll looks?"

From where he was standing, he could barely see Kristen's head above the counter, but she was holding... Vanessa? Rebecca? Whatever the doll with brown hair was called, high enough for Katie to notice.

"She's beautiful, Kristen," Katie answered. "Is that a new dress?"

"No, I've had it for a while. But she hasn't worn it lately."

"What's her name?"

"Vanessa," she said.

Vanessa, Alex thought. When he complimented Vanessa later, he would sound like a much more attentive father.

"Did you name her?"

"No, she came with the name. Can you help me get her boots on, though? I can't get them on all the way."

Alex watched as Kristen handed Katie the doll and she began to work on the soft plastic boots. From his own experience, Alex knew it was harder than it looked. There wasn't a chance a little girl could somehow muscle them on. He had trouble putting them on, but somehow Katie made it seem easy. She handed the doll back and asked, "How's that?"

"Perfect," Kristen said. "Do you think I should put a coat on her?"

"It's not that cold out."

"I know. But Vanessa gets cold sometimes. I think she needs one." Kristen's head vanished behind the counter and then popped up again. "Which one do you think? Blue or purple?"

Katie brought a finger to her mouth, her expression serious. "I think purple might be good."

Kristen nodded. "That's what I think, too. Thanks."

Katie smiled before turning away, and Alex focused his attention on the shelves before she caught him staring. He moved jars of mustard and relish toward the front of the shelf. From the corner of his eye, he saw Katie scoop up a small shopping basket before moving toward a different aisle.

Alex headed back to the register. When she saw him, he offered a friendly wave. "Good morning," he said.

"Hi." She tried to tuck a strand of hair behind her ear, but it was too short to catch. "I just have to pick up a few things."

"Let me know if you can't find what you need. Sometimes things get moved around."

She nodded before continuing down the aisle. As Alex stepped behind the register, he glanced at the video screen. Josh was fishing in the same spot, while a boat was slowly docking.

"What do you think, Daddy?" Kristen tugged on his pant leg as she held up the doll.

"Wow! She looks beautiful." Alex squatted down next to her. "And I love the coat. Vanessa gets cold sometimes, right?"

"Yup," Kristen said. "But she told me she wants to go on the swings, so she's probably going to change."

"Sounds like a good idea," Alex said. "Maybe we can all go to the park later? If you want to swing, too."

"I don't want to swing. Vanessa does. And it's all pretend, anyway, Daddy."

"Oh," he said, "okay." He stood again. *Scratch going to the park*, he thought.

Lost in her own world, Kristen began to undress the doll again. Alex checked on Josh in the monitor just as a teenager entered the store, wearing nothing but board shorts. He handed over a wad of cash.

"For the pump at the dock," he said before dashing out again.

Alex rang him up and set the pump as Katie walked to the register. Same items as always, with the addition of a tube of sunscreen. When she peeked over the counter at Kristen, Alex noticed the changeable color of her eyes.

"Did you find everything you needed?"

"Yes, thank you."

He began loading her bag. "My favorite Dickens novel is *Great Expectations*," he said. He tried to sound friendly as he put the items in her bag. "Which one is your favorite?"

Instead of answering right away, she seemed startled that he remembered that she'd told him she liked Dickens.

"*A Tale of Two Cities*," she answered, her voice soft.

"I like that one, too. But it's sad."

"Yes," she said. "That's why I like it."

Since he knew she'd be walking, he double-bagged the groceries.

"I figured that since you've already met my daughter, I should probably introduce myself. I'm Alex," he said. "Alex Wheatley."

"Her name is Miss Katie," Kristen chirped from behind him. "But I already told you that, remember?" Alex glanced over his shoulder at her. When he turned back, Katie was smiling as she handed the money to him.

"Just Katie," she said.

"It's nice to meet you, Katie." He tapped the keys and the register drawer opened with a ring. "I take it you live around here?"

She never got around to answering. Instead, when he looked up, he saw that her eyes had gone wide in fright. Swiveling around he saw what she'd caught on the monitor behind him: Josh in the water, fully clothed and arms flailing, in panic. Alex felt his throat suddenly close and he moved on instinct, rushing out from behind the counter and racing through the store and into the storeroom. Bursting through the door, he knocked over a case of paper towels, sending it flying, but he didn't slow down.

He flung open the back door, adrenaline surging through his system as he hurdled a row of bushes, taking a shortcut to the dock. He hit the wooden planks at full speed. As he launched himself from the dock, Alex could see Josh choking in the water, his arms thrashing.

His heart slamming against his rib cage, Alex sailed through the air, hitting the water only a couple of feet from Josh. The water wasn't deep—maybe six feet or so—and as he touched the soft, unsettled mud of the bottom, he sank up to his shins. He fought his way to the surface, feeling the strain in his arms as he reached for Josh.

"I've got you!" he shouted. "I've got you!"

But Josh was struggling and coughing, unable to catch his breath, and Alex fought to control him as he pulled him into shallower water. Then, with an enormous heave, he carried Josh up onto the grassy bank, his mind racing through options: CPR, stomach pumping, assisted breathing. He tried to lay Josh down, but Josh resisted. He was struggling and coughing, and though Alex could still feel the panic in his own system, he had enough presence of mind to know that it probably meant that Josh was going to be okay.

He didn't know how long it took—probably only a few seconds, but it felt a lot longer—until Josh finally gave a rattling cough, emitting a spray of water, and for the first time was able to catch his breath. He inhaled sharply and coughed again, then inhaled and coughed again, though this time it settled into something that sounded like he was clearing his throat. He drew a few long breaths, still panic-stricken, and only then did the boy seem to realize what had happened.

He reached for his dad and Alex folded him tightly in his arms. Josh began to cry, his shoulders shuddering, and Alex felt sick to his stomach at the thought of what might have been. What would have happened had he not noticed Katie staring at the monitor? What if another minute had passed? The answers to those questions left him shaking as badly as Josh.

In time, Josh's cries began to slow and he uttered the first words since Alex had pulled him from the water.

"I'm sorry, Daddy," he choked out.

"I'm sorry, too," Alex whispered in return, and still, he held on to his son, afraid that somehow, if he let go, time would start to run backward, but this time, the outcome would be different.

When he was finally able to loosen his hold on Josh, Alex found himself gazing at a crowd behind the store. Roger was there, as were the customers who'd been eating. Another pair of customers craned their necks, probably just having arrived. And of course, Kristen was there, too. Suddenly he felt like a terrible parent again, because he saw that his little girl was crying and afraid and needed him, too, even though she was nestled in Katie's arms.

It wasn't until both Josh and Alex had changed into dry clothes that Alex was able to piece together what had happened. Roger had cooked both kids hamburgers and fries, and they were all sitting at a table in the grill area, though neither of them showed any interest in eating.

"My fishing line got snagged on the boat as it was pulling out, and I didn't want to lose my fishing rod. I thought the line would snap right away but it pulled me in and I swallowed a bunch of water. Then I couldn't breathe and it felt like something was holding me down." Josh hesitated. "I think I dropped my rod in the river."

Kristen was sitting beside him, her eyes still red and puffy. She'd asked Katie to stay with her for a while, and Katie had remained at her side, holding her hand even now.

"It's okay. I'll head out there in a little while and if I can't find it, I'll get you a new one. But next time, just let go, okay?"

Josh sniffed and nodded. "I'm really sorry," he said.

"It was an accident," Alex assured him.

"But now you won't let me go fishing."

And risk losing him again? Alex thought. Not a chance. "We'll talk about that later, okay?" Alex said instead.

"What if I promise to let go the next time?"

"Like I said, we'll talk about it later. For now, why don't you eat something?"

"I'm not hungry."

"I know. But it's lunchtime and you've got to eat."

Josh reached for a French fry and took a small bite, chewing mechanically. Kristen did the same. At the table, she almost always mimicked Josh. It drove Josh crazy, but he didn't seem to have the energy right now to protest.

Alex turned to Katie. He swallowed, feeling suddenly nervous. "Can I talk to you for a minute?"

She stood up from the table and he led her away from the kids. When they were far enough away that he was sure they wouldn't hear, he cleared his throat. "I want to thank you for what you did."

"I didn't do anything," she protested.

"Yes," he said. "You did. Had you not been looking at the monitor, I wouldn't have known what was happening. I might not have reached him in time." He paused. "And also, thank you for taking care of Kristen. She's the sweetest thing in the world, but she's sensitive. I'm glad you didn't leave her alone. Even when we had to go up and change."

"I did what anyone would do," Katie insisted. In the silence that followed, she suddenly seemed to realize how close they were standing and took a half step backward. "I should really be going."

"Wait," Alex said. He walked toward the refrigerated cases at the rear of the store. "Do you like wine?"

She shook her head. "Sometimes, but—"

Before she could finish, he turned around and opened the case. He reached up and pulled out a bottle of chardonnay.

"Please," he said, "I want you to have it. It's actually a very good wine. I know you wouldn't think you could get a good bottle of wine here, but when I was in the army, I had a friend who introduced me to wine. He's kind of an amateur expert, and he's the one who picks what I stock. You'll enjoy it."

"You don't need to do that."

"It's the least I can do." He smiled. "As a way to say thank you."

For the first time since they'd met, she held his gaze. "Okay," she finally said.

After gathering her groceries, she left the store. Alex returned to the table. With a bit more cajoling, Josh and Kristen finished their lunches, while Alex went to the dock to retrieve the fishing pole. By the time he got back, Joyce was already slipping on her apron, and Alex took the kids for a bike ride. Afterward, he drove them to Wilmington, where they saw a movie and had pizza, the old standbys when it came to spending time with kids. The sun was down and they were tired when they got home, so they showered and put on their pajamas. He lay in bed between them for an hour, reading stories, before finally turning out the lights.

In the living room, he turned on the television and flipped through the channels for a while, but he wasn't in the mood to watch. Instead, he thought about Josh again, and though he knew that his son was safe upstairs, he felt a ripple of the same fear he'd felt earlier, the same sense of failure. He was doing the best he could and no one could love their kids more than he did, but he couldn't help feeling that somehow it wasn't enough.

Later, long after Josh and Kristen had fallen asleep, he went to the kitchen and pulled out a beer from the refrigerator. He nursed it as he sat on the couch. The memories of the day played in his mind, but this time, his thoughts were of his daughter and the way she'd clung to Katie, her little face buried in Katie's neck.

The last time he'd seen that, he reflected, was when Carly had been alive.

4

April gave way to May and the days continued to pass. The restaurant got steadily busier and the stash of money in Katie's coffee can grew reassuringly thick. Katie no longer panicked at the thought that she lacked the means to leave this place if she had to.

Even after paying her rent and utilities, along with food, she had extra money for the first time in years. Not a lot, but enough to make her feel light and free. On Friday morning, she stopped at Anna Jean's, a thrift shop that specialized in secondhand clothes. It took most of the morning to sift through all the clothing, but in the end, she bought two pairs of shoes, a couple of pairs of pants, shorts, three stylish T-shirts, and a few blouses, most of which were name brands of one sort or another and looked almost new. It amazed Katie to think that some women had so many nice clothes that they could donate what would probably cost a small fortune in a department store.

Jo was hanging a wind chime when Katie got home.

Since that first meeting, they hadn't talked much. Jo's job, whatever it was, seemed to keep her busy and Katie was working as many shifts as she could. At night, she'd notice that Jo's lights were on, but it was too late for her to drop by, and Jo hadn't been there the previous weekend.

"Long time, no talk," Jo said with a wave. She tapped the wind chime, making it ding before crossing the yard.

Katie reached the porch and put the bags down. "Where've you been?"

Jo shrugged. "You know how it goes. Late nights, early mornings, going here and there. Half the time, I feel like I'm being pulled in every direction." She motioned to the rockers. "You mind? I need a break. I've been cleaning all morning and I just hung that thing. I like the sound, you know."

"Go ahead," Katie said.

Jo sat and rolled her shoulders, working out the kinks. "You've been getting some sun," she commented. "Did you go to the beach?"

"No," Katie said. She scooted one of the bags aside to make room for her foot. "I picked up some extra day shifts the past couple of weeks and I worked outside on the deck."

"Sun, water…what else is there? Working at Ivan's must be like being on vacation."

Katie laughed. "Not quite. But how about you?"

"No sun, no fun for me these days." She nodded toward the bags. "I wanted to drop by and mooch a cup of coffee this morning, but you were already gone."

"I went shopping."

"I can tell. Did you find anything you liked?"

"I think so," Katie confessed.

"Well, don't just sit there, show me what you bought."

"Are you sure?"

Jo laughed. "I live in a cottage at the end of a gravel road in the middle of nowhere and I've been washing cabinets all morning. What else do I have to excite me?"

Katie pulled out a pair of jeans and handed them over. Jo held them up, turning them from front to back. "Wow!" she said. "You must have found these at Anna Jean's. I love that place."

"How did you know I went to Anna Jean's?"

"Because it's not like any of the stores around here sell things this nice. This came from someone's closet. A rich woman's closet. A lot of the stuff is practically new." Lowering the jeans, Jo ran her finger over the stitching on the pockets. "These are great. I love the designs!" She peeked toward the bag. "What else did you get?"

Katie handed over the items one by one, listening as Jo raved about every piece. When the bag was empty, Jo sighed. "Okay, it's official. I'm jealous. And let me guess, there's nothing like any of this left in the store, is there?"

Katie shrugged, feeling suddenly sheepish. "Sorry," she said. "I was there for a while."

"Well, good for you. These are treasures."

Katie nodded toward Jo's house. "How's it coming over there?" she asked. "Have you started painting?"

"Not yet."

"Too busy at work?"

Jo made a face. "The truth is, after I got the unpacking done and I cleaned the place from top to bottom, I sort of ran out of energy. It's a good thing you're my friend, since that means I can still come over here where it's bright and cheery."

"You're welcome anytime."

"Thanks. I appreciate that. But evil Mr. Benson is going to deliver some cans of paint tomorrow. Which also explains why I'm here. I'm dreading the very idea of spending my entire weekend covered in splatter."

"It's not so bad. It goes fast."

"Do you see these hands?" Jo said, holding them up. "These were made for caressing handsome men and meant to be adorned with pretty nails and diamond rings. They're not made for paint rollers and paint splatter and that kind of manual labor."

Katie giggled. "Do you want me to come over and help?"

"Absolutely not. I'm an expert in procrastination, but the last thing I want you to think is that I'm incompetent, too. Because I'm actually pretty good at what I do."

A flock of starlings broke from the trees, moving in an almost musical rhythm. The motion of the rockers was making the porch creak slightly.

"What *do* you do?" Katie asked.

"I'm a counselor of sorts."

"For the high school?"

"No," she said, shaking her head. "I'm a grief counselor."

"Oh," Katie said. She paused. "I'm not sure what that is."

Jo shrugged. "I visit with people and try to help them. Usually, it's because someone close to them has died." She paused, and when she went on, her voice was softer. "People react in a lot of different ways and it's up to me to figure out how to help them accept what happened—and I hate that word, by the way, since I've yet to meet anyone who *wants* to *accept it*—but that's pretty much what I'm supposed to do. Because in the end, and no matter how hard it is, acceptance helps people move on with the rest of their lives. But sometimes..."

She trailed off. In the silence, she scratched at a piece of flaking paint on the rocker. "Sometimes, when I'm with someone, other issues come up. That's what I've been dealing with lately. Because sometimes people need help in other ways, too."

"That sounds rewarding."

"It is. Even if it has challenges." She turned toward Katie. "But what about you?"

"You know I work at Ivan's."

"But you haven't told me anything else about yourself."

"There's not much to tell," Katie protested, hoping to deflect the line of questioning.

"Of course there is. Everyone has a story." She paused. "For instance, what really brought you to Southport?"

"I already told you," Katie said. "I wanted to start over."

Jo seemed to stare right through her as she studied the answer. "Okay," she finally said, her tone light. "You're right. It's not my business."

"That's not what I said..."

"Yes, you did. You just said it in a nice way. And I respect your answer because you're right; it isn't my business. But just so you know, when you say you wanted to start over, the counselor in me wonders why you felt the need to start over. And more important, what you left behind."

Katie felt her shoulders tense. Sensing her discomfort, Jo went on.

"How about this?" she asked gently. "Forget I even asked the question. Just know that if you ever want to talk, I'm here, okay? I'm good at listening. Especially with friends. And believe it or not, sometimes talking helps."

"What if I can't talk about it?" Katie said in an involuntary whisper.

"Then how about this? Ignore the fact that I'm a counselor. We're just friends, and friends can talk about anything. Like where you were born or something that made you happy as a kid."

"Why is that important?"

"It isn't. And that's the point. You don't have to say anything at all that you don't want to say."

Katie absorbed her words before squinting at Jo. "You're very good at your job, aren't you?"

"I try," Jo conceded.

Katie laced her fingers together in her lap. "All right. I was born in Altoona," she said.

Jo leaned back in her rocking chair. "I've never been there. Is it nice?"

"It's one of those old railroad towns," she said, "you know the kind. A town filled with good, hardworking people who are just trying to make a better life for themselves. And it was pretty, too, especially in the fall, when the leaves began to change. I used to think there was no place more beautiful in the world." She lowered her eyes, half lost in memories. "I used to have a friend named Emily, and together we'd lay pennies on the railroad tracks. After the train went past, we'd scramble around trying to find them, and when we did, we'd always marvel at how any trace of engraving would be completely gone. Sometimes the pennies were still hot. I remember almost burning my fingers one time. When I think back on my childhood, it's mostly about small pleasures like that."

Katie shrugged, but Jo remained silent, willing her to go on.

"Anyway, that's where I went to school. All the way through. I ended up graduating from high school there, but by then, I don't know...I guess I was tired of...all of it, you know? Small-town life, where every weekend was the same. The same people going to the same parties, the same boys drinking beer in the beds of their pickup trucks. I wanted something more, but college didn't work out and, long story short, I ended up in Atlantic City. I worked there for a while, moved around a bit, and now, years later, here I am."

"In another small town where everything stays the same."

Katie shook her head. "It's different here. It makes me feel..."

When she hesitated, Jo finished the thought for her.

"Safe?"

When Katie's startled gaze met hers, Jo seemed bemused. "It's not that hard to figure out. Like you said, you're starting over and what better place to start over than a place like this? Where nothing ever happens?" She paused. "Well, that's not quite true. I heard there was a little excitement a couple of weeks back. When you dropped by the store?"

"You heard about that?"

"It's a small town. It's impossible not to hear about it. What happened?"

"It was scary. One minute, I was talking to Alex, and when I saw what was happening on the monitor, I guess he noticed my expression because in the next instant, he was racing past me. He moved through that store like lightning, and then Kristen saw the monitor and started to panic. I scooped her up and followed her dad. By the time I got out there, Alex was already out of the water with Josh. I'm just glad he was okay."

"Me, too." Jo nodded. "What do you think of Kristen? Isn't she just the sweetest thing?"

"She calls me Miss Katie."

"I love that little girl," Jo said, drawing her knees up to her chest. "But it doesn't surprise me that the two of you get along. Or that she reached for you when she was scared."

"Why would you say that?"

"Because she's a perceptive little thing. She knows you've got a good heart."

Katie made a skeptical face. "Maybe she was just scared about her brother, and when her dad took off I was the only one there."

"Don't sell yourself short. Like I said, she's perceptive." Jo pressed on. "How was Alex? Afterward, I mean?"

"He was still shaken up, but other than that, he seemed all right."

"Have you talked to him much since then?"

Katie gave a noncommittal shrug. "Not too much. He's always nice when I come into the store, and he stocks what I need, but that's about it."

"He's good about things like that," Jo said with assurance.

"You sound like you know him pretty well."

Jo rocked a little in her chair. "I think I do."

Katie waited for more, but Jo was silent.

"You want to talk about it?" Katie inquired innocently. "Because talking sometimes helps, especially with a friend."

Jo's eyes sparkled. "You know, I always suspected you were a lot craftier than you let on. Throwing my own words back at me. You should be ashamed."

Katie smiled but said nothing, just as Jo had done with her. And, surprising her, it worked.

"I'm not sure how much I should say," Jo added. "But I can tell you this: he's a good man. He's the kind of man you can count on to do the right thing. You can see that in how much he loves his kids."

Katie brought her lips together for a moment. "Did you two ever see each other?"

Jo seemed to choose her words carefully. "Yes, but maybe not in the way you're thinking. And just so we're clear: it was a long time ago and everyone has moved on."

Katie wasn't sure what to make of her answer but didn't want to press it. "What's his story, by the way? I take it he's divorced, right?"

"You should ask him."

"Me? Why would I want to ask him?"

"Because you asked me," Jo said, arching an eyebrow. "Which means, of course, that you're interested in him."

"I'm not interested in him."

"Then why would you be wondering about him?"

Katie scowled. "For a friend, you're kind of manipulative."

Jo shrugged. "I just tell people what they already know, but are afraid to admit to themselves."

Katie thought about that. "Just so we're clear, I'm officially taking back my offer to help you paint your house."

"You already said you'd do it."

"I know, but I'm taking back the offer."

Jo laughed. "Okay," she said. "Hey, what are you doing tonight?"

"I have to go to work in a little while. Actually, I should probably start getting ready."

"How about tomorrow night? Are you working?"

"No. I have the weekend off."

"Then how about I bring over a bottle of wine? I'm sure I'm going to need it, and I really don't want to be inhaling the paint fumes any longer than I have to. Would that be okay?"

"Actually, that sounds like fun."

"Good." Jo unfolded herself from the chair and stood. "It's a date."

5

——— 🍃 ———

Saturday morning dawned with blue skies, but soon clouds began rolling in. Gray and thick, they swirled and twisted in the ever-rising wind. The temperature began to plummet, and by the time Katie left the house, she had to wear a sweatshirt. The store was a little shy of two miles from her house, maybe half an hour's walk at a steady pace, and she knew she'd have to hurry if she didn't want to get caught in a storm.

She reached the main road just as she heard the thunder rumbling. She picked up the pace, feeling the air thickening around her. A truck sped past, leaving a blast of dust in its wake, and Katie moved onto the sandy median. The air smelled of salt carried from the ocean. Above her, a red-tailed hawk floated intermittently on updrafts, testing the force of the wind.

The steady rhythm of her footfalls set her mind adrift and she found herself reflecting on her conversation with Jo. Not the stories she'd told, but some of the things Jo had said about Alex. Jo, she decided, didn't know what she was talking about. While she was simply trying to make conversation, Jo had twisted her words into something that wasn't quite true. Granted, Alex seemed like a nice guy, and as Jo said, Kristen was as sweet as could be, but she wasn't *interested* in him. She barely knew him. Since Josh had fallen in the river, they hadn't said more than a few words to each other, and the last thing she wanted was a relationship of any kind.

So why had it felt like Jo was trying to bring them together?

She wasn't sure, but honestly, it didn't matter. She was glad Jo was coming over tonight. Just a couple of friends, sharing some wine…it wasn't that special, she knew. Other people, other women, did things like that all the time. She wrinkled her brow. All right, maybe not *all* the time, but most of them probably felt like they could do it if they wanted to, and she supposed that was the difference between her and them. How long had it been since she'd done something that felt normal?

Since her childhood, she admitted. Since those days when she'd put pennies on the track. But she hadn't been completely truthful with Jo. She hadn't told her that she often went to the railroad tracks to escape the sound of her parents arguing, their slurred voices raging at each other. She didn't tell Jo that more than once, she'd been caught in the crossfire, and that when she was twelve, she'd been hit with a snow globe that her father had thrown at her mother. It made a gash in her head that bled for hours, but neither her mom nor her dad had shown any inclination to bring her to the hospital. She didn't tell Jo that her dad was mean when he was drunk, or that she'd never invited anyone, even Emily, over to her house, or that college hadn't worked out because her parents thought it was a waste of time and money. Or that they'd kicked her out of the house on the day she graduated from high school.

Maybe, she thought, she'd tell Jo about those things. Or maybe she wouldn't. It wasn't all that important. So what if she hadn't had the best childhood? Yes, her parents were alcoholics and often unemployed, but aside from the snow-globe incident, they'd never hurt her. No, she didn't get a car or have birthday parties, but she'd never gone to bed hungry, either, and in the fall, no matter how tight things were, she always got new clothes for school. Her dad might not have been the greatest, but he hadn't snuck into her bedroom at night to do awful things, things she knew had happened to her friends. At eighteen, she didn't consider herself scarred. A bit disappointed about college, maybe, and nervous about having to make her own way in the world, but not damaged beyond repair. And she'd made it. Atlantic City hadn't been all bad. She'd met a couple of nice guys, and she could remember more than one evening she spent laughing and talking with friends from work until the early hours of the morning.

No, she reminded herself, her childhood hadn't defined her, or had anything to do with the real reason she'd come to Southport. Even though Jo was the closest thing to a friend that she had in Southport, Jo knew absolutely nothing about her. No one did.

"Hi, Miss Katie," Kristen piped up from her little table. No dolls today. Instead, she was bent over a coloring book, holding crayons and working on a picture of unicorns and rainbows.

"Hi, Kristen. How are you?"

"I'm good." She looked up from her coloring book. "Why do you always walk here?"

Katie paused, then came around the corner of the

counter and squatted down to Kristen's level. "Because I don't have a car."

"Why not?"

Because I don't have a license, Katie thought. *And even if I did, I can't afford a car.* "I'll tell you what. I'll think about getting one, okay?"

"Okay," she said. She held up the coloring book. "What do you think of my picture?"

"It's pretty. You're doing a great job."

"Thanks," she said. "I'll give it to you when I'm finished."

"You don't have to do that."

"I know," she said with charming self-assurance. "But I want to. You can hang it on your refrigerator."

Katie smiled and stood up. "That's just what I was thinking."

"Do you need help shopping?"

"I think I can handle it today. And that way, you can finish coloring."

"Okay," she agreed.

Retrieving a basket, she saw Alex approaching. He waved at her, and though it made no sense she had the feeling that she was really seeing him for the first time. Though his hair was gray, there were only a few lines around the corners of his eyes, but they added to, rather than detracted from, an overall sense of vitality. His shoulders tapered to a trim waist, and she had the impression that he was a man who neither ate nor drank to excess.

"Hey, Katie. How are you?"

"I'm fine. And yourself?"

"Can't complain." He grinned. "I'm glad you came in. I wanted to show you something." He pointed toward the monitor and she saw Josh sitting on the dock holding his fishing pole.

"You let him go back out there?" she asked.

"See the vest he's wearing?"

She leaned closer, squinting. "A life jacket?"

"It took me awhile to find one that wasn't too bulky, or too hot. But this one is perfect. And really, I had no choice. You have no idea how miserable he was, not being able to fish. I can't tell you how many times he begged me to change my mind. I couldn't take it anymore, and I thought this was a solution."

"He's okay with wearing it?"

"New rule—it's either wear it, or don't fish. But I don't think he minds."

"Does he ever catch any fish?"

"Not as many as he'd like, but, yes, he does."

"Do you eat them?"

"Sometimes." He nodded. "But Josh usually throws them back. He doesn't mind catching the same fish over and over."

"I'm glad you found a solution."

"A better father probably would have figured it out beforehand."

For the first time, she looked up at him. "I get the sense you're a pretty good father."

Their eyes held for a moment before she forced herself to turn away. Alex, sensing her discomfort, began rummaging around behind the counter.

"I have something for you," he said, pulling out a bag and placing it on the counter. "There's a small farm I work with that has a hothouse, and they can grow things when other people can't. They just dropped off some fresh vegetables yesterday. Tomatoes, cucumbers, some different kinds of squash. You might want to try them out. My wife swore they were the best she'd ever tasted."

"Your wife?"

He shook his head. "I'm sorry. I still do that sometimes. I meant my late wife. She passed away a couple of years ago."

"I'm sorry," she murmured, her mind flashing back to her conversation with Jo.

What's his story?

You should ask him, Jo had countered.

Jo had obviously known that his wife had died, but hadn't said anything. Odd.

Alex didn't notice that her mind had wandered. "Thank you," he said, his voice subdued. "She was a great person. You would have liked her." A wistful expression crossed his face. "But anyway," he finally added, "she swore by the place. It's organic, and the family still harvests by hand. Usually, the produce is gone within hours, but I set a little aside for you, in case you wanted to try some." He smiled. "Besides, you're a vegetarian, right? A vegetarian will appreciate these. I promise."

She squinted up at him. "Why would you think I'm a vegetarian?"

"You're not?"

"No."

"Oh," he said, pushing his hands into his pockets. "My mistake."

"It's okay," she said. "I've been accused of worse."

"I doubt that."

Don't, she thought to herself. "Okay." She nodded. "I'll take the vegetables. And thank you."

6

─── 🍃 ───

As Katie shopped, Alex fiddled around the register, watching her from the corner of his eye. He straightened the counter, checked on Josh, examined Kristen's picture, and straightened the counter again, doing his best to seem busy.

She'd changed in recent weeks. She had the beginnings of a summer tan and her skin had a glowing freshness to it. She was also growing less skittish around him, today being a prime example. No, they hadn't set the world on fire with their scintillating conversation, but it was a start, right?

But the start of what?

From the very beginning, he'd sensed she was in trouble, and his instinctive response had been to want to help. And of course she was pretty, despite the bad hair-cut and plain-Jane attire. But it was seeing the way Katie had comforted Kristen after Josh had fallen in the water that had really moved him. Even more affecting had been Kristen's response to Katie. She had reached for Katie like a child reaching for her mother.

It had made his throat tighten, reminding him that as

much as he missed having a wife, his children missed having a mother. He knew they were grieving, and he tried to make up for it as best he could, but it wasn't until he saw Katie and Kristen together that he realized that sadness was only part of what they were experiencing. Their loneliness mirrored his own.

It troubled him that he hadn't realized it before.

As for Katie, she was something of a mystery to him. There was a missing element somewhere, something that had been gnawing at him. He watched her, wondering who she really was and what had brought her to Southport.

She was standing near one of the refrigerator cases, something she'd never done before, studying the items behind the glass. She frowned, and as she was debating what to buy, he noticed the fingers of her right hand twisting around her left ring finger, toying with a ring that wasn't there. The gesture triggered something both familiar and long forgotten.

It was a habit, a tic he'd noticed during his years at CID and sometimes observed with women whose faces were bruised and disfigured. They used to sit across from him, compulsively touching their rings, as though they were shackles that bound them to their husbands. Usually, they denied that their husband had hit them, and in the rare instances they admitted the truth, they usually insisted it wasn't his fault; that they'd provoked him. They'd tell him that they'd burned dinner or hadn't done the wash or that he'd been drinking. And always, always, these same women would swear that it was the first time it had ever happened, and tell him that they didn't want to press charges because his career would be ruined. Everyone knew the army came down hard on abusive husbands.

Some were different, though—at least in the beginning—and insisted that they wanted to press charges. He would start the report and listen as they questioned why paperwork was more important than making an arrest. Than enforcing the law. He would write up the report anyway and read their own words back to them before asking them to sign it. It was then, sometimes, that their bravado would fail, and he'd catch a glimpse of the terrified woman beneath the angry surface. Many would end up not signing it, and even those who did would quickly change their minds when their husbands were brought in. Those cases went forward, no matter what the woman decided. But later, when a wife wouldn't testify, little punishment was meted out. Alex came to understand that only those who pressed charges ever became truly free, because the life they were leading was a prison, even if most of them wouldn't admit it.

Still, there was another way to escape the horror of their lives, though in all his years he'd come across only one who actually did it. He'd interviewed the woman once and she'd taken the usual route of denial and self-blame. But a couple of months later, he'd learned that she'd fled. Not to her family and not to her friends, but somewhere else, a place where even her husband couldn't find her. Her husband, lost in his fury that his wife had left, had exploded after a long night of drinking and had bloodied an MP. He ended up in Leavenworth, and Alex remembered grinning in satisfaction when he'd heard the news. And when thinking of the man's wife, he smiled, thinking, *Good for you.*

Now, as he watched Katie toying with a ring that wasn't there, he felt his old investigative instincts kick in. There'd been a husband, he thought; her husband was the missing element. Either she was still married or she wasn't, but he had an undeniable hunch that Katie was still afraid of him.

The sky exploded while she was reaching for a box of crackers. Lightning flashed, and a few seconds later thunder crackled before finally settling into a loud, angry rumble. Josh dashed inside right before the downpour started, clutching his tackle box and fishing reel as he entered the store. His face was red and he was panting like a runner crossing the finish line.

"Hey, Dad."

Alex looked up. "Catch anything?"

"Just the catfish again. The same one I catch every time."

"I'll see you in a little bit for lunch, okay?"

Josh vanished back into the storeroom and Alex heard him padding up the steps to the house.

Outside, the rain came down hard and the wind whipped sheets of water against the glass. Branches bent in the wind, bowing to a higher power. The dark sky flashed bright with lightning, and thunder boomed, loud enough to shake the windows. From across the store, Alex saw Katie flinch, her face a mask of surprise and terror, and he found himself wondering whether it was the same way her husband had once seen her.

The door of the store opened and a man rushed in, trailing water on the old wood flooring. He shook rivulets of rain from his sleeves and nodded at Alex before finally moving toward the grill.

Katie turned back to the shelf that held crackers. He

didn't have a big selection, just saltines and Ritz, the only two that sold regularly, and she reached for the Ritz.

She selected her usual items as well and carried her basket to the register. When he finished ringing up and bagging her items, Alex tapped the bag he'd put on the counter earlier.

"Don't forget the vegetables."

She glanced at the total on the register. "Are you sure you rang them up?"

"Of course."

"Because the total isn't any more than it usually is."

"I gave you the introductory price."

She frowned, wondering whether to believe him, then finally reached into the bag. She pulled out a tomato and brought it to her nose.

"It smells good."

"I had some last night. They're great with a touch of salt, and the cucumbers don't need anything."

She nodded but her gaze was focused on the door. The wind was driving rain against it in furious waves. The door creaked open, the water fighting to get inside. The world beyond the glass was blurry.

People lingered in the grill. Alex could hear them mumbling to themselves about waiting for the storm to break.

Katie drew a fortifying breath and reached for her bags.

"Miss Katie!" Kristen cried, sounding almost panicked. She stood, brandishing the picture she'd colored. She'd already torn it from the book. "You almost forgot your picture."

Katie reached for it, brightening as she examined

the picture. Alex noted how—at least for an instant—everything else in the world seemed to be forgotten.

"This is beautiful," she murmured. "I can't wait to hang it up."

"I'll color another one for you the next time you come in."

"I'd like that very much," she said.

Kristen beamed before sitting at the table again. Katie rolled up the picture, making sure not to wrinkle it, and then tucked it into the bag. Lightning and thunder erupted, almost simultaneously this time. Rain hammered the ground and the parking lot was a sea of puddles. The sky was as dark as northern seas.

"Do you know how long the storm is supposed to last?" she asked.

"I heard it was supposed to last most of the day," Alex answered.

She stared out the door. As she debated what to do, she toyed again with the nonexistent ring. In the silence, Kristen tugged at her dad's shirt.

"You should drive Miss Katie home," she told him. "She doesn't have a car. And it's raining hard."

Alex looked at Katie, knowing she'd overheard Kristen. "Would you like a ride home?"

Katie shook her head. "No, that's okay."

"But what about the picture?" Kristen said. "It might get wet."

When Katie didn't answer immediately, Alex came out from behind the register. "Come on." He motioned with his head. "There's no reason to get soaked. My car's right out back."

"I don't want to impose…"

"You're not imposing." He patted his pocket and pulled out his car keys before reaching for the bags. "Let me get those for you," he said, taking them. "Kristen, sweetie? Will you run upstairs and tell Josh I'll be back in ten minutes?"

"Sure, Daddy," she said.

"Roger?" he called out. "Watch the store and the kids for a bit, would you?"

"No problem." Roger waved.

Alex nodded toward the rear of the store. "You ready?" he asked.

They made a frantic dash for the jeep, wielding bent umbrellas against the gale-force winds and blankets of rain. Lightning continued to flash, making the clouds blink. Once they had settled into their seats, Katie used her hand to wipe the condensation from the window.

"I didn't think it would be like this when I left the house."

"No one ever does, until the storm hits, anyway. We get a lot of *the sky is falling* on the weather reports, so when something big does hit, people never expect it. If it's not as bad as the reports predicted, we complain. If it's worse than expected, we complain. If it's just as bad as predicted, we complain about that, too, because we'll say that the reports are wrong so often, there was no way to know they'd be right this time. It just gives people something to complain about."

"Like the people in the grill?"

He nodded and grinned. "But they're basically good people. For the most part, they're hardworking, honest, and as kind as the day is long. Any one of them would have been glad to watch the store for me if I'd asked, and they'd account for every penny. It's like that down here. Because deep down, everyone here knows that in a small town like this, we all need one another. It's great, even if it did take some time for me to get used to it."

"You're not from here?"

"No. My wife was. I'm from Spokane. When I first moved here, I remember thinking that there wasn't a chance I'd ever stay in a place like this. I mean, it's a small Southern town that doesn't care what the rest of the world thinks. It takes a little getting used to, at first. But then ... it grows on you. It keeps me focused on what's important."

Katie's voice was soft. "What's important?"

He shrugged. "Depends on the person, doesn't it? But right now, for me, it's about my kids. This is home for them, and after what they've been through, they need predictability. Kristen needs a place to color and dress her dolls and Josh needs a place to fish, and they both need to know that I'm around whenever they need me. This place, and the store, gives them that, and right now, that's what I want. It's what I need."

He paused, feeling self-conscious about talking so much. "By the way, where am I going, exactly?"

"Keep going straight. There's a gravel road that you'll have to turn on. It's a little bit past the curve."

"You mean the gravel road by the plantation?"

Katie nodded. "That's the one."

"I didn't even know that road went anywhere." He wrinkled his forehead. "That's quite a walk," he said. "What is it? A couple of miles?"

"It's not too bad," she demurred.

"Maybe in nice weather. But today, you'd have to swim

home. There's no way you could have walked this far. And Kristen's picture would have been ruined."

He noted the flicker of a smile at Kristen's name but she said nothing.

"Someone said you work at Ivan's?" he prompted.

She nodded. "I started in March."

"How do you like it?"

"It's okay. It's just a job, but the owner has been good to me."

"Ivan?"

"You know him?"

"Everyone knows Ivan. Did you know he dresses up like a Confederate general every fall to reenact the famed Battle of Southport? When Sherman burned the town? Which is fine, of course…except that there was never a Battle of Southport in the Civil War. Southport wasn't even called Southport back then, it was called Smithville. And Sherman was never within a hundred miles of here."

"Seriously?" Katie asked.

"Don't get me wrong. I like Ivan—he's a good man, and the restaurant is a fixture in this town. Kristen and Josh love the hush puppies there, and Ivan's always welcoming whenever we show up. But sometimes, I've wondered what drives him. His family arrived from Russia in the fifties. First generation, in other words. No one in his extended family has probably even heard of the Civil War. But Ivan will spend an entire weekend pointing his sword and shouting orders right in the middle of the road in front of the courthouse."

"Why have I never heard about this?"

"Because it's not something the locals like to talk about. It's kind of…eccentric, you know? Even locals, people who really like him, try to ignore him. They'll see Ivan in the middle of downtown and they'll turn away and start saying things like, *Can you believe how beautiful those chrysanthemums are by the courthouse?*"

For the first time since she'd been in the car, Katie laughed. "I'm not sure I believe you."

"It doesn't matter. If you're here in October, you'll see for yourself. But again, don't get me wrong. He's a nice guy and the restaurant is great. After a day at the beach, we almost always stop in there. Next time we come in, we'll ask for you."

She hesitated. "Okay."

"She likes you," Alex said. "Kristen, I mean."

"I like her. She's a bright spirit—a real personality."

"I'll tell her you said that. And thanks."

"How old is she?"

"She's five. When she starts school in the fall, I don't know what I'm going to do. It'll be so quiet around the store."

"You'll miss her," Katie observed.

He nodded. "A lot. I know she'll enjoy school, but I kind of like having her around."

As he spoke, rain continued to sheet against the windows. The sky flashed on and off like a strobe, accompanied by an almost continuous rumble.

Katie peered out the passenger-side window, lost in her thoughts. He waited, somehow knowing she would break the silence.

"How long were you and your wife married?" Katie finally asked.

"Five years. We dated for a year before that. I met her when I was stationed at Fort Bragg."

"You were in the army?"

"Ten years. It was a good experience and I'm glad I did it. At the same time, I'm glad I'm done."

Katie pointed through the windshield. "There's the turn up ahead," she said.

Alex turned onto Katie's road and slowed down. The rough gravel surface had flooded during the downpour, and water splashed up to the windows and over the windshield. As he focused on steering the car through the deep puddles, Alex was suddenly struck by the thought that this was the first time he'd been alone in a car with a woman since his wife had died.

"Which one is it?" he asked, squinting at the outline of two small cottages.

"The one on the right," she said.

He turned into the makeshift drive and pulled as close to the house as he could. "I'll bring the groceries to the door for you."

"You don't have to do that."

"You don't know the way I was raised," he said, jumping out before she could object. He grabbed the bags and ran them to her porch. By the time he set them down and began to shake off, Katie was hurrying toward him, the umbrella Alex had lent her clutched in her hands.

"Thanks," she called out over the noise of the downpour.

When she offered him the umbrella, he shook his head. "Keep it for a while. Or forever. It doesn't matter. If you walk a lot around here, you're going to need it."

"I can pay you—" she began.

"Don't worry about it."

"But this is from the store."

"It's okay," he said. "Really. But if you don't think you should, then just settle up the next time you're in the store, okay?"

"Alex, really—"

He didn't let her finish. "You're a good customer, and I like to help my customers."

It took a moment for her to answer. "Thank you," she finally said, her eyes, now dark green, fixed on his. "And thanks for driving me home."

He tipped his head. "Anytime."

What to do with the kids: it was the endless, sometimes unanswerable question he faced on weekends, and as usual, he had absolutely no idea.

With the storm in full fury and showing no signs of letting up, doing anything outside was out of the question. He could take them to a movie, but there was nothing playing that they'd both be interested in. He could simply let them entertain themselves for a while. He knew lots of parents operated that way. On the other hand, his kids were still young, too young to be left completely to their own devices. More important, they were already on their own a lot, improvising ways to keep themselves entertained, simply because of his long hours at the store. He pondered the options as he made grilled cheese sandwiches, but he soon found his thoughts drifting to Katie. While she was obviously doing her best to maintain a low profile, he knew it was almost impossible in a town like this. She was too attractive to blend in, and when people caught on to the fact that she walked everywhere, it was inevitable that talk would start and questions would be asked about her past.

He didn't want that to happen. Not for selfish reasons, but because she was entitled to the kind of life she'd come here to find. A normal life. A life of simple pleasures, the kind that most people took for granted: the ability to go where she wanted when she wanted and live in a home where she felt safe and secure. She also needed a way to get around.

"Hey, kids," he said, putting their sandwiches on plates. "I have an idea. Let's do something for Miss Katie."

"Okay!" Kristen agreed.

Josh, always easygoing, simply nodded.

7

———— ❧ ————

Wind-driven rain blew hard across dark North Carolina skies, sweeping rivers against the kitchen windows. Earlier that afternoon, while Katie did her laundry in the sink and after she had taped Kristen's picture to the refrigerator, the ceiling in the living room had begun to leak. She'd placed a pot beneath the drip and had already emptied it twice. In the morning, she planned to call Benson, but she doubted whether he'd get around to repairing the leak right away. If, of course, he ever got around to fixing it at all.

In the kitchen, she sliced small cubes from a block of cheddar cheese, nibbling as she moved about. On a yellow plastic plate were crackers and slices of tomatoes and cucumbers, although she couldn't arrange them to look the way she wanted. Nothing looked quite the way she wanted. In her previous home, she'd had a pretty wooden serving board and a silver cheese knife with an engraving of a cardinal, and a full set of wineglasses. She'd had a dining room table made of cherry, and sheer curtains in the windows, but here the table wobbled and the chairs didn't match, the windows were bare, and she and Jo would have to drink wine from coffee mugs. As horrible as her life had been, she'd loved assembling the pieces of her household, but as with everything she'd left behind, she now viewed them as enemies that had gone over to the other side.

Through the window, she saw one of Jo's lights blink out. Katie made her way to the front door. Opening it, she watched as Jo splashed through puddles on the way to her house, umbrella in one hand and a bottle of wine in the other. Another couple of stomps and she was on the porch, her yellow slicker dripping wet.

"Now I understand how Noah must have felt. Can you believe this storm? I've got puddles all over my kitchen."

Katie motioned over her shoulder. "My leak is in the living room."

"Home sweet home, right? Here," she said, handing over the wine. "Just like I promised. And believe me, I'm going to need it."

"Rough day?"

"Like you couldn't imagine."

"Come on in."

"Let me leave my coat out here or you're going to have two puddles in your living room," she said, shimmying out of her slicker. "I got soaked in the few seconds I was out there."

Jo tossed her coat on the rocker along with the umbrella and followed Katie inside as she led the way to the kitchen.

Katie immediately set the wine on the counter. As Jo wandered to the table, Katie pulled open the drawer by the refrigerator. From the back of the drawer, she pulled out a rusted Swiss Army knife and readied the opener.

"This is great. I'm starved. I haven't eaten all day."

"Help yourself. How did it go with the painting?"

"Well, I got the living room done. But after that, it wasn't such a good day."

"What happened?"

"I'll tell you about it later. I need wine first. How about you? What did you do?"

"Nothing much. Ran to the store, cleaned up, did my laundry."

Jo took a seat at the table and reached for a cracker. "In other words, memoir material."

Katie laughed as she began to twist the corkscrew. "Oh, yeah. Real exciting."

"Do you want me to get that?" Jo asked.

"I think I've got it."

"Good." Jo smirked. "Because I'm the guest, and I expect to be pampered."

Katie propped the bottle between her legs and the cork came out with a pop.

"Seriously, though, thanks for having me over." Jo sighed. "You have no idea how much I've been looking forward to this."

"Really?"

"Don't do that."

"Don't do what?" Katie asked.

"Act surprised that I wanted to come over. That I wanted to bond over a bottle of wine. That's what friends do." She raised an eyebrow. "Oh, and by the way, before you start wondering whether or not we're actually friends and how well we know each other, trust me when I say

that yes, absolutely, I consider you a friend." She let that
sink in before going on. "Now how about some wine?"

The storm finally broke in the early evening, and Katie
opened the kitchen window. The temperature had dropped
and the air felt cool and clean. While pockets of mist rose
from the ground, rolling clouds drifted past the moon,
bringing light and shadow in equal measures. Leaves
turned from silver to black and to silver again as they shimmered in the evening breeze.

Katie drifted dreamily on the wine, the evening breeze,
and Jo's easy laughter. Katie found herself savoring every
bite of the buttery crackers and sharp, rich cheese, remembering how hungry she once had been. There was a time
when she'd been as thin as a heated strand of blown glass.

Her thoughts were wandering. She remembered her parents, not the hard times but the good ones, when the demons
were sleeping: when her mom made eggs and bacon, the
aroma filling the house, and she'd seen her father glide
into the kitchen, toward her mother. He would pull aside
her hair and kiss the side of her neck, making her giggle.
Once, she remembered, her dad had brought them to Get-
tysburg. He'd taken her hand as they walked around, and
she could still recall the rare sensation of strength and gentleness in his grasp. He was tall and broad-shouldered with
dark brown hair and there was a navy tattoo on his upper
arm. He'd served on a destroyer for four years and had been
to Japan, Korea, and Singapore, though he said little else
about his experience.

Her mom was petite with blond hair and had once
competed in a beauty pageant, finishing as the second
runner-up. She loved flowers, and in the spring she would

plant bulbs in ceramic flowerpots she placed in the yard.
Tulips and daffodils, peonies and violets would explode
in colors so bright they almost made Katie's eyes ache.
When they moved, the flowerpots would be placed on the
backseat and fastened with seat belts. Often, when she
cleaned, her mother would sing to herself, melodies from
childhood, some of them in Polish, and Katie would listen
secretly from another room, trying to make sense of the
words.

The wine Jo and Katie were drinking had hints of oak
and apricots, and it tasted wonderful. Katie finished her
cup and Jo poured her another. When a moth began to
dance around the light above the sink, fluttering with purpose and confusion, both of them began to giggle. Katie
cut more cheese and added more crackers to the plate.
They talked about movies and books, and Jo shrieked
with pleasure when Katie said her favorite movie was *It's
a Wonderful Life*, claiming that it was her favorite movie,
too. When she was younger, Katie remembered asking her
mom for a bell, so she could help angels get their wings.
Katie finished her second glass of wine, feeling as light as
a feather on a summer breeze.

Jo asked few questions. Instead, they stuck to super-
ficial topics, and Katie thought again that she was happy
for Jo's company. When silver highlighted the world
beyond the window, Katie and Jo stepped out onto the
front porch. Katie could feel herself swaying slightly and
she took hold of the railing. They sipped their wine as the
clouds continued to break, and all at once, the sky was
filled with stars. Katie pointed out the Big Dipper and
Polaris, the only stars she could name, but Jo began nam-
ing dozens of others. Katie stared at the sky in wonder,

amazed at how much Jo knew about the constellations, until she noticed the names Jo was reciting. "That one's called Elmer Fudd, and over there, right above that pine tree, you can make out Daffy Duck." When Katie finally realized that Jo knew as little about the stars as she did, Jo started to giggle like a mischievous kid.

Back in the kitchen, Katie poured the last of the wine and took a sip. It was warm in Katie's throat and made her feel dizzy. The moth continued to dance around the light, though if she tried to focus on it, there seemed to be two of them. She felt happy and safe and thought again how enjoyable the evening had been.

She had a friend, a real friend, someone who laughed and made jokes about the stars, and she wasn't sure if she wanted to laugh or cry because it had been so long since she'd experienced something so easy and natural.

"Are you okay?" Jo asked.

"I'm fine," Katie answered. "I was just thinking that I'm glad you came over."

Jo peered at her. "I think you might be tipsy."

"I think you might be right," Katie agreed.

"Well, okay then. What do you want to do? Since you're obviously tipsy and ready for fun."

"I don't know what you mean."

"Do you want to do something special? Head into town, find someplace exciting?"

Katie shook her head. "No."

"You don't want to meet people?"

"I'm better off alone."

Jo ran her finger around the rim of the mug before saying anything. "Trust me on this: no one is better off alone."

"I am."

Jo thought about Katie's answer before leaning closer. "So you're telling me that—assuming you had food, shelter, and clothing and anything else you needed to simply survive—you'd rather be stranded on a desert island in the middle of nowhere, all alone, forever, for the rest of your life? Be honest."

Katie blinked, trying to keep Jo in focus. "Why would you think I wouldn't be honest?"

"Because everybody lies. It's part of living in society. Don't get me wrong—I think it's necessary. The last thing anyone wants is to live in a society where total honesty prevails. Can you imagine the conversations? *You're short and fat*, one person might say, and the other might answer, *I know. But you smell bad*. It just wouldn't work. So people lie by omission all the time. People will tell you most of the story...and I've learned that the part they neglect to tell you is often the most important part. People hide the truth because they're afraid."

With Jo's words, Katie felt a finger touch her heart. All at once, it seemed hard to breathe.

"Are you talking about me?" she finally croaked out.

"I don't know. Am I?"

Katie felt herself pale slightly, but before she could respond, Jo smiled.

"Actually, I was thinking about my day today. I told you it was hard, right? Well, what I just told you is part of the problem. It gets frustrating when people won't tell the truth. I mean, how am I supposed to help people if they hold things back? If I don't really know what's going on?"

Katie could feel something twisting and tightening in her chest. "Maybe they want to talk about it but they know there's nothing you can do to help," she whispered.

"There's always something I can do."

In the moonlight shining through the kitchen window, Jo's skin glowed a luminous white, and Katie had the sense that she never went out in the sun. The wine made the room move, the walls buckle. Katie could feel tears beginning to form in her eyes and it was all she could do to blink them back. Her mouth was dry.

"Not always," Katie whispered. She turned to face the window. Beyond the glass, the moon hung low over the trees. Katie swallowed, suddenly feeling as if she were observing herself from across the room. She could see herself sitting at the table with Jo, and when she began to speak, her voice didn't seem to be her own. "I had a friend once. She was in a terrible marriage and she couldn't talk to anyone. He used to hit her, and in the beginning, she told him that if it ever happened again, she would leave him. He swore that it wouldn't and she believed him. But it only got worse after that, like when his dinner was cold, or when she mentioned that she'd visited with one of the neighbors who was walking by with his dog. She just chatted with him, but that night, her husband threw her into a mirror."

Katie stared at the floor. Linoleum was peeling up in the corners, but she hadn't known how to fix it. She'd tried to glue it, but the glue hadn't worked and the corners had curled again.

"He always apologized, and sometimes he would even cry because of the bruises he'd made on her arms or legs or her back. He would say that he hated what he'd done, but in the next breath tell her she'd deserved it. That if she'd been more careful, it wouldn't have happened. That if she'd been paying attention or hadn't been so stupid, he wouldn't have lost his temper. She tried to change. She worked hard at trying to be a better wife and to do things the way he wanted, but it was never enough."

Katie could feel the pressure of tears behind her eyes and though she tried again to stop them, she felt them sliding down her cheek. Jo was motionless across the table, watching her without moving.

"And she loved him! In the beginning, he was so sweet to her. He made her feel safe. On the night they met, she'd been working, and after she finished her shift, two men were following her. When she went around the corner, one of them grabbed her and clamped his hand over her mouth, and even though she tried to get away, the men were so much stronger and she didn't know what would have happened except that her future husband came around the corner and hit one of them hard on the back of the neck and he fell to the ground. And then he grabbed the other one and threw him into the wall, and it was over. Just like that. He helped her up and walked her home and the next day he took her out for coffee. He was kind and he treated her like a princess, right up until she was on her honeymoon."

Katie knew she shouldn't be telling Jo any of this, but she couldn't stop. "My friend tried to get away twice. One time, she came back on her own because she had nowhere else to go. And the second time she ran away, she thought she was finally free. But he hunted her down and dragged her back to the house. At home, he beat her and put a gun to her head and told her that if she ever ran away again, he'd kill her. He'd kill any man she cared for. And she believed him, because by then, she knew he was crazy. But she was trapped. He never gave her any money, he never allowed her to leave the house. He used to drive by the house when he was supposed to be working, just to make sure she was there. He monitored the phone records and called all the time, and he wouldn't let her get a driver's license. One time, when she woke up in the middle of the night, she found him standing over the bed, just staring at her. He'd been drinking and holding the gun again and she was too scared to say anything other than to ask him to come to bed. But that was when she knew that if she stayed, the husband would eventually kill her."

Katie swiped at her eyes, her fingers slick with salty tears. She could barely breathe but the words kept coming. "She started to steal money from his wallet. Never more than a dollar or two, because otherwise he would notice. Normally, he locked his wallet up at night, but sometimes, he would forget. It took so long to get enough money for her to escape. Because that's what she had to do. Escape. She had to go someplace where he would never find her, because she knew he wouldn't stop searching for her. And she couldn't tell anyone anything, because her family was gone and she knew the police wouldn't do anything. If he so much as suspected anything, he would kill her. So she stole and saved and found coins in the sofa cushions and in the washing machine. She hid the money in a plastic bag that she put beneath a flowerpot, and every time he went outside she was sure he would find it. It took so long to get the money she needed because she had to have enough to get far away so that he'd never find her. So that she could start over again."

Katie wasn't aware of when it had happened, but she realized that Jo had taken her hand and she was no longer watching herself from across the room. She could taste salt on her lips and imagined that her soul was leaking out. She wanted desperately to sleep.

In the silence Jo continued to hold her gaze. "Your friend has a lot of courage," she said quietly.

"No," Katie said. "My friend is scared all the time."

"That's what courage is. If she weren't scared, she wouldn't need courage in the first place. I admire what she did." Jo gave her hand a squeeze. "I think I'd like your friend. I'm glad you told me about her."

Katie glanced away, feeling utterly drained. "I probably shouldn't have told you all that."

Jo shrugged. "I wouldn't worry too much. One thing you'll learn about me is that I'm good with secrets. Especially when it comes to people I don't know, right?"

Katie nodded. "Right."

Jo stayed with Katie for another hour, but steered the conversation toward easier ground. Katie talked about working at Ivan's and some of the customers she was getting to know. Jo asked about the best way to get the paint out from under her fingernails. With the wine gone, Katie's dizziness began to fade, leaving in its wake a sense of exhaustion. Jo, too, began to yawn, and they finally rose from the table. Jo helped Katie clean up, though there wasn't much to do aside from washing a couple of dishes, and Katie walked her to the door.

As Jo stepped onto the porch, she paused. "I think we had a visitor," she said.

"What are you talking about?"

"There's a bicycle leaning against your tree."

Katie followed her outside. Beyond the yellow glow of the porch light, the world was dark and the outlines of the distant pine trees reminded Katie of the ragged edge of a black hole. Fireflies mimicked the stars, twinkling and blinking, and Katie squinted, realizing that Jo was right.

"Whose bicycle is that?" Katie asked.

"I don't know."

"Did you hear anyone come up?"

"No. But I think someone left it for you. See?" She pointed. "Isn't that a bow on the handlebars?"

Katie squinted, spotting the bow. A woman's bike, it had wire baskets on each side of the rear wheel, as well as another wire basket on the front. A chain was wrapped loosely around the seat, with the key still in the lock. "Who would bring me a bicycle?"

"Why do you keep asking me these questions? I don't know what's going on any more than you do."

Katie and Jo stepped off the porch. Though the puddles had largely vanished, sinking into the sandy loam, the grass held on to the rain and dampened the tips of her shoes as Katie moved through it. She touched the bicycle, then the bow, rubbing the ribbon between her fingers like a rug merchant. A card was tucked beneath it, and Katie reached for it.

"It's from Alex," she said, sounding baffled.

"Alex the store guy Alex, or another Alex?"

"The store guy."

"What does it say?"

Katie shook her head, trying to make sense of it before holding it out. *I thought you might enjoy this.*

Jo tapped the note. "I guess that means he's as interested in you as you are in him."

"I'm not interested in him!"

"Of course not." Jo winked. "Why would you be?"

8

Alex was sweeping the floor near the coolers when Katie entered the store. He had guessed that she would show up to talk to him about the bicycle first thing in the morning. After leaning the broom handle against the glass, he retucked his shirt and ran a quick hand through his hair. Kristen had been waiting for her all morning and she'd already popped up before the door had even closed.

"Hey, Miss Katie!" Kristen said. "Did you get the bicycle?"

"I did. Thank you," Katie answered. "That's why I'm here."

"We worked really hard on it."

"You did a great job," she said. "Is your dad around?"

"Uh-huh. He's right over there." She pointed. "He's coming."

Alex watched as Katie turned toward him.

"Hey, Katie," he said.

When he was close, she crossed her arms. "Can I talk to you outside for a minute?"

He could hear the coolness in her voice and knew she was doing her best not to show her anger in front of Kristen.

"Of course," he said, reaching for the door. Pushing it open, he followed her outside and found himself admiring her figure as she headed toward the bicycle.

Stopping near the bike, she turned to face him. In the front basket was the umbrella she'd borrowed the day before. She patted the seat, her face serious. "Can I ask what this is about?"

"Do you like it?"

"Why did you buy it for me?"

"I didn't buy it for you," he said.

She blinked. "But your note..."

He shrugged. "It's been in the shed collecting dust for the last couple of years. Believe me, the last thing I'd do is buy you a bicycle."

Her eyes flashed. "That's not the point! You keep giving me things and you've got to stop. I don't want anything from you. I don't need an umbrella or vegetables or wine. And I don't need a bike!"

"Then give it away." He shrugged. "Because I don't want it, either."

She fell silent and he watched as confusion gave way to frustration, then finally futility. In the end, she shook her head and turned to leave. Before she could take a step, he cleared his throat. "Before you go, though, would you at least do me the favor of listening to my explanation?"

She glared at him over her shoulder. "It doesn't matter."

"It might not matter to you, but it matters to me."

Her eyes held his, wavering before they finally dropped. When she sighed, he motioned to the bench in front of the store. He'd originally placed it there, wedged between the ice maker and a rack of propane tanks, as a joke, knowing that it would sit unused. Who would want to stare at a parking lot and the road out front? To his surprise, on most days it was almost always occupied; the only reason it was empty now was because it was so early.

Katie hesitated before taking a seat, and Alex laced his fingers together in his lap.

"I wasn't lying about the fact that the bike has been collecting dust for the last couple of years. It used to belong to my wife," Alex said. "She loved that bike and she rode it all the time. Once, she even rode it all the way to Wilmington, but of course, by the time she got there, she was tired and I had to go pick her up, even though I didn't have anyone to mind the store. I literally had to close the place up for a couple of hours." He paused. "That was the last ride she took on it. That night, she had her first seizure and I had to rush her to the hospital. After that, she got progressively sicker, and she never rode again. I put the bike in the garage, but every time I see it, I can't help but think back on that horrible night." He straightened up. "I know I should have already gotten rid of it, but I just couldn't give it to someone who'd ride it once or twice and then forget about it. I wanted it to go to someone who would appreciate it as much as she did. To someone who was going to use it. That's what my wife would have wanted. If you'd known her, you'd understand. You'd be doing me a favor."

When she spoke, her voice was subdued. "I can't take your wife's bike."

"So you're still giving it back?"

When she nodded, he leaned forward, propping his elbows on his knees. "You and I are a lot more alike than you realize. In your shoes, I would have done exactly the same thing. You don't want to feel like you owe anyone anything. You want to prove to yourself that you can make it on your own, right?"

She opened her mouth to answer but said nothing. In the silence, he went on.

"After my wife died, I was the same way. For a long time. People would drop by the store and a lot of them would tell me to call them if I ever needed anything. Most of them knew I didn't have any family here and they meant well, but I never called anyone because it just wasn't me. Even if I did want something, I wouldn't have known how to ask, but most of the time, I didn't even know what it was that I wanted. All I knew was that I was at the end of my rope, and to continue the metaphor, for a long time, I was barely hanging on. I mean, all at once, I had to take care of two young kids as well as the store, and the kids were younger then and needed even more attention than they do now. And then one day, Joyce showed up." He looked at her. "Have you met Joyce yet? Works a few afternoons a week including Sundays, older lady, talks to everyone? Josh and Kristen love her."

"I'm not sure."

"It's not important. But anyway, she showed up one afternoon, maybe around five or so, and she simply told me that she was going to take care of the kids while I spent the next week at the beach. She'd already arranged a place for me and she told me that I didn't have a choice in the matter because, in her opinion, I was heading straight for a nervous breakdown."

He pinched the bridge of his nose, trying to stifle the memory of those days. "I was upset about it at first.

I mean, they're my kids, right? And what kind of father was I to make people think that I couldn't handle being a father? But unlike anyone else, Joyce didn't ask me to call if I needed anything. She knew what I was going through and she went ahead and did what she thought was right. The next thing I knew, I was on my way to the beach. And she was right. The first two days, I was still a wreck. But over the next few days, I went for long walks, read some books, slept late, and by the time I got back, I realized that I was more relaxed than I'd been in a long time…"

He trailed off, feeling the weight of her scrutiny.

"I don't know why you're telling me this."

He turned toward her. "Both of us know that if I'd asked if you wanted the bicycle, you would have said no. So, like Joyce did with me, I just went ahead and did it because it was the right thing to do. Because I learned that it's okay to accept some help every now and then." He nodded toward the bike. "Take it," he said. "I have no use for it, and you have to admit that it would make getting to and from work a whole lot easier."

It took a few seconds before he saw her shoulders relax and she turned to him with a wry smile. "Did you practice that speech?"

"Of course." He tried to look sheepish. "But you'll take it?"

She hesitated. "A bike might be nice," she finally admitted. "Thank you."

For a long moment, neither of them said anything. As he stared at her profile, he noted again how pretty she was, though he had the sense that she didn't think so. Which only made her even more appealing.

"You're welcome," he said.

"But no more freebies, okay? You've done more than enough for me already."

"Fair enough." He nodded toward the bike. "Did it ride okay? With the baskets, I mean?"

"It was fine. Why?"

"Because Kristen and Josh helped me put them on yesterday. One of those rainy-day projects, you know? Kristen picked them out. Just so you know, she also thought you needed sparkly handlebar grips, too, but I drew the line at that."

"I wouldn't have minded sparkly handlebar grips."

He laughed. "I'll let her know."

She hesitated. "You're doing a good job, you know. With your kids, I mean."

"Thank you."

"I mean it. And I know it hasn't been easy."

"That's the thing about life. A lot of the time, it isn't easy at all. We just have to try to make the best of it. Do you know what I mean?"

"Yeah," she said. "I think I do."

The door to the store opened, and as Alex leaned forward he saw Josh scanning the parking lot, Kristen close behind him. With brown hair and brown eyes, Josh resembled his mom. His hair was a riotous mess, and Alex knew he'd just crawled out of bed.

"Over here, guys."

Josh scratched his head as he shuffled toward them. Kristen beamed, waving at Katie.

"Hey, Dad?" Josh asked.

"Yeah?"

"We wanted to ask if we're still going to the beach today. You promised to take us."

"That was the plan."

"With a barbecue?"

"Of course."

"Okay," he said. He rubbed his nose. "Hi, Miss Katie."

Katie waved at Josh and Kristen.

"Do you like the bike?" Kristen chirped.

"Yes. Thank you."

"I had to help my dad fix it," Josh informed her. "He's not too good with tools."

Katie glanced at Alex with a smirk. "He didn't mention that."

"It's okay. I knew what to do. But he had to help me with the new inner tube."

Kristen fixed her gaze on Katie. "Are you going to come to the beach, too?"

Katie sat up straighter. "I don't think so."

"Why not?" Kristen asked.

"She's probably working," Alex said.

"Actually, I'm not," she said. "I have a couple of things to do around the house."

"Then you have to come," Kristen cried. "It's really fun."

"That's your family time," she insisted. "I wouldn't want to be in the way."

"You won't be in the way. And it's really fun. You can watch me swim. Please?" Kristen begged.

Alex stayed quiet, loath to add pressure. He assumed Katie would say no, but surprising him, she nodded slightly. When she spoke, her voice was soft.

"Okay," she finally said.

9

———— ❧ ————

After getting back from the store, Katie parked the bike at the back of the cottage and went inside to change. She didn't have a bathing suit, but she wouldn't have worn one even if she did. As natural as it was for a teenager to walk around in front of strangers in the equivalent of underwear and a bra, she wasn't comfortable wearing something like that in front of Alex on a day out with his kids. Or frankly, even without the kids.

Though she resisted the idea, she had to admit he intrigued her. Not because of the things he'd done for her, as touching as that was. It had more to do with the sad way he smiled sometimes, the expression on his face when he'd told her about his wife, or the way he treated his kids. There was a loneliness within him that he couldn't disguise, and she knew that in some way it matched her own.

She knew he was interested in her. She'd been around long enough to recognize when men found her attractive; the clerk at the grocery store talking too much or a stranger glancing her way, or a waiter at a restaurant checking on their table just a bit too frequently. In time, she'd learned to pretend she was oblivious to the attention of those men; in other instances, she showed obvious disdain, because she'd known what would happen if she didn't. Later. Once they got home. Once they were alone.

But that life was gone now, she reminded herself. Opening the drawers, she pulled out a pair of shorts and the sandals she'd picked up at Anna Jean's. The night before, she'd had wine with a friend, and now she was going to the beach with Alex and his family. These were ordinary events in an ordinary life. The concept felt alien, like she was learning the customs of a foreign land, and it left her feeling strangely elated and wary at exactly the same time.

As soon as she finished dressing, she saw Alex's jeep coming up the gravel road and she drew a long breath as he pulled to a stop in front of her house. Now or never, she thought to herself as she stepped out onto the porch.

"You need to put on your seat belt, Miss Katie," Kristen said from behind her. "My dad won't drive unless you're wearing it."

Alex looked over at her, as if to say, *Are you ready for this?* She gave him her bravest smile.

"Okay," he said, "let's go."

They reached the coastal town of Long Beach, complete with saltbox houses and expansive views of the sea, in less than an hour. Alex pulled into a small parking lot nestled against the dunes; saw grass billowed nearby in the stiff sea breeze. Katie got out of the car and stared at the ocean, breathing deeply.

The kids climbed out and immediately made for the path between the dunes.

"I'm going to check the water, Dad!" Josh shouted, holding up his mask and snorkel.

"Me, too!" Kristen added, trailing behind.

Alex was busy unloading the back of the jeep. "Hold up," he called out. "Just wait, okay?"

Josh sighed, his impatience obvious as he shifted from one foot to the other. Alex began pulling out the cooler.

"Do you need some help?" Katie asked.

He shook his head. "I can handle this. But would you mind putting some sunscreen on the kids and keeping an eye on them for a few minutes? I know they're excited to be here."

"That's fine," she said, turning to Kristen and Josh. "Are you two ready?"

Alex spent the next few minutes ferrying the items from the car, setting up camp near the picnic table closest to the dune, where high tide wouldn't encroach. Though there were a few other families, for the most part they had this section of beach to themselves. Katie had slipped off her sandals and was standing at the water's edge as the kids splashed in the shallows. Her arms were crossed and even from a distance, Alex noticed a rare expression of contentment on her face.

He slung a couple of towels over his shoulder as he approached. "It's hard to believe there was a storm yesterday, isn't it?"

She turned at the sound of his voice. "I forgot how much I missed the ocean."

"Been awhile?"

"Too long," she said, listening to the steady rhythm of the waves as they gently rolled ashore.

Josh ran in and out of the waves, while off to the side Kristen crouched, searching for collectible seashells.

"It must be hard sometimes, raising them on your own," Katie observed.

Alex hesitated, considering it. When he spoke, his voice was soft. "Most of the time, it isn't so bad. We kind of get into a rhythm, you know? In our daily lives? It's when we do things like this—where there is no rhythm—that it sometimes gets frustrating." He kicked briefly at the sand, making a small furrow at their feet. "When my wife and I talked about having a third child, she tried to warn me that a third child would mean moving from 'man-to-man' to 'zone' defense. She used to joke that she wasn't sure I was up to it. But here I am, in zone defense every day..." he trailed off, shaking his head. "Sorry. I shouldn't have said that."

"Said what?"

"It seems like every time I talk to you, I end up talking about my wife."

For the first time, she turned to him. "Why shouldn't you talk about your wife?"

He pushed a pile of sand back and forth, smoothing over the ditch he'd just made. "Because I don't want you to think that I can't talk about anything else. That all I do is live in the past."

"You loved her very much, didn't you?"

"Yes," he answered.

"And she was a major part of your life and the mother of your kids, right?"

"Yes."

"Then it's okay to talk about her," she said. "You should talk about her. She's part of who you are."

Alex flashed a grateful smile but couldn't think of anything to say. Katie seemed to read his mind, and when she spoke, her voice was gentle. "How did the two of you meet?"

"We met in a bar, of all places. She was out with some girlfriends celebrating someone's birthday. It was hot and crowded and the lights were low and the music was loud, and she just . . . stood out. I mean, all her friends were a little out of control and it was obvious that all of them were having a good time, but she was as cool as can be."

"I'll bet she was beautiful, too."

"That goes without saying," he said. "So, swallowing my nervousness, I wandered over and proceeded to use every ounce of charm I had at my disposal."

When he paused, he noticed the smile playing at the corners of her lips.

"And?" she asked.

"And it still took me three hours to get so much as a name and phone number from her."

She laughed. "And let me guess. You called the next day, right? And asked her out?"

"How would you know that?"

"You seem like the type."

"Spoken like someone who's been hit on more than a few times."

She shrugged, leaving it open to interpretation. "Then what?"

"Why do you want to hear this?"

"I don't know," she admitted. "But I do."

He studied her. "Fair enough," he finally said. "So anyway—as you already magically knew—I asked her out to lunch and we spent the rest of the afternoon talking.

That weekend, I told her that the two of us would get married one day."

"You're kidding."

"I know it sounds crazy. Believe me, she thought it was crazy, too. But I just...knew. She was smart and kind and we had a lot in common and we wanted the same things in life. She laughed a lot and she made me laugh, too... honestly, of the two of us, I was the lucky one."

Rollers continued to ride the ocean breeze, pushing over her ankles. "She probably thought she was lucky, too."

"That's only because I was able to fool her."

"I doubt that."

"That's because I'm able to fool you, too."

She laughed. "I don't think so."

"You're just saying that because we're friends."

"You think we're friends?"

"Yeah," he said, holding her gaze. "Don't you?"

He could tell by her expression that the idea surprised her, but before she could answer, Kristen came splashing toward them, holding a fistful of seashells.

"Miss Katie!" she cried. "I found some really pretty ones!"

Katie bent lower. "Can you show me?"

Kristen held them out, dumping them into Katie's hand before turning toward Alex. "Hey, Daddy?" she asked. "Can we get the barbecue started? I'm really hungry."

"Sure, sweetie." He took a few steps down the beach, watching his son diving in and out of the waves. As Josh popped back up, Alex cupped his mouth. "Hey, Josh?" he shouted. "I'm going to start the coals, so why don't you come in for a while."

"Now?" Josh shouted back.

"Just for a little while."

Even from a distance, he saw his son's shoulders droop. Katie must have noticed it as well, because she was quick to speak up.

"I can stay down here if you want," she assured him.

"You sure?"

"Kristen's showing me her seashells," she said.

He nodded and turned back to Josh. "Miss Katie's going to watch you, okay? So don't go out too far!"

"I won't!" he said, grinning.

10

❦

A little while later, Katie led a shivering Kristen and excited Josh back toward the blanket Alex had spread out earlier. The grill had been set up and the briquettes were already glowing white on the edges.

Alex unfolded the last of the beach chairs onto the blanket and watched them approach. "How was the water, guys?"

"Awesome!" Josh answered. His hair, partially dried, was pointing in every direction. "When's lunch?"

Alex checked the coals. "Give me about twenty minutes."

"Can me and Kristen go back to the water?"

"You just got out of the water. Why don't you take a break for a few minutes?"

"We don't want to swim. We want to build sand castles," he said.

Alex noted Kristen's chattering teeth. "Are you sure you want to do that? You're purple."

Kristen nodded vehemently. "I'm okay," she said shivering. "And we're supposed to build castles at the beach."

"All right. But let's throw shirts on you two. And stay right there where I can see you," he said, pointing.

"I know, Dad." Josh sighed. "I'm not a little kid anymore."

Alex rummaged through a duffel bag and helped both Josh and Kristen put their shirts on. When he was finished, Josh grabbed a bag full of plastic toys and shovels and ran off, stopping a few feet from the water's edge. Kristen trailed behind him.

"Do you want me to head down there?" Katie asked.

He shook his head. "No, they'll be okay. This is the part they're used to. When I'm cooking, I mean. They know to stay out of the water."

Moving to the cooler, he squatted down and opened the lid. "Are you getting hungry, too?" he asked.

"A little," she said before realizing that she hadn't eaten anything since the cheese and wine she'd had the evening before. On cue, she heard her stomach growl and she crossed her arms over it.

"Good, because I'm starved." As Alex began rummaging through the cooler, Katie noticed the sinewy muscles of his forearm. "I was thinking hot dogs for Josh, a cheeseburger for Kristen, and for you and me, steaks." He pulled out the meat and set it aside, then leaned over the grill, blowing on the coals.

"Can I help with anything?"

"Would you mind putting the tablecloth on the table? It's in the cooler."

"Sure," Katie said. She pulled one of the bags of ice out of the cooler and simply stared. "There's enough food for half a dozen families in here," she said.

"Yeah, well, with kids, my motto has always been

bring too much rather than not enough, since I never know exactly what they'll eat. You can't imagine how many times we've come out here and I've forgotten something and have had to load the kids back up and run to the store. I wanted to avoid that today."

She unfolded the plastic tablecloth and, at Alex's direction, secured the corners with paperweights he had somehow thought to bring.

"What next? Do you want me to put everything else on the table?"

"We've got a few minutes. And I don't know about you, but I'm ready for a beer," he said. Reaching into the cooler, he pulled out a bottle. "You?"

"I'll take a soda," she said.

"Diet Coke?" he asked, reaching back in.

"Great."

When he passed the can to her, his hand brushed against hers, though she wasn't sure he even noticed.

He motioned to the chairs. "Would you like to sit?"

She hesitated before taking a seat next to him. When he'd set them up, he'd left enough distance between them so that they wouldn't accidentally touch. Alex twisted the cap from his beer and took a pull. "There's nothing better than a cold beer on a hot day at the beach."

She smiled, slightly disconcerted at being alone with him. "I'll take your word for it."

"You don't like beer?"

Her mind flashed to her father and the empty cans of Pabst Blue Ribbon that usually littered the floor next to the recliner where he sat. "Not too much," she admitted.

"Just wine, huh?"

It took her a moment to remember that he'd given her

a bottle. "I had some wine last night, as a matter of fact. With my neighbor."

"Yeah? Good for you."

She searched for a safe topic. "You said you were from Spokane?"

He stretched his legs out in front of him, crossing them at the ankles. "Born and raised. I lived in the same house until I went to college." He cast a sidelong glance at her. "University of Washington, by the way. Go, Huskies."

She smiled. "Do your parents still live there?"

"Yes."

"That must make it hard for them to visit the grandkids."

"I suppose."

Something in his tone caught her attention. "You suppose?"

"They're not the kind of grandparents who would come by, even if they were closer. They've seen the kids only twice, once when Kristen was born and the second time at the funeral." He shook his head. "Don't ask me to explain it," he went on, "but my parents have no interest in them, aside from sending them cards on their birthdays and gifts at Christmas. They'd rather travel or do whatever it is they do."

"Huh?"

"What can I do? And besides, I can't say they were all that different with me, even though I was their youngest child. The first time they visited me in college was graduation day, and even though I swam well enough to get a full scholarship, they saw me race only twice. Even if I lived across the street from them, I doubt they'd want to see the kids. That's one of the reasons I stayed here. I might as well, right?"

"What about the other set of grandparents?"

He scratched at the label on his bottle of beer. "That's trickier. They had two other daughters who moved to Florida, and after they sold me the store, they moved down there. They come up once or twice a year to visit for a few days, but it's still hard for them. And they won't stay at the house, either, because I think it reminds them of Carly. Too many memories."

"In other words, you're pretty much on your own."

"It's just the opposite," he said, nodding toward the kids. "I have them, remember?"

"It has to be hard sometimes, though. Running the store, raising your kids."

"It's not so bad. As long as I'm up by six in the morning and don't go to bed until midnight, it's easy to keep up."

She laughed easily. "Do you think the coals are getting close?"

"Let me check," he said. After setting the bottle in the sand, he stood up from his chair and walked over to the grill. The briquettes were white and heat rose in shimmering waves. "Your timing is impeccable," he said. He threw the steaks and the hamburger patty on the grill while Katie went to the cooler and started bringing the endless array of items to the table: Tupperware containers of potato salad, coleslaw, pickles, a green bean salad, sliced fruit, two bags of chips, slices of cheese, and assorted condiments.

She shook her head as she started arranging everything, thinking that Alex somehow forgot that his kids were still little. There was more food here than she'd kept in her house the entire time she'd lived in Southport.

Alex flipped the steaks and the hamburger patty and

then added the hot dogs to the grill. As he did, he found his gaze drifting to Katie's legs as she moved around the table, noting again how attractive she was.

She seemed to realize he was staring. "What?" she asked.

"Nothing," he said.

"You were thinking about something."

He sighed. "I'm glad you decided to come today," he finally said. "Because I'm having a great time."

As Alex hovered over the grill, they settled into easy conversation. Alex gave her an overview of what it was like to run a country store. He told her how his in-laws had started the business and described with affection some of the regulars, people who could best be described as eccentric, and Katie silently wondered whether she would have been included in that description had he brought someone else to the beach.

Not that it would have mattered. The more he talked, the more she realized that he was the kind of man who tried to find the best in people, the kind of man who didn't like to complain. She tried and failed to imagine what he'd been like when he was younger, and gradually she steered the conversation in that direction. He talked about growing up in Spokane and the long, lazy weekends he spent riding bikes along the Centennial Trail with friends; he told her that once he discovered swimming, it quickly became an obsession. He swam four or five hours a day and had Olympic dreams, but a torn rotator cuff in his sophomore year of college put an end to those. He told her about the fraternity parties he'd attended and the friends he'd made in college, and admitted that nearly all of those friendships had slowly but surely drifted away. As he talked, Katie noticed that he didn't seem to either embellish or downplay his past, nor did he appear to be overly preoccupied with what others thought of him.

She could see the traces of the elite athlete he once had been, noting the graceful, fluid way he moved and the easy way he smiled, as if long accustomed to both victory and defeat. When he paused, she worried that he would ask about her past, but he seemed to sense that it would make her uncomfortable and would instead launch into another story.

When the food was ready, he called the kids and they came running. They were covered in sand, and Alex had them stand to the side while he brushed them off. Watching him, she knew he was a better father than he gave himself credit for; good, she suspected, in all the ways that mattered.

Once the kids got to the table, the conversation shifted. She listened as they chattered on about their sand castle and one of the shows on the Disney Channel they both enjoyed. When they wondered aloud about the s'mores they were supposed to have later—marshmallows, chocolate bars, and graham crackers, warmed until melting—it was clear that Alex had created special, fun traditions for his kids. He was different, she thought, from the men she'd met in her past, different from anyone she'd met before, and as the conversation rambled on, any vestiges of the nervousness she'd once felt began to slip away.

The food was delicious, a welcome change from her recent austere diet. The sky remained clear, the blue expanse broken only by an occasional seabird passing overhead. The breeze rose and fell, enough to keep them cool, and the steady rhythm of the waves added to the sense of calm.

When they finished eating, Josh and Kristen helped clear the table and pack away the uneaten items. A few items that wouldn't spoil—the pickles and the chips— were left on the table. The kids wanted to go boogie boarding, and after Alex reapplied their suntan lotion, he slipped off his shirt and followed them into the waves.

Katie carried her chair to the water's edge and spent the next hour watching as he helped the kids through the breakers, moving one and then the other into position to catch the waves. The kids were squealing with delight, obviously having the time of their lives. She marveled at the way Alex was able to make each of them feel like the center of attention. There was a tenderness in the way he treated them, a depth of patience that she hadn't quite expected. As the afternoon wore on and the clouds began to drift in, she found herself smiling at the thought that for the first time in many years, she felt completely relaxed. And not only that, she knew she was having as much fun as the kids.

11

———— 🍂 ————

After they got out of the water, Kristen declared that she was cold and Alex led her to the bathroom to help her change into dry clothes. Katie stayed with Josh on the blanket, admiring the way the sunlight rippled on the water while Josh scooped sand into little piles.

"Hey, do you want to help me fly my kite?" Josh suddenly asked.

"I don't know that I've ever flown a kite before..."

"It's easy," he insisted, digging around in the pile of toys Alex had brought and pulling out a small kite. "I can show you how. C'mon."

He took off running down the beach, and Katie jogged a few steps before settling back into a brisk walk. By the time she reached him, he was already beginning to unwind the string and he handed her the kite. "Just hold this above your head, okay?"

She nodded as Josh started to back up slowly, continuing to loosen the string with practiced ease.

"Are you ready?" he shouted as he finally came to a stop. "When I take off running and yell, just let go!"

"I'm ready!" she shouted back.

Josh started running, and when Katie felt the tension in the kite and heard him shout, she released it immediately. She wasn't sure the breeze was strong enough, but the kite shot straight to the sky within seconds. Josh stopped and turned around. As she walked toward him, he let out even more line.

Reaching his side, she shielded her eyes from the sun as she watched the slowly rising kite. Black and yellow, the distinctive Batman logo was visible even from a distance.

"I'm pretty good at flying kites," he said, staring up at it. "How come you've never flown one?"

"I don't know. It just wasn't something I did as a kid."

"You should have. It's fun."

Josh continued to stare upward, his face a mask of concentration. For the first time, Katie noticed how much Josh and Kristen looked alike.

"How do you like school? You're in kindergarten, right?"

"It's okay. I like recess best. We have races and stuff."

Of course, she thought. Since they had arrived at the beach, he'd barely stopped moving. "Is your teacher nice?"

"She's really nice. She's kind of like my dad. She doesn't yell or anything."

"Your dad doesn't yell?"

"No," he said with great conviction.

"What does he do when he gets mad?"

"He doesn't get mad."

Katie studied Josh, wondering if he was serious before realizing that he was.

"Do you have a lot of friends?" he asked.

"Not too many. Why?"

"Because my dad says that you're his friend. That's why he brought you to the beach."

"When did he say that?"

"When we were in the waves."

"What else did he say?"

"He asked us if it bothered us that you came."

"Does it?"

"Why should it?" He shrugged. "Everybody needs friends, and the beach is fun."

No argument there. "You're right," she said.

"My mom used to come with us out here, you know."

"She did?"

"Yeah, but she died."

"I know. And I'm sorry. That must be hard. You must miss her very much."

He nodded and for an instant, he looked both older and younger than his age. "My dad gets sad sometimes. He doesn't think I know, but I can tell."

"I'd be sad, too."

He was quiet as he thought about her answer. "Thanks for helping me with my kite," he said.

"You two seemed to be having a good time," Alex observed.

After Kristen had changed, Alex helped her get her kite in the air and then went to stand with Katie on the compact sand near the water's edge. Katie could feel her hair moving slightly in the breeze.

"He's sweet. And more talkative than I thought he'd be."

As Alex watched his kids managing their kites, she had the sense that his eyes missed nothing.

"So this is what you do on weekends after you leave the store. You spend time with the kids?"

"Always," he said. "I think it's important."

"Even though it sounds like your parents felt differently?"

He hesitated. "That would be the easy answer, right? I felt slighted somehow and made a promise to myself to be different? It sounds good, but I don't know if it's totally accurate. The truth is that I spend time with them because I enjoy it. I enjoy them. I like watching them grow up and I want to be part of that."

As he answered, Katie found herself remembering her own childhood, trying and failing to imagine either of her parents echoing Alex's sentiments.

"Why did you join the army after you got out of school?"

"At the time, I thought it was the right thing to do. I was up for a new challenge, I wanted to try something different, and joining gave me an excuse to leave Washington. With the exception of a couple of swim meets here and there, I'd never even left the state."

"Did you ever see . . . ?"

When she trailed off, he finished her sentence. "Combat? No, I wasn't that kind of army. I was a criminal justice major in college and I ended up in CID."

"What's that?"

When he told her, she turned toward him. "Like the police?"

He nodded. "I was a detective," he said.

Katie said nothing. Instead, she turned away abruptly, her face closing down like a gate slamming shut.

"Did I say something wrong?" he asked.

She shook her head without answering. Alex stared at her, wondering what was going on. His suspicions about her past surfaced almost immediately.

"What's going on, Katie?"

"Nothing," she insisted, but as soon as the word came out, he knew she wasn't telling the truth. In another place and time, he would have followed up with another question, but instead, he let it drop.

"We don't have to talk about it," he said quietly. "And besides, it's not who I am anymore. Believe me when I say I'm a lot happier running a general store."

She nodded, but he sensed a trace of lingering anxiety. He could tell she needed space, even if he wasn't sure why. He motioned over his shoulder with his thumb. "Listen, I forgot to add more briquettes to the grill. If the kids don't get their s'mores, I'll never hear the end of it. I'll be right back, okay?"

"Sure," she answered, feigning nonchalance. When he jogged off, Katie exhaled, feeling like she'd somehow escaped. *He used to be a police officer*, she thought to herself, and she tried to tell herself that it didn't matter. Even so, it took almost a minute of steady breathing before she felt somewhat in control again. Kristen and Josh were in the same places, though Kristen had bent over to examine another seashell, ignoring her soaring kite.

She heard Alex approaching behind her.

"Told you it wouldn't take long," he said easily. "After we eat the s'mores, I was thinking about calling it a day. I'd love to stay out until the sun sets, but Josh has school tomorrow."

"Whenever you want to go is fine with me," she said, crossing her arms.

Noting her rigid shoulders and the tight way she'd spoken the words, he furrowed his brow. "I'm not sure what I said that bothered you, but I'm sorry, okay?" he finally said. "Just know that I'm here if you want to talk about it."

She nodded without answering, and though Alex waited for more, there was nothing. "Is this the way it's going to be with us?" he asked.

"What do you mean?"

"I feel like I'm suddenly walking on eggshells around you, but I don't know why."

"I'd tell you but I can't," she said. Her voice was almost inaudible over the sound of the waves.

"Can you at least tell me what I said? Or what I did?"

She turned toward him. "You didn't say or do anything wrong. But right now, I can't say any more than that, okay?"

He studied her. "Okay," he said. "As long as you're still having a good time."

It took some effort, but she finally managed a smile. "This is the best day I've spent in a long time. Best weekend in fact."

"You're still mad about the bike, aren't you?" he said, narrowing his eyes in mock suspicion. Despite the tension she felt, she laughed.

"Of course. It's going to take a long time for me to recover from that," she said, pretending to pout.

Turning his gaze to the horizon, he seemed relieved.

"Can I ask you something?" Katie asked, turning serious again. "You don't have to answer if you don't want to."

"Anything," he said.

"What happened to your wife? You said she had a seizure, but you haven't told me why she was sick."

He sighed, as if he'd known all along she was going to ask but still had to steel himself to answer. "She had a brain tumor," he began slowly. "Or, more accurately, she had three different types of brain tumors. I didn't know it then, but I learned that's fairly common. The one that was slow-growing was just what you'd think; it was about the size of an egg and the surgeons were able to take most of it out. But the other tumors weren't so simple. They were the kind of tumors that spread like spider legs, and there was no way to remove them without removing part of her brain. They were aggressive, too. The doctors did the best they could, but even when they walked out of surgery and told me that it had gone as well as it could, I knew exactly what they meant."

"I can't imagine hearing something like that." She stared down at the sand.

"I admit I had trouble believing it. It was so…unexpected. I mean, the week before, we were a normal family, and the next thing I knew, she was dying and there was nothing I could do to stop it."

Off to the side, Kristen and Josh were still concentrating on their kites but Katie knew that Alex could barely see them.

"After surgery, it took a few weeks for her to get back on her feet and I wanted to believe that things were okay. But after that, week by week, I began to notice little changes. The left side of her body started to get weaker and she was taking longer and longer naps. It was hard, but the worst part for me was that she began to pull away from the kids. Like she didn't want them to remember her being sick; she wanted them to remember the way she used to be." He paused before finally shaking his head. "I'm sorry. I shouldn't have told you that. She was a great mom. I mean, look how well they're turning out."

"I think their father has something to do with that, too."

"I try. But half the time, it doesn't feel like I know what I'm doing. It's like I'm faking it."

"I think all parents feel like that."

He turned toward her. "Did yours?"

She hesitated. "I think my parents did the best they could." Not a ringing endorsement, but the truth.

"Are you close with them?"

"They died in a car accident when I was nineteen."

He stared at her. "I'm sorry to hear that."

"It was tough," Katie said.

"Do you have any brothers and sisters?"

"No," she said. She turned toward the water. "It's just me."

A few minutes later, Alex helped the kids reel in their kites and they headed back to the picnic area. The coals weren't quite ready and Alex used the time to rinse the boogie boards and shake sand from the towels before pulling out what he needed for the s'mores.

Kristen and Josh helped pack up most of their things and Katie put the rest of the food back into the cooler while Alex began ferrying items to the jeep. By the time he was finished, only a blanket and four chairs remained. The kids had arranged them in a circle while Alex handed out long prongs and the bag of marshmallows. In his excitement, Josh ripped it open, spilling a small pile onto the blanket.

Following the kids' lead, Katie pushed three marshmallows onto the prong and the four of them stood over the grill, twirling the prongs, while the sugary puffs turned golden brown. Katie held hers a little too close to the heat and two of the marshmallows caught on fire, which Alex quickly blew out.

When they were ready, Alex helped the kids finish the treat: chocolate on the graham cracker, followed by the marshmallow and topped with another cracker. It was sticky and sweet and the best thing Katie had eaten in as long as she could remember.

Sitting between his kids, she noticed Alex struggling with his crumbling s'more, making a mess, and when he used his fingers to wipe his mouth, it made matters only worse. The kids found it hilarious, and Katie couldn't help giggling as well, and she felt a sudden, unexpected surge of hope. Despite the tragedy they'd all gone through, this was what a happy family looked like; this, she thought, is what a loving family did when they were together. For them, it was nothing but an ordinary day on an ordinary weekend, but for her, there was something revelatory about the notion that wonderful moments like these existed. And that maybe, just maybe, it would be possible for her to experience similar days in the future.

12

Then what happened?"

Jo was sitting across from her at the table, the kitchen glowing yellow, illuminated only by the light above the stove. After Katie had returned, she'd come over, specks of paint in her hair. Katie had started a pot of coffee and two cups were on the table.

"Nothing, really. After finishing the s'mores, we walked down the beach one last time, then got in the car and drove home."

"Did he walk you to the door?"

"Yes."

"Did you invite him in?"

"He had to get the kids back home."

"Did you kiss him good night?"

"Of course not."

"Why not?"

"Weren't you listening? He was bringing his kids to the beach and he invited me along. It wasn't a date."

Jo raised her coffee cup. "It sounds like a date."

"It was a family day."

Jo considered that. "It sounded like the two of you spent a lot of time talking."

Katie leaned back in her chair. "I think you wanted it to be a date."

"Why would I want that?"

"I have no idea. But ever since we've met, in every conversation, you bring him up somehow. It's like you've been trying to ... I don't know. Make sure I notice him."

Jo swirled the contents of her cup before setting it back on the table. "And have you?"

Katie threw up her hands. "See what I mean?"

Jo laughed before shaking her head. "All right. How about this?" She hesitated, then went on. "I've met a lot of people, and over time I've developed instincts that I've learned to trust. As we both know, Alex is a great guy, and once I got to know you, I felt the same way about you. Other than that, I haven't done anything more than tease you about it. It's not like I dragged you to the store and introduced the two of you. Nor was I around when he asked you to go to the beach, an invitation you were more than willing to accept."

"Kristen asked me to go ..."

"I know. You told me that," Jo said, arching an eyebrow. "And I'm sure that's the only reason you went."

Katie scowled. "You have a funny way of twisting things around."

Jo laughed again. "Did you ever think that it's because I'm envious? Oh, not that you went with Alex, but that you got to go to the beach on a perfect day, while I was stuck inside painting ... for the second day in a row? If I never touch a paint roller again in my life, it'll still be too soon. My arms and shoulders are *sore*."

Katie stood up from the table and went to the counter.

She poured another cup of coffee for herself and held up the pot. "More?"

"No, thank you. I need to sleep tonight and the caffeine would keep me up. I think I'm going to order some Chinese food. You want any?"

"I'm not hungry," Katie said. "I ate too much today."

"I don't think that's possible. But you did get a lot of sun. It looks good on you, even if it'll lead to wrinkles later."

Katie snorted. "Thanks for that."

"What are friends for?" Jo stood and gave a catlike stretch. "And listen, I had a good time last night. Although, I have to admit, I paid for it this morning."

"It was fun," Katie agreed.

Jo took a couple of steps before turning around. "Oh, I forgot to ask you. Are you going to keep the bike?"

"Yes," Katie said.

Jo thought about it. "Good for you."

"What do you mean by that?"

"Just that I don't think you should give it back. You obviously need it and he wanted you to have it. Why shouldn't you keep it?" She shrugged. "Your problem is that you sometimes read too much into things."

"Like with my manipulative friend?"

"Do you really think I'm manipulative?"

Katie thought about it. "Maybe a little."

Jo smiled. "So what's your schedule like this week? Are you working a lot?"

Katie nodded. "Six nights and three days."

Jo made a face. "Yuck."

"It's okay. I need the money and I'm used to it."

"And, of course, you had a great weekend."

Katie paused. "Yeah," she said. "I did."

13

The next few days passed uneventfully, which only made them feel longer to Alex. He hadn't spoken to Katie since he'd dropped her off on Sunday evening. It wasn't completely unexpected, since he knew she was working a lot this week, but more than once he found himself wandering out of the store and staring up the road, feeling vaguely disappointed when he didn't see her.

It was enough to squash the illusion that he'd dazzled her to the point that she couldn't resist stopping by. He was surprised, though, by the almost teenage-like enthusiasm he felt at the prospect of seeing her again, even if she didn't feel the same way. He pictured her on the beach, her chestnut hair fluttering in the breeze, her delicately boned features, and eyes that seemed to change color every time he saw them. Little by little, she'd relaxed as the day had worn on, and he had the sense that going to the beach had softened her resistance somehow.

He wondered not only about her past, but about all the other things he still didn't know about her. He tried to imagine what kind of music she liked, or what she thought about first thing in the morning, or whether or not she'd ever attended a baseball game. He wondered whether she slept on her back or on her side and, if given the choice, whether she preferred a shower to a bath. The more he wondered, the more curious he became.

He wished she would trust him with the details of her past, not because he was under the illusion that he could somehow rescue her or felt that she even needed to be rescued, but because giving voice to the truth of her past meant opening the door to the future. It meant they would be able to have a real conversation.

By Thursday, he was debating whether to drop by her cottage. He wanted to and had once even reached for his keys, but in the end he'd stopped because he had no idea what to say once he got there. Nor could he predict how she might respond. Would she smile? Or be nervous? Would she invite him inside or ask him to leave? As much as he tried to imagine what might happen, he couldn't, and he'd ended up putting the keys aside.

It was complicated. But then again, he reminded himself, she was a mysterious woman.

It didn't take long before Katie admitted that the bicycle was a godsend. Not only was she able to come home between her shifts on the days she pulled doubles, but for the first time, she felt as though she could really begin to explore the town, which was exactly what she did. On Tuesday, she visited a couple of antique stores, enjoyed the watercolor seascapes at a local art gallery, and rode through neighborhoods, marveling at the broad sweeping porches and porticos adorning the historic homes near the waterfront. On

Wednesday, she visited the library and spent a couple of hours browsing the shelves and reading the flaps of books, loading the bicycle baskets with novels that interested her.

In the evenings, though, as she lay in bed reading the books she'd checked out, she sometimes found her thoughts drifting to Alex. Sifting through her memories, those from Altoona, she realized he reminded her of her friend Callie's father. In her sophomore year in high school, Callie had lived down the street from her and though they didn't know each other that well—Callie was a couple of years younger—Katie could remember sitting on her porch steps every Saturday morning. Like clockwork, Callie's dad would open the garage, whistling as he rolled the lawn mower into place. He was proud of his yard—it was easily the most manicured in the neighborhood—and she'd watch as he pushed the mower back and forth with military precision. He stopped every so often to move a fallen branch out of the way, and in those moments, he would wipe his face with a handkerchief he kept in his back pocket. When he was finished, he would lean against the hood of the Ford in his driveway, sipping a glass of lemonade that his wife always brought to him. Sometimes, she would lean on the car alongside him, and Katie would smile as she saw him pat his wife's hip whenever he wanted to get her attention.

There was something contented in the way he sipped his drink and touched his wife that made her think he was satisfied with the life he was leading and that all his dreams had somehow been fulfilled. Often, as Katie studied him, she wondered how her life would have been had she been born into that family.

Alex had the same air of contentment about him when

his kids were around. Somehow he not only had been able to move past the tragedy of losing his wife but had done so with enough strength to help his kids move past the loss as well. When he'd spoken about his wife, Katie had listened for bitterness or self-pity, but there hadn't been any. There'd been sorrow, of course, and a loneliness in his expression as he spoke of her, but at the same time, he'd told Katie about his wife without making her feel like he'd been comparing the two of them. He seemed to accept her, and though she wasn't sure exactly when it had happened, she realized that she was attracted to him.

Beyond that, her feelings were complicated. Not since Atlantic City had she lowered her guard enough to let someone else get so close, and that ended up being a nightmare. But as hard as she'd tried to remain aloof, it seemed that every time she saw Alex, something happened to draw them together. Sometimes by accident, like when Josh fell in the river and she'd stayed with Kristen, but sometimes it seemed almost preordained. Like the storm rolling in. Or Kristen wandering out and pleading with her to come to the beach. To this point, she'd had enough sense to volunteer little about herself, but that was the thing. The more time she spent with Alex, the more she had the sense that he knew far more than he was letting on, and it frightened her. It made her feel naked and vulnerable and it was part of the reason she'd avoided going to the store at all this week. She needed time to think, time to decide what, if anything, she was going to do about it.

Unfortunately, she'd spent too much time dwelling on the way the fine lines at the corners of his eyes crinkled when he grinned or the graceful way he'd emerged from the surf. She thought about how Kristen would reach for his hand and the absolute trust Katie saw in that simple gesture. Early on, Jo had said something along the lines that Alex was a good man, the kind of man who would do the right thing, and though Katie couldn't claim to know him well, her instincts told her he was a man she could trust. That no matter what she told him, he would support her. That he would guard her secrets and never use what he knew to hurt her.

It was irrational and illogical and it went against everything she'd promised herself when she'd moved here, but she realized that she wanted him to know her. She wanted him to understand her, if only because she had the strange sense that he was the kind of man she could fall in love with, even if she didn't want to.

14

Butterfly hunting.

The notion had popped into his head soon after waking on Saturday morning, even before he'd gone downstairs to open the store. Strangely, as he'd been pondering the possibilities of what to do with the kids that day, he'd remembered a project he'd done in the sixth grade. The teacher had asked the students to make an insect collection. He flashed to a memory of running through a grassy field at recess, chasing after everything from bumblebees to katydids. He was certain that Josh and Kristen would enjoy it, and feeling proud of himself for coming up with something exciting and original to occupy a weekend afternoon, he sifted through the fishing nets he had in the store, choosing three that were about the right size.

When he told them at lunch, Josh and Kristen were less than enthusiastic about the idea.

"I don't want to hurt any butterflies," Kristen protested. "I like butterflies."

"We don't have to hurt them. We can let them go."

"Then why catch them in the first place?"

"Because it's fun."

"It doesn't sound fun. It sounds mean."

Alex opened his mouth to respond, but he wasn't sure what to say. Josh took another bite of his grilled cheese sandwich.

"It's pretty hot already, Dad," Josh pointed out, talking as he chewed.

"That's okay. Afterward, we can swim in the creek. And chew with your mouth closed."

Josh swallowed. "Why don't we just swim in the creek now?"

"Because we're going butterfly hunting."

"Can we go to a movie instead?"

"Yeah!" Kristen said. "Let's go to a movie."

Parenting, Alex thought, could be exasperating.

"It's a beautiful day and we're not going to spend it sitting inside. We're going butterfly hunting. And not only that, you're going to enjoy it, okay?"

After lunch, Alex drove them to a field on the outskirts of town that was filled with wildflowers. He handed them their nets and sent them on their way, watching as Josh sort of dragged his net while Kristen held hers tucked against her, in much the same way she held her dolls.

Alex took matters into his own hands and jogged ahead of both of them, his net at the ready. Up ahead, fluttering among the wildflowers, he spotted dozens of butterflies. When he got close enough, he swung his net, capturing one. Squatting down, he carefully began to shift the net, allowing the orange and brown colors to show through.

"Wow!" he shouted, trying to sound as enthusiastic as he could. "I got one!"

The next thing he knew, Josh and Kristen were peering over his shoulder.

"Be careful with it, Daddy!" Kristen cried.

"I will, baby. Look at how pretty the colors are."

They leaned in even closer.

"Cool!" Josh shouted, and a moment later, he was off and running, swinging the net with abandon.

Kristen continued to study the butterfly. "What kind is it?"

"It's a skipper," Alex said. "But I don't know exactly what kind."

"I think he's scared," Kristen said.

"I'm sure he's fine. But I'll let him go, okay?"

She nodded as Alex carefully pulled the net inside out. In the open air, the butterfly clung to the net before taking off in flight. Kristen's eyes went wide with wonder.

"Can you help me catch one?" she asked.

"I'd love to."

They spent a little more than an hour running among the flowers. They caught about eight different kinds of butterflies, including a buckeye, though the vast majority were skippers like the first. By the time they finished, the kids' faces were red and shiny, so Alex drove them to get ice cream cones before heading to the creek behind the house. The three of them jumped off the dock together—Josh and Kristen wearing life preservers—and floated downstream in the slow-moving water. It was the kind of day he'd spent as a kid. By the time they got out of the water, he was contented by the thought that, aside from going to the beach, it was the best weekend they'd had in a while.

But it was tiring, too. Afterward, once the kids had

showered, they wanted to watch a movie, and Alex popped in *Homeward Bound*, a movie they'd seen a dozen times but were always willing to watch again. From the kitchen, he could see them on the couch, neither one moving in the slightest, staring at the television in that dazed way particular to exhausted children.

He wiped the kitchen counters and loaded the dirty dishes into the dishwasher, started a load of laundry, straightened up the living room, and gave the kids' bathroom a good scrubbing before finally sitting beside them on the couch for a while. Josh curled up on one side, Kristen on the other. By the time the movie ended, Alex could feel his own eyelids beginning to droop. After working at the store and playing with the kids and cleaning the house, it felt good to simply relax for a while.

The sound of Josh's voice jarred him awake.

"Hey, Dad?"

"Yeah?"

"What's for dinner? I'm starved."

From the waitress stand, Katie peered out at the deck and then turned back again, staring as Alex and the kids followed the hostess to an open table near the railing. Kristen smiled and waved as soon as she saw Katie, and hesitated only a second before scooting between the tables and hurtling directly for her. Katie bent down as the little girl threw her arms around her.

"We wanted to surprise you!" Kristen said.

"Well, you did. What are you doing here?"

"My dad didn't want to cook for us tonight."

"He didn't?"

"He said he was too tired."

"There's more to the story," Alex announced. "Trust me."

Katie hadn't heard him come up, and she stood.

"Oh, hey," she said, blushing against her will.

"How are you?" Alex asked.

"Good." She nodded, feeling a bit flustered. "Busy, as you can tell."

"It seems like it. We had to wait before they could seat us in your section."

"It's been like that all day."

"Well, we won't keep you. C'mon, Kristen. Let's go to the table. We'll see you in a few minutes or whenever you're ready."

"Bye, Miss Katie." Kristen waved again.

Katie watched them walk to the table, strangely excited by their visit. She saw Alex open the menu and lean forward to help Kristen with hers, and for an instant, she wished she were sitting with them.

She retucked her shirt and glanced at her reflection in the stainless steel coffeepot. She couldn't make out much, only a blurry image, but it was enough to make her run a hand through her hair. Then, after a quick check to make sure her shirt hadn't been stained—nothing she could do about it, of course, but she still wanted to know—she walked over to the table.

"Hey, guys," she said, addressing the kids. "I hear your dad didn't want to cook dinner for you."

Kristen giggled but Josh simply nodded. "He said he was tired."

"That's what I heard," she said.

Alex rolled his eyes. "Thrown under the bus by my own kids. I just can't believe it."

"I wouldn't throw you under the bus, Daddy," Kristen said seriously.

"Thank you, sweetie."

Katie smiled. "Are you thirsty? Can I get you something to drink?"

They ordered sweet teas all around, along with a basket of hush puppies. Kristen brought the drinks to the table and as she walked away, she felt Alex's gaze on her. She fought the urge to peek over her shoulder, though she desperately wanted to.

For the next few minutes, she took orders and cleared plates from other tables, delivered a couple of meals, and finally returned with the basket of hush puppies.

"Be careful," she said. "They're still hot."

"That's when they're the best," Josh said, reaching into the basket. Kristen reached for one as well.

"We went butterfly hunting today," she said.

"You did?"

"Yep. But we didn't hurt them. We let them go."

"That sounds like fun. Did you have a good time?"

"It was awesome!" Josh said. "I caught, like, a hundred of them! And then we went swimming."

"What a great day," Katie said sincerely. "No wonder your dad is tired."

"I'm not tired," both Josh and Kristen said, almost simultaneously.

"Maybe not," Alex said, "but you're both still going to bed early. Because your poor old dad needs to go to sleep."

Katie shook her head. "Don't be so hard on yourself," she said. "You're not poor."

It took him a moment to realize she was teasing, and

he laughed. It was loud enough for the people at the next table to notice, though he didn't seem to care.

"I come in here to relax and enjoy my dinner, and I end up getting picked on by the waitress."

"It's a tough life."

"You're telling me. Next thing I know, you'll be telling me that I might want to order from the kids' menu, seeing as how I'm gaining weight."

"Well, I wasn't going to say anything," she said with a pointed glance at his midsection. He laughed again, and when he looked at her she saw an appreciative gleam in his eye, reminding her that he found her attractive.

"I think we're ready to order now," he said.

"What can I get you?"

Alex ordered for them and Katie jotted it down. She held his gaze for a moment before leaving the table and dropping the order off in the kitchen. As she continued to work the tables in her station—as quickly as people left, they were replaced—she found excuses to swing by Alex's table. She refilled their waters and their teas, she removed the basket when they were done with the hush puppies, and she brought Josh a new fork after his had dropped on the floor. She chatted easily with Alex and the kids, enjoying every moment, and eventually brought them their dinners.

Later, when they were through, she cleared the table and dropped off the check. By then, the sun was getting lower and Kristen had begun to yawn, and if anything, the restaurant had gotten busier. She had time for only a quick good-bye as the kids scrambled down the stairs, but when Alex hesitated, she had the sense that he was about to ask her out. She wasn't sure how she was going to handle it, but before he could get the words out, one of her customers spilled a beer. The customer stood quickly from the table, bumping it, and two more glasses toppled over. Alex stepped back, the moment broken, knowing she had to go.

"See you soon," he said, waving as he trailed after his kids.

The following day, Katie pushed open the door to the store only half an hour after opening.

"You're here early," Alex said, surprised.

"I was up early and just thought I'd get my shopping out of the way."

"Did it ever slow down last night?"

"Finally. But a couple of people have been out this week. One went to her sister's wedding, and another called in sick. It's been crazy."

"I could tell. But the food was great, even if the service was a little slow."

When she fixed him with an irate expression, he laughed. "Just getting you back for teasing me last night." He shook his head. "Calling me old. I'll have you know my hair went gray before I was thirty."

"You're very sensitive about that," she noted with a teasing tone. "But trust me. It looks good on you. It lends a certain air of respectability."

"Is that good or bad?"

She smiled without giving an answer before reaching for a basket. As she did, she heard him clear his throat. "Are you working as much this coming week?"

"Not as much."

"How about next weekend?"

She thought about it. "I'm off Saturday. Why?"

He shifted his weight from one foot to the other before meeting her eyes. "Because I was wondering if I might be able to take you to dinner. Just the two of us this time. No kids."

She knew they were at a crossroads, one that would change the tenor of things between them. At the same time, it was the reason she'd come to the store as early as she had. She wanted to figure out whether she'd been mistaken about what she'd seen in his expression the previous evening, because it was the first time she knew for certain that she wanted him to ask.

In the silence, though, he seemed to misread what she was thinking. "Never mind. It's not that big of a deal."

"Yes," she said, holding his gaze. "I'd love dinner. But on one condition."

"What's that?"

"You've already done so much for me that I'd rather do something for you this time. How about I make you dinner instead? At my house."

He smiled, relieved. "That sounds perfect."

15

———— ❧ ————

On Saturday, Katie woke later than usual. She'd spent the past few days frantically shopping and decorating her house—a new sheer lace curtain for the living room window, some inexpensive prints for the walls, a few small area rugs, and real place mats and glasses for their dinner. Friday night she'd worked until after midnight, plumping up her new throw pillows and giving the house a final cleaning. Despite the sun that slanted through her windows and striped her bed, she woke only when she heard the sounds of someone hammering. Checking the clock, she saw it was already after nine.

Stumbling out of bed, Katie yawned and then walked toward the kitchen to hit the switch on the coffeepot before stepping out onto the porch, squinting in the brightness of the morning sun. Jo was on her front porch, the hammer poised for another whack, when she spotted Katie.

Jo put the hammer down. "I didn't wake you, did I?"

"Yeah, but that's okay. I had to get up anyway. What are you doing?"

"I'm trying to keep the shutter from falling off. When I got home last night, it was hanging cockeyed, and I was sure it was going to give way in the middle of the night. Of course, thinking that the crash might wake me up any minute kept me from falling asleep for hours."

"Do you need some help?"

"No, I've just about got it."

"How about coffee?"

"Sounds great. I'll be over in a few minutes."

Katie went to her bedroom, slipped out of her pajamas, and threw on a pair of shorts and a T-shirt. She brushed her teeth and hair, just enough to get the tangles out. Through the window, she saw Jo walking toward the house. She opened the front door.

Katie poured two cups of coffee and handed one to Jo as soon as she entered the kitchen.

"Your house is really coming together! I love the rugs and the pictures."

Katie gave a modest shrug. "Yeah, well... Southport is starting to feel like home, I guess. I figured I should start making this house into something more permanent."

"It's really amazing. It's like you're finally beginning to nest."

"How's your place coming?"

"It's getting better. I'll bring you by when it's ready."

"Where've you been? I haven't seen you around lately."

Jo gave a dismissive wave. "I was out of town for a few days on business, and then I went to visit someone last weekend, and then I was working. You know the drill."

"I've been working a lot, too. I've had a ton of shifts lately."

"You working tonight?"

Katie took a sip of her coffee. "No. I'm having some-one over for dinner."

Jo's eyes lit up. "Do you want me to guess who it could be?"

"You already know who it is." Katie tried to stop the slow flush that was creeping up her neck.

"I knew it!" she said. "Good for you. Have you decided what you're going to wear?"

"Not yet."

"Well, no matter what you decide, you'll look beautiful, I'm sure. And you're going to cook?"

"Believe it or not, I'm actually a fairly good cook."

"What are you going to make?"

When Katie told her, Jo raised her eyebrows.

"Sounds yummy," Jo said. "That's great. I'm happy for you. Both of you, actually. Are you excited?"

"It's only dinner…"

"I'll take that as a yes." She winked. "It's too bad I can't stick around to spy on the two of you. I'd love to watch how it all unfolds, but unfortunately, I'm heading out of town."

"Yes," Katie said. "That's really too bad you're not going to be here."

Jo laughed. "Sarcasm doesn't become you, by the way. But just so you know, I'm not going to let you off the hook. As soon as I get back, I'm going to need the full play-by-play."

"It's just dinner," Katie said again.

"Which means that you won't have any trouble telling me all about it."

"I think you need another hobby."

"Probably," Jo agreed. "But right now, I'm having plenty of fun living vicariously through you since my love life is pretty much nonexistent. A girl needs to be able to dream, you know?"

Katie's first stop was the hair salon. There, a young woman named Brittany trimmed and styled her hair, chatting nonstop the entire time. Across the street was the only women's boutique in Southport, and Katie stopped there next. Though she'd ridden past the store, she'd never been inside before. It had been one of the stores she'd never imagined herself either wanting or needing to go into, but as she began to browse, she was pleasantly surprised not only by the selections, but by some of the prices. Well, on the sale items, anyway, which was where Katie focused her attention.

It was an odd experience to shop alone in a clothing store like this. She hadn't done such a thing in a long time, and as she changed in the dressing room, she felt more carefree than she had in years.

She bought a couple of sale items, including a tan form-fitting blouse with beading and stitching that scooped a bit in the front, not dramatically but enough to accent her figure. She also found a gorgeous patterned summer skirt that complemented the blouse perfectly. The skirt was a little too long, but she knew she could fix that. After paying for her purchases, she wandered two doors down, to what she knew was the only shoe store in town, where she picked up a pair of sandals. Again, they were on sale and although ordinarily she would have felt almost frantic about shopping, the tips had been good over the last few days and she'd decided to splurge. Within reason, of course.

From there, she went first to the drugstore to buy a few things and then finally rode across town to the grocery store. She took her time, content to browse the aisles, feeling the old, troubling memories trying and failing to reassert themselves.

When she was finished, she rode her bicycle home and started the preparations for dinner. She was making shrimp stuffed with crabmeat, cooked in a scampi sauce. She had to recall the recipe from memory, but she'd made it a dozen times over the years and was confident she hadn't forgotten anything. As side dishes, she'd decided on stuffed peppers and corn bread, and as an appetizer, she wanted to make a bacon-wrapped Brie, topped with a raspberry sauce.

It had been a long time since she'd prepared such an elaborate meal, but she'd always loved to cut recipes from magazines, even from a young age. Cooking was the one enthusiasm she'd been able to share occasionally with her mom.

She spent the rest of the afternoon hurrying. She mixed the bread and put it in the oven, then readied the ingredients for the stuffed peppers. Those went into the refrigerator along with the bacon-wrapped Brie. When the corn bread was done, she placed it on the counter to cool and started the raspberry sauce. Not much to it—sugar, raspberries, and water—but by the time it was ready, the kitchen smelled heavenly. That went into the fridge as well. Everything else could wait until later.

In her bedroom, she shortened the skirt to just above the knee, then made a last tour of the house to make sure everything was in place. Finally, she began to undress.

As she slipped into the shower, she thought about Alex.

She visualized his easy smile and the graceful way he moved, and the memory started a slow burn in her belly. Despite herself, she wondered whether he was taking a shower at the same time she was. There was something erotic in the idea, the promise of something exciting and new. It was just dinner, she reminded herself again, but even then, she knew she wasn't being completely honest with herself.

There was another force at work here, something she'd been trying to deny. She was attracted to him more than she wanted to admit, and as she stepped out of the shower she knew she had to be careful. He was the kind of man she knew she could fall for, and the notion frightened her. She wasn't ready for that. Not yet, anyway.

Then again, she heard a voice inside her whisper, maybe she was.

After toweling off, she moisturized her skin with a sweet-smelling body lotion, then put on her new outfit, including the sandals, before reaching for the makeup she'd purchased from the drugstore. She didn't need much, just some lipstick, mascara, and a trace of eye shadow. She brushed her hair and then put on a pair of dangly earrings she'd bought on a whim. When she was finished, she stepped back from the mirror.

That's it, she thought to herself, that's all I've got. She turned one way, then the other, tugging at the blouse before finally smiling. She hadn't looked this good in a long time.

Though the sun had finally moved toward the western sky, the house was still warm and she opened the kitchen window. The breeze was enough to keep her cool as she set the table. Earlier in the week, as she'd been leaving the store, Alex had asked her if he could bring a bottle of wine, and Katie put a couple of glasses out. In the center of the table, she placed a candle and as she stepped back, she heard the sound of an engine approaching. She saw from the clock that Alex was right on time.

She drew a deep breath, trying to calm her nerves. Then, after walking across the room and opening the door, she stepped out onto the porch. Dressed in jeans and a blue shirt rolled up to his elbows, Alex was standing at the driver's-side door and leaning into the car, obviously reaching for something. His hair was still a little damp near his collar.

Alex pulled out two bottles of wine and turned around. Seeing her, he seemed to freeze, his expression one of disbelief. She stood surrounded by the last rays of the setting sun, perfectly radiant, and for a moment all he could do was stare.

His wonder was obvious, and Katie let it wash over her, knowing she wanted the feeling to last forever.

"You made it," she said.

The sound of her voice was enough to break the spell, but Alex continued to stare. He knew he should say something witty, something charming to break the tension, but instead he found himself thinking, *I'm in trouble. Serious trouble.*

He wasn't exactly sure when it had happened. Or even when it started. It may have been the morning when he'd seen Kristen holding Katie after Josh had fallen in the river, or the rainy afternoon when he'd driven her home, or even during the day they had spent at the beach. All he knew for sure was that right here and now, he was falling hard for this woman, and he could only pray that she was feeling the same way.

In time, he was finally able to clear his throat. "Yeah," he said. "I guess I did."

16

The early evening sky was a prism of colors as Katie led Alex through the small living room and toward the kitchen.

"I don't know about you, but I could use a glass of wine," she said.

"Good idea," he agreed. "I wasn't sure what we were having, so I brought both a sauvignon blanc and a zinfandel. Do you have a preference?"

"I'll let you pick," she said.

In the kitchen, she leaned against the counter, one leg crossed over the other while Alex twisted the corkscrew into the cork. For once, he seemed more nervous than she was. With a series of quick movements, he opened the bottle of sauvignon blanc. Katie set the glasses on the counter next to him, conscious of how close together they were standing.

"I know I should have said it when I first got here, but you look beautiful."

"Thank you," she said.

He poured some wine, then set the bottle aside and handed her a glass. As she took it, he could smell the coconut-scented body lotion she'd used.

"I think you'll like the wine. At least, I hope so."

"I'm sure I'll love it," she said, raising her glass. "Cheers," she offered, clinking her glass against his.

Katie took a sip, feeling inordinately pleased about everything: how she looked and felt, the taste of the wine, the lingering scent of the raspberry sauce, the way Alex kept eyeing her while trying not to be obvious about it.

"Would you like to sit on the porch?" she suggested.

He nodded. Outside, they each sat in one of the rockers. In the slowly cooling air, the crickets began their chorus, welcoming the coming night.

Katie savored the wine, enjoying the fruity tang it left on her tongue. "How were Kristen and Josh today?"

"They were good." Alex shrugged. "I took them to a movie."

"But it was so pretty outside."

"I know. But with Memorial Day on Monday, I figure we can still spend a couple of days outside."

"Is the store open on Memorial Day?"

"Of course. It's one of the busiest days of the year, since everyone wants to spend the holiday on the water. I'll probably work until one o'clock or so."

"I'd say I feel sorry for you, but I'm working, too."

"Maybe we'll come in and bother you again."

"You didn't bother me at all." She peered at him over the top of her wineglass. "Well, the kids didn't bother me, anyway. As I recall, you were complaining about the quality of service."

"Us old guys will do that," he quipped.

She laughed before rocking back in the chair. "When I'm not working, I like to sit out here and read. It's just so quiet, you know? Sometimes I feel like I'm the only one around for miles."

"You are the only one around for miles. You live in the sticks."

She playfully slapped his shoulder. "Watch it. I happen to like my little house."

"You should. It's in better shape than I thought it would be. It's homey."

"It's getting there," she said. "It's a work in progress. And best of all, it's mine, and no one's going to take it away."

He looked over at her then. She was staring out over the gravel road, into the grassy field beyond.

"Are you okay?" he asked.

She took her time before answering. "I was just thinking that I'm glad you're here. You don't even know me."

"I think I know you well enough."

Katie said nothing to that. Alex watched as she lowered her gaze.

"You think you know me," she whispered, "but you don't."

Alex sensed that she was scared to say any more. In the silence, he heard the porch creaking as he rocked back and forth. "How about I tell you what I think I know, and you tell me if I'm right or wrong? Would that be okay?"

She nodded, her lips compressed. When Alex went on, his voice was soft.

"I think you're intelligent and charming, and that you're a person with a kind heart. I know that when you want to, you can look more beautiful than anyone I've ever met. You're independent, you've got a good sense of humor, and you show surprising patience with children. You're right in thinking that I don't know the specifics of your past, but I don't know that they're all that important unless you want to tell me about them. Everyone has a past, but that's just it—it's in the past. You can learn from it, but you can't change it. Besides, I never knew that person. The person I've come to know is the one I want to get to know even better."

As he spoke, Katie gave a fleeting smile. "You make it sound so simple," she said.

"It can be."

She twisted the stem of her wineglass, considering his words. "But what if the past isn't in the past? What if it's still happening?"

Alex continued to stare at her, holding her gaze. "You mean...what if he finds you?"

Katie flinched. "What did you say?"

"You heard me," he said. He kept his voice steady, almost conversational, something he'd learned in CID. "I'm guessing that you were married once...and that maybe he's trying to find you."

Katie froze, her eyes going wide. It was suddenly hard to breathe and she jumped up from the chair, spilling the rest of her wine. She took a step away from Alex, staring, feeling the blood drain from her face.

"How do you know so much about me? Who told you?" she demanded, her mind racing, trying to piece it together. There was no way he could know those things. It wasn't possible. She hadn't told anyone.

Except for Jo.

The realization was enough to leave her breathless and

she glanced at the cottage next door. Her neighbor, she thought, had betrayed her. Her *friend* had betrayed her—

As fast as her mind was working, Alex's was working as well. He could see the fear in her expression, but he'd seen it before. Too many times. And, he knew, it was time to stop playing games if they wanted to be able to move forward.

"No one told me," he assured her. "But your reaction makes it clear that I'm right. That's not the important question. I don't know that person, Katie. If you want to tell me about your past, I'm willing to listen and help in any way I can, but I'm not going to ask you about it. And if you don't want to tell me, that's okay, too, because, again—I never knew that person. You must have a good reason for keeping it secret, and that means I'm not going to tell anyone, either. No matter what happens, or doesn't happen, between us. Go ahead and make up a brand-new history if you want and I'll back you up word for word. You can trust me on that."

Katie stared at him as he spoke, confused and scared and angry, but absorbing every word.

"But...how?"

"I've learned to notice things that other people don't," he went on. "There was a time in my life when that was all I did. And you're not the first woman I've met in your position."

She continued to stare at him, wheels turning. "When you were in the army," she concluded.

He nodded, holding her gaze. Finally, he stood from the chair and took a cautious step toward her. "Can I pour you another glass of wine?"

Still in turmoil, she couldn't answer, but when he

reached for her glass, she let him take it. The porch door opened with a squeak and closed behind him, leaving her alone.

She paced to the railing, her thoughts chaotic. She fought the instinct to pack a bag and grab her coffee can full of money and leave town as soon as she could.

But what then? If Alex could figure out the truth simply by watching her, then it was possible for someone else to figure it out, too. And maybe, just maybe, they wouldn't be like Alex.

Behind her, she heard the door squeak open again. Alex stepped onto the porch, joining her at the railing. He set the glass in front of her.

"Did you figure it out yet?"

"Figure what out?"

"Whether you're going to take off to parts unknown as soon as you can?"

She turned to him, her face registering shock.

He held open his hands. "What else would you be thinking? But just so you know, I'm curious only because I'm kind of hungry. I'd hate for you to leave before we eat."

It took her a moment to realize he was teasing, and though she wouldn't have believed it possible considering the last few minutes, she found herself smiling in relief.

"We'll have dinner," she said.

"And tomorrow?"

Instead of answering, she reached for her wine. "I want to know how you knew."

"It wasn't one thing," he said. He mentioned a few of the things he'd noticed before finally shaking his head. "Most people wouldn't have put it all together."

She studied the depths of her glass. "But you did."

"I couldn't help it. It's kind of ingrained."

She thought about it. "That means you've known for a while, then. Or at least had suspicions."

"Yes," he admitted.

"Which is why you never asked about my past."

"Yes," he said again.

"And you still wanted to go out with me?"

His expression was serious. "I've wanted to go out with you from the first moment I saw you. I just had to wait until you were ready."

With the last of the sunlight fading from the horizon, twilight descended, turning the flat, cloudless sky a pale violet. They stood at the railing and Alex watched as the southern breeze gently lifted wayward strands of her hair. Her skin took on a peachy glow; he saw the subtle rise and fall of her chest as she breathed. She gazed into the distance, her expression unreadable, and Alex felt something catch in his throat as he wondered what she was thinking.

"You never answered my question," he finally said.

She stayed quiet for a moment before a shy smile finally appeared.

"I think I'm going to stay in Southport for a while, if that's what you're asking," she answered.

He breathed in her scent. "You can trust me, you know."

She leaned into him, feeling his strength as he slipped his arm around her. "I guess I'm going to have to, aren't I?"

They returned to the kitchen a few minutes later. Katie set her glass of wine aside as she slid the appetizer and stuffed peppers into the oven. Still reeling from Alex's disturbingly accurate assessment of her past, she was glad for tasks to keep her busy. It was hard to fathom that he *still* wanted to spend an evening with her. And more important, that she wanted to spend an evening with him. Deep in her heart, she wasn't sure she deserved to be happy, nor did she believe that she was worthy of someone who seemed...normal.

That was the dirty secret associated with her past. Not that she'd been abused but that somehow she felt that she deserved it because she'd let it happen. Even now, it shamed her, and there were times when she felt hideously ugly, as though the scars that had been left behind were visible to everyone.

But here and now, it mattered less than it once had, because she somehow suspected that Alex understood her shame. And accepted that, too.

From the refrigerator, she pulled out the raspberry sauce she'd made earlier, and began spooning it into a small saucepan to reheat. It didn't take long, and after setting it aside, she pulled the bacon-wrapped Brie from the oven, topped it with the sauce, and brought the cheese to the table. Suddenly remembering, she retrieved her wine from the counter and joined Alex at the table.

"This is just to start," she said. "The peppers are going to take a little longer."

He leaned toward the platter. "It smells amazing."

He moved a piece of Brie to his plate and took a bite. "Wow," he said.

She grinned. "Good, huh?"

"It's delicious. Where did you learn to do this?"

"I was friends with a chef once. He told me this would wow just about anyone."

He cut another piece with his fork. "I'm glad you're staying in Southport," he said. "I can easily imagine myself eating this regularly, even if I have to barter items at my store to get it."

"The recipe isn't complicated."

"You haven't seen me cook. I'm great with kid food, but after that, it starts going downhill fast."

He reached for his glass and took a sip of wine. "I think the cheese might go better with the red. Do you mind if I open the other bottle?"

"Not at all."

He walked over to the counter and opened the zinfandel while Katie went to the cupboard and removed two more glasses. Alex poured wine into each and handed one to her. They were standing close enough to brush up against each other and Alex had to fight the urge to pull her close and wrap his arms around her. Instead, he cleared his throat.

"I want to tell you something, but I don't want you to take it the wrong way."

She hesitated. "Why don't I like the sound of this?"

"I just wanted to tell you how much I've been looking forward to tonight. I mean...I've been thinking about it all week."

"Why would I take that the wrong way?"

"I don't know. Because you're a woman? Because it makes me sound desperate and women don't like desperate men?"

For the first time that evening, she laughed easily. "I don't think you're desperate. I get the sense you might be a bit overwhelmed at times because of the business and the kids, but it's not like you've been calling me every day."

"That's only because you don't have a phone. But anyway, I wanted you to know that it means a lot to me. I don't have a lot of experience in things like this."

"Dinner?"

"Dating. It's been a while."

Join the club, she thought to herself. But it made her feel good anyway. "Come on," she said, motioning to the appetizer. "It's better when it's warm."

When the appetizer was finished, Katie rose from the table and went to the oven. She peeked at the peppers before rinsing the saucepan she'd used earlier. She gathered the ingredients for the scampi sauce and got that started, then began to sauté the shrimp. By the time the shrimp were done, the sauce was ready as well. She put a pepper on each of their plates and added the main course. Then, after dimming the lights, she lit the candle she'd placed at the center of the table. The aroma of butter and garlic and the flickering light against the wall made the old kitchen feel almost new with promise.

They ate and talked while, outside, the stars emerged from hiding. Alex praised the meal more than once, claiming that he'd never tasted anything better. As the candle burned lower and the wine bottle emptied, Katie revealed bits and pieces about her life growing up in Altoona. While she'd held back about telling Jo the whole truth about her parents, she gave Alex the unvarnished version: the constant moves, her parents' alcoholism, the fact that she'd been on her own since she'd turned eighteen. Alex stayed silent throughout, listening without judgment. Even so, she wasn't sure what he thought about her past. When she finally trailed off, she found herself wondering whether she'd said too much. But it was then that he reached over and placed his hand on hers. Though she couldn't meet his gaze, they held hands across the table, neither of them willing to let go, as if they were the only two people remaining in the world.

"I should probably start cleaning the kitchen," Katie said finally, breaking the spell. She pushed back from the table. Alex heard her chair scrape against the floor, aware that the moment had been lost and wanting nothing more than to get it back.

"I want you to know I've had a wonderful time tonight," he began.

"Alex...I..."

He shook his head. "You don't have to say anything—"

She didn't let him finish. "I want to, okay?" She stood near the table, her eyes glittering with some unknown emotion. "I've had a wonderful time, too. But I know where this is leading, and I don't want you to get hurt." She exhaled, steeling herself for the words that were coming next. "I can't make promises. I can't tell you where I'll be tomorrow, let alone a year from now. When I first ran, I thought I'd be able to put everything behind me and start over, you know? I'd live my life and simply pretend that none of it ever happened. But how can I do that? You think you know me, but I'm not sure that even I know who I am anymore. And as much as you know about me, there's a lot you don't know."

Alex felt something collapse inside him. "Are you saying that you don't want to see me again?"

"No." She shook her head vehemently. "I'm saying all this because I do want to see you and it scares me because I know deep in my heart that you deserve someone better. You deserve someone you can count on. Someone your kids can count on. Like I said, there are things you don't know about me."

"Those things don't matter," Alex insisted.

"How can you say that?"

In the silence that followed, Alex could hear the faint hum of the refrigerator. Through the window, the moon had risen and hung suspended over the treetops.

"Because I know me," he finally said, realizing that he was in love with her. He loved the Katie he'd come to know and the Katie he'd never had the chance to meet. He rose from the table, moving closer to her.

"Alex . . . this can't . . ."

"Katie," he whispered, and for a moment, neither of them moved. Alex finally put a hand on her hip and pulled her closer. Katie exhaled, as if setting down an age-old burden, and when she looked up at him, it was suddenly easy for her to imagine that her fears were pointless. That he would love her no matter what she told him, and that he was the kind of man who loved her already and would love her forever.

And it was then she realized that she loved him, too.

With that, she let herself lean into him. She felt their bodies come together as he raised a hand to her hair. His touch was gentle and soft, unlike anything she'd known before, and she watched in wonder as he closed his eyes. He tilted his head, their faces drawing close.

When their lips finally came together, she could taste the wine on his tongue. She gave herself over to him then, allowing him to kiss her cheek and her neck, and she leaned back, reveling in the sensation. She could feel the moisture of his lips as they brushed against her skin, and she slid her arms around his neck.

This is what it feels like to really love someone, she thought, and to be loved in return, and she could feel the tears beginning to form. She blinked, trying to will them back, but all at once, they were impossible to stop. She loved him and wanted him, but more than that, she wanted him to love the real her, with all her flaws and secrets. She wanted him to know the whole truth.

They kissed for a long time in the kitchen, their bodies pressed together, his hand moving over her back and in her hair. She shivered at the feel of the slight stubble on his cheeks. When he ran a finger over the skin of her arm, she felt a flood of liquid heat course through her body.

"I want to be with you but I can't," she finally whispered, hoping that he wouldn't be angry.

"It's okay," he whispered. "There's no way tonight could have been any more wonderful than it's already been."

"But you're disappointed."

He brushed a strand of hair from her face. "It's not possible for you to disappoint me," he said.

She swallowed, trying to rid herself of her fears.

"There's something you should know about me," she whispered.

"Whatever it is, I'm sure I can handle it."

She leaned into him again.

"I can't be with you tonight," she whispered, "for the same reason I could never marry you." She sighed. "I have a husband."

"I know," he whispered.

"It doesn't matter to you?"

"It's not perfect, but trust me, I'm not perfect, either, so maybe it's best if we take all of this one day at a time. And when you're ready, if you're ever ready, I'll be waiting." He brushed her cheek with his finger. "I love you, Katie. You might not be ready to say those words now, and maybe you'll never be able to say them, but that doesn't change how I feel about you."

"Alex..."

"You don't have to say it," he said.

"Can I explain?" she asked, finally pulling back.

He didn't bother to hide his curiosity.

"I want to tell you something," she said. "I want to tell you about me."

17

Three days before Katie left New England, a brisk early January wind made the snowflakes freeze, and she had to lower her head as she walked toward the salon. Her long blond hair blew in the wind and she could feel the pinpricks of ice as they tapped against her cheeks. She wore high-heeled pumps, not boots, and her feet were already freezing. Behind her, Kevin sat in the car watching her. Though she didn't turn, she could hear the car idling and could imagine the mouth that was set into a hard, straight line.

The crowds that had filled the strip mall during Christmas were gone. On either side of the salon was a Radio Shack and a pet store, both of them empty; no one wanted to be out on a day like today. When Katie pulled the door, it flew open in the wind and she struggled to close it. Chilled air followed her into the salon and the shoulders of her jacket were coated with a fine layer of white. She slipped off her gloves and jacket, turning around as she did so. She waved good-bye to Kevin and smiled. He liked it when she smiled at him.

Her appointment was at two with a woman named Rachel. Most of the stations were already filled and Katie was unsure where to go. It was her first time here and she was uncomfortable. None of the stylists looked older than thirty and most had wild hair with red and blue tints. A moment later, she was approached by a girl in her mid-twenties, tanned and pierced with a tattoo on her neck.

"Are you my two o'clock? Color and trim?" she asked.

Katie nodded.

"I'm Rachel. Follow me."

Rachel glanced over her shoulder. "It's cold out there, huh?" Rachel said. "I almost died on my way to the door. They make us park on the far side of the lot. I hate that, but what can I do, right?"

"It is cold," Katie agreed.

Rachel led her to a station near the corner. The chair was purple vinyl and the floor was black tile. A place for younger people, Katie thought. Singles who wanted to stand out. Not married women with blond hair. Katie fidgeted as Rachel put a smock over her. She wiggled her toes, trying to warm her feet.

"Are you new in the area?" Rachel asked.

"I live in Dorchester," she said.

"That's kind of out of the way. Did someone give you a referral?"

Katie had passed by the salon two weeks earlier, when Kevin had taken her shopping, but she didn't say that. Instead, she simply shook her head.

"I guess I'm lucky I answered the phone then." Rachel smiled. "What sort of color do you want?"

Katie hated to stare at herself in the mirror but she didn't have a choice. She had to get this right. She *had* to.

Tucked into the mirror in front of her was a photograph of Rachel with someone Katie assumed to be her boyfriend. He had more piercings than she did and he had a Mohawk. Beneath the smock, Katie squeezed her hands together.

"I want it to look natural, so maybe some lowlights for winter? And fix the roots, too, so they blend."

Rachel nodded into the mirror. "Do you want it about the same color? Or darker or lighter? Not the lowlights, I mean."

"About the same."

"Foil okay?"

"Yes," Katie answered.

"Easy as pie," Rachel said. "Just give me a couple of minutes to get things ready and I'll be back, okay?"

Katie nodded. Off to the side, she saw a woman leaning back at the sink, another stylist beside her. She could hear the water as it was turned on and the hum of conversation from the other stations. Music played faintly over the speakers.

Rachel returned with the foil and the color. Near the chair, she stirred the color, making sure the consistency was right.

"How long have you lived in Dorchester?"

"Four years."

"Where'd you grow up?"

"Pennsylvania," Katie said. "I lived in Atlantic City before I moved here."

"Was that your husband who dropped you off?"

"Yes."

"He's got a nice car. I saw it when you were waving. What is it? A Mustang?"

Katie nodded again but didn't answer. Rachel worked for a little while in silence, applying color and wrapping the foil.

"How long have you been married?" Rachel asked as she coated and wrapped a particularly tricky strand of hair.

"Four years."

"That's why you moved to Dorchester, huh?"

"Yes."

Rachel kept up her patter. "So what do you do?"

Katie stared straight ahead, trying not to see herself. Wishing that she were someone else. She could be here for an hour and a half before Kevin came back and she prayed he wouldn't arrive early.

"I don't have a job," Katie answered.

"I'd go crazy if I didn't work. Not that it's always easy. What did you do before you were married?"

"I was a cocktail waitress."

"In one of the casinos?"

Katie nodded.

"Is that where you met your husband?"

"Yes," Katie said.

"So what's he doing now? While you're getting your hair done?"

He's probably at a bar, Katie thought. "I don't know."

"Why didn't you drive, then? Like I said, it's kind of out of the way."

"I don't drive. My husband drives me when I need to go somewhere."

"I don't know what I'd do without a car. I mean, it's not much but it gets me to where I need to go. I'd hate to have to depend on someone else like that."

Katie could smell perfume in the air. The radiator below the counter had begun to click. "I never learned to drive."

Rachel shrugged as she worked another piece of foil into Katie's hair. "It's not hard. Practice a little, take the test, and you're good to go."

Katie stared at Rachel in the mirror. Rachel seemed to know what she was doing, but she was young and starting out and Katie still wished she were older and more experienced. Which was odd, because she was probably only a couple of years older than Rachel. Maybe less than that. But Katie felt old.

"Do you have kids?"

"No."

Perhaps the girl sensed that she'd said something wrong, because she worked in silence for the next few minutes, the foils making Katie look like she had alien antennae, before finally leading Katie to another seat. Rachel turned on a heat lamp.

"I'll be back to check in a few minutes, okay?"

Rachel wandered off, toward another stylist. They were talking but the chatter in the salon made it impossible to overhear them. Katie glanced at the clock. Kevin would be back in less than an hour. Time was going fast, too fast.

Rachel came back and checked on her hair. "A little while longer," she chirped, and resumed her conversation with her colleague, gesturing with her hands. Animated. Young and carefree. Happy.

More minutes passed. Then, a dozen. Katie tried not to stare at the clock. Finally, it was time, and Rachel removed the foil before leading Katie to the sink. Katie sat and leaned back, resting her neck against the towel. Rachel turned the water on and Katie felt a splash of cool water against her cheek. Rachel massaged the shampoo in her hair and scalp and rinsed, then added conditioner and rinsed again.

"Now let's trim you up, okay?"

Back at the station, Katie thought her hair looked okay, but it was hard to tell when it was wet. It had to be right or Kevin would notice. Rachel combed Katie's hair straight, getting out the tangles. There were forty minutes left.

Rachel stared into the mirror at Katie's reflection. "How much do you want taken off?"

"Not too much," Katie said. "Just enough to clean it up. My husband likes it long."

"How do you want it styled? I've got a book over there if you want something new."

"How I had it when I came in is fine."

"Will do," Rachel said.

Katie watched as Rachel used a comb, running her hair through her fingers, then snipped it with the scissors. First the back, then the sides. And finally the top. Somewhere, Rachel had found a piece of gum and she chewed, her jaw moving up and down as she worked.

"Okay so far?"

"Yes. I think that's enough."

Rachel reached for the hair dryer and a circular brush. She ran the brush slowly through Katie's hair, the noise of the dryer loud in her ear.

"How often do you get your hair done?" Rachel asked, making small talk.

"Once a month," Katie answered. "But sometimes I just get it cut."

"You have beautiful hair, by the way."

"Thank you."

Rachel continued to work. Katie asked for some light curls and Rachel brought out the curling iron. It took a couple of minutes to heat up. There were still twenty minutes left.

Rachel curled and brushed until she was finally satisfied and studied Katie in the mirror.

"How's that?"

Katie examined the color and the style. "That's perfect," she said.

"Let me show you the back," Rachael said. She spun Katie's chair around and handed her a mirror. Katie stared into the double reflection and nodded.

"Okay, that's it, then," Rachel said.

"How much is it?"

Rachel told her and Katie dug into her purse. She pulled out the money she needed, including the tip. "Could I have a receipt?"

"Sure," Rachel said. "Just come with me to the register."

The girl wrote it up. Kevin would check it and ask for the change when she got back in the car, so she made sure Rachel included the tip. She glanced at the clock. Twelve minutes.

Kevin had yet to return and her heart was beating fast as she slipped her jacket and gloves back on. She left the salon while Rachel was still talking to her. Next door, at Radio Shack, she asked the clerk for a disposable cell phone and a card that allowed her twenty hours of service. She felt faint as she said the words, knowing that after this, there was no turning back.

He pulled one out from under the counter and began

to ring her up while he explained how it worked. She had extra money in her purse tucked into a tampon case because she knew Kevin would never look there. She pulled it out, laying the crumpled bills on the counter. The clock was continuing to tick and she looked out at the lot again. She was beginning to feel dizzy and her mouth had gone dry.

It took the clerk forever to ring her up. Though she was paying cash, he asked for her name, address, and zip code. Pointless. Ridiculous. She wanted to pay and get out of there. She counted to ten and the clerk still typed. On the road, the light had turned red. Cars were waiting. She wondered if Kevin was getting ready to turn into the lot. She wondered if he would see her leaving the store. It was hard for her to breathe again.

She tried to open the plastic packaging, but it was impossible—as strong as steel. Too big for her small handbag, too big for her pocket. She asked the clerk for a pair of scissors and it took him a precious minute to find one. She wanted to scream, to tell him to hurry because Kevin would be here any minute. She turned toward the window instead.

When the phone was free, she jammed it into her jacket pocket along with the prepaid card. The clerk asked if she wanted a bag but she was out the door without answering. The phone felt like lead, and the snow and ice made it hard to keep her balance.

She opened the door of the salon and went back inside. She slipped off her jacket and gloves and waited by the register. Thirty seconds later, she saw Kevin's car turn into the lot, angling toward the salon.

There was snow on her jacket and she quickly brushed

at it as Rachel came toward her. Katie panicked at the thought that Kevin might have noticed. She concentrated, urging herself to stay in control. To act natural.

"Did you forget something?" Rachel asked.

Katie exhaled. "I was going to wait outside but it's too cold," she explained. "And then I realized I didn't get your card."

Rachel's face lit up. "Oh, that's right. Hold on a second," she said. She walked toward her station and pulled a card from the drawer. Katie knew that Kevin was watching her from inside the car, but she pretended not to notice.

Rachel returned with her business card and handed it over. "I usually don't work on Sundays or Mondays," she said.

Katie nodded. "I'll give you a call."

Behind her, she heard the door open and Kevin was standing in the doorway. He usually didn't come inside and her heart pounded. She slipped her jacket back on, trying to control the trembling of her hands. Then, she turned and smiled.

18

The snow was falling harder as Kevin Tierney pulled the car into the driveway. There were bags of groceries in the backseat and Kevin grabbed three of them before walking toward the door. He'd said nothing on the drive from the salon, had said little to her in the grocery store. Instead, he'd walked beside her as she scanned the shelves looking for sales and trying not to think about the phone in her pocket. Money was tight and Kevin would be angry if she spent too much. Their mortgage took nearly half his salary, and credit card bills consumed another chunk. Most of the time, they had to eat in, but he liked restaurant-type meals, with a main course and two side dishes and sometimes a salad. He refused to eat leftovers and it was hard to make the budget stretch. She had to plan the menu carefully, and she cut coupons from the newspaper. When Kevin paid for the groceries, she handed him the change from the salon and the receipt. He counted the money, making sure everything was there.

At home, she rubbed her arms to stay warm. The house

was old and frigid air wormed its way through the window seams and beneath the front door. The bathroom floor was cold enough to make her feet ache, but Kevin complained about the cost of heating oil and never let her adjust the thermostat. When he was at work, she wore a sweatshirt and slippers around the house, but when he was home, he wanted her to look sexy.

Kevin placed the bags of groceries on the kitchen table. She put her bags beside his as he moved to the refrigerator. Opening the freezer, he pulled out a bottle of vodka and a couple of ice cubes. He dropped the cubes into a glass and poured the vodka. The glass was nearly full by the time he stopped pouring. Leaving her alone, he went to the living room and she heard the television come on and the sounds of ESPN. The announcer was talking about the Patriots and the play-offs and the chances of winning another Super Bowl. Last year, Kevin had gone to a Patriots game; he'd been a fan since childhood.

Katie slipped her jacket off and reached into the pocket. She had, she suspected, a couple of minutes and she hoped it was enough. After peeking in the living room, she hurried to the sink. In the cupboard below, there was a box of SOS scrubbing pads. She placed the cell phone at the bottom of the box and put the pads over the top of it. She closed the cupboard quietly before grabbing her jacket, hoping her face wasn't flushed, praying he hadn't seen her. With a long breath to steel herself, she looped it over her arm, carrying it through the living room toward the foyer closet. The room seemed to stretch as she moved through it, like a room viewed through a fun-house mirror at a carnival, but she tried to ignore the sensation. She knew he'd be able to see through her, to read her mind and know what she'd done, but he never turned away from the television. Only when she was back in the kitchen did her breathing begin to slow.

She began to unpack the groceries, still feeling dazed but knowing she had to act normal. Kevin liked a tidy house, especially the kitchen and bathrooms. She put away the cheese and eggs in their separate compartments in the refrigerator. She pulled the old vegetables from the drawer and wiped it down before putting the new vegetables on the bottom. She kept out some green beans and found a dozen red potatoes in a basket on the pantry floor. She left a cucumber on the counter, along with iceberg lettuce and a tomato for a salad. The main course was marinated strip steaks.

She'd put the steaks in the marinade the day before: red wine, orange juice, grapefruit juice, salt, and pepper. The acidity of the juices made the meat tender and gave it extra flavor. It was in a casserole dish on the bottom shelf of the refrigerator.

She put the rest of the groceries away, rotating the older items to the front, then folded the bags and put them under the sink. From a drawer, she removed a knife; the cutting board was beneath the toaster and she set that near the burner. She cut the potatoes in half, only enough for the two of them. She oiled a baking pan, turned the oven on, and seasoned the potatoes with parsley, salt, pepper, and garlic. They would go in before the steaks and she would have to reheat them. The steaks needed to be broiled.

Kevin liked his salads finely diced, with blue cheese crumbles and croutons and Italian dressing. She cut the tomato in half and cut a quarter of the cucumber before wrapping the remainder in plastic wrap and putting it back in the refrigerator. As she opened the door, she noticed Kevin in the kitchen behind her, leaning against the doorjamb that led to the dining room. He took a long drink, finishing his vodka and continuing to watch her, his presence all-encompassing.

He didn't know she'd left the salon, she reminded herself. He didn't know she'd bought a cell phone. He would have said something. He would have done something.

"Steaks tonight?" he finally asked.

She closed the refrigerator door and kept moving, trying to appear busy, staying ahead of her fears. "Yes," she said. "I just turned on the oven, so it'll be a few minutes. I've got to put the potatoes in first."

Kevin stared at her. "Your hair looks good," he said.

"Thank you. She did a good job."

Katie went back to the cutting board. She began to cut the tomato, making a long slice.

"Not too big," he said, nodding in her direction.

"I know," she said. She smiled as he moved to the freezer again. Katie heard the clink of cubes in his glass.

"What did you talk about when you were getting your hair done?"

"Not much. Just the usual. You know how stylists are. They'll talk about anything."

He shook his glass. She could hear the cubes clink against the glass. "Did you talk about me?"

"No," she said.

She knew he wouldn't have liked that and he nodded. He pulled the bottle of vodka out again and set it beside his glass on the counter before moving behind her. He stood, watching over her shoulder as she diced the tomatoes. Small pieces, no larger than a pea. She could feel his breath on her neck and tried not to cringe as he placed his hands on her hips. Knowing what she had to do, she set the knife down and turned toward him, putting her arms around his neck. She kissed him with a little tongue knowing he wanted her to, and didn't see the slap coming until she felt the sting against her cheek. It burned, hot and red. Sharp. Bee stings.

"You made me waste my entire afternoon!" he shouted at her. He gripped her arms tight, squeezing hard. His mouth was contorted, his eyes already bloodshot. She could smell the booze on his breath, and spittle hit her face. "My only day off and you pick that day to get your damn hair done in the middle of the city! And then go grocery shopping!"

She wiggled, trying to back away, and he finally let her go. He shook his head, the muscle of his jaw pulsing. "Did you ever stop to think that I might have wanted to relax today? Just take it easy on my only day off?"

"I'm sorry," she said, holding her cheek. She didn't say that she'd checked with him twice earlier in the week if it would be okay, or that he was the one who made her switch salons because he didn't want her making friends. Didn't want anyone knowing their business.

"I'm sorry," he mimicked her. He stared at her before shaking his head again. "Christ almighty," he said. "Is it so hard for you to think about anyone other than yourself?"

He reached out, trying to grab her, and she turned, trying to run. He was ready for her and there was nowhere to go. He struck fast and hard, his fist a piston, firing at her lower back. She gasped, her vision going black in the corners, feeling as though she'd been pierced with a knife. She collapsed to the floor, her kidney on fire, the pain shooting through her legs and up her spine. The world was spinning, and when she tried to get up, the movement only made it worse.

"You're so damn selfish all the time!" he said, towering over her.

She said nothing. Couldn't say anything. Couldn't breathe. She bit her lip to keep from screaming and wondered if she would pee blood tomorrow. The pain was a razor, slashing at her nerves, but she wouldn't cry because that only made him angrier.

He continued to stand over her, then let out a disgusted sigh. He reached for his empty glass and grabbed the bottle of vodka on the way out of the kitchen.

It took her almost a minute to summon the strength to get up. When she started cutting again, her hands were shaking. The kitchen was cold and the pain was intense in her back, pulsing with every heartbeat. The week before, he'd hit her so hard in the stomach that she'd spent the rest of the night vomiting. She'd fallen to the floor and he'd grabbed her by the wrist to pull her up. The bruise on her wrist was shaped like fingers. Branches of hell.

Tears were on her cheeks and she had to keep shifting her weight to keep the pain at bay as she finished dicing the tomato. She diced the cucumber as well. Small pieces. Lettuce, too, diced and chopped. The way he wanted it. She wiped the tears away with the back of her hand and moved slowly toward the refrigerator. She pulled out a packet of blue cheese before finding the croutons in the cupboard.

In the living room, he'd turned the volume up again.

The oven was ready and she put the baking sheet in and set the timer. When the heat hit her face, she realized her skin was still stinging, but she doubted that he'd left a mark there. He knew exactly how hard to strike and she wondered where he'd learned that, whether it was something that all men knew, whether there were secret classes with instructors who specialized in teaching such things. Or whether it was just Kevin.

The pain in her back had finally begun to lessen to a throb. She could breathe normally again. Wind blew through the seams in the window and the sky had turned a dark gray. Snow tapped gently on the glass. She peeked toward the living room, saw Kevin seated on the couch, and went to lean against the counter. She took off one pump and rubbed her toes, trying to get the blood flowing, trying to warm her feet. She did the same with the other foot before slipping her pumps back on.

She rinsed and cut the green beans and put some olive oil in the frying pan. She would start the beans when the steaks went in the broiler. She tried again not to think about the phone beneath the sink.

She was removing the baking sheet from the oven when Kevin came back in the kitchen. He was holding his glass and it was half empty. His eyes were already glassy. Four or five drinks so far. She couldn't tell. She put the sheet on the stove.

"Just a little bit longer," she said, her tone neutral, pretending that nothing had happened. She'd learned that if she acted angry or hurt, it only enraged him. "I have to finish the steaks and then dinner will be ready."

"I'm sorry," he said. He swayed slightly.

She smiled. "I know. It's okay. It's been a hard few weeks. You've been working a lot."

"Are those new jeans?" The words came out slurry.

"No," she said. "I just haven't worn them for a while."

"They look good."

"Thank you," she said.

He took a step toward her. "You're so beautiful. You know I love you, right?"

"I know."

"I don't like hitting you. You just don't *think* sometimes."

She nodded, looking away, trying to think of something to do, needing to stay busy, then remembered she had to set the table. She moved to the cupboard near the sink.

He moved behind her as she was reaching for the plates and rotated her toward him, pulling her close. She inhaled before offering a contented sigh, because she knew he wanted her to make those kinds of sounds. "You're supposed to say that you love me, too," he whispered. He kissed her cheek and she put her arms around him. She could feel him pressed against her, knew what he wanted.

"I love you," she said.

His hand traveled to her breast. She waited for the squeeze, but it didn't come. Instead, he caressed it gently. Despite herself, her nipple began to harden and she hated it but she couldn't help it. His breath was hot. Boozy.

"God, you're beautiful. You've always been beautiful, from the first time I saw you." He pressed himself harder against her and she could feel him. "Let's hold off on putting the steaks in," he said. "Dinner can wait for a little while."

"I thought you were hungry." She made it sound like a tease.

"I'm hungry for something else right now," he

whispered. He unbuttoned her shirt and pulled it open before moving to the snap on her jeans.

"Not here," she said, leaning her head back, letting him continue to kiss her. "In the bedroom, okay?"

"How about the table? Or on the counter instead?"

"Please, baby," she murmured, her head back as he kissed her neck. "That's not very romantic."

"But it's sexy," he said.

"What if someone sees us through the window?"

"You're no fun," he said.

"Please?" she said again. "For me? You know how hot you make me in bed."

He kissed her once more, his hands traveling to her bra. He unsnapped it from the front; he didn't like bras that snapped in the back. She felt the cold air of the kitchen on her breasts; saw the lust in his face as he stared at them. He licked his lips before leading her to the bedroom.

He was almost frenzied as soon as they got there, working her jeans down around her hips, then to her ankles. He squeezed her breasts and she bit her lip to keep from crying out before they fell onto the bed. She panted and moaned and called his name, knowing he wanted her to do those things, because she didn't want him to be angry, because she didn't want to be slapped or punched or kicked, because she didn't want him to know about the phone. Her kidney was still shooting pain and she changed her cries into moans, saying the things he wanted her to say, turning him on until his body started to spasm. When it was over, she got up from the bed, dressed, and kissed him, then she went back to the kitchen and finished making dinner.

Kevin went back to the living room and drank more

vodka before going to the table. He told her about work and then went to watch television again while she cleaned the kitchen. Afterward, he wanted her to sit beside him and watch television so she did, until it was finally time to turn in.

In the bedroom, he was snoring within minutes, oblivious to Katie's silent tears, oblivious to her hatred of him, her hatred of herself. Oblivious to the money she'd been stashing away for almost a year or the hair dye she'd snuck into the grocery cart a month ago and hidden in the closet, oblivious to the cell phone hidden in the cupboard beneath the kitchen sink. Oblivious to the fact that in just a few days, if all went the way she hoped, he would never see or hit her ever again.

19

Katie sat beside Alex on the porch, the sky above them a black expanse dotted with light. For months, she'd tried to block out the specific memories, focusing only on the fear that had been left behind. She didn't want to remember Kevin, didn't want to think about him. She wanted to erase him entirely, to pretend he never existed. But he would always be there.

Alex had stayed silent throughout her story, his chair angled toward hers. She'd spoken through her tears, though he doubted she even knew she was crying. She'd told him without emotion, almost in a trance, as if the events had happened to someone else. He felt sick to his stomach by the time she'd trailed off.

She couldn't look at him as she told him. He'd heard versions of the same story before, but this time it was different. She wasn't simply a victim, she was his friend, the woman he'd come to love, and he tucked a loose strand of hair behind her ear.

At his touch, she flinched slightly before relaxing. He

heard her sigh, tired now. Tired of talking. Tired of the past.

"You did the right thing by leaving," he said. His tone was soft. Understanding.

It took her a moment to respond. "I know," she said.

"It had nothing to do with you."

She stared into the darkness. "Yes," she said, "it did. I chose him, remember? I married him. I let it happen once and then again, and after that, it was too late. I still cooked for him and cleaned the house for him. I slept with him whenever he wanted, did whatever he wanted. I made him think I *loved* it."

"You did what you had to do to survive," he said, his voice steady.

She grew silent again. The crickets were chirping and locusts hummed from the trees. "I never thought something like this could happen, you know? My dad was a drunk, but he wasn't violent. I was just so ... weak. I don't know why I let it happen."

His voice was soft. "Because at one time you loved him. Because you believed him when he promised it wouldn't happen again. Because he gradually grew more violent and controlling over time, slowly enough that you felt like he would change until you finally realized he wouldn't."

With his words, she inhaled sharply and lowered her head, her shoulders heaving up and down. The sound of her anguish made his throat clench with anger at the life she'd lived and sadness because she was still living it. He wanted to hold her, but knew that right now, at this moment, he was doing all she wanted. She was fragile, on edge. Vulnerable.

It took a few minutes before she was finally able to stop

crying. Her eyes were red and puffy. "I'm sorry I told you all that," she said, her voice still choked up. "I shouldn't have."

"I'm glad you did."

"The only reason I did was because you already knew."

"I know."

"But you didn't need to know the details about the things I had to do."

"It's okay."

"I hate him," she said. "But I hate myself, too. I tried to tell you that I'm better off alone. I'm not who you thought I was. I'm not the woman you think you know."

She was on the verge of crying again and he finally stood. He tugged at her hand, willing her to stand. She did but wouldn't look at him. He suppressed his anger at her husband and kept his voice soft.

"Listen to me," he said. He used a finger to raise her chin. She resisted at first then gave in, finally looking at him. He went on. "There's nothing you can tell me that will change how I feel about you. Nothing. Because that isn't you. It's never been you. You're the woman I've come to know. The woman I love."

She studied him, wanting to believe him, knowing somehow he was telling the truth, and she felt something give way inside her. Still...

"But..."

"No buts," he said, "because there are none. You see yourself as someone who couldn't get away. I see the courageous woman who escaped. You see yourself as someone who should be ashamed or guilty because she let it happen. I see a kind, beautiful woman who should feel proud because she stopped it from happening ever again. Not many women have the strength to do what you did. That's what I see now, and that's what I've always seen when I look at you."

She smiled. "I think you need glasses."

"Don't let the gray hair fool you. My eyes are still perfect." He moved toward her, making sure it was okay before leaning in to kiss her. It was brief and soft. Caring. "I'm just sorry you had to go through it at all."

"I'm still going through it."

"Because you think he's looking for you?"

"I know he's looking for me. And he'll never stop." She paused. "There's something wrong with him. He's... insane."

Alex thought about that. "I know I shouldn't ask, but did you ever think of calling the police?"

Her shoulders dropped slightly. "Yes," she said. "I called once."

"And they didn't do anything?"

"They came to the house and talked to me. They convinced me not to press charges."

Alex considered it. "That doesn't make sense."

"It made perfect sense to me." She shrugged. "Kevin warned me that it wouldn't do any good to call the police."

"How would he know?"

She sighed, thinking she might as well tell him everything. "Because he *is* the police," she finally said. She looked up at him. "He's a detective with the Boston Police Department. And he didn't call me Katie." Her eyes telegraphed despair. "He called me Erin."

20

On Memorial Day, hundreds of miles to the north, Kevin Tierney stood in the backyard of a house in Dorchester, wearing shorts and a Hawaiian-style shirt he'd bought when he and Erin had visited Oahu on their honeymoon.

"Erin's back in Manchester," he said.

Bill Robinson, his captain, flipped burgers on the grill. "Again?"

"I told you that her friend has cancer, right? She feels like she's got to be there for her friend."

"That cancer's bad stuff," Bill said. "How's Erin holding up?"

"Okay. I can tell she's tired, though. It's hard to keep going back and forth like she's been doing."

"I can imagine," Bill said. "Emily had to do something like that when her sister got lupus. Spent two months up in Burlington in the middle of winter cooped up in a tiny apartment, just the two of them. Drove them both crazy. In the end, the sister packed up Em's suitcases and set them outside the front door and said she was better off alone. Not that I could blame her, of course."

Kevin took a pull on his beer, and because it was expected of him, he smiled. Emily was Bill's wife and they'd been married almost thirty years. Bill liked to tell people they'd been the happiest six years of his life. Everyone at the precinct had heard the joke about fifty times in the past eight years, and a big chunk of those people were here now. Bill hosted a barbecue at his house every Memorial Day and pretty much everyone who wasn't on duty showed up, not only out of obligation, but because Bill's brother distributed beer for a living, a lot of which ended up here. Wives and husbands, girlfriends and boyfriends, and kids were clustered in groups, some in the kitchen, others on the patio. Four detectives were playing horseshoes and sand was flying around the stakes.

"Next time she's back in town," Bill added, "why don't you bring her by for dinner? Em's been asking about her. Unless, of course, you two would rather make up for lost time." He winked.

Kevin wondered if the offer was genuine. On days like these, Bill liked to pretend he was just one of the guys instead of the captain. But he was hard-edged. Cunning. More a politician than a cop. "I'll mention it to her."

"When did she take off?"

"Earlier this morning. She's already there."

The burgers were sizzling on the grill, the drippings making the flames jump and dance.

Bill pressed down on one of the patties, squeezing out the juice, drying it out. The man knew nothing about barbecuing, Kevin thought. Without the juice they would taste like rocks—dry, flavorless, and hard. Inedible. "Hey, about the Ashley Henderson case," Bill said, changing the subject. "I think we're finally going to be able to indict. You did good work, there."

"It's about time," Kevin said. "I thought they had enough a while ago."

"I did, too. But I'm not the DA." Bill pressed down on another patty, ruining it. "I also wanted to talk to you about Terry."

Terry Canton had been Kevin's partner for the last three years, but he'd had a heart attack in December and had been out of work since. Kevin had been working alone since then.

"What about him?"

"He's not coming back. I just found out this morning. His doctors recommended that he retire and he decided they were right. He figures he's already put in his twenty and his pension is waiting for him."

"What does that mean for me?"

Bill shrugged. "We'll get you a new partner, but we can't right now with the city on a budget freeze. Maybe when the new budget passes."

"Maybe or probably?"

"You'll get a partner. But it probably won't be until July. I'm sorry about that. I know it means more work for you, but there's nothing I can do. I'll try my best to keep your load manageable."

"I appreciate that."

A group of kids ran across the patio, their faces dirty. Two women exited the house carrying bowls of chips, probably gossiping. Kevin hated gossips. Bill motioned with his spatula toward the railing on the deck. "Hand me that plate over there, would you? I think these are getting close to being done."

Kevin grabbed the serving platter. It was the same one that had been used to bring the hamburger patties out to the grill and he noted smears of grease and bits of raw hamburger. Disgusting. He knew that Erin would have brought a clean platter, one without bits of raw hamburger and grease. Kevin set the platter next to the grill.

"I need another beer," Kevin said, raising his bottle. "You want one?"

Bill shook his head and ruined another burger. "I'm still working on mine right there. But thanks."

Kevin headed toward the house, feeling the grease from the platter on his fingertips. Soaking in.

"Hey," Bill shouted from behind him. Kevin turned.

"Cooler's over there, remember?" Bill pointed to the corner of the deck.

"I know. But I want to wash my hands before dinner."

"Make it back quick then. Once I set the platter out, it's every man for himself."

Kevin paused at the back door to wipe his feet on the mat before heading inside. In the kitchen, he walked around a group of chattering wives and toward the sink. He washed his hands twice, using soap both times. Through the window, he saw Bill set the platter of hot dogs and burgers on the picnic table, near the buns, condiments, and bowls of chips. Almost immediately flies caught the scent and descended on the feast, buzzing over the food and landing on the burgers. People didn't seem to care as they formed a crazy line. Instead, they shooed the flies and loaded their plates, pretending that flies weren't swarming.

Ruined burgers and a cloud of flies.

He and Erin would have done it differently. He wouldn't have pressed the burgers with the spatula and Erin would have placed the condiments and chips and pickles in the kitchen so people could serve up there, where it was clean. Flies were disgusting and the burgers were as hard as rocks and he wasn't going to eat them because the thought made him nauseated.

He waited until the platter of burgers had been emptied before heading back outside. He wandered to the table, feigning disappointment.

"I warned you they'd go fast." Bill beamed. "But Emily's got another platter in the refrigerator, so it won't be long until round two. Grab me a beer, would you, while I go get it?"

"Sure," Kevin said.

When the next batch of burgers was done, Kevin loaded a plate of food and complimented Bill and told him it looked fantastic. Flies were swarming and the burgers were dry and when Bill turned away, Kevin tossed the food into the metal garbage can on the side of the house. He told Bill that the burger tasted fantastic.

He stayed at the barbecue for a couple of hours. He talked with Coffey and Ramirez. They were detectives like him, except they ate the burgers and didn't care that the flies were swarming. Kevin didn't want to be the first one to leave, or even the second one, because the captain wanted to pretend he was one of the guys and he didn't want to offend the captain. He didn't like Coffey or Ramirez. Sometimes, when Kevin was around, Coffey and Ramirez stopped talking, and Kevin knew they had been talking about him behind his back. Gossips.

But Kevin was a good detective and he knew it. Bill knew it, and so did Coffey and Ramirez. He worked homicide and knew how to talk to witnesses and suspects. He knew when to ask questions and when to listen; he knew when people were lying to him and he put murderers behind bars because the Bible says *Thou shalt not kill* and he believed in God and he was doing God's work by putting the guilty in jail.

Back at home, Kevin walked through the living room. He resisted the urge to call for Erin. If Erin had been here, the mantel would have been dusted and the magazines would have fanned out on the end table and there wouldn't have been an empty bottle of vodka on the couch. If Erin had been here, the drapes would have been opened, allowing the sunlight to stretch across the floorboards. If Erin had been here, the dishes would have been washed and put away and dinner would have been waiting on the table and she would have smiled at him and asked him how his day had gone. Later they would make love because he loved her and she loved him.

Upstairs in the bedroom, he stood at the closet door. He could still catch a whiff of the perfume she'd worn, the one he'd bought her for Christmas. He'd seen her lift a tab on an ad in one of her magazines and smile when she smelled the perfume sample. When she went to bed, he tore the page out of the magazine and tucked it into his wallet so he'd know exactly which perfume to buy. He remembered the tender way she'd dabbed a little behind each ear and on her wrists when he'd taken her out on New Year's Eve, and how pretty she'd looked in the black cocktail dress she was wearing. In the restaurant, Kevin had noticed the way other men, even those with dates, had glanced in her direction as she passed by them on the way to the table. Afterward, when they'd returned home, they made love as the New Year rolled in.

The dress was still there, hanging in the same place, bringing back those memories. A week ago, he remembered removing it from the hanger and holding it as he'd sat on the edge of the bed and cried.

Outside, he could hear the steady sound of crickets but it did nothing to soothe him. Though it was supposed to have been a relaxing day, he was tired. He hadn't wanted to go to the barbecue, hadn't wanted to answer questions about Erin, hadn't wanted to lie. Not because lying bothered him, but because it was hard to keep up the pretense that Erin hadn't left him. He'd invented a story and had been sticking to it for months: that Erin called every night, that she'd been home the last few days but had gone back to New Hampshire, that the friend was undergoing chemotherapy and needed Erin's help. He knew he couldn't keep that up forever, that soon the helping-a-friend excuse would begin to sound hollow and people would begin to wonder why they never saw Erin in church or at the store or even around the neighborhood or how long she would continue to help her friend. They'd talk about him behind his back and say things like, *Erin must have left him,* and *I guess their marriage wasn't as perfect as I thought it was.* The thought made his stomach clench, reminding him that he hadn't eaten.

There wasn't much in the refrigerator. Erin always had turkey and ham and Dijon mustard and fresh rye bread from the bakery, but his only choice now was whether to reheat the Mongolian beef he'd picked up from the Chinese restaurant a couple of days earlier. On the bottom shelf, he saw food stains and he felt like crying again, because it made him think about Erin's screams and the way her head had sounded when it had hit the edge of the table after he'd thrown her across the kitchen. He'd been slapping and kicking her because there were food stains in the refrigerator and he wondered now why he'd become so angry about such a little thing.

Kevin went to the bed and lay down. Next thing he knew, it was midnight, and the neighborhood outside his window was still. Across the street, he saw a light on in the Feldmans' house. He didn't like the Feldmans. Unlike the other neighbors, Larry Feldman never waved at him if both of them happened to be in their yards, and if his wife, Gladys, happened to see him, she'd turn away and head back into the house. They were in their sixties, the kind of people who rushed outside to scold a kid who happened to walk across their grass to retrieve a Frisbee or baseball. And even though they were Jewish, they decorated their house with Christmas lights in addition to the menorah they put in the window at the holidays. They confounded him and he didn't think they were good neighbors.

He went back to bed but couldn't fall asleep. In the morning, with sunlight streaming in, he knew that nothing had changed for anyone else. Only his life was different. His brother, Michael, and his wife, Nadine, would be getting the kids ready for school before heading out to their jobs at Boston College, and his mom and dad were probably reading the *Globe* as they had their morning coffee. Crimes had been committed, and witnesses would be in the precinct. Coffey and Ramirez would be gossiping about him.

He showered and had vodka and toast for breakfast. At

the precinct, he was called out to investigate a murder. A woman in her twenties, most likely a prostitute, had been found stabbed to death, her body tossed in a Dumpster. He spent the morning talking to bystanders while the evidence was collected. When he finished with the interviews, he went to the precinct to start the report while the information was fresh in his mind. He was a good detective.

The precinct was busy. End of a holiday weekend. The world gone crazy. Detectives were speaking into phones and writing at their desks and talking to witnesses and listening as victims told detectives about their victimization. Noisy. Active. People coming and going. Phones ringing. Kevin walked toward his desk, one of four in the middle of the room. Through the open door, Bill waved but stayed in his office. Ramirez and Coffey were at their desks, sitting across from him.

"You okay?" Coffey asked. Coffey was in his forties, overweight and balding. "You look like hell."

"I didn't sleep well," Kevin said.

"I don't sleep well without Janet, either. When's Erin coming back?"

Kevin kept his expression neutral.

"Next weekend. I've got a few days coming and we've decided to go to the Cape. We haven't been there in years."

"Yeah? My mom lives there. Where at the Cape?"

"Provincetown."

"So does she. You'll love it there. I go there all the time. Where are you staying?"

Kevin wondered why Coffey kept asking questions. "I'm not sure," he finally said. "Erin's making the arrangements."

Kevin walked toward the coffeepot and poured himself a cup, even though he didn't want any. He'd have to find the name of a bed-and-breakfast and a couple of restaurants, so if Coffey asked about it, he'd know what to say.

His days followed the same routine. He worked and talked to witnesses and finally went home. His work was stressful and he wanted to relax when he finished, but everything was different at home and the work stayed with him. He'd once believed that he would get used to the sight of murder victims, but their gray, lifeless faces were etched in his memory, and sometimes the victims visited him in his sleep.

He didn't like going home. When he finished his shift, there was no beautiful wife to greet him at the door. Erin had been gone since January. Now, his house was messy and dirty and he had to do his own laundry. He hadn't known how to work the washing machine, and the first time he ran it he added too much soap and the clothes came out looking dingy. There were no home-cooked meals or candles on the table. Instead, he grabbed food on the way home and ate on the couch. Sometimes, he put on the television. Erin liked to watch HGTV, the home and garden channel on cable, so he often watched that and when he did, the emptiness he felt inside was almost unbearable.

After work he no longer bothered to store his gun in the gun box he kept in his closet; in the box, he had a second Glock for his personal use. Erin had been afraid of guns, even before he'd placed the Glock to her head and threatened to kill her if she ever ran away again. She'd screamed and cried as he'd sworn that he'd kill any man she slept with, any man she cared about. She'd been so stupid and he'd been so angry with her for running away and he demanded the name of the man who had helped her so he could kill him. But Erin had screamed and cried and begged for her life and swore there wasn't a man and he believed her because she was his wife. They'd made their vows in front of God and family and the Bible says *Thou shalt not commit adultery.* Even then, he hadn't believed that Erin had been unfaithful. He'd never believed another man was involved. While they were married, he'd made sure of that. He made random calls to the house throughout the day and never let her go to the store or to the hair salon or to the library by herself. She didn't have a car or even a license and he swung by their house whenever he was in the area, just to make sure she was at home. She hadn't left because she wanted to commit adultery. She left because she was tired of getting kicked and punched and thrown down the cellar stairs and he knew he shouldn't have done those things and he always felt guilty and apologized but it still hadn't mattered.

She shouldn't have run away. It broke his heart because he loved her more than life and he'd always taken care of her. He bought her a house and a refrigerator and a washer and dryer and new furniture. The house had always been clean, but now the sink was full of dishes and his hamper was overflowing.

He knew he should clean the house but he didn't have the energy. Instead, he went to the kitchen and pulled a bottle of vodka from the freezer. There were four bottles left; a week ago, there'd been twelve. He knew he was drinking too much. He knew he should eat better and stop drinking but all he wanted to do was take the bottle and sit on the couch and drink. Vodka was good because it didn't make your breath smell, and in the mornings, no one would know he was nursing a hangover.

He poured a glass of vodka, finished it, and poured another before walking through the empty house. His heart ached because Erin wasn't here and if she suddenly showed up at the door, he knew he'd apologize for hitting her and they'd work things out and then they'd make love in the bedroom. He wanted to hold her and whisper how much he adored her, but he knew she wasn't coming back, and even though he loved her, she made him so angry sometimes. A wife didn't just leave. A wife didn't just walk away from a marriage. He wanted to hit and kick and slap her and pull her hair for being so stupid. For being so damn selfish. He wanted to show her it was pointless to run away.

He drank a third and fourth glass of vodka.

It was all so confusing. The house was a wreck. There was an empty pizza box on the floor of the living room and the casing around the bathroom door was splintered and cracked. The door would no longer close all the way. He'd kicked it in after she'd locked it, trying to get away from him. He'd been holding her by the hair as he punched her in the kitchen and she'd run to the bathroom and he'd chased her through the house and kicked the door in. But now he couldn't remember what they'd been fighting about.

He couldn't remember much about that night. He couldn't remember breaking two of her fingers, even though it was obvious that he had. But he wouldn't let her go to the hospital for a week, not until the bruises on her face could be covered by makeup, and she'd had to cook and clean one-handed. He bought her flowers and apologized and told her that he loved her and promised it would never happen again, and after she got the cast off, he'd taken her into Boston for a dinner at Petroni's. It was expensive and he'd smiled across the table at her. Afterward, they'd gone to a movie and on the way home he remembered thinking about how much he loved her and how lucky he was to have someone like her as his wife.

21

Alex had stayed with Katie until after midnight, listening as she'd told the story of her prior life. When she was too spent and exhausted to talk anymore, he put his arms around her and kissed her good night. On his drive home, he thought that he had never met anyone braver or stronger or more resourceful.

They spent much of the next couple of weeks together—or as much as they could, anyway. Between the hours he worked at the store and her shifts at Ivan's, it wasn't usually more than a few hours a day, but he anticipated his visits to her place with a sense of excitement he hadn't felt in years. Sometimes, Kristen and Josh went with him. Other times, Joyce would shoo him out the door with a wink, urging him to have himself a good time before he headed over.

They seldom spent time at his house and when they did, it was only for short periods. In his mind, he wanted to believe it was because of the kids, that he wanted to take things slowly, but part of him realized it also had to do with Carly. Though he knew he loved Katie—and he grew more certain with every passing day—he wasn't sure he was ready for that just yet. Katie seemed to understand his reluctance and didn't seem to mind, if only because it was easier to be alone at her place.

Even so, they'd yet to make love. Though he often found himself imagining how wonderful it would be, especially in those moments before sleep, he knew Katie wasn't ready for that. They both seemed to realize it would signal a change in their relationship, a hopeful permanence of sorts. For now, it was enough to kiss her, to feel her arms wrapped around him. He loved the scent of jasmine shampoo in her hair and the way her hand nestled so perfectly in his; the way their every touch was charged with delicious anticipation, as if they were somehow saving themselves for each other. He hadn't slept with anyone since his wife had died, and now he felt that in some way he had unknowingly been waiting for Katie.

He took pleasure in showing her around the area. They walked the waterfront and past the historic homes, examining the architecture, and one weekend he took her to the Orton Plantation Gardens, where they wandered among a thousand blooming rosebushes. Afterward, they went to lunch at a small oceanfront bistro at Caswell Beach, where they held hands across the table like teenagers.

Since their dinner at her house, she hadn't broached her past again, and he didn't bring it up. He knew she was still working things out in her mind: how much she'd told him already and how much there still was to tell, whether or not she could trust him, how much it mattered that she was still married, and what would happen if Kevin somehow found her here. When he sensed she was brooding over such things, he would remind her gently that no matter what happened, her secret would always be safe with him. He would never tell anyone.

Watching her, he would sometimes be overcome with an overwhelming rage at Kevin Tierney. Such men's instincts to victimize and torture were as foreign to him as the ability to breathe underwater or fly; more than anything, he wanted revenge. He wanted justice. He wanted Kevin to experience Katie's anguish and terror, the unending bouts of brutal physical pain. During his time in the army, he'd killed one man, a soldier strung out on methamphetamines who was threatening a hostage with a gun. The man was dangerous and out of control and when the opportunity arose, Alex had pulled the trigger without hesitation. The death had given his job a sobering new meaning, but in his heart he knew that there were moments in life when violence was necessary to save lives. He knew that if Kevin ever showed up, Alex would protect Katie, no matter what. In the army, he'd slowly come to the realization that there were people who added goodness to the world and people who lived to destroy it. In his mind, the decision to protect an innocent woman like Katie from a psychopath like Kevin was as clear as black and white—a simple choice.

On most days, the specter of Katie's past life didn't intrude, and they spent each day together in a state of relaxed and growing intimacy. The afternoons with the kids were particularly special for him. Katie was a natural with children—whether helping Kristen feed the ducks at the pond or playing catch with Josh, she always seemed to fall effortlessly into rhythm with them, by turns playful, comforting, rowdy, or quiet. In this way she was much like Carly, and he somehow felt certain that Katie was the kind of woman Carly had once spoken about.

In the final weeks of Carly's life, he had maintained a vigil beside her bed. Even though she slept most of the time, he was afraid of missing those times when she was conscious, no matter how short they might be. By then, the left side of her body was almost paralyzed, and speech was difficult for her. But one night, during a brief lucid period in the hour just before dawn, she'd reached for him.

"I want you to do something for me," she said with effort, licking her cracked lips. Her voice was hoarse from disuse.

"Anything."

"I want you to be . . . happy." At this, he saw the ghost of her old smile, the confident, self-possessed smile that had captivated him at their first meeting.

"I am happy."

She gave a faint shake of her head. "I'm talking about the future." Her eyes gleamed with the intensity of hot coals in her sunken face. "We both know what I'm talking about."

"I don't."

She ignored his response. "Marrying you . . . being with you every day and having children with you . . . it's the best thing I've ever done. You're the best man I've ever known."

His throat closed up. "Me, too," he said. "I feel the same way."

"I know," she said. "And that's why this is so hard for me. Because I know that I've failed—"

"You haven't failed," he broke in.

Her expression was sad. "I love you, Alex, and I love our kids," she whispered. "And it would break my heart to think that you'll never be completely happy again."

"Carly—"

"I want you to meet someone new." She struggled to take a deep breath, her fragile rib cage heaving with the effort. "I want her to be smart and kind...and I want you to fall in love with her, because you shouldn't spend the rest of your life alone."

Alex couldn't speak, could barely see her through his tears.

"The kids need a mom." To his ears, it sounded almost like a plea. "Someone who loves them as much as I do, someone who thinks of them as her own children."

"Why are you talking about this?" he asked, his voice cracking.

"Because," she said, "I have to believe that it's possible." Her bony fingers clutched at his arm with desperate intensity. "It's the only thing I have left."

Now, as he saw Katie chasing after Josh and Kristen on the grassy shoulder of the duck pond, he felt a bittersweet pang at the thought that maybe Carly had gotten her last wish after all.

She liked him too much for her own good. Katie knew that she was walking a dangerous line. Telling him about her past had seemed like the right thing to do at the time, and speaking the words had freed her somehow from the crushing burden of her secrets. But the morning after their first dinner, she was paralyzed with anxiety by what she had done. Alex used to be an investigator, after all, which probably meant he could easily make a phone call or two, no matter what he'd said to her. He'd talk to someone and they'd talk to someone and eventually, Kevin would learn of it. She hadn't told him that Kevin had an almost eerie ability to connect seemingly random information; she hadn't mentioned that when a suspect was on the run, Kevin almost always knew where to find him. Simply thinking about what she'd done made her sick to her stomach.

But gradually, over the next couple of weeks, she felt her fears ebb. Instead of asking her more questions when they were alone, Alex acted as if her revelations had no bearing on their lives in Southport. The days passed with easy spontaneity, untroubled by shadows from her prior life. She couldn't help it: she trusted him. And when they kissed, which happened with surprising frequency, there were times when her knees went shaky and it was all she could do to stop from taking his hand and dragging him into the bedroom.

On Saturday, two weeks after their first date, they stood on her front porch, his arms wrapped around her, his lips against hers. Josh and Kristen were at an end-of-the-year swimming party hosted by a kid in Josh's class. Later, Alex and Katie planned to take them to the beach for an evening barbecue, but for the next few hours, they'd be alone.

When they finally separated, Katie sighed. "You really have to stop doing that."

"Doing what?"

"You know exactly what you're doing."

"I can't help it."

I know the feeling, Katie thought. "Do you know what I like about you?"

"My body?"

"Yes. That, too." She laughed. "But I also like that you make me feel special."

"You are special," he said.

"I'm serious," she said. "But it makes me wonder why you never found someone else. Since your wife passed away, I mean."

"I haven't been looking," he said. "But even if there was someone else, I would have dumped her so I could be with you instead."

"That's not nice." She poked him in the ribs.

"It's true, though. Believe it or not, I'm picky."

"Yeah," she said, "real picky. You only go out with emotionally scarred women."

"You're not emotionally scarred. You're tough. You're a survivor. It's actually kind of sexy."

"I think you're just trying to flatter me in the hopes I'll rip off your clothes."

"Is it working?"

"You're getting closer," she admitted, and the sound of his laughter reminded her again how much he loved her.

"I'm glad you ended up in Southport," he said.

"Uh-huh." For an instant she seemed to disappear inside herself.

"What?" He scrutinized her face, suddenly alert.

She shook her head. "It was so close..." She sighed, hugging her arms around herself at the memory. "I almost didn't make it."

22

Brittle snow coated the yards of Dorchester, forming a glittering shell over the world outside her window. The January sky, gray the day before, had given way to an icy blue and the temperature was below freezing.

It was Sunday morning, the day after she'd had her hair done. She peeked in the toilet for blood, sure she'd see some after she peed. Her kidney still throbbed, radiating pain from her shoulder blades to the backs of her legs. It had kept her up for hours as Kevin snored beside her, but thankfully, it wasn't as serious as it could have been. After closing the bedroom door behind her, she limped to the kitchen, reminding herself that in just a couple of days, it would be over. But she had to be careful not to arouse Kevin's suspicions, to play things exactly right. If she ignored the beating he had given her the night before, he would be suspicious. If she went too far, he would be suspicious. After four years of hell, she'd learned the rules.

Kevin had to go into work at noon, even though it was

Sunday, and she knew he'd be up soon. The house was cold and she pulled on a sweatshirt over her pajamas; in the mornings, Kevin didn't mind, usually because he was too hung over to care. She started the coffee and put the milk and sugar on the table, along with butter and jelly. She set his silverware out and placed a cup of ice water beside the fork. After that, two pieces of toast went in the toaster, though she couldn't toast them just yet. She put three eggs on the counter, where she could reach them quickly. When that was done, she placed half a dozen slices of bacon in the frying pan. They were sizzling and popping when Kevin finally wandered into the kitchen. He took a seat at the empty table and drank his water as she brought him a cup of coffee.

"I was dead to the world last night," he said. "What time did we end up going to bed?"

"Maybe ten?" she answered. She put the coffee beside his empty glass. "It wasn't late. You've been working hard and I know you've been tired."

His eyes were bloodshot. "I'm sorry about last night. I didn't mean it. I've just been under a lot of pressure lately. Since Terry's heart attack, I've been having to do the work of two people, and the Preston case starts this week."

"It's okay," she said. She could still smell the alcohol on his breath. "Your breakfast will be ready in a few minutes."

At the stove, she turned the bacon with a fork and a splash of grease scalded her arm, making her temporarily forget the pain in her back.

When the bacon was crispy, she put four pieces on Kevin's plate and two on hers. She drained the grease into a soup can, wiped the frying pan with a paper towel, and oiled it again with cooking spray. She had to move fast, so the bacon wouldn't get cold. She started the toaster and cracked the eggs. He liked his over medium, with the yolk intact, and she'd grown adept at the process. The pan was still hot and the eggs cooked quickly. She turned them once before sliding two onto his plate and one onto hers. The toast came up and she placed both slices on his plate.

She sat across from him at the table because he liked them to have breakfast together. He buttered his toast and added grape jelly before using his fork to break the eggs. The yolk pooled like yellow blood and he used his toast to sop it up.

"What are you going to do today?" he asked. He used his fork to cut another piece of egg. Chewing.

"I was going to do the windows and the laundry," she said.

"The sheets probably need a wash, too, huh? After our fun last night?" he said, waggling his eyebrows. His hair was pointing in different directions and there was a piece of egg at the corner of his mouth.

She tried not to show her revulsion. Instead, she changed the subject.

"Do you think you'll get a conviction in the Preston case?" she asked.

He leaned back and rolled his shoulders before hunching over his plate again.

"That's up to the DA. Higgins is good, but you never know. Preston has a shyster lawyer and he's going to try to twist all the facts around."

"I'm sure you'll do fine. You're smarter than he is."

"We'll see. I just hate that it's in Marlborough. Higgins wants to prep me Tuesday night, after court finishes for the day."

Erin knew all of this already and she nodded. The Preston case had been widely publicized and the trial was due to start on Monday in Marlborough, not Boston. Lorraine Preston had supposedly hired a man to kill her husband. Not only was Douglass Preston a billionaire hedge-fund manager, but his wife was a scion of society, involved in charities ranging from art museums and the symphony to inner-city schools. The pretrial publicity had been staggering; a day hadn't gone by in weeks without one or two articles on the front page and a top story on the evening news. Megamoney, lurid sex, drugs, betrayal, infidelity, assassination, and an illegitimate child. Because of the endless publicity, the trial had been moved to Marlborough. Kevin had been one of several detectives assigned to the investigation and all were scheduled to testify Wednesday. Like everyone else, Erin had been following the news but she'd been asking Kevin questions every now and then about the case.

"You know what you need after you're finished in court?" she asked. "A night out. We should get dressed up and go out to dinner. You're off on Friday, right?"

"We just did that on New Year's," Kevin grumbled, sopping up more yolk on his plate. There were smears of jelly on his fingers.

"If you don't want to go out, I can make you something special here. Whatever you want. We can have wine and maybe start a fire and I could wear something sexy. It could be really romantic." He looked up from his plate and she went on. "The point is, I'm open to whatever," she purred, "and you need a break. I don't like it when you work so hard. It's like they expect you to solve every case out there."

He tapped his fork against his plate, studying her. "Why are you acting all lovey-dovey? What's going on?"

Telling herself to stick to the script, she pushed back from the table.

"Just forget it, okay?" She grabbed her plate and the fork clattered off it, hitting the table and then the floor. "I was trying to be supportive since you're going out of town, but if you don't like it, fine. I'll tell you what—you figure out what you want to do and let me know sometime, okay?"

She stormed over to the sink and turned the faucet on hard. She knew she'd surprised him, could feel him vacillating between anger and confusion. She ran her hands under the water then brought them to her face. She drew a series of rapid breaths, hiding her face, and made a choking sound. She let her shoulders heave a little.

"Are you crying?" he asked. She heard his chair slide back. "Why the hell are you crying?"

She choked out the words, doing her best to make them sound broken. "I don't know what to do anymore. I don't know what you want. I know how big this case is and how important it is and how much pressure you're under..."

She choked off the final words, sensing his approach. When she felt him touch her, she shuddered.

"Hey, it's okay," he said grudgingly. "You don't have to cry."

She turned toward him, squeezing her eyes shut, putting her face against his chest. "I just want to make you happy," she stammered. She wiped her wet face on his shirt.

"We'll figure it out, okay? We'll have a nice weekend. I promise. To make up for last night."

She put her arms around him, pulling him close, sniffling. She drew another rasping inhale. "I'm really sorry. I know you didn't need that today. Me getting all blubbery for nothing. You've got so much on your plate already."

"I can handle it," he said. He tilted his head and she leaned up to kiss him, her eyes still shut. When she pulled back, she wiped her face with her fingers and pulled close to him again. As he pressed against her, she could feel him getting excited. She knew how her vulnerability turned him on.

"We've got a little time before I have to head into work," he said.

"I should clean the kitchen first."

"You can do it later," he said.

Minutes later, with Kevin moving atop her, she made the sounds he wanted while staring out the window of the bedroom and thinking of other things.

She had learned to hate winter, with the endless cold and a yard half-buried in snow, because she couldn't go outside. Kevin didn't like her to walk around the neighborhood but he let her garden in the backyard because of the privacy fence. In the spring, she always planted flowers in pots and vegetables in a small plot near the back of the garage, where the sun was full and strong, unshaded by the maple trees. In the fall, she would pull on a sweater and read books from the library as fallen leaves, brown and crinkly, drifted around the yard.

But winter made her life a prison, cold and gray and gloomy. Misery. Most days were spent without setting foot outside the door because she never knew when Kevin would show up unexpectedly. She knew the names of a single neighbor, the Feldmans, who lived across the street. In her first year of marriage, Kevin rarely hit her and sometimes she went for walks without him. The Feldmans, an older couple, liked to work in their garden, and in the first year she'd lived here, she'd often stopped to talk to them for a while. Kevin gradually tried to put an end to those friendly visits. Now she saw the Feldmans only when she knew Kevin was busy at work, when she knew he couldn't call. She would make sure no other neighbors were watching before darting across the street to their front door. She felt like a spy when she visited with them. They showed her photos of their daughters growing up. One had died and the other had moved away and she had the sense that they were as lonely as she was. In the summer, she made them blueberry pies and would spend the rest of the afternoon mopping up the flour in the kitchen so Kevin wouldn't know.

After Kevin went to work, she cleaned the windows and put fresh sheets on the bed. She vacuumed, dusted, and cleaned the kitchen. As she worked, she practiced lowering her voice so she could sound like a man. She tried not to think about the cell phone she had charged overnight and put under the sink. Even though she knew that she might never get a better chance, she was terrified because there was still so much that could go wrong.

She made Kevin breakfast on Monday morning, just as she always did. Four slices of bacon, eggs over medium, and two pieces of toast. He was grumpy and distracted and he read the paper without saying much to her. When he was about to leave, he put a coat on over his suit and she told him she was going to hop into the shower.

"Must be nice," he grunted, "to wake up every day

knowing you can do whatever the hell you want to do whenever you want to do it."

"Is there anything special you want for dinner?" she asked, pretending not to have heard him.

He thought about it. "Lasagna and garlic bread. And a salad," he said.

When he left, she stood at the window watching as his car reached the corner. As soon as he turned, she walked to the phone, dizzy at the thought of what was to come next.

When she called the phone company, she was directed to customer service. Five minutes passed, then six. It would take Kevin twenty minutes to get to work, and no doubt he would call as soon as he arrived. She still had time. Finally, a rep got on the line and asked her name and the billing address and, for purposes of identification, Kevin's mother's maiden name. The account was in Kevin's name, and she spoke in a low voice as she recited the information, in the voice she'd been practicing. She didn't sound like Kevin, maybe not even masculine, but the representative was harried and didn't notice.

"Is it possible to get call forwarding on my line?" she asked.

"It's an extra charge, but with that, you also get call waiting and voice mail. It's only—"

"That's fine. But is it possible to have it turned on today?"

"Yes," the representative said. She heard him beginning to type. It was a long time before he spoke again. He told her the extra charge would show up on the next bill, which would be sent out next week, but that it would still reflect the full monthly amount, even though she activated the service today. She told him it was fine. He took some more information and then told her it was done and that she would be able to use the service right away. She hung up and glanced at the clock. The whole transaction had taken eighteen minutes.

Kevin called from the precinct three minutes later.

As soon as she got off the phone with Kevin, she called Super Shuttle, a van service that transported people to the airport and bus station. She made a reservation for the following day. Then, after retrieving the cell phone, she finally activated it. She called a local movie theater, one that had a recording, to make sure it worked. Next, she activated the landline's call-forwarding service, sending incoming calls to the number of the movie theater. As a test, she dialed the home number from her cell phone. Her heart was pounding as the landline rang. On the second ring, the ring cut off and she heard the recording from the movie theater. Something broke free inside her and her hands were shaking as she powered off the cell phone and replaced it in the box of SOS pads. She reset the landline.

Kevin called again forty minutes later.

She spent the rest of the afternoon in a daze, working steadily to keep from worrying. She ironed two of his shirts and brought the suit bag and suitcase in from the garage. She set out clean socks and she polished his other pair of black shoes. She ran the lint brush over his suit, the black one he wore to court, and laid out three ties. She scrubbed the bathroom until the floor was shiny, and scrubbed the baseboards with vinegar. She dusted every item in the china cabinet and then started preparing the lasagna. She boiled the pasta and made a meat sauce and layered all of it with cheese. She brushed four pieces of sourdough bread with butter, garlic, and oregano and diced everything she needed for the salad. She showered and dressed sexy, and at five o'clock, she put the lasagna in the oven.

When he got home, dinner was ready. He ate the lasagna and talked about his day. When he asked for a second serving, she rose from the table and brought it to him. After dinner, he drank vodka as they watched reruns of *Seinfeld* and *The King of Queens*. Afterward, the Celtics were playing the Timberwolves and she sat beside him, her head on his shoulder, watching the game. He fell asleep in front of the television and she wandered to the bedroom. She lay in bed, staring at the ceiling, until he finally woke and staggered in, flopping onto the mattress. He fell asleep immediately, one arm draped over her, and his snores sounded like a warning.

She made him breakfast on Tuesday morning. He packed his clothes and toiletries and was finally ready to head to Marlborough. He loaded his things into the car, then went back to the front door, where she was standing. He kissed her.

"I'll be home tomorrow night," he said.

"I'll miss you," she said, leaning into him, putting her arms around his neck.

"I should be home around eight."

"I'll make something that I can reheat when you get home," she said. "How about chili?"

"I'll probably eat on the way home."

"Are you sure? Do you really want to eat fast food? It's so bad for you."

"We'll see," he said.

"I'll make it anyway," she said. "Just in case."

He kissed her as she leaned into him. "I'll call you," he said, his hands drifting downward. Caressing her.

"I know," she answered.

In the bathroom, she took off her clothes and set them on the toilet, then rolled up the rug. She'd placed a garbage bag in the sink, and naked, she stared at herself in the mirror. She fingered the bruises on her ribs and on her wrist. All of her ribs stood out, and dark circles beneath her eyes gave her face a hollowed-out look. She was engulfed by a wave of fury mixed with sadness as she imagined the way he'd call for her when he walked through the house upon his return. He'd call her name and walk to the kitchen. He'd look for her in the bedroom. He'd check the garage and the back porch and the cellar. *Where are you?* he'd call out. *What's for dinner?*

With the scissors, she began to chop savagely at her hair. Four inches of blond hair fell onto the garbage bag. She seized another chunk, using her fingers to pull it tight, telling herself to measure, and snipped. Her chest felt constricted and tight.

"I hate you!" she hissed, her voice trembling. "Degraded me all the time!" She lopped off more hair, her eyes flooding with rage-fueled tears. "Hit me because I had to go shopping!" More hair gone. She tried to slow down, even out the ends. "Made me steal money from your wallet and kicked me because you were drunk!"

She was shaking now, her hands unsteady. Uneven lengths of hair collected at her feet. "Made me hide from you! Hit me so hard that I vomit!"

She snapped the scissors. "I loved you!" She sobbed.

"You promised me you'd never hit me again and I believed you! I wanted to believe you!" She cut and cried, and when her hair was all the same length, she pulled out the hair dye from its hiding place behind the sink. Dark Brown. Then she got in the shower and wet her hair. She tilted the bottle and began massaging the dye into her hair. She stood at the mirror and sobbed uncontrollably while it set. When it was done, she climbed into the shower again and rinsed it out. She shampooed and conditioned and stood before the mirror. Carefully, she applied mascara to her eyebrows, darkening them. She added bronzer to her skin, darkening it. She dressed in jeans and a sweater and stared at herself.

A dark, short-haired stranger looked back at her.

She cleaned the bathroom scrupulously, making sure no hair remained in the shower or on the floor. Extra strands went into the garbage bag, along with the box of hair dye. She wiped the sink and counter down and tied up the garbage bag. Last, she put eyedrops in, trying to erase the evidence of her tears.

She had to hurry now. She packed her things in a duffel bag. Three pairs of jeans, two sweatshirts, shirts. Panties and bras. Socks. Toothbrush and toothpaste. A brush. Mascara for her eyebrows. The little jewelry she owned. Cheese and crackers and nuts and raisins. A fork and a knife. She went to the back porch and dug out the money from beneath the flowerpot. The cell phone from the kitchen. And finally, the identification she needed to start a new life, identification she'd stolen from people who trusted her. She'd hated herself for stealing and knew it was wrong, but she'd had no other choice and she'd prayed to God for forgiveness. It was too late to turn back now.

She had rehearsed the scenario in her head a thousand

times, and she moved fast. Most of the neighbors were off at work: she'd watched them in the mornings and knew their routines. She didn't want anyone to see her leave, didn't want anyone to recognize her.

She threw on a hat and her jacket, along with a scarf and gloves. She rounded the duffel bag and stuffed it beneath her sweatshirt, kneading and working it until it was round. Until she looked pregnant. She put on her long coat, one that was roomy enough to cover the bump.

She stared at herself in the mirror. Short, dark hair. Skin the color of copper. Pregnant. She put on a pair of sunglasses, and on her way out the door, she turned on her cell phone and set the landline on call forwarding. She left the house through the gate at the side. She walked between her house and the neighbors', following the fence line, and deposited the garbage bag in their garbage can. She knew that both of them worked, that neither was at home. Same thing for the house behind hers. She walked through their yard and past the side of the house, finally emerging onto the icy sidewalk.

Snow had begun to fall again. By tomorrow, she knew, her footprints would be gone.

She had six blocks to go but she was going to make it. She kept her head down and walked, trying to ignore the biting wind, feeling dazed and free and terrified, all at the same time. Tomorrow night, she knew, Kevin would walk through the house, calling for her, and he wouldn't find her because she wasn't there. And tomorrow night, he would begin his hunt.

Snow flurries swirled as Katie stood at the intersection, just outside a diner. In the distance, she saw Super

Shuttle's blue van round the corner and her heart pounded in her chest. Just then, she heard the cell phone ring.

She paled. Cars roared past her, their tires loud as they rolled through the slush. In the distance, the van changed lanes, angling toward her side of the road. She had to answer; there was no choice but to answer. But the van was coming and it was noisy on the street. If she answered now, he would know she was outside. He would know she'd left him.

Her phone rang a third time. The blue van stopped at a red light. One block away.

She turned around, walking into the diner, the sounds muffled but still noticeable—a symphony of plates clanking and people talking; directly ahead was the hostess stand, where a man was asking for a table. She felt sick to her stomach. She cupped the phone and faced the window, praying that he couldn't hear the commotion behind her. Her legs went wobbly as she pressed the button and answered.

"What took you so long to answer?" he demanded.

"I was in the shower," she said. "What's going on?"

"I'm about ten minutes out," he said. "How are you?"

"I'm okay," she said.

He hesitated. "You sound kind of funny," he said. "Is something wrong with the phone?"

Up the street, the signal light turned green. The Super Shuttle van's turn signal indicated that it was pulling over. She prayed that it would wait. Behind her, people in the diner had gone surprisingly quiet.

"I'm not sure. But you sound fine," she said. "It's probably bad service where you are. How's the drive?"

"Not too bad once I got out of the city. But it's still icy in places."

"That doesn't sound good. Be careful."

"I'm fine," he said.

"I know," she said. The van was pulling over to the curb, the driver craning his neck, looking for her. "I hate to do this, but can you call me in a few minutes? I still have conditioner in my hair and I want to rinse it out."

"Yeah," he grumbled. "Okay. I'll call you in a bit."

"I love you," she said.

"Love you, too."

She let him hang up before she pressed the button on her phone. Then she walked out of the diner and hurried to the van.

At the bus terminal, she bought a ticket to Philadelphia, hating the way the man who sold her the ticket kept trying to talk to her.

Rather than waiting at the terminal, she went across the street to have breakfast. Money for the shuttle and the bus ticket had taken more than half of the savings she'd collected during the year, but she was hungry and she ordered pancakes and sausage and milk. At the booth, someone had left a newspaper and she forced herself to read it. Kevin called her while she was eating and when he told her again that the phone sounded funny, she suggested that it was the storm.

Twenty minutes later, she got on the bus. An elderly woman motioned to her bulge as she moved down the aisle.

"How much longer?" the woman asked.

"Another month."

"First one?"

"Yes," she answered, but her mouth was so dry it was hard to keep talking. She started down the aisle again and took a seat toward the rear. People sat in the seats in front of and behind her. Across the aisle was a young couple. Teenagers, draped over each other, both of them listening to music. Their heads bobbed up and down.

She stared out the window as the bus pulled away from the station, feeling as if she were dreaming. On the highway, Boston began to recede into the distance, gray and cold. Her lower back ached as the bus rolled forward, miles from home. Snow continued to fall and cars whipped up slush as they passed the bus.

She wished she could talk to someone. She wanted to tell them that she was running away because her husband beat her and that she couldn't call the police because he *was* the police. She wanted to tell them that she didn't have much money and she could never use her real name again. If she did, he would find her and bring her home and beat her again, only this time he might not stop. She wanted to tell them that she was terrified because she didn't know where she was going to sleep tonight or how she was going to eat when the money ran out.

She could feel cold air against the window as towns drifted past. Traffic on the highway thinned and then the roads became crowded again. She didn't know what she was going to do. All her plans had stopped at the bus and there was no one to call for help. She was alone and had nothing but the things she carried with her.

An hour from Philadelphia, her cell phone rang again. She cupped the phone and talked to him. Before he hung up, he promised to call her before he went to bed.

She arrived in Philadelphia in the late afternoon. It was cold, but not snowy. Passengers got off the bus and she hung back, waiting for all of them to leave. In the rest-room, she removed the duffel bag and then went into the waiting room and took a seat on a bench. Her stomach was growling and she sliced off a little cheese and ate it with crackers. She knew she had to make it last, though, so she put the rest of it away, even though she was still hungry. Finally, after buying a map of the city, she stepped outside.

The terminal wasn't located in a bad part of town; she saw the convention center and Trocadero Theater, which made her feel safe, but it also meant she could never afford a hotel room in the area. The map indicated that she was close to Chinatown, and for lack of a better plan she headed in that direction.

Three hours later, she'd finally found a place to sleep. It was dingy and reeked of smoke, and her room was barely large enough for the small bed that had been crammed inside. There was no lamp; instead, a single bulb pro-truded from the ceiling and the communal bathroom was down the hall. The walls were gray and water stained and the window had bars. From the rooms on either side of her, she could hear people talking in a language she couldn't understand. Still, it was all she could afford. She had enough money to stay three nights, four if she could somehow survive on the little food she'd brought from home.

She sat on the edge of the bed, trembling, afraid of this place, afraid of the future, her mind whirling. She had to pee but she didn't want to leave the room. She tried to tell herself that it was an adventure and everything would be okay. As crazy as it sounded, she found herself wonder-ing if she'd made a mistake by leaving; she tried not to think about her kitchen and bedroom and all the things she'd left behind. She knew she could buy a ticket back to Boston and get home before Kevin even realized she was gone. But her hair was short and dark and there was no way she could explain that.

Outside, the sun was down but streetlights shone through the dirty window. She heard horns honking and she looked out. At the street level, all the signs were in Chinese and some businesses were still open. She could hear conversations rising in the darkness and there were plastic bags filled with garbage piled near the street. She was in an unfamiliar city, a city filled with strangers. She couldn't do this, she thought. She wasn't strong enough. In three days, she'd have no place to stay unless she could find a job. If she sold her jewelry, she might buy herself another day, but then what?

She was so tired and her back throbbed. She lay down on the bed and drifted off to sleep almost immediately. Kevin called later, the bleating of the cell phone waking her up. It took everything she had to keep her voice steady, to betray nothing, but she sounded as tired as she felt and she knew that Kevin believed that she was in their bed. When he hung up, she fell asleep again within minutes.

In the morning, she could hear people walking down the hall, heading for the bathroom. Two Chinese women stood at the sinks and there was green mold in the grout and wet toilet paper on the floor. The door to the stall wouldn't lock and she had to hold it closed with her hand.

In the room, she had cheese and crackers for breakfast. She wanted to shower but she realized she'd forgotten to pack shampoo and soap, so there wasn't much point. She changed her clothes and brushed her teeth and hair.

She repacked the duffel bag, unwilling to leave it in the room while she wasn't there, and slung the strap over her shoulder and walked down the steps. The same clerk who'd given her the key was at the desk and she wondered whether he ever left this place. She paid for another night and asked him to hold her room.

Outside, the sky was blue and the streets were dry. She realized the pain in her back had all but vanished. It was cold but not as cold as Boston, and despite her fears she found herself smiling. She'd done it, she reminded herself. She'd escaped and Kevin was hundreds of miles away and didn't know where she was. Didn't even know she'd left yet. He would call a couple more times, then she'd throw away the cell phone and never speak with him again.

She stood straighter and breathed in the crisp air. The day felt almost new, with endless possibilities. Today, she told herself, she was going to find a job. Today, she decided, she was going to start living the rest of her life.

She had run away twice before and she wanted to think she'd learned from her mistakes. The first time was a little less than a year after she was married, after he'd beaten her while she was cowering in the corner of the bedroom. The bills had come in and he was angry with her because she'd turned up the thermostat to make the house warmer. When he'd finally stopped, he'd grabbed his keys and headed out to buy more liquor. Without thinking, she'd grabbed her jacket and left the house, limping down the road. Hours later, with sleet coming down and nowhere to go, she'd called him and he went to pick her up.

The next time she'd gotten as far as Atlantic City before he found her. She'd taken money from his wallet and

purchased a ticket on the bus, but he'd found her within
an hour of her arrival. He'd driven his car at breakneck
speed, knowing she would run to the only place where she
might still find friends. He'd handcuffed her in the backseat of the car on the drive back. He stopped once, pulling
the car over to the side of a closed office building, and
beat her; later that night, the gun came out.

After that, he'd made it harder to leave. He usually
kept the money locked away and started tracking her
whereabouts obsessively. She knew that he would go to
extraordinary lengths to find her. As crazy as he was, he
was persistent and diligent and his instincts were usually
right. He would find out where she'd gone, she knew; he
would come to Philadelphia to find her. She had a head
start, that was all, but with no extra money to start over
somewhere else, all she could do was watch for him over
her shoulder for the time being. Her time in Philadelphia
was limited.

She found a job as a cocktail waitress on her third day
in town. She made up a name and social security number.
Eventually, it would be checked, but she'd be long gone
by then. She found another room to rent on the far side
of Chinatown. She worked for two weeks, accumulated
some tip money while searching for and finding another
job, and quit without bothering to pick up her paycheck.
There was no point; without identification, she wouldn't
be able to cash it. She worked another three weeks at a
small diner and eventually moved out of Chinatown to a
run-down motel that rented by the week. Although it was
in a seedier section of town, the room was more expensive, but she had her own shower and bathroom and it
was worth it, if only to have some privacy and a place to

leave her things. She'd saved a few hundred dollars, more than she had when she'd left Dorchester, but not enough to start over. Again, she left before picking up her paycheck, without even going back to quit. She found yet another job at yet another diner a few days later. In the new job, she told the manager her name was Erica.

The constant job changing and moves had kept her vigilant, and it was there, only four days after she started, that she'd rounded the corner on her way to work and saw a car that seemed somehow out of place. She stopped.

Even now, she wasn't sure how she'd realized it, other than the fact that it was shiny enough to reflect the early morning light. As she stared at the car, she noticed movement in the driver's seat. The engine wasn't running and it struck her as odd that someone would be sitting in an unheated car on a cold morning. The only people, she knew, who did that were those who were waiting for someone.

Or watching for someone.

Kevin.

She knew it was him, knew it with a certainty that surprised her, and she backed around the corner, the way she'd come, praying that he hadn't glanced in the rearview mirror. Praying he hadn't seen her. As soon as the car was out of sight, she began to run back toward the motel, her heart hammering. She hadn't run so fast in years, but all the walking she'd been doing had strengthened her legs and she moved quickly. One block. Two. Three. She looked constantly over her shoulder but Kevin didn't follow.

No matter. He knew she was here. He knew where she worked. He would know if she didn't show up. Within hours, he would find out where she was staying.

In her room, she threw her things into the duffel bag and was out the door within minutes. She started toward the bus station. It would take forever, though. An hour, maybe more, to walk there, and she didn't have the time. That would be the first place he went when he realized she wasn't there. Turning around, she went back into the motel and had the clerk call her a cab. It arrived ten minutes later. The longest ten minutes of her life.

At the bus station, she frantically searched the schedule and selected a bus to New York. It was scheduled to leave in half an hour. She hid in the women's restroom until it was time to board. When she got on the bus she lowered herself into a seat. It didn't take long to get to New York. Again, she scanned the schedules and bought a ticket that would take her as far as Omaha.

In the evening, she got off the bus somewhere in Ohio. She slept in the station, and the next morning she found her way to a truck stop. There she met a man who was delivering materials to Wilmington, North Carolina.

A few days later, after selling her jewelry, she wandered into Southport and found the cottage. After she paid the first month's rent, there was no money left to buy food.

23

It was mid-June and Katie was leaving Ivan's after finishing up a busy dinner shift when she spotted a familiar figure standing near the exit.

"Hey there." Jo waved from beneath the lamppost where Katie had locked up her bike.

"What are you doing here?" Katie asked, leaning in to give her friend a hug. She'd never run into Jo in town before, and seeing her out of context felt strange for some reason.

"I came to see you. Where've you been, stranger?"

"I could ask you the same question."

"I've been around enough to know you've been seeing Alex for a few weeks." Jo winked. "But as a friend, I've never been one to impose. I figured you two needed some time alone."

Katie blushed despite herself. "How did you know I was here?"

"I didn't. But your lights weren't on at the house and I took a chance." Jo shrugged. She motioned over her shoulder. "Are you doing anything? Do you want to grab a drink before you head home?" When she saw Katie's hesitation, she went on. "I know it's late. One drink, I promise. Then I'll let you go to bed."

"One drink," Katie agreed.

A few minutes later, they stepped inside the pub, a local favorite paneled in dark wood scarred with decades of use, with a long mirror behind the bar. It was quiet tonight; only a few tables were occupied and the two women took a seat at a corner table in the back. Since there didn't seem to be table service, Katie ordered two glasses of wine at the bar and brought them back to the table.

"Thanks," Jo said, taking her glass. "Next time, it's on me." She leaned back. "So you and Alex, huh?"

"Is that really what you wanted to talk to me about?" Katie asked.

"Well, since my own love life is in the dumps, I have to live vicariously through you. It seems to be going well, though. He was over there...what? Two or three times last week? And the same thing the week before that?"

Actually more, Katie thought. "Something like that."

Jo twisted the stem of her wineglass. "Uh-oh."

"Uh-oh what?"

"If I didn't know better, I'd think it was getting serious." She raised an eyebrow.

"We're still getting to know each other," Katie offered, not sure where Jo was going with this line of questioning.

"That's how every relationship starts. He likes you, you like him. Then you both go from there."

"Is this why you came down?" Katie tried not to sound exasperated. "To hear all the details?"

"Not *all* of them. Just the juicy ones."

Katie rolled her eyes. "How about we talk about your love life instead?"

"Why? Are you in the mood to be depressed?"

"When was the last time you went on a date?"

"A good date? Or just a date-date?"

"A good date."

Jo hesitated. "I'd have to say that it's been at least a couple of years."

"What happened?"

Jo dipped a finger in her wine, then ran it around the rim of her glass, making it hum. Finally, she looked up. "A good man is hard to find," she said wistfully. "Not everyone is as lucky as you are."

Katie didn't know quite how to respond to that, so instead she touched Jo's hand. "What's really going on?" she asked gently. "Why did you want to talk to me?"

Jo looked around the empty bar as if trying to draw inspiration from her surroundings. "Do you ever sit back and wonder what it all means? Whether this is it or if there's something greater out there? Or if you were meant for something better?"

"I think everyone does," Katie answered, her curiosity growing.

"When I was a girl, I used to make believe that I was a princess. One of the good ones, I mean. Someone who always does the right thing and has the power to make people's lives better so that, in the end, they live happily ever after."

Katie nodded. She could remember doing the same thing, but she still wasn't sure where Jo was going so she stayed quiet.

"I think that's why I do what I do now. When I started,

I just wanted to help. I'd see people who were struggling with the loss of someone they loved—a parent, a child, a friend—and my heart just overflowed with sympathy. I tried to do everything in my power to make things better for them. But as time passed, I came to realize that there was only so much I could do myself. That in the end, people who are grieving have to *want* to move on—that first step, that motivating spark, has to come from within them. And when it does, it opens the door to the unexpected."

Katie took a deep breath, trying to make sense of Jo's rambling. "I don't know what you're trying to tell me."

Jo swirled her wine, studying the little whirlpool in her glass. For the first time, her tone became utterly serious. "I'm talking about you and Alex."

Katie couldn't hide her surprise. "Me and Alex?"

"Yes." She nodded. "He's told you about losing his wife, right? About how hard it was for him—for the whole family—to get past it?"

Katie stared across the table, suddenly uncomfortable. "Yes..." she began.

"Then be careful with them," Jo said, her tone serious. "All of them. Don't break their hearts."

In the awkward silence that followed, Katie found herself recalling their first conversation about Alex.

Did you two ever see each other? she remembered asking Jo.

Yes, but maybe not in the way you're thinking, Jo had answered. *And just so we're clear: it was a long time ago and everyone has moved on.*

At the time, she'd assumed that it meant that Jo and Alex had dated in the past, but now...

She was struck by the obviousness of the conclusion.

The counselor Alex had mentioned, who had seen the kids and consulted with him in the aftermath of Carly's death—it must have been Jo. Katie sat up straight. "You worked with Alex and the kids, didn't you? After Carly died, I mean."

"I'd rather not say," Jo answered. Her tone was measured and calm. Just like a counselor's. "I can say that all of them...mean a lot to me. And if you're not serious about a possible future with them, I think you should end it now. Before it's too late."

Katie felt her cheeks flush; it seemed inappropriate—presumptuous, even—for Jo to be talking to her like this. "I'm not sure any of this is really your concern," she said, her voice tight.

Jo acknowledged her point with a reluctant nod. "You're right. It's not my concern—and I'm crossing some important boundaries here. But I really do think they've been through enough. And the last thing I want for them is to become attached to someone who has no intention of staying in Southport. Maybe I'm worried that the past is never really in the past and that you might decide to leave, no matter how much sadness you leave in your wake."

Katie was speechless. This conversation was so unexpected, so uncomfortable, and Jo's words had definitely thrown her emotions into turmoil.

If Jo sensed Katie's discomfort, she pressed on anyway.

"Love doesn't mean anything if you're not willing to make a commitment," she said, "and you have to think not only about what you want, but about what he wants. Not just now, but in the future." She continued to stare at Katie across the table, her brown eyes unwavering. "Are you ready to be a wife to Alex and a mother to his kids?

Because that's what Alex wants. Maybe not right now, but he will in the future. And if you're not willing to make a commitment, if you're only going to toy with his feelings and those of his children, then you're not the person he needs in his life."

Before Katie could say anything, Jo got up from the table as she went on. "It might have been wrong of me to say all this, and maybe we won't be friends any longer, but I wouldn't feel right about myself if I didn't speak plainly. As I've said from the very beginning, he's a good man—a rare man. He loves deeply and never stops loving." She let those words sink in before her expression suddenly softened. "I think you're the same way, but I wanted to remind you that if you care about him, then you have to be willing to commit to him. No matter what the future might bring. No matter how scared you might be."

With that, she turned and left the bar, leaving Katie sitting at the table in stunned silence. It was only as she got up to leave that she noticed that Jo hadn't touched her wine.

24

Kevin Tierney didn't go to Provincetown on the weekend he'd told Coffey and Ramirez that he would. Instead, he stayed home with the curtains closed, brooding over how close he'd come to finding her in Philadelphia.

He wouldn't have succeeded in tracking her that far, except that she'd made a mistake in going to the bus station. He knew it was the only transportation choice she could have made. Tickets were cheap and identification wasn't necessary, and though he wasn't sure how much she'd stolen from him, he knew it couldn't have been much. From the first day they were married, he'd controlled the money. He always made her keep receipts and give him any change, but after she'd run away the second time, he'd also started locking his wallet in the gun box with his guns when he went to sleep. Sometimes, though, he fell asleep on the couch and he imagined her slipping the wallet from his pocket and stealing his money. He imagined the way she silently laughed at him as she did it, and how, in the morning, she would make him breakfast and pretend that she'd done nothing wrong. She would smile and kiss him, but inside she was laughing. Laughing at *him*. She'd stolen from him and he knew that was wrong because the Bible says *Thou shalt not steal*.

In the darkness, he chewed his lips, remembering his initial hope that she might come back. It was snowing and she couldn't get far; the first time she'd run away it had also been on a bitter cold night, and she'd called him within a few hours and asked him to pick her up because she had nowhere else to go. When she got home, she apologized for what she'd done and he made her a cup of hot cocoa as she sat shivering on the couch. He brought her a blanket and watched as she covered herself, trying to get warm. She smiled at him and he smiled at her, but once she stopped shivering, he crossed the room and slapped her until she cried. By the time he rose for work in the morning, she'd cleaned the spilled cocoa from the floor, though there was still a stain on the rug that she couldn't get out, and sometimes the sight of it made him angry.

On the night he realized she was missing last January, he drank two glasses of vodka while he waited for her to come back, but the phone didn't ring and the front door stayed closed. He knew she hadn't been gone long. He'd spoken to her less than an hour before and she'd told him she was making dinner. But there was no dinner on the stove. No sign of her in the house or in the cellar or in the garage. He stood on the porch and looked for footprints in the snow, but it was obvious that she hadn't left through the front door. But the snow in the backyard was equally pristine, so she hadn't left that way, either. It was as if she'd floated away or vanished into thin air. Which meant she had to be here...except that she wasn't.

Two more vodkas later and another half hour passed. By then, he was in a rage and he punched a hole in the bedroom door. He stormed from the house and banged on the neighbors' doors, asking if they'd noticed her leaving, but none of them could tell him anything. He hopped in his car and drove up and down the streets of the neighborhood, looking for traces of her, trying to figure out how she'd been able to leave the house without leaving any clues behind. By then, he figured she had a two-hour head start, but she was walking, and in this weather she couldn't have gotten far. Unless someone had come to pick her up. Someone she cared about. A man.

He pounded the wheel, his face contorted in fury. Six blocks away was the commercial district. He went to the businesses there, flashing a wallet-size photograph and asking if anyone had seen her. No one had. He told them she might have been with a man and still they shook their heads. The men he asked were adamant about it: *A pretty blond like that?* they said. *I would have noticed her, especially on a night like tonight.*

He drove each and every road within five miles of the house two or three times before finally going back home. It was three a.m. and the house was empty. After another vodka he cried himself to sleep.

In the morning, when he woke, he was enraged again, and with a hammer he smashed the flowerpots she kept in the backyard. Breathing hard, he went to the phone and called in sick, then went to the couch and tried to figure out how she'd gotten away. Someone had to have picked her up; someone must have driven her someplace. Someone she knew. A friend from Atlantic City? Altoona? Possible, he supposed, except that he checked the phone bills every month. She never placed long-distance phone calls. Someone local, then. But who? She never went anywhere, never talked to anyone. He made sure of that.

He went to the kitchen and was pouring himself another drink when he heard the phone ring. He lunged for it, hoping it was Erin. Strangely, however, the phone rang only once, and when he picked up he heard a dial tone. He stared at the receiver, trying to figure it out before hanging up the phone.

How had she gotten away? He was missing something. Even if someone local had picked her up, how had she gotten to the road without leaving footprints? He stared out the window, trying to piece together the sequence of events. Something seemed off, though he couldn't identify what it was. He turned away from the window and found himself focused on the telephone. It was then that the pieces suddenly came together and he pulled out his cell phone. He dialed his home number and listened as it rang once. The cell phone kept ringing. When he picked up the landline, he heard a dial tone and realized that she'd forwarded the calls to a cell phone. Which meant she hadn't been here when he'd called her last night. Which also explained the bad reception he'd noticed over the past two days. And, of course, the lack of footprints in the snow. She'd been gone, he now knew, since Tuesday morning.

At the bus station, she made a mistake, even if she couldn't really help it. She should have purchased her tickets from a woman, since Erin was pretty and men always remembered pretty women. It didn't matter whether their hair was long and blond or short and dark. Nor did it matter if she'd pretended she was pregnant.

He went to the bus station. He showed his badge and carried a larger photograph of her. The first two times he visited, none of the ticket sellers had recognized her. The third time, though, one of them hesitated and said that it might have been her, except that her hair was short and brown and that she was pregnant. He didn't, however, remember her destination. Back at home, Kevin found a photograph of her on the computer and used Photoshop to change her hair from blond to brown and then shortened it. He called in sick again on Friday. *That's her*, the ticket seller confirmed, and Kevin felt a surge of energy. She thought she was smarter than he was, but she was stupid and careless and she'd made a mistake. He took a couple of vacation days the following week and continued to hang around the bus station, showing the new photograph to drivers. He arrived in the morning and left late, since the drivers came and went all day long. There were two bottles in the car, and he poured the vodka into a Styrofoam cup and sipped it with a straw.

On Saturday, eleven days after she'd left him, he found the driver. The driver had taken her to Philadelphia. He remembered her, he said, because she was pretty and pregnant and she didn't have any luggage.

Philadelphia. She might have left again from there to parts unknown, but it was the only lead he had. Plus, he knew she didn't have much money.

He'd packed a bag and hopped in his car and drove to Philadelphia. He parked at the bus station and tried to think like her. He was a good detective and he knew that if he could think like her, he'd be able to find her. People, he'd learned, were predictable.

The bus had arrived a few minutes before four o'clock, and he stood in the bus station, looking from one direction to the next. She had stood here days earlier, he thought, and he wondered what she would do in a strange city with no money and no friends and no place to go. Quarters and dimes and dollar bills wouldn't go far, especially after purchasing a bus ticket.

It was cold, he remembered, and it would have been getting dark soon. She wouldn't want to walk far and she would need a place to stay. A place that took cash. But where? Not here, in this area. Too expensive. Where would she go? She wouldn't want to get lost or head in the wrong direction, which meant that she probably looked in the phone book. He went back inside the terminal and looked under hotels. Pages and pages, he realized. She might have picked one, but then what? She'd have to walk there. Which meant she'd need a map.

He went to the convenience store at the station and bought himself a map. He showed the clerk the photograph but he shook his head. He hadn't been working on Tuesday, he said. But it felt right to Kevin. This, he knew, was what she did. He unfolded the map and located the station. It bordered on Chinatown and he guessed she had headed in that direction.

He got back in his car and drove the streets of Chinatown, and again it felt right. He drank his vodka and walked the streets. He started at those businesses closest to the bus station and showed her picture around. No one knew anything but he had the sense that some of them were lying. He found cheap rooms, places he never would have taken her, dirty places with dirty sheets, managed by men who spoke little English and took only cash. He implied that she was in danger if he couldn't find her. He found the first place she'd stayed, but the owner didn't know where she'd gone after that. Kevin put a gun to the man's head, but even though he cried, he couldn't tell Kevin anything more.

Kevin had to go back to work on Monday, furious that she'd eluded him. But the following weekend, he was back in Philadelphia. And the weekend after that. He expanded his search, but the problem was that there were too many places and he was only one person and not everyone trusted an out-of-town cop.

But he was patient and diligent and he kept coming back and took more vacation days. Another weekend passed. He widened his search, knowing she would need cash. He stopped in bars and restaurants and diners. He would check every one in the city if he had to. Finally, a week after Valentine's Day, he met a waitress named Tracy who told him that Erin was working at a diner, except she was calling herself Erica. She was scheduled to work the following day. The waitress trusted him because he was a detective, and she'd even flirted with him, handing him her phone number before he left.

He rented a car and waited up the block from the diner the following morning, before the sun was up. Employees entered through a door in the alley. He sipped from his Styrofoam cup in the front seat, watching for her. Eventually, he saw the owner and Tracy and another woman head down the alley. But Erin never showed, and she didn't show up the following day, either, and no one knew where she lived. She never came back to pick up her paycheck.

He found where she lived a few hours later. It was walking distance from the diner, a piece-of-crap hotel.

The man, who accepted only cash, knew nothing except that Erin had left the day before and come back and left again in a hurry. Kevin searched her room but there was nothing inside, and when he finally raced to the bus station there were only women in the ticket booths and none of them remembered her. Buses in the last two hours were traveling north, south, east, and west, going everywhere.

She'd disappeared again, and in the car Kevin screamed and beat his fists against the wheel until they were bruised and swollen.

In the months that Erin had been gone, he felt the ache inside grow more poisonous and all-consuming, spreading like a cancer every day. He had returned to Philadelphia and questioned the drivers over the next few weeks, but it hadn't amounted to much. He eventually learned that she'd gone on to New York, but from there, the trail went cold. Too many buses, too many drivers, too many passengers; too many days had passed since then. Too many options. She could be anywhere, and the thought that she was gone tormented him. He flew into rages and broke things; he cried himself to sleep. He was filled with despair and sometimes felt like he was losing his mind.

It wasn't fair. He'd loved her since the first time they met in Atlantic City. And they'd been happy, hadn't they? Early on in the marriage, she used to sing to herself as she put on her makeup. He used to bring her to the library and she would check out eight or ten books. Sometimes she would read him passages and he would hear her voice and watch the way she leaned against the counter and think to himself that she was the most beautiful woman in the world.

He'd been a good husband. He bought her the house she wanted and the curtains she wanted and the furniture she wanted, even though he could barely afford it. After they were married, he often bought flowers from street vendors on the way home, and Erin would put them in a vase on the table along with candles, and the two of them would have romantic dinners. Sometimes, they ended up making love in the kitchen, her back pressed against the counter.

He never made her work, either, and she didn't know how good she had it. She didn't understand the sacrifices he made for her. She was spoiled and selfish and it used to make him so angry because she didn't understand how *easy* her life was. Clean the house and make a meal and she could spend the rest of her days reading stupid books she checked out from the library and watching television and taking naps and never having to worry about a utility bill or mortgage payment or people who talked about him behind his back. She never had to see the faces of people who had been murdered. He kept that from her because he loved her, but it had made no difference. He never told her about the children who'd been burned with irons or tossed from the roofs of buildings or women stabbed in the alley and thrown in Dumpsters. He never told her that sometimes he had to scrape the blood from his shoes before he got in the car, and when he looked into the eyes of murderers he knew he was coming face-to-face with evil because the Bible says *To kill a person is to kill a living being made in God's image.*

He loved her and she loved him and she had to come home because he couldn't find her. She could have her happy life again and he wouldn't hit or punch or slap or kick her if she walked in the door because he'd always been a good husband. He loved her and she loved him and he remembered that on the day he asked her to marry him, she reminded him of the night they'd met outside the casino when the men were following her. Dangerous men. He'd stopped them from hurting her that night, and in the morning they'd walked along the boardwalk and he took her for coffee. She told him that of course she would marry him. She loved him, she'd said. He made her feel safe.

Safe. That was the word she used. Safe.

25

—⟡—

The third week of June was a series of glorious high summer days. The temperature crept up over the course of the afternoon, bringing with it humidity heavy enough to thicken the air and blur the horizon. Heavy clouds would then form as if by magic, and violent thunderstorms would drop torrents of rain. The showers never lasted long, though, leaving behind only dripping leaves and a layer of ground mist.

Katie continued to work long evening shifts at the restaurant. She was tired when she rode home, and in the morning her legs and feet often ached. She put half the money she earned in tips in the coffee can, and it was almost filled to the brim. She had more money than she'd imagined she'd be able to save, more than enough to get away if she had to. For the first time, she wondered whether she needed to add more.

Lingering over her last few bites of breakfast, she stared out the window at Jo's house. She hadn't spoken with her since their encounter, and last night, after her shift, she'd seen lights burning in Jo's kitchen and living room. Earlier this morning, she'd heard her car start up and listened to the crunching of dirt and gravel as it pulled away. She didn't know what to say to Jo, or even whether she wanted to say anything at all. She couldn't even decide whether she was angry with her. Jo cared about Alex and the kids; she was worried about them and had expressed her concerns to Katie. It was hard to find malice in anything she'd done.

Alex, she knew, would be by later today. His visits had settled into something of a routine, and when they were together, she was constantly reminded of all the reasons she'd fallen for him in the first place. He accepted her occasional silences and varying moods, and he treated her with a gentleness that astonished and touched her. But since her conversation with Jo, she wondered if she was being unfair to him. What would happen, after all, if Kevin showed up? How would Alex and the kids react if she disappeared, never to return? Was she willing to leave all of them behind and never talk to them again?

She hated the questions Jo had raised, because she wasn't ready to face them. *You have no idea what I've been through*, she'd wanted to say afterward, once she had time to think about it. *You have no idea what my husband is like.* But even she knew that begged the question.

Leaving her breakfast dishes in the sink, she walked through the small cottage, thinking how much had changed in the last few months. She owned virtually nothing, but felt like she had more than ever. She felt loved for the first time in years. She'd never been a parent, but she found herself thinking and worrying about Kristen and Josh when she least expected it. She knew she couldn't predict the future, and yet she was struck with the sudden certainty that leaving this new existence behind was inconceivable.

What had Jo once said to her? *I just tell people what they already know but are afraid to admit to themselves.*

Reflecting on her words, she knew exactly what she had to do.

"Sure," Alex said to her, after she related her request. She could tell he was surprised, but he also seemed encouraged. "When do you want to start?"

"How about today?" she suggested. "If you have any time."

He looked around the store. There was only one person eating in the grill area, and Roger was leaning against the counter, chatting with him.

"Hey, Roger? Do you think you could watch the register for an hour?"

"No problem, boss," Roger said. He stayed where he was; Alex knew he wouldn't come up front unless necessary. But on a weekday morning, after the initial rush, he didn't expect many people in the store, so Alex didn't mind. He moved out from behind the register.

"You ready?"

"Not really." She hugged herself nervously. "But it's something I should know how to do."

They left the store, walking toward his jeep. Climbing in, she could feel his gaze on her.

"Why the sudden rush to learn how to drive?" he asked. "Is the bike not good enough?" he teased.

"The bike is all I need," she said. "But I want to get a driver's license."

He reached for the car keys before pausing. He turned back to her again, and as he stared at her, she caught a glimpse of the investigator he used to be. He was alert and she sensed his caution. "Learning how to drive is only part of it. To get a license, the state requires identification. Birth certificate, social security card, things like that."

"I know," she said.

He chose his words carefully. "Information like that can be tracked," he pointed out. "If you get a license, people might be able to find you."

"I'm already using a safe social security number," she said. "If Kevin knew about it, he would have tracked me down already. And if I'm going to stay in Southport, it's something I need to do."

He shook his head. "Katie..."

She leaned over and kissed him on the cheek. "It's okay," she said. "My name's not Katie, remember?"

He traced the curve of her cheek with his finger. "To me, you'll always be Katie."

She smiled. "I have a secret," she said. "My hair isn't naturally brown. I'm really a blond."

He sat back, processing this new information. "Are you sure you want to be telling me this?"

"I figure you'll find out eventually, anyway. Who knows? Maybe I'll go back to being a blond one day."

"What's this all about? Wanting to learn how to drive, volunteering information?"

"You told me I could trust you." She shrugged. "I believe you."

"That's it?"

"Yes," she said. "I feel like I can tell you anything."

He studied their hands, locked together on the seat

divider, before looking at her. "Then I'll cut to the chase. Are you sure your documents will hold up? They can't be copies. They have to be originals."

"I know," she said.

He knew better than to ask anything more. He reached for the keys but didn't start the engine.

"What is it?" she asked.

"Since you want to learn how to drive, we may as well start now." He opened the door and got out. "Let's get you behind the wheel."

They switched places. As soon as Katie was behind the wheel, Alex pointed out the basics: gas and brake pedals, how to put the car in gear, turn signals, lights and wipers, gauges on the dashboard. It was always best to start at the beginning.

"You ready?" he asked.

"I think so," she said, concentrating.

"Since it's not a manual transmission, you use only one foot. It's either on the accelerator or the brake, okay?"

"Okay," she said. She moved her left foot near the door.

"Now, push down on the brake and start the car. When you're ready, keep the brake on while you put the transmission in reverse. Don't use the accelerator, and slowly release the brake. Then turn the wheel to back out, keeping your foot lightly on the brake."

She did exactly as she was told and backed the car out gingerly before he guided her out of the parking lot. For the first time, she paused. "Are you sure I should drive onto the main road?"

"If there was a lot of traffic, I'd say no. If you were sixteen, I'd say no. But I think you can handle it, and I'm right here to help. You ready? What you're going to do is turn right, and we'll follow that until the next turn. Then we'll turn right again. I want you to get a feel for the car."

They spent the next hour driving along rural roads. Like most beginners, she had trouble with oversteering, she sometimes veered onto the shoulder, and parking took a little while to get used to, but other than that, she did better than probably either of them expected. As they were getting close to finishing, Alex had her park on one of the downtown streets.

"Where are we going?"

He pointed to a small coffee shop. "I figured you might want to celebrate. You did well."

"I don't know," she said. "I didn't feel like I knew what I was doing."

"That comes with practice," he said. "The more you drive, the more natural it feels."

"Can I drive tomorrow?" she asked.

"Of course," he said. "Can we do it in the morning, though? Now that Josh is out of school, he and Kristen are at day camp for a couple of weeks. They get home around noon."

"Mornings are perfect," she said. "Do you really think I did okay?"

"You could probably pass the driving portion of the exam with a couple more days of practice. Of course, you have to pass the written test, too, but all that takes is some prep time."

She reached out and gave him a spontaneous hug. "Thanks for this, by the way."

He hugged her back. "I'm glad to help. Even if you don't have a car, it's something you should probably know how to do. Why didn't you . . . ?"

"Learn to drive when I was younger?" She shrugged. "Growing up, we had only one car and my dad was usually using it. Even if I got my license, I wouldn't have been able to drive, so it never struck me as all that important. After I moved out, I couldn't afford a car, so again, I didn't bother. And then, when I was married, Kevin didn't want me to have one." She turned. "And here I am. A twenty-seven-year-old bike rider."

"You're twenty-seven?"

"You knew that."

"Actually, I didn't."

"And?"

"You don't look a day over thirty."

She punched him lightly in the arm. "For that, I'm going to make you buy me a croissant, too."

"Fair enough. And since you're in the mood for full disclosure, I'd like to hear the story of how you finally got away."

She hesitated only briefly. "Okay," she said.

At a small table outside, Katie related the account of her escape—the forwarded phone calls, the trip to Philadelphia, the ever-changing jobs and miserable flophouses, the eventual trip to Southport. Unlike the first time, now she was able to describe her experiences calmly, as though talking about someone else. When she finished, he shook his head.

"What?"

"I was just trying to imagine how you must have felt after hanging up on that final call from Kevin. When he still thought you were at home. I'll bet you were relieved."

"I was. But I was also terrified. And at that point, I still didn't have a job and didn't know what I was going to do."

"But you made it."

"Yes," she said. "I did." Her gaze was focused on some distant point. "It's not the kind of life I ever imagined for myself."

Alex's tone was gentle. "I'm not sure anyone's life turns out exactly the way they imagine. All we can do is to try to make the best of it. Even when it seems impossible."

She knew he was talking as much about himself as he was about her, and for a long moment neither of them said anything.

"I love you," he finally whispered.

She leaned forward and touched his face. "I know. And I love you, too."

26

By late June, the flower gardens in Dorchester that had been ablaze with color in the spring were beginning to wilt, the blooms turning brown and curling inward. The humidity had begun to creep up and the alleys in downtown Boston began to smell of rotting food and urine and decay. Kevin told Coffey and Ramirez that he and Erin were going to spend the weekend at home, watching movies and doing a little gardening. Coffey had asked about Provincetown and Kevin had lied and told him about the bed-and-breakfast where they'd stayed and some of the restaurants they'd gone to. Coffey had said that he'd been to all of those places and asked if Kevin had ordered the crab cakes at one of them. Kevin said that he hadn't but would the next time.

Erin was gone, but Kevin still looked for her everywhere. He couldn't help it. As he drove the streets of Boston and saw the glint of gold brushing a woman's shoulders, he would feel his heart catch in his throat. He would watch for the delicate nose and green eyes and the graceful way she walked. Sometimes he would stand outside the bakery, pretending that he was waiting for her.

He should have been able to find her, even if she'd gotten away in Philadelphia. People left trails. Paper left trails. In Philadelphia, she'd used a phony name and phony social security number, but that couldn't last forever unless she was willing to keep on living in cheap hotels and changing jobs every few weeks. To this point, though, she hadn't used her own social security number. An officer from another precinct who had connections checked for him, and that officer was the only one who knew that Erin was gone, but he'd keep his mouth shut because Kevin knew he was having an affair with his underage babysitter. Kevin felt dirty whenever he had to talk to him because the guy was a pervert and he belonged in prison, since the Bible says *Let there be no sexual immorality among you.* But right now, Kevin needed him so that he could find Erin and bring her home. Man and wife were supposed to stay together because they'd made their vows in front of God and family.

He'd known he would find her in March; he'd felt sure she would turn up in April. He was certain that her name would surface in May, but the house stayed empty. Now it was June and his thoughts were often scattered and sometimes it was all he could do to go through the motions. It was hard to concentrate and the vodka didn't seem to help and he had to lie to Coffey and Ramirez and walk away while they gossiped.

This he knew: she wasn't running any longer. She wouldn't move from place to place or job to job forever. It wasn't like her. She liked nice things and wanted to have them around her. Which meant she had to be using someone else's identity. Unless she was willing to live a life continually on the run, she needed a real birth certificate and a real social security number. These days, employers required identification, but where and how would she have assumed another's identity? He knew the most common way was to find someone of a similar age who'd recently died, and then to take on the identity of the deceased. The first part of that was conceivable, if only because of Erin's frequent visits to the library. He could imagine her scanning the obituaries on microfiche, looking for a name to steal. She schemed and planned in the library while pretending to peruse the bookshelves, and she'd done those things after he'd taken time out of his busy day to drive her there. He showed her kindness and she repaid him with treachery, and it infuriated him to think of the way she must have laughed while she did it. It made him so angry to imagine those things, and with a hammer he smashed the set of china they'd been given for their wedding. Having let off steam, he was able to focus on what he had to do. Throughout March and April, Kevin spent hours in the library just as she must have done, trying to find her new identity. But even if she had found a name, how had she retrieved the identification? Where was she now? And why hadn't she come home?

These were the questions that tormented him, and sometimes it was so confusing he couldn't stop crying because he missed her and wanted her to come home and he hated to be alone. But other times, the thought that she had left him made him dwell on how selfish she was and all he wanted to do was kill her.

July rolled in with the breath of dragons: hot and moist and horizons that shimmered like a mirage when seen from a distance. The holiday weekend passed and another week started. The air conditioner had broken in his home and Kevin hadn't called the repairman. He had a headache every morning when he went to work. Trial and error proved that vodka worked better than Tylenol, but the pain was always there, pounding in his temple. He'd stopped going to the library, and Coffey and Ramirez asked about his wife again and he said that she was fine but said nothing else about her and then he changed the subject. He got a new partner named Todd Vannerty, who'd just been promoted. He was happy to let Kevin do most of the questioning when they talked to witnesses and victims, and that was fine with Kevin.

Kevin told him that, almost always, the victim knew the murderer. But not always in an obvious way. At the end of their first week together, they were called out to an apartment less than three blocks from the precinct, where they found a ten-year-old boy who'd died of a bullet wound. The shooter was a recent emigrant from Greece who had been celebrating a Greek soccer victory when he'd fired his gun at the floor. The bullet passed through the ceiling of the apartment below him and killed the boy just as he was taking a bite of pizza. The bullet entered the top of his head and the boy fell face-first into his pizza. When they saw the boy, there was cheese and tomato sauce on the boy's forehead. His mother had screamed and cried for two hours and had tried to tackle the Greek as he was led down the stairs in handcuffs. She ended up tumbling down to the landing and they'd had to call an ambulance.

Kevin and Todd went to a bar after their shift ended and Todd tried to pretend he could forget what he'd seen, but he drank three beers in less than fifteen minutes. He told Kevin that he'd failed his detective exam once, before finally passing it. Kevin drank vodka, though because Todd was with him, he told the bartender to add a splash of cranberry juice.

It was a cop bar. Lots of cops, low prices, dim lights, and women who liked to hook up with cops. The bartender let people smoke, even though it was against the law, since most of the smokers were cops. Todd wasn't married and had been there often. Kevin had never been there before and wasn't sure he liked it, but he didn't want to go home, either.

Todd went to the bathroom and when he came back, he leaned closer to Kevin.

"I think those two at the end of the bar are checking us out."

Kevin turned. Like him, the women appeared to be around thirty. The brunette noticed him staring before she turned back to her redheaded friend.

"Too bad you're married, huh? They look pretty good."

They looked worn, Kevin thought. Not like Erin, who had clear skin and smelled of lemon and mint and the perfume he'd bought her for Christmas.

"Go ahead and talk to them if you want," Kevin said.

"I think I will," Todd said. Todd ordered another beer and walked to the end of the bar and smiled. He probably said something stupid, but it was enough to make the women laugh. Kevin ordered a double vodka, no cranberry juice, and saw their reflection in the mirror behind the bar. The brunette met his eyes in the mirror, and he didn't turn away. Ten minutes later, she sauntered over and took a seat on the stool that Todd had been occupying.

"Not feeling social tonight?" the brunette asked.

"I'm not good at small talk."

The brunette seemed to consider this. "I'm Amber," she said.

"Kevin," he replied, and again, he didn't know what to say. He took a drink, thinking it tasted almost like water.

The brunette leaned toward him. She smelled musky, not like lemon and mint. "Todd says that the two of you work homicide."

"We do."

"Is that hard?"

"Sometimes," he said. He finished his drink and raised the glass. The bartender brought another over. "What do you do?"

"I'm an office manager at my brother's bakery. He makes rolls and bread products for restaurants."

"That sounds interesting."

She gave a cynical smile. "No, it doesn't. And it's not, but it pays the bills." Her teeth flashed white in the gloom. "I haven't seen you here before."

"Todd brought me."

She nodded in Todd's direction. "Him, I've seen. He hits on anything in a skirt who's still breathing. And I think the breathing part is optional. My friend loves it here, but usually I can't stand the place. She makes me come with her."

Kevin nodded and shifted on his stool. He wondered if Coffey and Ramirez ever came here.

"Am I boring you?" she asked. "I can leave you alone if you'd like."

"You're not boring me."

She flipped her hair and Kevin thought she was prettier

than he'd first realized. "Would you like to buy me a drink?" she suggested.

"What would you like?"

"Cosmopolitan," she said, and Kevin signaled to the bartender. The Cosmopolitan arrived.

"I'm not very good at this," Kevin admitted.

"Not good at what?"

"This."

"We're just talking," she said. "And you're doing fine."

"I'm married."

She smiled. "I know. I saw your ring."

"Does that bother you?"

"Like I said, we're just talking."

She ran a finger along her glass and he could see the moisture collect on the tip.

"Does your wife know you're here?" she asked.

"My wife is out of town," he said. "Her friend is sick and she's helping her out."

"And so you thought you'd hit the bars? Meet some women?"

"I'm not like that," Kevin said tightly. "I love my wife."

"You should. Since you married her, I mean."

He wanted another double vodka but didn't want to order it in front of her, since he'd already done so. Instead, as if reading his mind, she signaled to the bartender and he brought over another one. Kevin took a large gulp, still thinking it tasted like water.

"Is it okay that I did that?" she asked.

"It's okay," he said.

She stared at him, her expression sultry. "I wouldn't tell your wife that you were here if I were you."

"Why not?" he asked.

"Because you're way too handsome for a place like this. You never know who would try to hit on you."

"Are you hitting on me?"

It took her a moment to answer. "Would you be offended if I said yes?"

He spun the glass slowly on the bar. "No," he said, "I wouldn't be offended."

After drinking and flirting for another two hours, they ended up at her place. Amber understood that he wanted to be discreet and gave him her address. After Amber and her friend left, Kevin stayed in the bar with Todd for another half hour before he told Todd that he had to get home so he could call Erin.

When he drove, the world blurred around the edge of his vision. His thoughts were jumbled and confusing and he knew he was swerving but he was a good detective. Even if he was stopped, he wouldn't be arrested because cops don't arrest other cops, and what were a few drinks?

Amber lived in an apartment a few blocks away from the bar. He knocked at the door, and when she opened it she was wearing nothing beneath the sheet she had wrapped around her. He kissed her and carried her to the bedroom and felt her fingers unbuttoning his shirt. He placed her on the bed and undressed and turned out the light because he didn't want to be reminded that he was cheating on his wife. Adultery was a sin and now that he was here he didn't want to have sex with her, but he'd been drinking and the world appeared smudged and she'd been wearing nothing except a sheet and it was all so confusing.

She wasn't like Erin. Her body was different, her shape was different, and her scent was different. She smelled spicy, animal-like almost, and her hands moved too much, and everything with Amber was new and he didn't like it but he couldn't stop, either. He heard her calling out his name and saying dirty things and he wanted to tell her to shut up so he could think about Erin, but it was hard to concentrate because everything was so confusing.

He squeezed her arms and heard her gasp and say, "Not so hard," and he loosened his grip, but then he squeezed her arms again because he wanted to. This time she said nothing. He thought about Erin and where she was and whether she was okay and thought again how much he missed her.

He shouldn't have hit Erin because she was sweet and kind and gentle and she didn't deserve to be punched or kicked. It was his fault she was gone. He'd driven her away, even though he loved her. He'd searched for her and hadn't been able to find her and he'd been to Philadelphia and now he was with a woman named Amber who didn't know what to do with her hands and made strange noises and it felt all wrong.

When they were done, he didn't want to stay. Instead, he got out of bed and started to get dressed. She turned on the lamp and sat up in bed. The sight of her reminded him that she wasn't Erin and he suddenly felt sick to his stomach. The Bible says *The man who commits adultery is an utter fool, for he destroys his own soul.*

He had to get away from Amber. He didn't know why he'd come, and as he stared at her, his stomach was in knots.

"Are you okay?" she asked.

"I shouldn't be here," he said. "I shouldn't have come."

"It's a little late now," she said.

"I have to go."

"Just like that?"

"I'm married," he said again.

"I know." She gave a weary smile. "And it's okay."

"No, it's not," he said, and after getting dressed, he left her apartment and raced down the steps and jumped in his car. He drove fast but didn't swerve because the guilt he felt was like a sharp tonic to his senses. He made it home and saw a light on at the Feldmans' and he knew they would peek out their window as he pulled in his driveway. The Feldmans were bad neighbors and never waved at him and told kids to stay off their lawn. They would know what he'd done because they were bad people and he had done a bad thing and birds of a feather flocked together.

When he went inside, he needed a drink but the thought of vodka made him sick and his mind was racing. He'd cheated on his wife and the Bible says *His shame will never be erased*. He'd broken a commandment of God and broken his vow to Erin and he knew the truth would come out. Amber knew and Todd knew and the Feldmans knew and they'd tell someone who'd tell someone else and Erin would learn what he had done. He paced the living room, his breaths coming fast because he knew he wouldn't be able to explain it to Erin in a way she would understand. She was his wife and she would never forgive him. She'd be angry and she'd tell him to sleep on the couch and in the morning she would look at him with disappointment because he was a sinner and she would never trust him again. He shivered, feeling nauseated. He slept with another woman and the Bible says *Have nothing to*

do with sexual sin, impurity, lust, and shameful desires.
It was all so confusing and he wanted to stop thinking but
he couldn't. He wanted to drink but he couldn't and he
had the feeling that Erin would suddenly appear at their
doorstep.

The house was messy and dirty and Erin would know
what he'd done, and even though his thoughts were jumbled, he knew those two things were linked. He paced the
living room frantically. Dirty and cheating were linked
because cheating was dirty and Erin would know that
he'd cheated because the house was dirty, and the two
of them went together. Suddenly, he stopped pacing and
he strode to the kitchen and found a garbage bag beneath
the sink. In the living room, he dropped to his knees and
crawled around, filling it with empty takeout containers
and magazines and plastic utensils and empty bottles of
vodka and pizza boxes. It was well past midnight and he
didn't have to work in the morning, so he stayed awake
cleaning the house and doing the dishes and running
the vacuum that he'd bought for Erin. He cleaned so she
wouldn't know, because he knew that cheating and dirty
went together. He put the dirty clothes in the washer and
when they were done he dried them and folded them while
other loads were washing and drying. The sun came up
and he pulled the cushions from the sofa and vacuumed
until all the crumbs were gone. As he worked, he glanced
out the window, knowing Erin would be home any minute. He scrubbed the toilet and washed the food stains
from the refrigerator and mopped the linoleum. Dawn
turned to morning and then to late morning. He washed
the sheets and opened the drapes and dusted the frame
that held the photograph of their wedding day. He mowed

the lawn and emptied the clippings in the garbage can and when he was done he went shopping and bought turkey and ham and Dijon mustard and fresh rye bread from the bakery. He bought flowers and set them on the table. He added candles. When he was finished he was breathing hard. He poured himself a tall, icy glass of vodka and sat at the kitchen table and waited for Erin. He was happy because he'd cleaned the house because it meant that Erin would never know what he'd done and they would have the kind of marriage he'd always wanted. They would trust each other and be happy and he would love her forever and never cheat on her again because why on earth would he ever do something as disgusting as that?

27

Katie got her driver's license in the second week of July. In the days leading up to her test, Alex had taken her driving regularly, and despite some pretest jitters, she'd passed with a nearly perfect score. The license arrived in the mail within a few days and when Katie opened the envelope, she felt almost dizzy. There was a photograph of her next to a name she'd never imagined having, but according to the state of North Carolina, she was as real as any other resident of the state.

That night, Alex took her to dinner in Wilmington. Afterward, they'd walked the downtown streets holding hands and browsing the shops. Every now and then, she saw Alex regarding her with amusement.

"What?" she finally demanded.

"I was just thinking that you don't look like an Erin. You look like a Katie."

"I should look like a Katie," she said. "That's my name and I've got a driver's license to prove it."

"I know you do," he said. "Now all you need is a car."

"Why do I need a car?" She shrugged. "It's a small town and I've got a bike. And when it's raining, there's this guy who's willing to drive me anywhere I need to go. It's almost like having a chauffeur."

"Really?"

"Uh-huh. And I'm pretty sure that if I asked, he'd even let me borrow his car. I have him wrapped around my little finger."

Alex cocked an eyebrow. "He doesn't sound like much of a man."

"He's all right," she teased. "He seemed a little desperate in the beginning, what with all the freebies he gave me, but I eventually got used to it."

"You have a heart of gold."

"Obviously," she said. "I'm pretty much one in a million."

He laughed. "I'm beginning to think that you're finally coming out of your shell and I'm beginning to glimpse the real you."

She walked a few steps in silence. "You know the real me," she said, stopping to peer up at him. "More than anyone else."

"I know," he said, pulling her toward him. "And that's why I think that somehow we were meant to find each other."

Though the store was as busy as ever, Alex took a vacation. It was his first in a while, and he spent most afternoons with Katie and the kids, relishing the lazy days of summer in a way he hadn't since childhood. He fished with Josh and built dollhouses with Kristen; he took Katie to a jazz festival in Myrtle Beach. When the fireflies were out in force, they caught dozens with nets and put them in a jar; later that night, they watched the eerie glow with a mixture of wonder and fascination before Alex finally opened the lid.

They rode their bikes and went to the movies, and when Katie wasn't working evenings, Alex liked to fire up the grill. The kids would eat and then swim in the creek until it was almost dark. After they'd showered and gone to bed, Alex would sit with Katie on the small dock out back, their legs dangling over the water, while the moon slowly traversed the sky. They sipped wine and talked about nothing important, but Alex grew to savor those quiet moments together.

Kristen particularly loved spending time with Katie. When the four of them were walking together, Kristen often reached for Katie's hand; when she fell down in the playground, she'd begun to run to Katie. While it warmed Alex's heart to see those things, he always felt a pang of sadness, too, because it reminded him that he could never be everything that his daughter needed, no matter how hard he tried. Still, when Kristen came running up to him and asked if Katie could take her shopping, Alex couldn't say no. Though Alex made a point to take her shopping once or twice a year, he tended to view it more as a parental duty than an opportunity for fun. By contrast, Katie seemed delighted by the idea. After giving Katie some money, Alex handed her the keys to the jeep and waved from the parking lot as they left.

As happy as Katie's presence had made Kristen, Josh's feelings weren't quite as obvious. The day before, Alex had picked him up from a friend's swimming party, and he hadn't said anything to either Katie or Alex the rest of the evening. Earlier, at the beach, he'd been subdued as well. Alex knew that something was bothering him and suggested that they get out their fishing poles, just as dusk was settling in. Shadows began to stretch across the blackened water and the creek was still, a darkened mirror reflecting the slowly drifting clouds.

They cast their lines for an hour while the sky turned violet, then indigo, the lures making circular ripples as they splashed into the water. Josh remained strangely quiet. At other times the tableau might have seemed peaceful, but now Alex had the nagging feeling that something was wrong. Just when he was about to ask Josh about it, however, his son half-swiveled in his direction.

"Hey, Dad?"

"Yeah?"

"Do you ever think about Mom?"

"All the time," he said.

Josh nodded. "I think about her, too."

"You should. She loved you very much. What do you think about?"

"I remember when she made us cookies. She let me put the frosting on."

"I remember that. You had pink frosting all over your face. She took your picture. It's still on the refrigerator."

"I think that's why I remember." He propped the rod in his lap. "Do you miss her?"

"Of course I do. I loved her very much," Alex said, holding Josh's gaze. "What's going on, Josh?"

"At the party yesterday…" Josh rubbed his nose, hesitating.

"What happened?"

"Most of the moms stayed the whole time. Talking and stuff."

"I would have stayed if you wanted me to."

Josh dropped his eyes, and in the silence, Alex suddenly knew what he hadn't said. "I was supposed to stay, too, wasn't I. Some parent-child thing." His tone was more a statement than a question. "But you didn't want to tell me because I would have been the only dad there, right?"

Josh nodded, looking guilty. "I don't want you to be mad at me."

Alex slipped an arm around his son. "I'm not mad," he said.

"Are you sure?"

"I'm positive. I couldn't be mad at you for that."

"Do you think Mom would have gone? If she was still here?"

"Of course she would have. She wouldn't have missed it."

On the far side of the creek, a mullet jumped and the tiny ripples began moving toward them.

"What do you do when you go out with Miss Katie?" he asked.

Alex shifted slightly. "It's kind of like what we did at the beach today. We eat and talk and maybe go for a walk."

"You've been spending a lot of time with her lately."

"Yes."

Josh considered that. "What do you talk about?"

"Just regular stuff." Alex tilted his head. "And we talk about you and your sister, too."

"What do you say?"

"We talk about how much fun it is to spend time with you two, and how well you did in school, or how good you are at keeping your room clean."

"Will you tell her that I didn't tell you that you were supposed to stay at the party?"

"Do you want me to?"

"No," he said.

"Then I won't say anything."

"Promise? Because I don't want her to be mad at me."

Alex raised his fingers. "Scout's honor. But just so you know, she wouldn't be mad at you even if I did. She thinks you're a great kid."

Josh sat up straighter and began reeling in his line. "Good," he said. "Because I think she's pretty great, too."

The conversation with Josh kept Alex awake that night. He found himself studying the portrait of Carly in his bedroom as he sipped his third beer of the evening.

Kristen and Katie had returned to the house, full of energy and excitement as they showed him the clothes they'd purchased. Surprisingly, Katie had returned nearly half the money, saying only that she was pretty good at finding things on sale. Alex sat on the couch as Kristen modeled an outfit for him, only to vanish back into her bedroom before returning wearing something completely different. Even Josh, who ordinarily wouldn't have cared in the slightest, set his Nintendo game aside, and when Kristen had left the room, he approached Katie.

"Could you take me shopping, too?" he asked, his voice barely above a whisper. "Because I need some new shirts and stuff."

Afterward, Alex ordered Chinese food and they sat around the table, eating and laughing. At one point during dinner, Katie pulled a leather wristband from her purse and turned toward Josh. "I thought this was pretty cool-looking," she said, handing it to Josh. His surprise gave way to pleasure as he put it on, and Alex noticed how

Josh's eyes continually flickered toward Katie for the rest of the evening.

Ironically, it was at times like tonight that he missed Carly most. Even though she'd never experienced nights like these as a family—the kids were too young when she died—he found it easy to imagine her being at the table.

Perhaps that was the reason he couldn't sleep, long after Katie went home and Kristen and Josh were asleep in their beds. Tossing back the covers, he went to the closet and opened the safe he'd installed a few years earlier. In it were important financial and insurance documents, stacked beside treasures from his marriage. They were items that Carly had collected: photos from their honeymoon, a four-leaf clover they'd found while vacationing in Vancouver, the bouquet of peonies and calla lilies she'd carried on her wedding day, ultrasound images of Josh and Kristen while each was still in her womb, along with the outfits that each had worn on the way home from the hospital. Photo negatives and camera disks, chronicling their years together. The articles were heavy with meaning and memories, and since Carly's death, Alex had added nothing to the safe, except for the letters that Carly had written. One had been addressed to him. The second had no name on it, however, and it remained unopened. He couldn't open it—a promise, after all, was a promise.

He pulled out the letter he'd read a hundred times, leaving the other in the safe. He'd known nothing about the letters until she'd handed the envelopes to him less than a week before she died. By that point, she was bedridden and could only sip liquids. When he carried her to the bathroom, she was light, as if somehow she'd been hollowed out. He spent her few waking hours sitting quietly beside her. Usually, she would fall asleep again within minutes, and Alex would stare at her, afraid to leave in case she needed him and afraid to stay in case he might rob her of rest. On the day she gave him the envelopes, he saw that they had been tucked into the blankets, appearing as if by magic. Only later would he learn that she'd written them two months earlier and her mom had been holding them.

Now, Alex opened the envelope and pulled out the much-handled letter. It was written on yellow legal paper. Bringing it to his nose, he was still able to discern the scent of the lotion she often wore. He remembered his surprise and the way her eyes pleaded with him for understanding.

"You want me to read this one first?" he remembered asking. He pointed to the one inscribed with his name and she nodded slightly. She relaxed as he pulled the letter out, her head sinking into the pillow.

My dearest Alex,

There are dreams that visit us and leave us fulfilled upon waking, there are dreams that make life worth living. You, my sweet husband, are that dream, and it saddens me to have to put into words the way I feel about you.

I'm writing this letter now, while I still can, and yet I'm not sure how to capture what I want to say. I'm not a writer, and words seem so inadequate right now. How can I describe how much I love you? Is it even possible to describe a love like that? I don't know, but as I sit here with pen in hand, I know that I have to try.

I know you like to tell the story of how I played

hard to get, but when I think back on the night we first met, I think I realized even then that we were meant to be together. I remember that night clearly, just as I can recall the exact sensation of your hand in mine, and every detail of the cloudy afternoon at the beach when you dropped to one knee and asked me to become your wife. Until you came along, I never knew how much I'd been missing. I never knew that a touch could be so meaningful or an expression so eloquent; I never knew that a kiss could literally take my breath away. You are, and always have been, everything I've always wanted in a husband. You're kind and strong and caring and smart; you lift my spirits and you're a better father than you know. You have a knack with children, a way of making them trust you, and I can't express the joy it has brought me to see you holding them as they fall asleep on your shoulder.

My life is infinitely better for having you in it. And that's what makes all of this so hard; it's why I can't seem to find the words I need. It scares me to know that all of this will be ending soon. I'm not simply scared for me, though—I'm scared for you and our children, too. It breaks my heart to know that I'm going to cause you all such grief, but I don't know what I can do, other than to remind you of the reasons I fell in love with you in the first place and express my sorrow at hurting you and our beautiful children. It pains me to think that your love for me will also be the source of so much anguish.

But I truly believe that while love can hurt, love can also heal...and that's why I'm enclosing another letter.

Please don't read it. It's not meant for you, or our families, or even our friends. I highly doubt that either of us has met the woman to whom you will give this letter. You see, this one is meant for the woman who eventually heals you, the one who makes you whole again.

Right now, I know you can't imagine something like that. It might take months, it might take years, but someday, you'll give that letter to another woman. Trust your instincts, just as I did on the night you first walked up to me. You'll know when and where to do that, just as you'll know which woman deserves it. And when you do, trust me when I say that somewhere, somehow, I'll be smiling down on both of you.

Love,
Carly

After reading the letter again, Alex slipped it back into the envelope and returned it to the safe. Beyond the window, the sky was filled with moonlit clouds and it glowed with an eerie incandescence. He stared upward, thinking of Carly and of Katie. Carly had told him to trust his instincts; Carly had told him that he would know what to do with the letter.

And Carly, he suddenly realized, had been exactly right, about half of it, anyway. He knew he wanted to give the letter to Katie. He just wasn't sure whether she was ready to receive it.

28

Hey, Kevin." Bill gestured to him. "Can you come into my office for a minute?"

Kevin had almost reached his desk, and Coffey and Ramirez followed him with their eyes. His new partner, Todd, was already at his desk and offered a weak smile, but it faded quickly before Todd suddenly turned away.

His head was throbbing and he didn't want to talk to Bill first thing in the morning but Kevin wasn't worried. He was good with witnesses and victims and knew when criminals were lying and he made lots of arrests and the criminals were convicted.

Bill motioned for him to sit in the chair and though Kevin didn't want to sit, he took a seat and wondered why Bill wanted him to sit because usually he stood when the two of them were talking. The pain in his temple felt as if he were being stabbed with a pencil, and for a moment Bill simply stared. Bill finally got up and closed the door before propping himself on the edge of his desk.

"How are you doing, Kevin?"

"I'm fine," Kevin answered. He wanted to close his eyes to lessen the pain, but he could tell that Bill was studying him. "What's up?"

Bill crossed his arms. "I called you in here to let you know that we received a complaint about you."

"What kind of complaint?"

"This is serious, Kevin. Internal Affairs is involved, and as of now, you're being suspended pending an investigation."

The words sounded jumbled, making no sense at all, not at first, anyway, but as he concentrated, he could see Bill's expression and wished he hadn't woken with a headache and didn't need so much vodka.

"What are you talking about?"

Bill lifted a few pages from his desk. "The Gates murder," he said. "The little boy who was shot through the floor? Earlier this month?"

"I remember," Kevin said. "He had pizza sauce on his forehead."

"Excuse me?"

Kevin blinked. "The boy. That's how we found him. It was horrible. Todd was pretty shaken up."

Bill furrowed his brow. "An ambulance was called," he said.

Kevin breathed in and out. Concentrating.

"It came for the mom," Kevin said. "She was upset, obviously, and she went after the Greek who'd fired the bullet. They struggled and she fell down the stairs. We called it in immediately...as far as I know, she was taken to the hospital."

Bill continued to stare at him before finally setting the pages aside. "You talked to her beforehand, right?"

"I tried to...but she was pretty hysterical. I tried to

calm her down, but she went crazy. What else is there to tell? It's all in the report."

Bill reached for the papers on his desk again. "I saw what you wrote. But the woman is claiming that you told her to push the perp down the stairs."

"What?"

Bill read from the pages. "She claims you were talking about God and told her, quote, 'The man was a sinner and deserved to be punished because the Bible says *Thou shalt not kill.*' She says that you also told her that the guy was probably going to get probation, even though he killed her kid, so she should take matters into her own hands. Because wrongdoers deserve to be punished. Does any of this ring a bell?"

Kevin could feel the blood in his cheeks. "That's ridiculous," he said. "You know she's lying, right?"

He expected Bill to immediately agree with him, to say that he knew Internal Affairs would clear him. But Bill didn't. Instead, his boss leaned forward.

"What exactly did you tell her? Word for word."

"I didn't *tell* her anything. I asked her what happened and she told me and I saw the hole in the ceiling and went upstairs and I arrested the neighbor after he admitted to firing the gun. I cuffed him and started bringing him down the stairs; the next thing I know, she went after him."

Bill was silent, his gaze locked on Kevin. "You never talked to her about sin?"

"No."

He held up the paper he had been reading from. "You never said the words *Vengeance is mine, I will repay, says the Lord.*"

"No."

"None of this sounds familiar at all?"

Kevin felt the anger rising but forced it back down. "Nothing. It's a lie. You know how people are. She probably wants to sue the city so she can get a big payday."

Bill's jaw muscle was flexing and it took a long time before he spoke.

"Had you been drinking before you talked to the woman?"

"I don't know where this is coming from. No. I don't do that. I wouldn't do that. You know my clear rate. I'm a good detective." Kevin held out his hands, almost blind from the throbbing pain in his head. "C'mon, Bill. We've worked together for years."

"That's why I'm talking to you instead of firing you. Because in the past few months, you haven't been yourself. And I've been hearing rumors."

"What rumors?"

"That you're drunk when you come into work."

"It's not true."

"So if I gave you a Breathalyzer, you'd blow a zero, right?"

Kevin could feel his heart hammering in his chest. He knew how to lie and he was good at it but he had to keep his voice steady. "Last night, I was up late with a buddy and we were drinking. There might still be some alcohol in my system, but I'm not drunk and I didn't drink before coming into work this morning. Or that day, either. Or any day, for that matter."

Bill stared at him. "Tell me what's going on with Erin," he said.

"I've already told you. She's helping a friend in Manchester. We went to the Cape just a few weeks ago."

"You told Coffey that you went to a restaurant in Provincetown with Erin, but the restaurant closed six months ago and there was no record of you checking into the bed-and-breakfast you mentioned. And no one has seen or heard from Erin in months."

Kevin felt his head filling with blood, making the pounding worse. "You checked up on me?"

"You've been drinking on the job and you've been lying to me."

"I haven't—"

"Stop lying to me!" the captain suddenly shouted. "I can smell your breath from here!" His eyes flared anger. "And as of now, you're suspended from duty. You should call your union rep before you meet with Internal Affairs. Leave your gun and your badge on my desk and go home."

"How long?" Kevin managed to croak out.

"Right now, suspension is the least of your worries."

"Just so you know, I didn't say anything to that woman."

"They heard you!" Bill shouted. "Your partner, the medical examiner, the crime scene investigators, the boyfriend." He paused, visibly trying to regain his calm. "Everyone heard you," he said with finality, and all at once, Kevin felt as though he'd lost control of everything and he knew it was all Erin's fault.

29

August rolled in, and although Alex and Katie were enjoying the hot, slow summer days they spent together, the kids were beginning to get bored. Wanting to do something unusual, Alex took Katie and the kids to see the rodeo monkeys in Wilmington. Much to Katie's disbelief, it turned out to be exactly what it sounded like: monkeys, dressed in cowboy outfits, rode dogs and herded rams for almost an hour before a show of fireworks that rivaled the Fourth of July. On their way out, Katie turned toward him with a smile.

"That has to be the craziest thing I've ever seen," she said, shaking her head.

"And you probably thought we lacked culture in the South."

She laughed. "Where do people come up with these ideas?"

"I have no idea. But it's a good thing I heard about it. They're in town for only a couple of days." He scanned the parking lot for his car.

"Yes, it's hard to imagine how unfulfilling my life would have been had I never seen monkeys riding dogs."

"The kids liked it!" Alex protested.

"The kids loved it," Katie agreed. "But I can't figure out whether the monkeys liked it. They didn't look all that happy to me."

Alex squinted at her. "I'm not sure I'd be able to tell whether a monkey was happy or not."

"My point exactly," she said.

"Hey, it's not my fault that there's still another month until school, and I'm just about out of new things for the kids to do."

"They don't need to do something special every day."

"I know. And they don't. But I don't want them watching television all the time, either."

"Your kids don't watch a lot of television."

"That's because I take them to see the rodeo monkeys."

"And next week?"

"That's easy. The carnival will be in town. One of those traveling things."

She smiled. "Those kinds of rides always made me sick to my stomach."

"And the kids love them, anyway. But that reminds me. Are you working next Saturday?"

"I'm not sure. Why?"

"Because I was hoping you'd come to the carnival with us."

"You want me to be sick to my stomach?"

"You don't have to go on the rides if you don't want to. But I would like to ask a favor."

"What's that?"

"I was hoping you'd watch the kids later that evening.

Joyce's daughter is flying into Raleigh, and Joyce asked if I could drive her to the airport to pick her up. Joyce doesn't like to drive at night."

"I'd be glad to watch them."

"It'll have to be at my place, so they go to bed at a reasonable hour."

She looked at him. "Your place? I never get to spend time at your house."

"Yeah, well..."

He didn't seem to know what to say next and she smiled. "No problem," she said. "That sounds like fun. Maybe we'll watch a movie together and have some popcorn."

Alex walked in silence for a few steps before he asked, "Do you ever want to have kids?"

Katie hesitated. "I'm not sure," she finally said. "I haven't really thought about it."

"Ever?"

She shook her head. "In Atlantic City I was too young, with Kevin I couldn't bear the idea, and I've had my mind on other things the last few months."

"But if you did think about it?" he persisted.

"I still don't know. I guess it would depend on a lot of things."

"Like what?"

"Like whether I was married, for starters. And, as you know, I can't get married."

"Erin can't get married," he said. "But Katie probably could. She has a driver's license, remember."

Katie took a few steps in silence. "She might be able to, but she wouldn't do it unless she met the right guy."

He laughed and slipped his arm around her. "I know that working at Ivan's was just what you needed at the time you took the job, but did you ever think about doing something else?"

"Like what?"

"I don't know. Going back to college, getting a degree, finding a job that you really love."

"What makes you think I don't love waiting tables?"

"Nothing." He shrugged. "I was just curious as to what you might be interested in."

She thought about it. "Growing up, like every other girl I knew, I loved animals and I thought I'd be a veterinarian. But there's no way I'd be willing to go back to school for that now. It would take too long."

"There are other ways to work with animals. You could train rodeo monkeys, for instance."

"I don't think so. I still haven't decided whether the monkeys liked it."

"You've got a soft spot for those monkeys, don't you?"

"Who wouldn't? I mean, who on earth came up with that idea in the first place?"

"Correct me if I'm wrong, but I think I heard you laughing."

"I didn't want to make the rest of you feel bad."

He laughed again, pulling her even closer. Ahead of them, Josh and Kristen were already slumped against the jeep. She knew they would probably fall asleep before they got back to Southport.

"You never answered my question," Alex said. "About what you want to do with your life."

"Maybe my dreams aren't that complicated. Maybe I think that a job is just a job."

"What does that mean?"

"Maybe I don't want to be defined by what I do. Maybe I'd like to be defined by what I am."

He considered the response. "Okay," he said. "Then who do you want to be?"

"Do you really want to know?"

"I wouldn't have asked you otherwise."

She stopped and met his gaze. "I'd like to be a wife and mother," she finally said.

He frowned. "But I thought you said that you weren't sure whether you wanted to have children."

She cocked her head, looking as beautiful as he'd ever seen. "What does that have to do with anything?"

The kids fell asleep before they reached the highway. It wasn't a long trip back, maybe half an hour, but neither Alex nor Katie wanted to risk waking the kids with their conversation. Instead, they were content to hold hands in silence as they made the drive back to Southport.

As Alex pulled to a stop in front of her house, Katie spotted Jo sitting on the steps of her porch, as if waiting for her. In the darkness, she wasn't sure whether Alex recognized her, but at that moment Kristen stirred and he turned around in his seat to make sure she hadn't woken up. Katie leaned over and kissed him.

"I should probably talk to her," Katie whispered.

"Who? Kristen?"

"My neighbor." Katie smiled, gesturing over her shoulder. "Or rather, she probably wants to talk to me."

"Oh." He nodded. "Okay." He glanced toward Jo's porch and back again. "I had a great time tonight."

"I did, too."

He kissed her before she opened the door, and when

Alex pulled out of the driveway she started toward Jo's house. Jo smiled and waved, and Katie felt herself relax slightly. They hadn't talked since that night in the bar, and as she approached, Jo stood and came to the railing.

"First off, I want to apologize for the way I talked to you," she said without preamble. "I was out of line. I was wrong and it won't happen again."

Katie climbed the steps to her porch and sat down, waving Jo to a spot next to her on the top step. "It's okay," she said. "I wasn't mad."

"I still feel terrible about it," Jo said, her remorse obvious. "I don't know what got into me."

"I do," Katie said. "It's obvious. You care about them. And you want to watch out for them."

"I still shouldn't have talked to you the way I did. That's why I haven't been around. It embarrassed me and I knew you'd never forgive me."

Katie touched her arm. "I appreciate the apology, but it's not necessary. You actually made me realize some important things about myself."

"Yeah?"

Katie nodded. "And just so you know, I think I'm going to stay in Southport for a while."

"I saw you driving the other day."

"Hard to believe, isn't it? I still don't feel comfortable behind the wheel."

"You will," she said. "And it's better than the bike."

"I still ride my bike every day," she said. "I can't afford a car."

"I'd say you could use mine, but it's back in the shop again. Thing's always breaking down. I'd probably be better off with a bike."

"Be careful what you wish for."

"Now you sound like me again." Jo nodded toward the road. "I'm happy for you and Alex. And the kids. You're good for them, you know."

"How can you be so sure?"

"Because I can see the way he looks at you. And the way you look at all of them."

"We've spent a lot of time together," Katie hedged.

Jo shook her head. "It's more than that. The two of you look like you're in love." She squirmed a bit under Katie's blushing gaze. "Okay, I'll admit it. Even if you haven't seen me, let's just say that I've seen the way the two of you kiss when you say good-bye."

"You spy on us?" Katie pretended to be outraged.

"Of course." Jo snorted. "How else am I supposed to occupy myself? It's not like anything else interesting ever happens around here." She paused. "You do love him, don't you?"

Katie nodded. "And I love the kids, too."

"I'm so glad." Jo clasped her hands together, prayer-style.

Katie paused. "Did you know his wife?"

"Yes," Jo said.

Katie stared down the road. "What was she like? I mean, Alex's talked about her and I can sort of picture in my mind what she was like—"

Jo didn't let her finish. "Based on what I've seen, she was a lot like you. And I mean that in a good way. She loved Alex and she loved the kids. They were the most important things in her life. That's really all you have to know about her."

"Do you think she would have liked me?"

"Yes," Jo said. "I'm sure she would have loved you."

30

⟶ ❧ ⟵

August, and Boston was sweltering.

Kevin vaguely remembered seeing the ambulance outside the Feldmans' home, but he hadn't thought much about it because the Feldmans were bad neighbors and he didn't care about them. Only now did he realize that Gladys Feldman had died and cars were parked along both sides of the street. Kevin had been suspended for two weeks and he didn't like cars parked in front of his house, but people were in town for the funeral and he lacked the energy to ask any of them to move.

He'd showered infrequently since he'd been suspended, and he sat on the porch, drinking straight from the bottle, watching people walk in and out of the Feldmans' house. He knew the funeral was later in the afternoon and people were at the Feldmans' house because they would be going to the funeral as a group. People clustered like flocks of geese whenever there was a funeral.

He hadn't talked to Bill or Coffey or Ramirez or Todd or Amber or even his parents. There were no pizza boxes on the living room floor and no leftover Chinese in the refrigerator because he hadn't been hungry. Vodka was enough and he drank until the Feldmans' house was a blur. Across the street, he saw a woman walk out of their house to smoke a cigarette. She was wearing a black dress and Kevin wondered if she knew the Feldmans yelled at neighborhood kids.

He watched the woman because he didn't want to watch the home and garden channel on the television. Erin used to watch that channel but she ran away to Philadelphia and called herself Erica and then she disappeared and he'd been suspended from his job but before that he'd been a good detective.

The woman in black finished her cigarette and dropped it in the grass and stepped on it. She scanned the street and noticed him sitting on the porch. She hesitated before crossing the street toward him. He didn't know her; had never seen her before.

He didn't know what she wanted but he put the bottle down and climbed down the porch steps. She stopped on the sidewalk out front.

"Are you Kevin Tierney?" the woman asked.

"Yes," he said, and his voice sounded strange because he hadn't spoken in days.

"I'm Karen Feldman," she said. "My parents live across the street. Larry and Gladys Feldman?" She paused but Kevin said nothing and she went on. "I was just wondering if Erin was planning to attend the funeral."

He stared at her.

"Erin?" he finally said.

"Yes. My mom and dad used to love it when she came by to visit. She used to make them pies and sometimes she helped them clean up, especially once my mom started getting sick. Lung cancer. It was awful." She shook her head. "Is Erin around? I've been hoping to meet her. The funeral starts at two."

"No, she's not. She's helping a sick friend in Manchester," he said.

"Oh...well, okay then. That's too bad. I'm sorry to have bothered you."

His mind began to clear and he noticed that she was about to leave. "I'm sorry for your loss, by the way. I told Erin and she's upset that she can't be here. Did you get the flowers?"

"Oh, probably. I haven't checked. The funeral home is full of them."

"No big deal. I just wish Erin could have been here."

"Me, too. I've always wanted to meet her. My mom told me that she reminded her of Katie."

"Katie?"

"My younger sister. She passed away six years ago."

"I'm sorry to hear that."

"Me, too. We all miss her—my mom did especially. That's why she got along so well with Erin. They even looked alike. Same age and everything." If Karen noticed Kevin's blank expression, she gave no sign. "My mom used to show Erin the scrapbook she'd put together about Katie...She was always so patient with my mom. She's a sweet woman. You're a lucky man."

Kevin forced himself to smile. "Yes, I know."

He'd been a good detective but in truth sometimes the answers came down to luck. New evidence surfacing, an unknown witness stepping forward, a street camera catching a license plate. In this case the lead came from a woman in black named Karen Feldman, who crossed the street on a morning he'd been drinking and told him about her dead sister.

Even though his head still ached, he poured the vodka down the drain and thought about Erin and the Feldmans. Erin knew them and visited them, even though she'd never mentioned going to their house. He'd called her and dropped by unexpectedly and she'd always been home, but somehow, he'd never found out. She'd never told him and when he'd complained that they were bad neighbors, she'd never said a word.

Erin had a secret.

His mind was clearer than it had been in a long time and he got in the shower and washed and put on a black suit. He made a ham-and-turkey sandwich with Dijon mustard and ate it, then made another and ate it as well. The street was filled with cars and he watched people walking in and out of the house. Karen came outside and smoked another cigarette. While he waited, he tucked a small pad of paper and a pen in his pocket.

In the afternoon, people started filing toward their cars. He heard the engines start up and one by one they began to pull away. It was past one o'clock and they were going to the service. It took fifteen minutes for everyone to leave and he saw Larry Feldman being helped to the car by Karen. Karen got in the driver's seat and drove off, and finally there were no more cars on the street or in the driveway.

He waited ten more minutes, making sure everyone had left before finally walking out his front door. He crossed his lawn and paused at the street and headed for the Feldmans' house. He didn't hurry and didn't try to hide. He'd noticed that a lot of the neighbors had gone to the funeral and those who hadn't would simply remember a mourner wearing a black suit. He went to the front door and it was locked, but there'd been a lot of people in the house so he walked around the side and headed to the back. There he found another door and it was unlocked and he stepped into the house.

It was quiet. He paused, listening for the sound of voices or footsteps but heard nothing. There were plastic cups on the countertop and platters of food on the table. He walked through the house. He had time, but he didn't know how much time, and he decided to start in the living room. He opened cabinet doors and closed them, leaving everything the way it had been before. He searched in the kitchen and the bedroom and finally went to the study. There were books on the shelves and a recliner and a television. In the corner, he spotted a small file cabinet.

He went to the file cabinet and opened it. Quickly, he scanned the tabs. He found a file labeled KATIE and pulled it out, opened it, and examined what was inside. There was a newspaper article—it turns out that she'd drowned after breaking through the ice of a local pond—and there were pictures of her that had been taken at school. In her graduation photo, she looked remarkably like Erin. In the back of the file, he found an envelope. He opened it and found an old report card. On the front of the envelope was a social security number, and he took the pad of paper and his pen and wrote it down. He didn't find the social security card, but he had the number. The birth certificate was a copy, though it was wrinkled and worn, as if someone had crumpled it up and then tried to flatten it again.

He had what he needed and he left the house. As soon as he reached home he called the officer from the other precinct, the one who was sleeping with the babysitter. The following day, he received a call in return.

Katie Feldman had recently been issued a driver's license, with an address listed in Southport, North Carolina.

Kevin hung up the phone without another word, knowing he'd found her.

Erin.

31

———— ❧ ————

Remnants of a tropical storm blew through Southport, rain falling most of the afternoon and into the evening. Katie worked the lunch shift, but the weather kept the restaurant only half full and Ivan let her leave early. She had borrowed the jeep and after spending an hour at the library, she'd dropped it off at the store. When Alex drove her home, she'd invited him to come by later with the kids for dinner.

She'd been on edge the rest of the afternoon. She wanted to believe it had something to do with the weather, but as she stood at her kitchen window, watching the branches bend in the wind and rain falling in sheets, she knew it had more to do with the uneasy feeling that everything in her life these days seemed almost too perfect. Her relationship with Alex and the afternoons she spent with the kids filled a void she hadn't known existed, but she'd learned long ago that nothing wonderful lasted forever. Joy was as fleeting as a shooting star that crossed the evening sky, ready to blink out at any moment.

Earlier that day, at the library, she'd perused the *Boston Globe* online at one of the computers and had come across Gladys Feldman's obituary. She'd known Gladys was ill, had known about her terminal diagnosis of cancer before she left. Even though she'd been checking the Boston obituaries regularly, the sparse description of her life and survivors struck her with unexpected force.

She hadn't wanted to take the identification from the Feldmans' files, hadn't even considered the possibility until Gladys had pulled out the file to show her Katie's graduation photo. She'd seen the birth certificate and the social security card next to the photo and recognized the opportunity they presented. The next time she'd gone to the house, she'd excused herself to go to the bathroom and had gone to the file cabinet instead. Later, as she ate blueberry pie with them in the kitchen, the documents felt like they were burning in her pockets. A week later, after making a copy of the birth certificate at the library and folding and wrinkling it to make it appear dated, she put the document in the file. She would have done the same with the social security card, but she couldn't make a good enough copy and she hoped that if they noticed it was missing, they would believe it had been lost or misplaced.

She reminded herself that Kevin would never know what she'd done. He didn't like the Feldmans and the feeling was mutual. She suspected that they knew he beat her. She could see it in their eyes as they watched her dart across the road to visit them, in the way they pretended never to notice the bruises on her arms, in the way their faces tightened whenever she mentioned Kevin. She wanted to think that they would have been okay with what she'd done, that they would have wanted her to take the identification, because they knew she needed it and wanted her to escape.

They were the only people she missed from Dorchester and she wondered how Larry was doing. They were her friends when she had no one else, and she wanted to tell Larry that she was sorry for his loss. She wanted to cry with him and talk about Gladys and to tell him that because of them, her life was better now. She wanted to tell him that she'd met a man who loved her, that she was happy for the first time in years.

But she would do none of those things. Instead, she simply stepped out onto the porch and, through eyes that were blurry with tears, watched the storm tear leaves from the trees.

"You've been quiet tonight," Alex said. "Is everything okay?"

She'd made tuna casserole for dinner and Alex was helping her with the dishes. The kids were in the living room, both of them playing handheld computer games; she could hear the beeps and buzzes over the sound of the faucet.

"A friend of mine passed away," she said. She handed him a plate to dry. "I knew it was coming, but it's still sad."

"It's always sad," he agreed. "I'm sorry." He knew enough not to ask for further details. Instead, he waited on the chance she wanted to say more, but she washed another glass and changed the subject.

"How long do you think the storm is going to last?" she asked.

"Not long. Why?"

"I was just wondering whether the carnival tomorrow

is going to be canceled. Or whether the flight is going to be canceled."

Alex glanced out the window. "It should be fine. It's already blowing through. I'm pretty sure we're on the tail end of it now."

"Just in time," Katie remarked.

"Of course. The elements wouldn't dare mess with the well-laid plans of the carnival committee. Or Joyce for that matter."

She smiled. "How long is it going to take you to pick up Joyce's daughter?"

"Probably four or five hours. Raleigh's not exactly convenient to this place."

"Why didn't she fly into Wilmington? Or just rent a car?"

"I don't know. I didn't ask, but if I had to guess I'd say she wanted to save some money."

"You're doing a good thing, you know. Helping Joyce like that."

He gave a nonchalant shrug, indicating that it wasn't a big deal. "You'll have fun tomorrow."

"At the carnival or with the kids?"

"Both. And if you ask me nice, I'll treat you to some deep-fried ice cream."

"Fried ice cream? It sounds disgusting."

"It's actually tasty."

"Is everything fried down here?"

"If it can be fried, believe me, someone will find a way. Last year, there was a place serving deep-fried butter."

She almost gagged. "You're kidding."

"Nope. It sounded terrible, but people were lining up to buy it. They might as well have been lining up for heart attacks."

She washed and rinsed the last of the cups, then passed it to him. "Do you think the kids liked the dinner I made? Kristen didn't eat very much."

"Kristen never eats much. And more important, I liked it. I thought it was delicious."

She shook her head. "Who cares about the kids, right? As long as you're happy?"

"I'm sorry. I'm a narcissist at heart."

She ran the soapy sponge over a plate and rinsed it. "I'm looking forward to spending some time at your house."

"Why?"

"Because we're always here, not there. Don't get me wrong—I understand it was the right thing to do because of the kids." *And because of Carly*, she also thought, but she didn't mention that part. "It'll give me the chance to see how you live."

Alex took the plate. "You've been there before."

"Yes, but not for more than a few minutes, and then only in the kitchen or living room. It's not like I've had the chance to check out your bedroom or peek in your medicine cabinet."

"You wouldn't do that." Alex feigned outrage.

"Maybe if I had the chance, I might."

He dried the plate and put it in the cupboard. "Feel free to spend as much time in my bedroom as you like."

She laughed. "You're such a man."

"I'm just saying that I wouldn't mind. And feel free to peek in the medicine cabinet, too. I have no secrets."

"So you say," she teased. "You're talking to someone who only has secrets."

"Not from me."

"No," she agreed, her face serious. "Not from you."

She washed two more plates and handed them to him, feeling a wave of contentment wash over her as she watched him dry and put them away.

He cleared his throat.

"Can I ask you something?" he said. "I don't want you to take it the wrong way, but I've been curious."

"Go ahead."

He used the towel on his arms, dabbing at stray droplets, buying time. "I was wondering if you'd given more thought to what I said last weekend. In the parking lot, after seeing the rodeo monkeys?"

"You said a lot of things," she said cautiously.

"Don't you remember? You told me that Erin couldn't get married, but I said that Katie probably could?"

Katie felt herself stiffen, less at the memory than at the serious tone he was using. She knew exactly where this was leading. "I remember," she said with forced lightness. "I think I said I would have to meet the right guy."

At her words, his lips tightened, as if he were debating whether to continue. "I just wanted to know if you thought about it. Us eventually getting married, I mean."

The water was still warm as she started on the silverware. "You'd have to ask first."

"But if I did?"

She found a fork and scrubbed it. "I suppose I'd tell you that I love you."

"Would you say yes?"

She paused. "I don't want to get married again."

"You don't want to, or you don't think you can?"

"What's the difference?" Her expression remained stubborn, closed. "You know I'm still married. Bigamy is illegal."

"You're not Erin anymore. You're Katie. As you pointed out, your driver's license proves it."

"But I'm not Katie, either!" she snapped before turning toward him. "Don't you get that? I stole that name from people I cared about! People who trusted me." She stared at him, feeling the surge of tension from earlier in the day, recalling with fresh intensity Gladys's kindness and pity, her escape, and the nightmarish years with Kevin. "Why can't you just be happy with the way things are? Why do you have to push so hard for me to be the person you want me to be rather than the person that I am?"

He flinched. "I love the person that you are."

"But you're making it conditional!"

"I'm not!"

"But you are!" she insisted. She knew she was raising her voice but she couldn't seem to stop it. "You have this idea of what you want in life and you're trying to make me fit into it!"

"I don't," Alex protested. "I simply asked you a question."

"But you wanted a specific answer! You wanted the *right* answer, and if you didn't get it, you were going to try to convince me otherwise. That I should do what you want! That I should do everything you want!"

For the first time ever, Alex narrowed his eyes at her. "Don't do this," he said.

"Do what? Tell the truth? Tell you how I feel? Why? What are you going to do? Hit me? Go ahead."

He physically recoiled as though she'd slapped him. She knew her words had hit their mark, but instead of getting angry, Alex set the dish towel on the counter and took a step backward. "I don't know what's going on, but I'm sorry that I even brought it up. I didn't mean to put you on the spot or try to convince you of anything. I was just trying to have a conversation."

He paused, waiting for her to say something, but she stayed silent. Shaking his head, he started to leave the kitchen before coming to a stop. "Thank you for dinner," he whispered.

In the living room, she heard him tell the kids it was getting late, heard the front door open with a squeak. He closed the door softly behind him and the house was suddenly quiet, leaving her alone with her thoughts.

32

Kevin was having trouble staying between the lines on the highway. He'd wanted to keep his mind sharp, but his head had begun to pound and he'd been sick to his stomach, so he'd stopped at a liquor store and bought a bottle of vodka. It numbed the pain, and as he sipped it through a straw, all he could think about was Erin and how she'd changed her name to Katie.

The interstate was a blur. Headlights, double pinpricks of white, rose in intensity as they approached from the opposite direction and then vanished when they passed him. One after another. Thousands. People going places, doing things. Kevin driving to North Carolina, heading south to find his wife. Leaving Massachusetts, driving through Rhode Island and Connecticut. New York and New Jersey. The moon rose, orange and angry before turning white, and crossed the blackened sky above him. Stars overhead.

Hot wind blew through the open window and Kevin held the wheel steady, his thoughts a jigsaw of mismatched pieces. The bitch had left him. She'd abandoned the marriage and left him to rot and believed she was smarter than he was. But he'd found her. Karen Feldman had crossed the street and he'd learned that Erin had a secret. But not anymore. He knew where Erin lived, he knew where she was hiding. Her address was scribbled on a piece of paper on the seat beside him, held in place by the Glock he'd brought from home. On the backseat was a duffel bag filled with clothes and handcuffs and duct tape. On his way out of town, he stopped at an ATM and withdrew a few hundred dollars. He wanted to smash Erin's face with his fists as soon as he found her, bloody it to an ugly pulp. He wanted to kiss her and hold her and beg her to come home. He filled the tank near Philadelphia and remembered how he'd tracked her there.

She'd made a fool of him, carrying on a secret life he hadn't even known about. Visiting the Feldmans, cooking and cleaning for them while she plotted and schemed and lied. What else, he wondered, had she lied about? A man? Maybe not then, but there had to be a man by now. Kissing her. Caressing her. Taking her clothes off. Laughing at him. They were probably in bed together right now. Her and the man. Both of them laughing at him behind his back. *I showed him, didn't I?* she was saying as she laughed. *Kevin didn't even see it coming.*

It made him crazy to think about. Furious. He'd been on the road for hours already, but Kevin kept driving. He sipped his vodka and blinked rapidly to clear his vision. He didn't speed, didn't want to get pulled over. Not with a gun on the seat beside him. She was afraid of guns and always asked him to lock his up when he finished his shift, which he did.

But it wasn't enough. He could buy her a house, furniture, and pretty clothes and take her to the library and the hair salon and it still wasn't enough. Who could understand it? Was it so hard to clean the house and cook dinner? He never wanted to hit her, only did it when he had no other choice. When she was stupid or careless or selfish. She brought it on herself.

The engine droned, the noise steady in his ears. She had a driver's license now and she was a waitress at a restaurant called Ivan's. Before he left, he'd spent some time on the Internet and had made some calls. It hadn't been hard to track her down because the town was small. It took him less than twenty minutes to find out where she worked. All he had to do was dial the number and ask if Katie was there. On the fourth call, someone said yes. He hung up without a word. She thought she could hide forever, but he was a good detective and he'd found her. *I'm coming*, he thought to himself. *I know where you live and where you work and you won't get away again.*

He passed billboards and exit ramps, and in Delaware the rain started to fall. He rolled up the window and felt the wind begin to push the car sideways. A truck ahead of him was swerving, the trailer wheels riding the lines. He turned on the wipers and the windshield cleared. But the rain began to fall even harder and he leaned over the wheel, squinting into the fuzzy orbs of oncoming headlights. His breath began to fog the glass and he turned on the defroster. He would drive all night and find Erin tomorrow. He'd bring her home and they'd start over again. Man and wife, living together, the way it was supposed to be. Happy.

They used to be happy. Used to do fun things together.

Early on in the marriage, he remembered, he and Erin would visit open houses on the weekends. She was excited about buying a house and he would listen as she talked to the Realtors, her voice trilling like music in the empty homes. She liked to take her time as she walked through the rooms, and he knew she was imagining where to put furniture. When they found the house in Dorchester, he'd known she wanted it by the way her eyes were sparkling. That night, lying in bed, she traced small circles on his chest as she pleaded with him to make an offer and he could remember thinking that he would do anything she wanted because he loved her.

Except have children. She'd told him that she wanted kids, wanted to start a family. In the first year of marriage, she'd talked about it all the time. He tried to ignore her, didn't want to tell her that he didn't want her to get fat and puffy, that pregnant women were ugly, that he didn't want to hear her whining about how tired she was or how her feet were swollen. He didn't want to hear a baby fussing and crying when he got home from work, didn't want toys scattered around the house. He didn't want her to get frumpy and saggy or hear her ask him whether he thought her butt was getting fat. He married her because he wanted a wife, not a mother. But she kept bringing it up, kept harping day after day until he finally slapped her and told her to shut up. After that, she never talked about it again, but now he wondered whether he should have given her what she wanted. She wouldn't have left if she had a child, wouldn't have been able to run away in the first place. By the same token, she could never run away again.

They would have a child, he decided, and the three of them would live in Dorchester and he would work as a detective. In the evenings, he'd come home to his pretty wife and when people saw them in the grocery store, they would marvel and say, *They look like the all-American family.*

He wondered whether her hair was blond again. Hoped it was long and blond and that he could run his fingers through it. She liked when he did that, always whispering to him, saying the words he liked, turning him on. But it hadn't been real, not if she'd been planning to leave him, not if she hadn't come back. She'd lied to him, been lying all along. For weeks. Months, even. Stealing from the Feldmans, the cell phone, taking money from his wallet. Scheming and plotting and he'd had no idea at all and now another man was sharing her bed. Running his fingers through her hair, listening to her moans, feeling her hands on him. Kevin bit his lip and tasted blood, hating her, wanting to kick and punch her, wanting to throw her down the stairs. He took another sip from the bottle next to him, rinsing the metallic taste from his mouth.

She'd fooled him because she was beautiful. Everything about her was pretty. Her breasts, her lips, even the small of her back. At the casino, in Atlantic City, when he'd first met her, he'd thought she was the prettiest woman he'd ever seen, and in their four years of marriage, nothing had changed. She knew he desired her, and she used it to her advantage. Dressing sexy. Getting her hair done. Wearing lacy underwear. It made him lower his guard, made him think she loved him.

But she didn't love him. She didn't even care about him. She didn't care about the broken flowerpots and smashed-up china, didn't care that he'd been suspended from his job, didn't care that he'd cried himself to sleep for months. Didn't care that his life was falling apart. All that mattered was what she wanted, but she'd always been selfish and now she was laughing at him. Laughing for months and thinking only about herself. He loved her and hated her and he couldn't make sense of it. He felt tears beginning to form and he blinked them back.

Delaware. Maryland. The outskirts of Washington, DC. Virginia. Hours lost to the never-ending night. Raining hard at first, then gradually the rain dissipated. He stopped near Richmond at dawn and ate breakfast. Two eggs, four pieces of bacon, wheat toast. He drank three cups of coffee. He put more gas in the car and went back to the interstate. He crossed into North Carolina under blue skies. Bugs were cemented against the windshield and his back had begun to ache. He had to wear sunglasses to keep from squinting and his whiskers had begun to itch.

I'm coming, Erin, he thought. *I'll be there soon.*

33

———— 🌿 ————

Katie awoke exhausted. She had tossed and turned for hours during the night, replaying the horrible things she'd said to Alex. She didn't know what had come over her. Yes, she was upset about the Feldmans, but for the life of her, she couldn't remember how the argument had started in the first place. Or rather, she did remember, but it didn't make sense. She'd known he hadn't been pressuring her or trying to force her to do anything she wasn't ready for. She knew he wasn't remotely like Kevin, but what had she said to him?

What are you going to do? Hit me? Go ahead.

Why would she have said something like that?

She eventually dozed off sometime after two a.m., when the wind and rain were beginning to taper off. By dawn, the sky was clear and birdsong was drifting from the trees. From the porch, she noticed the effects of the storm: broken branches strewn out front, a carpet of pinecones littered across the yard and drive. The air was already thick with humidity. It was going to be a scorcher, maybe the hottest day of the summer yet. She made a note to herself to remind Alex not to keep the kids out in the sun too long before she realized that he might not want her with them. That maybe he was still mad at her.

Not maybe, she corrected herself. He was almost certainly mad at her. And hurt as well. He hadn't even let the kids say good-bye last night.

She took a seat on the steps and turned toward Jo's, wondering if she was up and about. It was early, probably too early to knock on her door. She didn't know what she would say to her or what good it would do. She wouldn't tell her what she'd said to Alex—that was a memory she'd rather erase in its entirety—but maybe Jo could help her understand the anxiety she'd been feeling. Even after Alex left, she noted the tension in her shoulders, and last night, for the first time in weeks, she'd wanted the light on.

Her intuition told her that something was wrong but she couldn't pinpoint what it was, other than that her thoughts kept returning to the Feldmans. To Gladys. To the inevitable changes in the house. What would happen if someone realized Katie's information was missing? Simply imagining it made her sick to her stomach.

"It's going to be okay," she suddenly heard. Whirling around, she saw Jo standing off to the side in her running shoes, cheeks flushed and perspiration staining her shirt.

"Where did you come from?"

"I went for a jog," Jo said. "I was trying to beat the heat, but obviously, it didn't work. It's so steamy I could barely breathe and I thought I was going to die of heatstroke. Even so, I think I'm doing better than you. You seem downright glum." She motioned to the steps and Katie scooted over. Jo took a seat beside her.

"Alex and I had a fight last night."

"And?"

"I said something terrible to him."

"Did you apologize?"

"No," Katie answered. "He left before I could. I should have, but I didn't. And now..."

"What? You think it's too late?" She squeezed Katie's knee. "It's never too late to do the right thing. Go over there and talk to him."

Katie hesitated, her anxiety plain. "What if he won't forgive me?"

"Then he's not who you thought he was."

Katie drew her knees up, propping her chin on them. Jo peeled her shirt away from her skin, trying to fan herself before going on. "He'll forgive you, though. You know that, right? He might be angry and you might have hurt his feelings, but he's a good man." She smiled. "Besides, every couple needs to argue now and then. Just to prove that the relationship is strong enough to survive it."

"That sounds like the counselor talking."

"It is, but it's also true. Long-term relationships—the ones that matter—are all about weathering the peaks and the valleys. And you *are* still thinking long-term, right?"

"Yes." Katie nodded. "I am. And you're right. Thanks."

Jo patted Katie's leg and winked as she unfolded herself from the steps and stood. "What are friends for, right?"

Katie squinted up. "Do you want some coffee? I was going to start a pot."

"Not this morning. Too hot. What I need is a glass of ice water and a cool shower. I feel like I'm melting."

"Are you going to the carnival today?"

"Maybe. I haven't decided yet. But if I do, I'll try to

find you," she promised. "Now head on over there before you change your mind."

Katie sat on the steps a few minutes longer before retreating into the house. She showered and made herself a cup of coffee—but Jo was right, it was too hot to drink it. Instead, she changed into shorts and sandals before walking around to the back of the house and getting on her bicycle.

Despite the recent downpour, the gravel road was already drying and she was able to pedal without exerting much energy. Good thing. She had no idea how Jo had been able to jog in this heat, even first thing in the morning. Everything, it seemed, was trying to escape the heat. Normally, there were squirrels or birds, but as she turned onto the main road, she saw no movement at all.

On the road, traffic was light. A couple of cars zipped past, leaving fumes in their wake. Katie pedaled onward and as she rounded a bend, the store came into view. Already, there were half a dozen cars parked out front. Regulars who came to eat biscuits.

Talking to Jo had helped, she thought. A little, anyway. She was still anxious, but it had less to do with the Feldmans or other troubling memories than what she was going to say to Alex. Or rather, what he was going to say to her in return.

She pulled to a stop out front. A couple of older men were fanning themselves on the benches and she walked past them toward the door. Behind the register, Joyce was ringing up a customer and she smiled.

"Good morning, Katie," she said.

Katie quickly scanned the store. "Is Alex around?"

"He's upstairs with the kids. You know the way, right? The stairs out back?"

Katie left the store and went around the side, toward the rear of the building. At the dock, a line of boats queued, waiting to fill up.

She hesitated at the door before finally knocking. Inside, she could hear footfalls approaching. When the door swung open, Alex stood before her.

She offered a tentative smile. "Hi," she said.

He nodded, his expression unreadable. Katie cleared her throat.

"I wanted to tell you that I'm sorry about what I said. I was wrong."

His expression remained neutral. "Okay," he said. "I appreciate the apology."

For a moment, neither of them said anything, and Katie suddenly wished she hadn't come. "I can go. I just need to know whether you still need me to watch the kids tonight."

Again, he said nothing, and in the silence Katie shook her head. When she turned to leave, she heard him take a step toward her. "Katie... wait," he said. He peeked over his shoulder at the kids before closing the door behind him.

"What you said last night..." he began. He trailed off, uncertain.

"I didn't mean it," she said, her voice soft. "I don't know what got into me. I was upset about something else and I took it out on you."

"I admit it—it bothered me. Not so much that you said it, but that you imagined me capable of... that."

"I don't think that," Katie said. "I would never think that about you."

He seemed to take that in, but she knew he had more to say.

"I want you to know that I value what we have right now, and more than anything, I want you to be comfortable. Whatever that means. I'm sorry for making you feel like I was putting you on the spot. That wasn't what I was trying to do."

"Yes, you were." She gave him a knowing smile. "A little, anyway. But it's okay. I mean, who knows what the future might bring, right? Like tonight, for instance."

"Why? What happens tonight?"

She leaned against the doorjamb. "Well, once the kids are asleep and depending when you get back, it might be too late for me to ride back to my house. You might just find me in your bed..."

When he realized she wasn't kidding, he brought a hand to his chin in mock contemplation. "That is a dilemma."

"Then again, traffic might be light and you'll get home early enough to bring me home."

"I'm generally a pretty safe driver. As a rule, I don't like to speed."

She leaned into him and breathed into his ear. "That's very conscientious of you."

"I try," he whispered, before their lips met. When he pulled back, he noticed half a dozen boaters watching them. He didn't care. "How long did it take you to rehearse that speech?"

"I didn't. It just sort of ... came to me."

He could still feel the remnants of their kiss. "Have you had breakfast yet?" he whispered.

"No."

"Would you like to have cereal with me and the kids? Before we head off to the carnival?"

"Cereal sounds delicious."

34

———— ❧ ————

North Carolina was ugly, a strip of road sandwiched between monotonous strands of pine trees and rolling hills. Along the highway, there were clusters of mobile homes and farmhouses and rotting barns overgrown with weeds. He left one interstate and got on another, turning toward Wilmington, and drank some more out of sheer boredom.

As he passed through the unchanging landscape, he thought about Erin. Thought about what he was going to do when he found her. He hoped she would be at home when he arrived, but even if she was at work, it would only be a matter of time before she came home.

The interstate wove past uninteresting towns with forgettable names. He was in Wilmington by ten. He drove through the city and turned onto a small, rural highway. Heading south, with the sun coming hard through the driver's-side window. He put the gun in his lap and then back on the seat again and kept on going.

And finally, he was there, in the town where she was living. Southport.

*   *   *

He drove slowly through town, detouring around a street fair, occasionally consulting the directions he'd printed out on the computer before he left. He pulled a shirt from the duffel bag and placed it over the gun to conceal it.

It was a small town with neat, well-kept houses. Some were typically Southern, with wide porches and magnolia trees and American flags waving from poles, others reminded him of homes in New England. There were mansions on the waterfront. Sunlight dappled the water in the spaces between them and it was hot as hell. Like a steam bath.

Minutes later, he found the road where she lived. On the left, up ahead, was a general store and he pulled in to buy some gas and a can of Red Bull. He stood behind a man buying charcoal and lighter fluid. At the register, he paid the old woman. She smiled and thanked him for coming, and commented in that nosy way that old women have that she hadn't seen him around before. He told her he was in town for the fair.

As he turned back onto the road, his pulse raced at the knowledge that it wasn't far now. He rounded a bend and slowed the car. In the distance, a gravel road came into view. The directions indicated that he was supposed to turn but he didn't stop the car. If Erin was home, she would recognize his car immediately, and he didn't want that. Not until he had everything ready.

He turned the car around, searching for an out-of-the-way place to park. There wasn't much. The store parking lot, maybe, but wouldn't someone notice if he parked it there? He passed the store again, scanning the area. The trees on either side of the road might provide cover ... or they might not. He didn't want to take the chance that someone would grow suspicious of an abandoned car in the trees.

The caffeine was making him jittery and he switched to vodka to settle his nerves. For the life of him, he couldn't find a place to stash the car. What the hell kind of a place was this? He turned around again, getting angry now. It shouldn't have been this hard and he should have rented a car but he hadn't and now he couldn't find a way to get close enough to her without her noticing.

The store was the only option and he pulled back into the lot, stopping along the side of the building. It was at least a mile to the house from here but he didn't know what else to do. He brooded before turning off the engine. When he opened the door, the heat enveloped him. He emptied the duffel bag, tossing his clothes on the backseat. Into the duffel bag went the gun, the ropes, the handcuffs, and the duct tape—and a spare bottle of vodka. Tossing the bag over his shoulder, he glanced around. No one was watching. He figured he could keep his car here for maybe an hour or two before someone got suspicious.

He left the lot, and as he walked down the shoulder of the road he could feel the pain starting in his head. The heat was ridiculous. Like something alive. He walked the road, staring at the drivers in passing cars. He didn't see Erin, even a brown-haired one.

He reached the gravel road and turned. The road, dusty and potholed, seemed to lead nowhere until he finally spotted a pair of small cottages a half mile down. He felt his heart speed up. Erin lived in one of them. He moved to the side of the road, hugging the trees, staying out of sight as much as possible. He was hoping for shade but the sun was high and the heat remained constant. His shirt was drenched, sweat dripped down his cheeks and plastered his hair to his skull. His head pounded and he stopped for a drink, straight from the bottle.

From a distance, neither of the cottages appeared occupied. Hell, neither one looked habitable. It was nothing like their house in Dorchester, with its shutters and corbels and red front door. On the cottage closest to him, the paint was peeling and the planks were rotting in the corners. Moving forward, he watched the windows, looking for signs of movement. There was nothing.

He didn't know which cottage was hers. He stopped to study them closely. Both were bad, but one looked practically abandoned. He moved toward the better one, angling away from the window.

It had taken thirty minutes to get here from the store. Once he surprised Erin, he knew she'd try to get away. She wouldn't want to go with him. She would try to get away, might even try to fight, and he would tie her up and tape her mouth shut and then go get the car. Once he returned with the car, he would put her in the trunk until they were far away from this town.

He reached the side of the house and flattened himself against it, staying away from the window. He listened for movement, the sound of opening doors or water running or dishes clattering, but heard nothing.

His head still hurt and he was thirsty. The heat poured down and his shirt was wet. He was breathing too fast but he was so close to Erin now and he thought again how she'd left him and hadn't cared that he'd cried. She'd laughed behind his back. Her and the man, whoever he was. He knew there had to be a man. She couldn't make it on her own.

He peeked around the back of the house and saw nothing. He crept forward, watching. Ahead, there was a small window and he took a chance and looked in. No lights on, but it was clean and tidy, with a dish towel draped over the kitchen sink. Just like Erin used to do. He silently approached the door and turned the knob. Unlocked.

Holding his breath, he opened the door and stepped inside, pausing again to listen and hearing nothing. He crossed the kitchen and entered the living room—then the bedroom and bathroom. He cursed aloud, knowing she wasn't home.

Assuming he was in the right home, of course. In the bedroom, he spied the chest of drawers and pulled the top one open. Finding a stack of her panties, he sifted through them, rubbed them between his thumb and forefinger, but it had been so long, he wasn't sure he could remember if they were the ones she had back home. The other clothes he didn't recognize, but they were her size.

He recognized the shampoo and conditioner, he recognized the brand of toothpaste. In the kitchen, he rifled through the drawers, opening them one by one until he found a utility bill. It was listed in the name of Katie Feldman, and now he leaned against the cupboard, staring at the name and feeling a sense of completion.

The only problem was that she wasn't here, and he didn't know when she would return. He knew he couldn't leave his car at the store indefinitely, but all at once, he was just so tired. He wanted to sleep, needed to sleep. He'd driven all night and his head was pounding. Instinctively, he wandered back to her bedroom. She'd made the bed, and when he peeled back the cover, he could smell her scent in the sheets. He crawled into the bed, breathing deeply, breathing her in. He felt the tears flood his eyes as he realized how much he missed her and loved her and that they could have been happy if she hadn't been so selfish.

He couldn't stay awake and he told himself that he would sleep for just a little while. Not long. Just enough so that when he came back later in the evening, his mind would be sharp and he wouldn't make mistakes and he and Erin could be husband and wife once more.

35

Alex, Katie, and the kids rode their bikes to the carnival because parking downtown was almost impossible. Trying to get home, once cars started pulling out, would be even worse.

Booths displaying arts and crafts lined either side of the street, and the air was thick with the scent of hot dogs and burgers, popcorn and cotton candy. On the main stage, a local band was playing "Little Deuce Coupe" by the Beach Boys. There were sack races and a banner promising a watermelon-eating contest later in the afternoon. Games of chance, too—throwing darts at balloons, tossing rings around bottles, sinking three shots with a basketball to win a stuffed animal. The Ferris wheel at the far end of the park towered above all of it, drawing families like a beacon.

Alex stood in line to buy tickets while Katie followed behind with the kids, heading toward the bumper cars and tilt-a-whirl. Long lines were everywhere. Mothers and fathers clung to the hands of children, and teens clustered in groups. The air sounded with the roar of generators and clacking noises as the rides went round and round.

The world's tallest horse could be viewed for a dollar. Another dollar bought admission to the tent next door, which housed the smallest horse. Ponies, walking in circles and tethered to a wheel, were hot and tired, their heads hanging low.

The kids were antsy and wanted to ride everything, so Alex purchased a small fortune in tickets. The tickets went fast, because most of the rides required three or four. The cumulative cost was ridiculous, and Alex tried to make them last by insisting they do other things as well.

They watched a man juggle bowling pins and cheered for a dog that could walk across a tightrope. They had pizza for lunch at one of the local restaurants, eating inside to escape the heat, and listened to a country-western band play a number of songs. Afterward, they watched people racing jet skis in the Cape Fear River before heading back to the rides. Kristen wanted cotton candy and Josh got a press-on tattoo.

And so the hours passed, in a blur of heat and noise and small-town pleasures.

Kevin woke two hours later, his body slick with sweat, his stomach knotted with cramps. His heat-induced dreams had been vivid and colorful, and it was hard to remember where he was. His head felt like it was splitting in two. He staggered from the bedroom and into the kitchen, slaking his thirst directly from the tap. He was dizzy and weak and felt more tired than when he lay down in the first place.

But he couldn't linger. He shouldn't have slept at all,

and he went to the bedroom and remade the bed so that she wouldn't know he'd been there. He was about to leave when he remembered the tuna casserole he'd spied in her refrigerator earlier, when he'd searched her kitchen. He was ravenous, and he remembered that she hadn't cooked him dinner in months.

It had to be close to a hundred degrees in this airless shack, and when he opened the refrigerator, he stood for a long minute in the cool air as it spilled out. He grabbed the tuna casserole and rummaged through the drawers until he found a fork. After peeling back the plastic wrap, he took a bite and then a second one. Eating did nothing for the pain in his head but his stomach felt better and the cramps began to subside. He could have eaten all of the casserole, but he forced himself to take just one more bite before putting it back in the refrigerator. She couldn't know that he'd been here.

He rinsed the fork, dried it, and put it back in the drawer. He straightened the towel and checked the bed again, making sure it looked the way it had when he entered.

Satisfied, he left the house and headed up the gravel road, toward the store.

The roof of the car was scalding to the touch and when he opened the door, it felt like a furnace. No one was in the parking lot. Too hot to be outside. Sweltering, without a cloud or hint of breeze. Who in God's name would want to live in a place like this?

In the store, he grabbed a bottle of water and drank it while standing near the coolers. He paid for the empty container and the old woman threw it out. She asked him if he enjoyed the carnival. He told the nosy old woman that he had.

Back in the car, he drank more vodka, not caring that it was now the temperature of a cup of coffee. As long as it made the pain go away. It was too hot to think and he could have been on his way back to Dorchester if Erin had been home. Maybe when he brought Erin back and Bill realized how happy they were together, he would give him his job back. He was a good detective and Bill needed him.

As he drank, the throbbing in his temples began to recede, but he started to see two of everything when he knew there should be only one. He needed to keep his mind sharp, but the pain and the heat were making him sick and he didn't know what to do.

He started the car and turned onto the main road, heading back to downtown Southport. Many streets were closed off and he made countless detours before he found a spot to park. No shade for miles, just sun and endless, stifling heat. He felt like he might vomit.

He thought about Erin and where she might be. Ivan's? At the carnival? He should have called to ask whether she was working today, should have stopped at a hotel last night. No reason to rush, because she wasn't at home, but he hadn't known that then, and it made him angry to think she was probably laughing about that, too. Laughing and laughing at poor Kevin Tierney while she cheated on him with another man.

He changed his shirt and tucked the gun into the waistband of his jeans and started toward the waterfront. He knew that's where he'd find Ivan's, because he'd searched for the location on the computer. He knew he was taking a risk if he went there and he turned around twice, but he had to find her, had to make sure she was still real.

He'd been in her house and inhaled her scent but it wasn't enough.

Crowds of people were everywhere. The streets reminded him of a county fair, without the pigs and horses and cows. He bought a hot dog and tried to eat it, but his stomach rebelled and he threw most of it away. Weaving among the people, he spotted the waterfront in the distance, and then Ivan's. His progress through the throngs was excruciatingly slow. His mouth was dry by the time he reached the door of the restaurant.

Ivan's was packed, people waiting outside the entrance for tables. He should have brought a hat and sunglasses, but he hadn't been thinking. He knew she would recognize him instantly, but he worked his way to the door anyway and stepped inside.

He spotted a waitress, but she wasn't Erin. Saw another, but she wasn't Erin, either. The hostess was young and harried and trying to figure out where to put the next group of customers. It was loud—people talking, forks clanking against plates, glasses sloshing in the bus tubs. Loud and confusing and the damn pounding in his head wouldn't go away. His stomach burned.

"Is Erin working today?" he called out to the hostess, raising his voice above the noise.

She blinked at him in confusion. "Who?"

"Katie," he said. "I meant Katie. Katie Feldman."

"No," the hostess shouted back. "She's off. She's working tomorrow, though." She nodded toward the windows. "She's probably out there somewhere, along with everyone else. I thought I saw her walk past here earlier."

Kevin turned and left, bumping into people as he went. Ignoring it. Outside, he paused at a sidewalk vendor. He bought a baseball hat and a pair of inexpensive sunglasses. And then he began to walk.

The Ferris wheel went round and round, Alex and Josh in one seat and Kristen and Katie in another, hot wind in their faces. Katie had her arm draped over Kristen's shoulders, knowing that despite Kristen's smile, she was nervous about the height. As the seat rotated to its peak, unveiling a panorama of the town, Katie realized that while she wasn't exactly thrilled with the height, either, she was more concerned with the Ferris wheel itself. The thing looked like it was held together with bobby pins and chicken wire, even if it had supposedly passed inspection earlier that morning.

She wondered if Alex had been telling the truth about the inspection, or if he'd heard her saying aloud whether it might be dangerous. It was too late to worry about it now, she supposed, so instead she occupied herself by staring at the throngs of people below. The carnival had become even more crowded as the afternoon wore on, but aside from boating, there wasn't a lot to do in Southport. It was a sleepy little town, and she surmised that an event like this was probably the highlight of the year.

The Ferris wheel slowed and stopped, stranding them as the first of the passengers got out and others crawled on. It rotated a bit, and she found herself scrutinizing the crowd more closely. Kristen seemed more relaxed and was doing the same.

She recognized a couple of people eating snow cones as regulars at Ivan's, and she wondered how many others were out there. Her eyes began to travel from group to group, and for some reason she remembered that she used to do the same thing when she first started working at Ivan's. Back when she was watching for Kevin.

Kevin walked past the booths that lined either side of the street, just wandering and trying to think like Erin. He should have asked the hostess if she'd seen Erin with a man because he knew she wouldn't be at the carnival alone. It was hard to keep reminding himself that she might have short brown hair because she'd cut and dyed it. He should have had the pedophile at the other precinct get a copy of the driver's license photo, but he hadn't been thinking at the time, and it didn't matter now because he knew where she lived and he would go back.

He could feel the gun in his waistband, pressing against his skin. It felt uncomfortable, pinching his flesh, and it was hot under the ball hat, especially since it was pulled low and tight. His head felt like it would explode.

He moved around groups of people, lines that formed. Arts and crafts. Decorated pinecones, stained glass in frames, wind chimes. Old-fashioned toys carved from wood. People were stuffing their faces with food: pretzels and ice cream, nachos, cinnamon rolls. He saw babies in strollers and remembered again that Erin wanted to have a baby. He decided he would give her one. A girl or a boy, it didn't matter, but he preferred a boy because girls were selfish and wouldn't appreciate the life he gave them. Girls were like that.

People talked and whispered all around him and he thought some of them were staring at him, like Coffey and Ramirez used to do. He ignored them, focused on his search. Families. Teens with their arms around one another. A guy in a sombrero. A couple of the carnival

workers stood near a streetlight, smoking. Thin and tat-
tooed, with bad teeth. Probably drug users, with long
records. They gave him a bad feeling. He was a good
detective and knew how to read people and he didn't trust
them but they did nothing as he brushed past them.

He veered left and right, working his way steadily
through the crowd, studying people's faces. He paused
while an overweight couple waddled past him, eating
corn dogs, their faces red and blotchy. He hated fat people, thought they were weak and had no discipline, people
who complained about their blood pressure and diabetes
and heart problems and whined about the cost of medicine, but couldn't summon the strength to put the fork
down. Erin was always thin but her breasts were big and
now she was here with another man who fondled them at
night and the thought made him burn inside. He hated her.
But he wanted her, too. Loved her. It was hard to keep it
straight in his head. He'd been drinking too much and it
was just so damn hot. Why had she moved to a place as
hellish as this?

He wandered among the carnival rides and noticed the
Ferris wheel up ahead. He moved closer, bumping into
a man in a tank top, ignoring his muttered outrage. He
checked the seats on the ride, his gaze flashing on every
face. Erin wasn't there, or in the line, either.

He moved on, walking in the heat among the fat people, looking for skinny Erin and the man who touched
her breasts at night. With every step, he thought about the
Glock.

The swings, spinning clockwise, were a big hit with the
kids. They'd ridden them twice in the morning, and after

the Ferris wheel Kristen and Josh begged to ride them once more. There were only a few tickets left and Alex agreed, explaining that after this last ride they would have to go home. He wanted to have time to shower and eat and maybe relax before he had to drive to Raleigh.

Despite his best efforts, he couldn't stop thinking about Katie's earlier suggestive remark. She seemed to sense the direction of his thoughts, because he'd caught her staring at him a number of times, a provocative smile playing at the corner of her lips.

Now she stood beside him, smiling up at the kids. He scooted closer, slipping his arm around her, and felt her lean into him. He said nothing, for there was no need for words, and she said nothing, either. Instead, she tilted her head, resting it against his shoulder, and Alex was struck by the notion that there was nothing better in the world.

Erin wasn't at the tilt-a-whirl or the maze of mirrors or the haunted house. He watched from the ticket line, trying to blend in, wanting to see her before she spotted him. He had the advantage because he knew she was here and she didn't know about him, but sometimes people got lucky and strange things happened. He flashed on the memory of Karen Feldman and the day she revealed Erin's secret.

He wished he hadn't left his vodka in the car. There didn't seem to be anywhere to buy more, not a bar in sight. He hadn't even seen a booth selling beer, which he didn't like but would have bought if he had no other choice. The smell of food made him nauseated and hungry at the same time and he could feel the sweat plastering his shirt to his back and armpits.

He walked by the games of chance, run by con artists.

Waste of money because the games were rigged, but morons packed around them. He searched faces. No Erin.

He wandered toward the other rides. There were kids in bumper cars, people fidgeting in the line. Beyond that were the swings, and he started in that direction. He circumvented a cluster of people, straining for a better view.

The swings had begun to slow, but Kristen and Josh were still grinning with excitement. Alex was right about needing to call it a day; the heat had drained Katie and it would be nice to be able to cool off for a while. If there was one bad thing about the cottage—well, there was actually more than one bad thing, she supposed—it was that it didn't have air-conditioning. She'd gotten used to keeping the windows open at night, but it didn't help much.

The ride came to a stop and Josh unhooked the chain and jumped down. It took Kristen a little longer before she could manage it, but a moment later, the two children were scrambling back toward Katie and their dad.

Kevin saw the swings come to a stop and a bunch of kids jump down from their seats, but that wasn't where he focused his attention. Instead, he concentrated on the adults who were crowding the perimeter of the ride.

He kept walking, his eyes moving from one woman to the next. Blond or brunette, it didn't matter. He watched for Erin's lean figure. From his angle, he couldn't see the faces of the people directly in front of him, so he changed directions. In a few seconds, once the kids reached the exit, everyone would scatter again.

He walked quickly. A family stood in front of him, holding tickets, debating where to go next, arguing in confusion. Idiots. He skirted them, straining to see faces near the swings.

No skinny women, except for one. A short-haired brunette, standing next to a man with gray hair, his arm around her waist.

She was unmistakable. Same long legs, same face, same sinewy arms.

Erin.

36

———— ❧ ————

Alex and Katie held hands as they walked toward Ivan's with the kids. They'd stored their bicycles near the back door, Katie's regular spot. On the way out, Alex bought some water for Josh and Kristen before they started toward home.

"Good day, guys?" Alex asked, bending over to unlock the bikes.

"Great day, Daddy," Kristen answered, her face red with the heat.

Josh wiped his mouth on his arm. "Can we come back tomorrow?"

"Maybe," Alex fudged.

"Please? I want to ride the swing again."

Finished with the locks, Alex slung the chains over his shoulder. "We'll see," he said.

An overhang in the back of the restaurant provided some shade, but it was still warm. After seeing how crowded it had been as she'd walked past the windows, Katie was glad she'd taken the day off, even if she had to work a double shift tomorrow and Monday. It was worth it. It had been a good day, and she'd get to relax and watch a movie with the kids while Alex was away tonight. And then later, when he got back...

"What?" Alex said.

"Nothing."

"You were staring at me like you were going to eat me up."

"Just drifting off there for a second," she said with a wink. "I think the heat kind of got to me."

"Uh-huh." He nodded. "If I didn't know better..."

"I'd like to remind you that there are some young ears tuning in right now, so I'd watch what you say." She kissed him before patting him lightly on the chest.

Neither of them noticed the man in the baseball hat and sunglasses watching them from the deck of the neighboring restaurant.

Kevin felt dizzy as he watched Erin and the gray-haired man kiss, seeing the way Erin flirted with him. He saw her lean down and smile at the little girl. Watched as he tousled the hair of the little boy. Noticed the gray-haired man pat her on her butt when the children's attention was elsewhere. And Erin—his wife—was playing along. Liking it. Encouraging it. Cheating on him with her new family, as if Kevin and their marriage had never existed at all.

They got on their bikes and started pedaling, heading around the side of the building, away from Kevin. Erin rode beside the gray-haired man. She was wearing shorts and sandals, showing skin, looking sexy for someone else.

Kevin followed them. Her hair was blond and long and

flowing... but then he blinked, and it was short and brown again. Pretending she wasn't Erin and riding bikes with her new family and kissing another man and smiling and smiling, without a care in the world. It wasn't real, he told himself. It was nothing but a dream. A nightmare. Docked boats wobbled in their slips as they passed.

He rounded the corner. They were riding and he was on foot, but they were moving slowly to allow the little girl to keep up. He was closing the distance and he was near enough to hear Erin laugh, sounding happy. He reached for the Glock in his waistband and pulled it out, then slid it beneath his shirt, keeping it pressed against his skin. He took off the baseball hat and used it to hide the gun from the people around him.

His thoughts ricocheted like pachinko balls, bouncing fast, left and right, downward, downward. Erin lying and cheating and plotting and scheming. Running away to find a lover. Talking and laughing behind his back. Whispering to the gray-haired man, saying dirty things, the man's hands on her breasts, her breaths coming hard. Pretending she wasn't married, ignoring all he'd done for her and the sacrifices he'd made and that he had to scrape the blood from his shoes and that Coffey and Ramirez were always gossiping about him and there were flies buzzing on the burgers because she'd run away and he'd had to go to the barbecue alone and she couldn't tell Bill the captain that he wasn't just one of the guys.

And there she was, pedaling easily, her hair short and dyed, as pretty as ever, never thinking about her husband at all. Never caring about him. Forgetting him and the marriage so she could have a life with the gray-haired man and pat his chest and kiss him with a dreamy expression on her face. Happy and serene, without a concern in the world. Going to carnivals, riding bikes. She probably sang to herself in the shower while he'd been crying and remembering the perfume he'd bought her for Christmas, and none of it mattered because she was selfish and thought she could throw a marriage away, like an empty pizza box.

He unconsciously picked up his pace. The crowds were slowing them down, and he knew that he could raise the gun and kill her right now. His finger moved to the trigger and he slipped the safety off because the Bible says *Let marriage be held in honor among all, and let the bed be undefiled*, but he realized that it meant he had to kill the gray-haired man as well. He could kill him in front of her. All he had to do was pull the trigger, but then hitting moving targets from a distance was almost impossible with a Glock, and there were people everywhere. They would see the gun and scream and shout and the shot was almost impossible, so he removed his finger from the trigger.

"Quit veering toward your sister!" the gray-haired man said, up ahead, his voice almost lost in the distance. But his words were real and Kevin imagined the dirty things he whispered to Erin. He could feel the rage building inside him. Then, all at once, the kids turned the corner and they were followed by Erin and the gray-haired man.

Kevin stopped, panting and feeling ill. As she'd rounded the corner, her profile had flashed in the bright light and he thought again that she was beautiful. She'd always reminded him of a delicate flower, so pretty and refined, and he remembered that he'd saved her from being raped by thugs after she left the casino and how she used to tell him that he made her feel safe but even that hadn't been enough to keep her from leaving him.

Gradually, he began to hear the voices of people walking on either side of him as they passed by. Chattering about nothing, going nowhere, but it jolted him into action. He started to jog, trying to reach the spot where they'd turned, feeling like he was going to vomit with every footfall under the blazing sun. His palm felt slick and sweaty around the gun. He reached the corner and peered up the street.

No one in sight, but two blocks up, there were barricades blocking the road for the street fair. They must have turned on the street before it. No other choice. He figured they had turned right, the only way to leave the downtown area.

He had a choice. Chase them on foot and risk being spotted or run back to the car and try to follow them that way. He tried to think like Erin and figured they would go to the house where the gray-haired man lived. Erin's house was too small, too hot for the four of them, and Erin would want to go to a pretty house with expensive furniture, because she believed she deserved a life like that, instead of appreciating the life she had.

Pick and choose. Follow on foot or in the car. He stood, blinking and trying to think, but it was hot and confusing and his head pounded and all he could think was that Erin was sleeping with a gray-haired man and the realization made him sick to his stomach.

She probably dressed in lace and danced for him, whispered words that made him hot. Begged him to let her please him, so she could live in his house with fancy things. She'd become a prostitute, selling her soul for luxuries. Selling herself for pearls and caviar. Probably slept in a mansion now, after the gray-haired man took her out for fancy dinners.

He felt sick, imagining it. Hurt and betrayed. The fury helped his thoughts clear and he realized that he was standing in place as they were getting farther and farther away. His car was blocks away, but he turned and started to run. At the carnival, he pushed through people wildly, ignoring their shouts and protests. "Move, move!" he shouted, and some people moved and others were shoved aside. He reached a spot clear of the throngs of people, but he was breathing hard and he had to stop to vomit near a fire hydrant. A couple of teenage boys laughed at him and he felt like shooting them right then and there, but after wiping his mouth, he simply pulled the gun and pointed it at them and they shut up fast enough.

He stumbled forward, feeling the ice pick chip away at his head. Stab and pain, stab and pain. Every damn step it was stab and pain and Erin was probably telling the gray-haired man about the sexy things they would do in bed. Telling the gray-haired man about Kevin and laughing, whispering, *Kevin could never please me the way you do*, even though it wasn't true.

It took forever to get to his car. When he reached it, the sun was baking it like a loaf of bread. Heat spilled out in clouds, and the steering wheel was scalding to the touch. Hellhole. Erin had chosen to live in a hellhole. He started the car and opened the windows, making a U-turn back toward the carnival and honking at people in the street.

Detours again. Barricades. He wanted to blow through them, to blast them into pieces, but even here, there were cops and they would arrest him. Stupid cops, fat and lazy cops. Barney Fife cops. Idiots. None of them were good detectives but they had guns and badges. Kevin drove the side streets, trying to zero in on where Erin was heading.

Erin and her lover. Both of them adulterers, and the Bible says *Whoever gazes at a woman with lust has committed adultery in his heart.*

People everywhere. Crossing the street haphazardly. Making him stop. He leaned over the steering wheel, straining to see through the windshield, and caught sight of them, tiny figures in the distance. They were just beyond another barricade, heading toward the road that led to her house. A cop was standing at the corner, another Barney Fife.

He surged forward, only to be stopped when a man suddenly appeared at the front of his car, banging on the hood. A redneck with a mullet, skulls on his shirt, tattoos. Fat wife and greasy-looking kids. Losers, all of them.

"Watch where you're going!" the redneck shouted.

Kevin mentally shot all of them, *bang-bang-bang-bang*, but forced himself not to react because the cop at the corner was eyeballing him. *Bang*, Kevin thought again.

He turned, speeding up, heading through the neighborhood. Turned left and sped up again. Turned left again. More barricades up ahead. Kevin made another U-turn, went right, and turned left at the next block.

More barricades. He was stuck in a maze, like a rodent undergoing an experiment. The town conspiring against him while Erin got away. He slammed the car into reverse and backed up. He found the road again and turned, then raced straight to the next intersection. It had to be close now and he turned left again, saw a line of traffic ahead, moving in the direction he wanted. He turned, muscling his car between a couple of trucks.

He wanted to accelerate but couldn't. Cars and trucks

stretched before him, some with Confederate flags on the bumper stickers, others with gun racks on the roof. Rednecks. People in the road made it impossible for the cars to move forward, walking as if they weren't aware that any of the cars existed. People sauntered past, moving faster than he was. Fat people, still eating. Probably eating all day long and slowing the traffic while Erin got farther and farther away.

His car went forward one length and stopped again. Went forward and stopped. Over and over. He felt like screaming, wanted to pound the wheel, but people were everywhere. If he wasn't careful someone would say something and Barney Fife would investigate and remember his out-of-state plates and probably arrest him on the spot, simply because he wasn't a local.

Forward and stopping, over and over, movement measured in inches until he reached the corner. The traffic had to ease up now, he thought, but it didn't, and up ahead, Erin and the gray-haired man were gone. There was only a long line of cars and trucks ahead of him on a road that led nowhere and everywhere at exactly the same time.

37

―❦―

A dozen cars were parked in front of the store as Katie trailed the kids up the stairs to the house. Josh and Kristen had whined most of the ride home about how tired their legs were, but Alex ignored it, reminding them periodically that they were getting closer. When that didn't work, he simply commented that he was getting tired, too, and didn't want to hear any more about it.

The complaining ended when they got to the store. Alex let them grab Popsicles and Gatorade before they went upstairs, and the burst of cool air as they opened the door was ridiculously refreshing. Alex led Katie to the kitchen and she watched as he drenched his face and neck at the kitchen sink. In the living room, the kids were already sprawled on the couch, the television on.

"Sorry," he said. "I thought I was about to die about ten minutes ago."

"You didn't say anything."

"That's because I'm tough," he said, pretending to puff out his chest. He retrieved two glasses from the cupboard and added ice cubes before pouring water from a pitcher he kept in the refrigerator.

"You're a trouper," he added, handing her a glass. "It's like a sauna out there."

"I can't believe how many people are still at the carnival," she said, taking a drink.

"I've always wondered why they don't move up the date to either May or October, but then again, the crowds seem to come no matter what."

She glanced at the clock on the wall. "What time do you have to leave?"

"In an hour or so. But I should be back before eleven."

Five hours, she thought. "Do you want me to make the kids anything special for dinner?"

"They like pasta. Kristen likes hers with butter, Josh likes his with marinara, and I've got a bottle of that in the refrigerator. They've been snacking all day, though, so they might not eat much."

"What time do they go to bed?"

"Whenever. It's always before ten, but sometimes it's as early as eight. You'll have to use your best judgment."

She held the cool glass of water against her cheek and glanced around the kitchen. She hadn't spent much time in their home, and now that she was here she noticed remnants of a woman's touch. Little things—red stitching on the curtains, china prominently displayed in a cabinet, Bible verses on painted ceramic tiles near the stove. The house was filled with evidence of his life with another woman, but to her surprise, it didn't bother her.

"I'm going to go hop into the shower," Alex said. "Will you be okay for a few minutes?"

"Of course," she said. "I can snoop around your kitchen and think about dinner."

"The pasta's in the cupboard over there," he said, pointing. "But listen, when I get out, if you want me to drive you over to your place so you can shower and change, I'd be glad to do it. Or you can shower here. Whatever you want."

She struck a sultry pose. "Is that an invitation?"

His eyes widened and then flashed to the kids.

"I was kidding." She laughed. "I'll shower after you're gone."

"Do you want to pick up a change of clothes first? If not, you can borrow sweats and a T-shirt...the sweats will be too big for you, but you can adjust the drawstring."

Somehow the idea of wearing his clothes sounded extremely sexy to her. "That's fine," she assured him. "I'm not picky. I'm just watching movies with the kids, remember?"

Alex drained his glass before putting it in the sink. He leaned forward and kissed her, then headed toward the bedroom.

Once he was gone, Katie turned toward the kitchen window. She watched the road outside, feeling a nameless anxiety come over her. She'd felt the same way earlier in the morning and assumed it was an aftershock of the argument she'd had with Alex, but now she found herself thinking of the Feldmans again. And about Kevin.

She'd thought of him when she was on the Ferris wheel. As she'd scanned the crowd, she knew she hadn't been searching for people from the restaurant. Not really. She'd been looking for Kevin. Believing for some inexplicable reason that he might be in the crowd. Thinking he was there.

But that was just her paranoia surfacing again. There

was no way he could know where she was, no way to know her identity. It was impossible, she reminded herself. He never would have connected her to the Feldmans' daughter; he never even spoke to them. But why, then, had she felt all day like someone was following her, even as they left the carnival?

She wasn't psychic and didn't believe in such things. But she did believe in the power of the subconscious mind to put together pieces that the conscious mind might miss. Standing in Alex's kitchen, however, the pieces were still scrambled, without shape or order of any kind, and after watching a dozen cars pass by on the road out front, she finally turned away. It was probably just her old fears raising their ugly head again.

She shook her head and thought of Alex in the shower. The thought of joining him made her flush hot with anticipation. And yet...it wasn't quite that simple, even if the kids hadn't been around. Even if Alex thought of her as Katie, Erin was still married to Kevin. She wished that she were another woman, a woman who could simply move into her lover's arms without hesitation. After all, it was Kevin who had broken all the rules of marriage when he first raised his fists against her. When God looked into her heart, she was pretty sure that He would agree that what she was doing wasn't a sin. Wouldn't He?

She sighed. Alex...he was all she could think about. *Later* was all she could think about. He loved her and wanted her and she wanted, more than anything, to show him that she felt the same way. She wanted to feel his body against hers, wanted all of him for as long as he wanted her. Forever.

Katie forced herself to stop picturing herself with Alex,

to stop dreaming about what was to come. She shook her head to clear it and went to the living room, where she took a seat on the couch next to Josh. They were watching a Disney Channel television show she didn't recognize. After a while she looked up at the clock, and noticed that only ten minutes had gone by. It felt like an hour.

Once he finished with his shower, Alex made a sandwich and sat beside her on the couch as he ate. He smelled clean and his hair was still wet at the ends, clinging to his skin in a way that made her want to trace the line of dampness with her lips. The kids, glued to the screen, ignored them, even after he put the plate on the end table and began to run his finger slowly up and down her thigh.

"You look beautiful," he whispered into her ear.

"I look terrible," she countered, trying to ignore the line of fire burning its way up her thigh. "I haven't showered yet."

When it was time for him to leave, he kissed the kids in the living room. She followed him to the door and when he kissed her good-bye, he let his hand wander lower, past her waist, his lips soft against hers. Obviously in love with her, obviously wanting her, making sure she knew it. He was driving her crazy, and he seemed to be enjoying it.

"See you in a bit," he said, pulling back.

"Drive safely," she whispered. "The kids will be fine."

When she heard his footsteps descending the steps outside, she leaned against the door for a long, slow breath. Good Lord, she thought. Good Lord. Vows or not, guilt or not, she decided that even if *he* wasn't in the mood, she definitely was.

She peeked up at the clock again, certain that this would be the longest five hours of her life.

38

Damn!" Kevin kept saying. "Damn!" He'd been driving for hours. He'd stopped to buy four bottles of vodka at the ABC store. One of them was half gone, and as he drove he saw two of everything unless he squinted, keeping one eye closed.

He was searching for bicycles. Four of them, including one with baskets. He might as well have been looking for a specific piece of plankton in the ocean. Up one road and down the next, as the afternoon wound down and dusk settled in. He looked from left to right and back again. He knew where she lived, knew he would eventually find her at home. But in the meantime the gray-haired man was out there with Erin, laughing at him, saying, *I'm so much better than Kevin, baby.*

He screamed curses in the car, pounding on the steering wheel. He flipped the safety on the Glock from the off to the on position and back again, imagining Erin kissing him, his arm around her waist. Remembering how happy she'd looked, thinking she had tricked her husband.

Cheated on him. Moaned and murmured beneath her lover while he panted atop her.

He could barely see, fighting the blurriness with one eye. A car came up behind him on the neighborhood streets, tailgating for a while, then flashing his lights. Kevin slowed the car and pulled over, fingering the gun. He hated rude people, people who thought they owned the road. *Bang.*

Dusk turned the streets into shadowy mazes, making it difficult to see the spindly outlines of bicycles. When he drove past the gravel road for the second time, he decided on impulse to turn around and visit her house again, just in case. He stopped just out of sight of the cottage and got out. A hawk circled overhead, and he heard cicadas humming, but otherwise the place seemed deserted. He started toward the house but could see already from a distance that there was no bicycle parked out front. No lights on, either, but it wasn't dark yet, so he crept to the back door. Unlocked, just like before.

She wasn't home, and he didn't think she'd been home since he'd been here earlier. The house was sweltering, all the windows shut tight. She would have opened the windows, he felt sure, would have had a glass of water, might have taken a shower. Nothing. He left through the back door, staring at the neighboring house. A dump. Probably deserted. Good. But the fact that Erin wasn't home meant she was with the gray-haired man, had gone to his house. Cheating, pretending she wasn't married. Forgetting the home that Kevin had bought for her.

His head throbbed in time with his heartbeats, a knife going in and out. Stab. Stab. Stab. It was hard to focus as he pulled the door closed behind him. Mercy of all mercies, it was cooler outside. She lived in a sweatbox, sweated with a gray-haired man. They were sweating together now, somewhere, writhing in sheets, bodies intertwined. Coffey and Ramirez were laughing about that, slapping their thighs, having a good old time at his expense. *I wonder if I could do her, too*, Coffey was saying to Ramirez. *Don't you know?* Ramirez answered back. *She let half the precinct do her while Kevin was working. Everyone knows about it.* Bill waving from his office, holding suspension papers. *I did her, too, every Tuesday for a year. She's wild in bed. Says the dirtiest things.*

He stumbled back to his car, his finger on the gun. Bastards, all of them. Hated them, imagined walking into the precinct and unloading the Glock, emptying the clip, showing them. Showing all of them. Erin, too.

He stopped and bent over, vomiting onto the side of the road. Stomach cramping, a clawing in his gut like a rodent was trapped inside him. Puked again, and then dry heaves and the world spun when he tried to stand. The car was close and he staggered to it. Grabbed the vodka and drank and tried to think like Erin, but then he was at the barbecue holding a burger covered in flies and everyone was pointing and laughing at him.

Back to the car. Bitch had to be somewhere. She'd watch gray-hair die. Watch them all die. Burn in hell. Burn and burn, all of them. Carefully, he climbed in and started the car. He backed into a tree as he was trying to turn around, and then, cursing, tore out on the gravel, spinning rocks.

Night would soon be falling. She came in this direction, had to be down this way. Little kids couldn't ride far. Three or four miles, maybe five. He'd been down every road this way, looked at every house. No bicycles.

They could be in the garage, could be parked in fenced yards. He'd wait and she'd come home sometime. Tonight. Tomorrow. Tomorrow night. He'd stick the gun in her mouth, aim it at her breasts. *Tell me who he is*, he'd say. *I just want to talk to him.* He'd find gray-hair and show him what happened to men who slept with other men's wives.

He felt like he had been weeks without sleep, weeks without food. He couldn't understand why it was dark and he wondered when that happened. Couldn't remember when he got here exactly. He remembered seeing Erin, remembered trying to follow her and driving, but wasn't even sure where he was.

A store loomed on the right, looking like a house with a porch out front. GAS FOOD, the sign said. He remembered that from earlier, but how long ago he couldn't say. He slowed the car involuntarily. He needed food, needed to sleep. Had to find a place to stay the night. His stomach lurched. He grabbed the bottle and tilted the bottom up, feeling the burn in his throat, soothing him. But as soon as he lowered the bottle, his stomach heaved again.

He pulled into the lot, fighting to keep the liquor down, his mouth watering. Running out of time. He skidded to a stop alongside the store and jumped out. Ran to the front of his car and heaved into the darkness. His body shivered, his legs wobbled. His stomach coming up. His liver. All of it. Somehow, he was still holding the bottle, hadn't put it down. He breathed hard in and out and drank, using it to rinse his mouth, swallowing it. Finishing another bottle.

And there, like an image from a dream, in the darkened shadows behind the house, he saw four bicycles parked side by side.

39

Katie had the kids take a bath before getting them into their pajamas. Afterward, she showered, lingering under the spray and enjoying the luxurious feeling of shampoo and soap rinsing the salt from her body after a day in the sun.

She made the kids their pasta, and after dinner they sorted through the collection of DVDs, trying to find one that both kids wanted to watch, until they finally agreed on *Finding Nemo*. She sat between Josh and Kristen on the couch, a bowl of popcorn in her lap, their little hands reaching in automatically from either direction. She wore a comfy pair of sweats that Alex had laid out and a worn Carolina Panthers jersey, tucking her legs up under her as they watched the movie, utterly at ease for the first time that day.

Outside, the heavens bloomed like fireworks, displaying vibrant rainbow colors that faded to pastel washes before finally giving way to bluish-gray and then indigo skies. Stars began to flicker as the last shimmering waves of heat rose from the earth.

Kristen had begun to yawn as the movie progressed,

but every time Dory appeared on-screen, she managed to chirp, "She's my favorite, but I can't remember why!" On the other side of her, Josh was struggling to stay awake.

When the movie ended and Katie leaned forward to turn it off, Josh raised his head and let it fall to the couch. He was too big for her to carry, so she nudged his shoulder, telling him it was time for bed. He grunted and whined before sitting up. He yawned and rose to his feet and, with Katie by his side, staggered to the bedroom. He crawled into bed without complaint and she kissed him good night. Unsure whether he needed a night-light, she kept the light in the hallway on but closed the door partway.

Kristen was next. She asked Katie to lie beside her for a few minutes, and Katie did, staring at the ceiling, feeling the heat of the day beginning to take its toll. Kristen fell asleep within minutes, and Katie had to force herself to stay awake before tiptoeing out of the room.

Afterward, she cleaned up the remnants of their dinner and emptied the bowl of popcorn. As she glanced around the living room, she noticed evidence of the kids everywhere: a stack of puzzles on a bookshelf, a basket of toys in the corner, comfortable leather couches that were gloriously spill-proof. She studied the knickknacks scattered about: an old-fashioned clock that had to be wound daily, an ancient set of encyclopedias on a shelf near the recliner, a crystal vase on the table near the windowsill. On the walls hung framed black-and-white architectural photographs of decaying tobacco barns. They were quintessentially Southern, and she remembered seeing many of these rustic scenes on her journey through North Carolina.

There were also signs of the chaotic life Alex led: a red stain on the runner in front of the couch, gouges in the wood floor, dust on the baseboards. But as she surveyed the house, she couldn't help smiling, because those things, too, seemed to reflect who Alex was. He was a widowed father, doing his best to raise two kids and keep a tidy, if imperfect, house. The house was a snapshot of his life, and she liked its easy, comfortable feel.

She turned out the lights and collapsed on the couch. She picked up the remote and surfed TV channels, trying to find something interesting but not too demanding. It was coming up on ten o'clock, she noted. An hour to go. She lay back on the couch and started watching a show on the Discovery Channel, something about volcanoes. She noticed a glare on the screen and stretched to turn off the lamp on the end table, darkening the room. She leaned back again. Better.

She watched for a few minutes, barely aware that every time she blinked, her eyes stayed closed a fraction longer. Her breath slowed and she began to melt into the cushions. Images began to float through her mind, disjointed at first, thoughts of the carnival rides, the view from the Ferris wheel. People standing in random clusters, young and old, teens and couples. Families. And somewhere in the distance, a man in a baseball hat and sunglasses, weaving among the crowd, moving with purpose before she lost sight of him again. Something she'd recognized: the walk, the jut of his jaw, the way he swung his arms.

She was drifting now, relaxing and remembering, the images beginning to blur, the sound of the television fading. The room growing darker, quieter. She drifted further, her mind flashing back again and again to the view from the Ferris wheel. And, of course, to the man she'd seen, a man who'd been moving like a hunter through the brush, in search of game.

40

Kevin stared up at the windows, nursing his half-empty bottle of vodka, his third of the night. No one gave him a second glance. He was standing on the dock at the rear of the house; he'd changed into a black long-sleeved shirt and dark jeans. Only his face was visible, but he stood in the shade of a cypress tree, hidden behind the trunk. Watching the windows. Watching the lights, watching for Erin.

Nothing happened for a long while. He drank, working on finishing the bottle. People came through the store every few minutes, often using their credit cards to buy gas at the pump. Busy, busy, even out here, in the middle of nowhere. He moved around to the side of the store, gazing up at the windows. He recognized the flickering blue glow of a television. The four of them, watching TV, acting like a happy family. Or maybe the kids were already in bed, tired from the carnival, tired from the bike ride. Maybe it was just Erin and the gray-haired man snuggling on the couch, kissing and touching each other while Meg Ryan or Julia Roberts fell in love on the screen.

Everything hurt and he was tired and his stomach kept churning. He could have walked up the stairs and kicked the door in, could have killed them half a dozen times already, and he wanted to get it over with, but there were people in the store. Cars in the lot. He'd pushed his own car forward with the engine off to a spot beneath a tree at the rear of the store, out of sight from passing cars. He wanted to aim the Glock and pull the trigger, wanted to watch them die, but he also wanted to lie down and go to sleep because he'd never been more tired in his life and when he woke up he wanted to find Erin beside him and think to himself that she had never left him.

Later, he spotted her profile at the window, saw her smiling as she turned away and knew she was thinking about the gray-haired man. Thinking about sex, and the Bible says *Those who gave themselves over to fornication and strange flesh are set forth for an example and suffering the vengeance of eternal fire.*

He was an angel of the Lord. Erin had sinned and the Bible says *She shall be tormented with fire and brimstone in the presence of holy angels.*

In the Bible there was always fire because it purified and condemned, and he understood that. Fire was powerful, the weapon of angels. He finished the bottle of vodka and kicked it under the bushes. A car pulled up to the gasoline pumps and a man stepped out. He slid his credit card in and began to pump gas. The sign near the pump informed people it was illegal to smoke, because gasoline was flammable. Inside the store, there was lighter fluid for use with charcoal. He remembered the man in line ahead of him earlier, holding a can of it.

Fire.

*   *   *

Alex shifted and adjusted his hands on the wheel, trying to get comfortable. Joyce and her daughter were in the backseat and hadn't stopped talking from the moment they'd gotten in the car.

The clock on the dashboard showed it was getting late. The kids were either in bed or soon would be, which sounded good right now. On the drive back, he'd had a bottle of water, but he was still thirsty and debated whether to stop again. He was sure that neither Joyce nor her daughter would mind, but he didn't want to stop. He just wanted to get home.

As he drove, he felt his mind drifting. He thought about Josh and Kristen, about Katie, and he sifted through memories of Carly. He tried to imagine what Carly would say about Katie and whether Carly would have wanted him to give the letter to her. He remembered the day he'd seen Katie helping Kristen with her doll, and recalled how beautiful she had looked on the night she'd made him dinner. The knowledge that she was at his house waiting for him made him want to floor the accelerator.

On the other side of the highway, distant pinpricks of light appeared at the horizon, slowly separating and growing larger, forming headlamps of oncoming cars. They grew brighter until they flashed past. In the rearview mirror, red lights receded into the distance.

Heat lightning crackled to the south, making the sky blink like a slide show. Off to the right was a farmhouse, lights on downstairs. He passed a truck with Virginia plates and rolled his shoulders, trying to shake off the fatigue he felt. He passed the sign indicating the number of miles to Wilmington and sighed. He still had a ways to go.

*   *   *

Katie's eyelids fluttered as she dreamed, her subconscious working overtime. Bits and pieces, fragments, trying to connect with each other.

The dream ended, and a few minutes later she tucked her knees up and shifted onto her side, almost waking. Her breathing began to slow again.

At ten o'clock the lot was nearly empty. It was just before closing time, and Kevin walked around to the front of the store, squinting at the light coming through the front door. He pushed the door open and heard a bell jingle. At the register was a man in an apron. Kevin vaguely recognized him, but couldn't place him. He was wearing a white apron, the name ROGER stenciled on the right.

Kevin walked past the register, trying not to slur his words. "I ran out of gas up the road."

"Gas cans are along the far wall," Roger answered without looking up. When he finally did, he blinked. "You okay?"

"Just tired," Kevin said from the aisle, trying not to draw attention to himself but knowing the man was watching. The Glock was in his waistband and all Roger had to do was mind his own business. At the far wall, Kevin saw three five-gallon plastic cans and reached for two of them. He brought them to the register and put money on the counter.

"I'll pay after I fill 'em," he said.

Outside, he pumped the gas into the can, watching the numbers roll past. He filled the second and went back inside. Roger was staring at him, hesitating to make change.

"That's a lot of gas to carry."

"Erin needs it."

"Who's Erin?"

Kevin blinked. "Can I buy the damn gas or not?"

"You sure you're okay to drive?"

"I've been sick," Kevin muttered. "Puking all day."

He wasn't sure whether Roger believed him, but after a moment, Roger took the money and made change. Kevin had left the cans near the gas pumps and went to pick them up. It was like lifting cans of lead. He strained, his stomach churning, pulsating pain between his ears. He started up the road, leaving behind the lights of the store.

In the darkness, he set the cans down in the tall grass just off the road. After that, he circled back behind the store. Waiting for Roger to close up, waiting for the lights to go out. Waiting for everyone to fall asleep upstairs. He retrieved another bottle of vodka from the car and took a sip.

In Wilmington, Alex began to perk up, knowing he was getting close. It wouldn't be long now, maybe half an hour before he reached Southport. It would take another few minutes to drop off Joyce and her daughter, but then he would be home.

He wondered if he would find Katie waiting up for him in the living room or whether, as she'd teased, he would find her in his bed.

It was the kind of thing that Carly used to say. They might have been talking about the business or whether her parents were enjoying Florida, when out of the blue, she'd announce that she was bored and ask him whether he wanted to go to the bedroom and fool around.

He stared at the clock. A quarter after ten and Katie was waiting. On the side of the road, Alex saw half a dozen deer frozen on the grass, their eyes reflecting the headlights, glowing like something unnatural. Haunted.

Kevin watched the fluorescent lights above the gas pumps flicker off. Lights in the store went out next. From his hidden vantage point, he watched Roger locking the door. He tugged on it, making sure it was secure, before turning away. He walked to a brown pickup truck parked on the far side of the gravel lot and got in.

The engine started with a whine and squeak. A loose fan belt. Roger revved the engine, turned on the headlights, then put the truck in gear. He turned onto the main road, heading toward downtown.

Kevin waited five minutes, making sure Roger wouldn't turn around and come back. The road in front of the store was quiet now, no cars or trucks coming from either direction. He jogged over to the bushes, where he'd hidden the cans. Checked the road again, and then carried one of them to the back of the store. He did the same with the second can, setting them next to a couple of metal garbage cans filled with rotting food. The stench was overwhelming.

Upstairs, the TV continued to bathe one of the windows in blue light. There were no other lights and he knew they were naked. He felt the rage well up inside him. Now, he thought. It was time. When he reached for the gas cans, he saw four of them. He closed one eye and it was back to two. He stumbled as he took a step and jerked forward, off balance, swaying as he tried to grab the corner of the wall to keep from falling. He missed and fell, landing hard, his head hitting the gravel. Sparks and stars, shooting pains. It was hard to breathe. Tried to stand up and fell again. He rolled over onto his back, staring up at the stars.

He wasn't drunk because he never got drunk, but something was wrong. Twinkling lights were whirling round and round, caught in an accelerating tornado. He squeezed his eyes shut, but the spinning got worse. He rolled to his side and vomited onto the gravel. Someone must have slipped him drugs because he'd barely had anything to drink all day and he'd never been sick like this.

He reached out blindly for the garbage can. He grabbed the lid and tried to use it for balance, but he pulled too hard. The lid clattered off and a bag of garbage spilled out, making an unholy racket.

Upstairs, Katie flinched at the sound of something crashing. She was lost in her dream, and it took a moment for her eyes to flutter open. Groggy, she listened but wasn't sure why, wasn't sure whether she'd dreamed the sound or not. But there was nothing.

She leaned back, giving way to sleep again, and the dream picked up from where it left off. She was at the carnival, on the Ferris wheel, but it was no longer Kristen sitting beside her.

It was Jo.

Kevin was finally able to struggle to his feet and stay upright. He couldn't figure out what was happening to him, why he couldn't keep his balance. He concentrated on catching his breath, in and out, in and out. He spotted the cans of gas and stepped toward them, almost falling again.

But he didn't fall. He lifted a can, then staggered toward

the stairs at the back of the house. He reached out for the railing and missed it, then tried again. Got it. He lugged the can of gas up the stairs, toward the door, a Sherpa in the Himalayas. He finally reached the landing at the top, panting, and bent over to remove the cap. His head filled with blood, making him swoon, but he used the gas can to keep from falling. It took awhile before he could get the cap off because it kept slipping between his fingers.

Once open, he picked up the can and doused the landing, splashing its contents against the door. With every heave, the can got lighter, gas spilling out in arcs, drenching the wall. Getting easier now. He splashed left and right, trying to coat either side of the building. He started back down the stairs, splashing left and right. The fumes made him sick but he kept going.

There wasn't much gas left in the can when he reached the bottom and he rested at ground level. He was breathing hard and the fumes were making him feel sick again but he began moving again, with purpose now. Determination. He tossed the empty can aside and reached for the other. He couldn't douse the upper reaches of the walls, but he did what he could. He splashed one side and then circled around the back to the other side. Above him, the window still flickered with light from the television but all was quiet.

He drained the can on the other side of the building and had nothing left for the front. He scanned the road; no cars were coming from either direction. Upstairs, Erin and the gray-haired man were naked and laughing at him and Erin ran away and he almost found her in Philadelphia but back then she was calling herself Erica, not Erin, and now she pretended her name was Katie.

He stood in front of the store, thinking about the

windows. Maybe they were alarmed and maybe not. He
didn't care. He needed lighter fluid, motor oil, turpentine,
anything that would burn. But once he broke the window,
he wouldn't have much time.

He shattered the window with his elbow but heard no
alarm. Pulling out pieces of glass, he barely felt his fingers getting cut and beginning to bleed. More chunks, the
window coming apart in sections. He thought the opening
was big enough for him to climb inside, but his arm caught
on a jagged shard, deep. He pulled, tearing flesh. But he
couldn't stop now. Blood flowed from his arm, dripping
and mingling with the cuts on his fingers.

The coolers along the back wall were still illuminated
and he walked the aisles, wondering idly if Cheerios
would burn, if Twinkies would burn. DVDs. He located
the charcoal and the lighter fluid—only two cans, not
much. Not enough. He blinked, looking around for something else. He spotted the grill in the rear of the store.

Natural gas. Propane.

He approached the grill area, lifted the divider, and
stood facing the grill itself. He turned a burner on, then
another. There had to be a valve somewhere, but he didn't
know where to find it and he didn't have time because
someone might be coming and Coffey and Ramirez were
talking about him, laughing and asking whether he'd had
the crab cakes in Provincetown.

Roger's apron hung on a rack and he tossed it onto the
flame. He opened the can of lighter fluid he was holding
and sprayed it on the walls of the grill. The can was slippery with blood and he wondered where the blood had
come from. He hopped up onto the counter and squirted
some lighter fluid on the ceiling and got down again. He

ran a trail of fluid along the front of the store, noticing that the apron had begun to burn in earnest. He emptied the can and tossed it aside. Opening the second can, he squirted more fluid at the ceiling. The flames from the apron began leaping toward the walls and the ceiling. He went to the register and searched for a lighter and found a bunch of them in a plastic bin, near the cigarettes. He squirted lighter fluid on the register and on the little table behind him. The can was empty now, too, and he stumbled toward the window he'd broken earlier. He climbed out, stepping on broken glass, hearing it crack and pop. Standing by the side of the house, he flicked the lighter and held it against the gas-soaked wall, watching as the wood caught fire. At the back of the house, he touched the flame to the stairs and the flames rose quickly, shooting up to the door and spreading to the roof. Next came the far side.

Fire blossomed everywhere, the exterior rippling with flame, and Erin was a sinner and her lover was a sinner and the Bible says *They will suffer the punishment of eternal destruction.*

He stood back, watching the fire start to consume the building, wiping his face, leaving trails of blood. In the glowing orange light, he looked like a monster.

In her dream, Jo wasn't smiling as she sat beside Katie on the Ferris wheel. She seemed to be searching the crowd below, a frown of concentration on her face.

There, she said, pointing. *Over there. Do you see him?*

What are you doing here? Where's Kristen?

She's sleeping. But you have to remember, now.

Katie looked but there were so many people, so much movement. *Where?* she asked. *I don't see anything.*

He's here, Jo said.

Who?

You know.

In her dream, the Ferris wheel lurched to a stop. The sound was loud, like the shattering of glass, and it seemed to signal a change. The carnival's colors began to fade, the scene below dissolving into cloud banks that hadn't been there a moment before. As if the world were slowly being erased, and then everything suddenly dimmed. She was surrounded by impenetrable darkness, broken only by an odd flickering at the periphery of her vision, and the sound of someone talking.

Katie heard Jo's voice again, almost a whisper.

Can you smell it?

Katie sniffed, still lost in the haze. Her eyes fluttered open, stinging for some reason as she tried to clear her sight. The television was still on and she realized she must have fallen asleep. The dream was already fading away but she heard Jo's words clearly in her head.

Can you smell it?

Katie took a deep breath as she pushed herself to a sitting position and immediately started coughing. It took only an instant to realize that the room was filled with smoke. She bolted off the couch.

Smoke meant fire, and now she could see the flames outside the window, dancing and twisting orange. The door was on fire, smoke billowing from the kitchen in thick clouds. She heard roaring, a sound like a train, heard cracks and pops and splintering, her mind taking it in at once.

Oh, my God. The kids.

She ran toward the hallway, panicked at the sight of heavy smoke billowing from both rooms. Josh's room was closest and she rushed in, waving her arms against the stinging black fog.

She reached the bed and grabbed Josh's arm, dragging him up.

"Josh! Get up! The house is on fire! We've got to get out!"

He was about to whine, but she pulled him up, cutting him off. "C'mon!" she screamed. He immediately began to cough, doubled over as she dragged him out. The hallway was an impenetrable wall of smoke, but she rushed forward nonetheless, pulling Josh behind her. Groping, she found the doorjamb to Kristen's room across the hall.

It wasn't as bad as Josh's room, but she could feel the enormous heat building behind them. Josh continued to cough and wail, struggling to keep up, and she knew better than to let go. She raced to Kristen's bedside and shook her, pulling her out of bed with her other hand.

The roaring of the fire was so loud, she could barely hear the sound of her own voice. Half-carrying, half-dragging the kids back out into the hallway, she saw an orange glow, barely visible through the smoke, where the entrance to the hallway was. The wall crawled with fire, flames on the ceiling, moving toward them. She didn't have time to think, only had time to react. She turned and pushed the kids back down the hallway toward the master bedroom, where the smoke was less thick.

She rushed into the room, flicking on the light. Still working. Alex's bed stood against one wall, a chest of drawers against another. Straight ahead was a rocking chair and windows, thankfully untouched as yet by fire. She slammed the door behind her.

Racked by coughing spasms, she stumbled forward,

dragging Josh and Kristen. Both of them were wailing between hoarse bouts of coughing. She tried to free herself to raise the bedroom window, but Kristen and Josh clung to her.

"I need to open the window!" she screamed, shaking herself free. "This is the only way out!" In their panic, they didn't understand, but Katie didn't have time to explain. Frantically, she tore at the old-fashioned window lock and tried to heave the heavy pane up. It wouldn't budge. Peering closer, Katie realized that the frame had been painted shut, probably years ago. She didn't know what to do, but the sight of the two children staring at her in terror cleared her head. She looked around, frantic, finally seizing the rocking chair.

It was heavy, but somehow she lifted it above her shoulder and heaved it at the window with all her might. It cracked but didn't break. She tried again, sobbing through a last burst of adrenaline and fear, and this time the rocking chair went flying out, crashing onto the overhang below. Moving fast, Katie raced to the bed and tore off the comforter. She bundled it around Josh and Kristen and began pushing them toward the window.

There was a loud splintering sound behind her as part of the wall burst into flame, tendrils licking the ceiling. Katie turned in panic, pausing long enough to notice the portrait that hung on the wall. She stared at it, already knowing it was of Alex's wife, because there was no one else it could be. She blinked, thinking it was an illusion, a distortion created by the smoke and fear. She took an involuntary step toward the eerily familiar face when she heard a roar above her as the ceiling started to give way.

Whirling around, she pushed through the window,

holding the kids in the circle of her arms and praying that the comforter would protect them from glass shards. They seemed to hang in the air for an eternity, Katie twisting as they fell so that the kids would land on top of her. She hit the overhang on her back with a whump. It wasn't far, maybe four or five feet, but the impact left her breathless before pain rolled over her in waves.

Josh and Kristen were hiccuping in fear, wailing and coughing. But they were alive. She blinked, trying not to pass out, sure she'd broken her back. But she hadn't; she moved one leg, then the other. She shook her head to clear her vision. Josh and Kristen were struggling on top of her, trying to get free of the comforter. Above her, tongues of flame began to flare from the broken bedroom window. Flames were everywhere now, all over the house, and she knew they had only seconds to live unless she somehow summoned the strength to move.

On his way back from Joyce's house, Alex noticed the sky glowing orange just above the blackened tree line on the outskirts of town. He hadn't seen that as they drove into town and navigated the streets to Joyce's home. Now, however, he frowned as he turned in that direction. Something in his gut told him that danger lay ahead, and he debated only an instant before pressing down on the accelerator.

Josh and Kristen were already sitting up as Katie rolled over. The ground was perhaps a ten-foot drop from the overhang, but she had to risk it. They were running out of time. Josh continued to sob but didn't protest as Katie quickly explained what was going to happen next. She seized his arms, trying to keep her voice steady.

"I'm going to lower you as far as I can, but then you're going to have to jump."

He nodded, seemingly in shock, and she quickly scooted toward the edge, dragging Josh with her. He moved to the edge and she grabbed his hand. The overhang was shaking now, fire climbing up both support columns. Josh climbed over, legs first, holding on, Katie sliding on her belly toward the edge. Lowering him... God, the agony in her arms... four feet, no more, she told herself. He wouldn't fall far and he would land on his feet.

She let go as the roof shuddered. Kristen crawled toward her, trembling.

"Okay, baby, your turn," Katie urged. "Give me your hand."

She did the same thing with Kristen, holding her breath as she let go. A moment later, both of them were on their feet, staring up at her. They were waiting for her.

"Run!" she screamed. "Move back!"

Her words were swallowed by another coughing spasm, and she knew she had to move. She grabbed the edge of the overhang and swung one leg off, then the other. She dangled for only an instant before her grip weakened.

She hit the ground and felt her knees buckle before she rolled to a stop in front of the store entrance. Her legs screamed with pain, but she had to get the kids to safety. She scrambled toward them, seizing their hands and beginning to drag them away.

Fire was dancing, leaping, spurting toward the sky. Nearby trees caught fire, their upper branches sparking like firecrackers. There was a sharp clap, loud enough to make her ears ring. She chanced a peek over her shoulder, just in time to see the walls of the building collapse inward. Then there was the deafening sound of an explosion, and Katie and the kids were knocked over in the scorching blast of air.

By the time the three of them caught their breath and turned to look, the store was nothing but a gigantic cone of fire.

But they'd made it. She pulled both Josh and Kristen toward her. They were whimpering as she put her arms around them and she kissed the tops of their heads. "You're okay," she murmured. "You're safe now."

It was only when a shadow appeared before her that she realized she was wrong.

It was him, looming over them, a gun at his side.

Kevin.

In the jeep, Alex kept his foot clamped down on the gas pedal, growing more worried with every passing second. Though the fire was still too far away to pinpoint the location with accuracy, his stomach began to seize up. There weren't too many structures in that direction, mostly a few isolated farmhouses. And, of course, the store.

He leaned over the steering wheel, as if to urge the car forward. *Faster.*

Katie had trouble processing what she was seeing.

"Where is he?" Kevin rasped out. The words came out slurred, but she recognized the voice, even with his face partly in shadow. The inferno blazed behind him and his face was covered in soot and blood. There were smears of what she thought was blood on his shirt as well. In his hand the Glock shone, like it had been dipped in a barrel of oil.

He's here, Jo had said in Katie's dream.

Who?

You know.

Kevin raised the gun, pointing it at her. "I just want to talk to him, Erin."

Katie got to her feet. Kristen and Josh clung to her, fear etched on their faces. Kevin's eyes were feral, his movements jerky. He took a step toward them, almost losing his balance. The gun swung back and forth. Unsteady.

He was ready to kill them all, Katie realized. He'd already tried to kill them with the fire. But drunk, very drunk. Worse than she'd ever seen him. He was out of control, beyond reason.

She had to get the kids away, had to give them a chance to run.

"Hi, Kevin," she purred. She forced herself to smile. "Why are you holding that gun? Did you come to get me? Are you all right, baby?"

Kevin blinked. The voice, soft and sultry, sweet. He liked it when she sounded like that, and he thought it was a dream. But he wasn't dreaming and Erin was standing in front of him. She smiled as she took a step forward. "I love you, Kevin, and I always knew you'd come."

He stared. There were two of her now and then only one. He had told people she was in New Hampshire taking care of a sick friend, but there weren't any footprints in the snow and his calls were forwarded and a little boy had been shot and there was pizza sauce on his forehead and now Erin was here, telling him that she loved him.

Closer, Katie thought. *Almost there.* She took another step forward, pushing the kids behind her.

"Can you bring me home?" Her voice pleaded with him, begged like Erin used to, but her hair was short and brown and she was moving closer and he wondered why she wasn't scared and he wanted to pull the trigger but he loved her. If only he could stop the hammering inside his head—

Suddenly, Katie lunged forward, pushing the gun away. It fired, the sound like a vicious slap, but she kept moving forward, clinging to his wrist, not letting go. Kristen started to scream.

"RUN!" Katie shouted over her shoulder. "Josh, take Kristen and run! He's got a gun! Get as far away as you can and hide!"

The panic in Katie's voice seemed to galvanize Josh and he grabbed Kristen's hand and took off running. They headed toward the road, racing for Katie's house. Fleeing for their lives.

"Bitch!" Kevin screamed, trying to free his arm. Katie lowered her mouth and bit down as hard as she could and Kevin let out a ferocious cry. Trying to pull the arm free, he slammed his other fist into her temple. Instantly, she saw flashes of white light. She bit down again, finding his thumb this time, and he screamed, letting go of the gun. It clattered to the ground and he punched her again, catching her on her cheekbone, knocking her to the ground.

He kicked her in the back and she arched with pain. But she kept moving, in panic now, fueled by the certainty that he meant to kill her and the kids. She had to give them time to get away. She rose to all fours and started crawling, moving fast, gaining speed. Finally, she surged to her feet, a sprinter coming out of the blocks.

She ran as fast as she could, forcing herself forward, but she felt his body slam into her from behind and she lay breathless on the ground again. He grabbed her by the hair and hit her again. He seized an arm and twisted it, trying to work it behind her back, but he was off balance and she was slippery enough to turn onto her back. Reaching up, she clawed at his eyes, catching one in the corner, tearing hard.

Fighting for her life, adrenaline flooding her limbs. Fighting now, for all the times she hadn't. Fighting to give the kids time to run away and hide. Screaming curses at him, hating him, refusing to let him beat her again.

He snatched at her fingers, tottering off balance, and she used the opportunity to wiggle away. She felt him clawing at her legs, but his grip wasn't good enough and she pulled one leg free. Pulling her knee up toward her chin, she kicked him with all her force, stunning him as she connected with his chin. She did it again, watching this time as he toppled sideways, his arms grabbing at nothing.

She scrambled to her feet and started to run again, but Kevin was up just as quickly. A few feet away, she saw the gun and she lunged for it.

Alex was driving recklessly now, praying for the safety of Kristen and Josh and Katie, whispering their names in panic.

He passed the gravel road and rounded the bend, his stomach dropping as his premonition proved right. Before him the entire tableau spread out beyond his windshield, like a portrait of hell.

He noticed movement on the side of the road, up ahead. Two small figures, dressed in white pajamas. Josh and Kristen. He slammed on the brakes.

He was out of the car and rushing toward them almost

before the jeep came to a halt. They cried out for him as they ran, and he bent down to scoop them into his arms.

"You're okay," he murmured over and over, holding them in the tight circle of his arms. "You're okay, you're okay."

Kristen and Josh were both sobbing and hiccuping and at first he didn't understand what they were saying because they weren't talking about the fire. They were crying about a man with a gun, that Miss Katie was fighting him, and then he suddenly knew with chilling clarity what had happened.

He pushed them into the jeep and wheeled it around, racing toward Katie's house as his fingers punched the speed dial on his cell phone. He reached a startled Joyce on the second ring and told her to have her daughter drive her to Katie's house now, that it was an emergency, that she should call the police immediately. Then he hung up.

Gravel sprayed as he came to a skidding halt in front of Katie's house.

He dropped the kids off and told them to run inside, that he would be back for them as quick as he could. He counted off the seconds as he turned around and gunned the engine for the store, praying that he wasn't too late.

Praying that Katie was still alive.

Kevin saw the gun in the same instant she did and dove for it, reaching it first. He snatched it up and pointed it at her, enraged. He grabbed her by the hair and put the gun to her head as he began dragging her across the lot.

"Leave me? You can't leave me!"

Behind the store, beneath a tree, she saw his car, with its Massachusetts plates. The heat from the fire scorched her face, singeing the hair on her arms. Kevin was raging at her, his voice slurred and raw.

"You're my wife!"

In the distance, she could faintly make out sirens, but they seemed so far away.

When they reached the car, she tried to fight again but Kevin slammed her head onto the roof and she almost passed out. He opened the trunk and tried to force her in. Somehow she turned and managed to drive her knee into his groin. She heard him gasp and felt his grip loosen momentarily.

She pushed blindly, tearing out of his grasp, and started running for her life. She knew the bullet was coming, that she was about to die.

He couldn't understand why she was fighting, could barely breathe through the pain. She'd never fought him before, had never scratched at his eyes or kicked or bitten him. She wasn't acting like his wife and her hair was brown but she sounded like Erin...He started staggering after her, raising the gun, aiming, but there were two Erins and both were running.

He pulled the trigger.

Katie gasped as she heard the shot, waiting for the flash of pain, but it didn't come. She kept running and suddenly it occurred to her that he'd missed. She veered left and then right, still in the lot, desperate for some kind of shelter. But there was nothing.

Kevin staggered after her, his hands slippery with blood, slipping on the trigger. He felt like he was about to vomit again. She was getting farther away, moving from side to side, and he couldn't keep her in sight. She was trying to get away but she wouldn't because she was his wife. He would bring her home because he loved her, and then he would shoot her dead because he hated her.

Katie saw the headlights of a car on the road, moving as fast as a race car. She wanted to get to the road, to flag the car down, but she knew she wouldn't reach the road in time. Surprising her, the car suddenly began to slow, and all at once, she recognized the jeep as it careened into the lot, recognized Alex behind the wheel.

Roaring past her, toward Kevin.

The sirens were getting closer now. People were coming and she felt a surge of hope.

Kevin saw the jeep coming and raised the gun. He began firing, but the jeep kept coming toward him. He leapt out of the way as the jeep roared past, but it clipped his hand, breaking all the bones and knocking the gun somewhere into the darkness.

Kevin screamed in agony, instinctively cradling his hand as the jeep careened forward, past the burning wreckage of the store, skidding on the gravel and crashing headlong into the storage shed.

There were sirens in the distance. He wanted to chase Erin but he would get arrested if he stayed. The fear took over and Kevin began to limp and jog to his car, knowing that he had to get out of there and wondering how everything had gone so wrong.

Katie watched Kevin tear out of the lot, gravel spinning, onto the main road. Turning around, she saw that Alex's jeep was half buried in the storage shed, its engine still spewing exhaust, and she raced toward it. The fire cast its flickering light on the rear of the car and she felt panic rising inside her, as she prayed for Alex to show himself.

She was closing in on the car when her foot hit something hard, making her stumble. Spotting the gun she'd tripped on, she picked it up and started toward the car again.

Ahead, the door of the car pushed open slightly, but it was blocked by debris on either side. She felt a surge of relief that Alex was alive at the same instant she remembered that Josh and Kristen were missing.

"Alex!" she cried. She reached the back of the jeep and started to pound on it. "You have to get out! The kids are out there—need to find them!"

The door was still jammed but he was able to roll down the window. When he leaned out, she saw he was bleeding from his forehead and his voice was weak. "They're okay...I brought them to your house..."

Ice flooded her veins. "Oh, my God," she croaked out, thinking, *No, no, no* ... "Hurry up!" She pounded the rear of the car. "Get out! Kevin just left!" She could hear the raw fear in her own voice. "That's the direction he went!"

The pain in his hand was beyond anything he'd ever experienced, and he felt dizzy from blood loss. Nothing was making any sense, and his hand was useless now. He heard the sirens coming but he would wait for Erin at her house, because he knew she would be home tonight or tomorrow.

He parked behind the other, deserted cottage. Strangely, he saw Amber standing behind a tree, asking if he wanted to buy her a drink, but then her image vanished. He remembered that he had cleaned the house and mowed the lawn but he had never learned how to do laundry and now Erin was calling herself Katie.

There was nothing to drink and he was getting so tired. Blood stained his pants and he realized that his fingers and arm were bleeding, too, but he couldn't remember how that had happened. He wanted so much to sleep. He needed to rest for a while because the police would be searching for him and he needed to be fresh if they got close.

The world around him was growing faint and distant, as if viewed through the far end of a telescope. He heard the trees swaying back and forth, but instead of a breeze, all he felt was the hot summer air. He began to shiver, but he was sweating, too. So much blood, and it drained out of his hands and arm, wouldn't seem to stop. He needed to rest, couldn't stay awake, and his eyes began to close.

Alex slammed the jeep into reverse and revved the engine, listening to the wheels spinning, but the jeep was going nowhere. His mind raced frantically with the knowledge that Josh and Kristen were in danger.

He lifted his foot off the gas, engaged the four-wheel drive, and tried again. This time the jeep began to move, the side mirrors ripping off, debris scraping and bending its body. The jeep came free with a final lurch. Katie pulled futilely at the passenger door until Alex rotated in his seat and kicked at it, flinging it open. Katie jumped in.

Alex turned the jeep around and accelerated hard, gaining the road as the fire trucks pulled in. Neither said a word as he slammed the pedal to the floor. Alex had never been more frightened in his life.

Around the bend, the gravel road. Alex turned sharply, the car skidding out. The rear fishtailed and he accelerated again. Up ahead, he spotted the cottages, lights glowing in the windows of Katie's. No sign of Kevin's car, and he exhaled before he even realized he'd been holding his breath.

Kevin heard the sound of an engine coming down the gravel road and he jerked awake.

The police, he thought, and he automatically reached for his gun using his crippled hand. He screamed in pain and confusion as he realized that the gun wasn't there. It had been on the front seat but it wasn't there now and none of this made sense.

He got out of the car and looked up the road. The jeep pulled into view, the one from the store parking lot, the one that had almost killed him. It came to a stop and Erin leapt out. At first he couldn't believe his good fortune, but then he remembered that she lived here and it was the reason he'd come.

His good hand was shaking hard as he opened the trunk and removed the crowbar. He saw Erin and her lover racing to the porch. He staggered and limped toward the house, unwilling and unable to stop, because Erin was his wife and he loved her and the gray-haired man had to die.

Alex skidded to a stop in front of the house and both of them jumped out simultaneously, running for the door, calling the kids' names. Katie still held the gun. They reached the door just as Josh opened it, and as soon as he saw his son, Alex swept him up in his arms. Kristen came out from behind the couch and rushed toward them. Alex opened his arms to her as well, catching her easily as she jumped.

Katie stood just inside the doorway, watching with tears of relief in her eyes. Kristen reached out for her, too, and Katie moved closer, accepting Kristen's hug with a blind rush of happiness.

Lost in the tidal wave of emotion, none of them noticed Kevin appear in the doorway, crowbar raised high. He swung hard, sending Alex crashing to the floor and the kids stumbling and falling backward in horror and shock.

Kevin heard the satisfying thud of the crowbar, felt the vibration up his arm. The gray-haired man lay crumpled on the floor and Erin screamed.

In that instant, Alex and the kids were all that mattered to her, and Katie instinctively rushed toward Kevin, driving him back out the door. There were only two porch steps, but it was enough, and Kevin toppled backward into the dirt.

Katie spun around. "Lock the door!" she screamed, and this time it was Kristen who moved first, even as she screamed.

The crowbar had fallen to the side and Kevin struggled to roll over and stand. Katie raised the gun, pointing it as Kevin finally made it to his feet. He swayed, almost losing his balance, his face a skeletal white. He seemed unable to focus and Katie could feel the tears in her eyes.

"I used to love you," she said. "I married you because I loved you."

He thought it was Erin, but her hair was short and dark, and Erin was a blond. A foot lurched forward as he almost fell again. Why was she telling him this?

"Why did you start to hit me?" she cried. "I never knew why you couldn't stop even when you promised." Her hand was shaking and the gun felt so, so heavy. "You hit me on our honeymoon because I left my sunglasses by the pool..."

The voice was Erin's and he wondered if he was dreaming.

"I love you," he mumbled. "I've always loved you. I don't know why you left me."

She could feel the sobs building in her chest, choking her. Her words flooded out in a torrent, unstoppable and nonsensical, years' worth of sorrow. "You wouldn't let me drive or have any friends and you kept the money and made me beg you for it. I want to know why you thought you could do that to me. I was your wife and I loved you!"

Kevin could barely stay upright. Blood dripped from his fingers and arm to the ground, slippery and distracting. He wanted to talk to Erin, wanted to find her, but this wasn't real. He was sleeping, Erin was beside him in bed, and they were in Dorchester. Then his thoughts leapfrogged, and he was standing in a dingy apartment and a woman was crying.

"There was pizza sauce on his forehead," he muttered, stumbling forward. "On the boy who was shot, but the mom fell down the stairs and we arrested the Greek."

She couldn't make sense of what he was saying, couldn't understand what he wanted from her. She hated him with a rage that had been building up for years. "I cooked for you and cleaned for you and none of it mattered! All you did was drink and hit me!"

Kevin was swaying, like he was about to fall. His words

were slurred, unintelligible. "There were no footprints in the snow. But the flowerpots are broken."

"You should have let me go! You shouldn't have followed me! You shouldn't have come here! Why couldn't you just let me go? You never loved me!"

Kevin lurched toward her, but this time he reached for the gun, trying to knock it away. He was weak now, though, and she managed to hold on. He tried to grab her, but he screamed in agony when his damaged hand connected with her arm. Acting on instinct, he threw his shoulder into her, driving her against the side of the house. He needed to take the gun away from her and press it into her temple. He stared at her with wide, hate-filled eyes, pulling her close, reaching for the gun with his good hand, using his weight against her.

He felt the barrel graze his fingertips and instinctively scrambled for the trigger. He tried to push the gun toward her, but it was moving in the wrong direction, pointing down now.

"I loved you!" she sobbed, fighting him with every ounce of rage and strength left in her, and he felt something give way, momentary clarity returning.

"Then you never should have left me," he whispered, his breath heavy with alcohol. He pulled the trigger and the gun sounded with a loud crack and then he knew it was almost over. She was going to die because he'd told her that he'd find her and kill her if she ever ran away again. He would kill any man who loved her.

But strangely, Erin didn't fall, didn't even flinch. Instead, she stared at him with fierce green eyes, holding his gaze without blinking.

He felt something then, burning in his stomach, fire.

His left leg gave way and he tried to stay upright, but his body was no longer his own. He collapsed on the porch, reaching for his stomach.

"Come back with me," he whispered. "Please."

Blood pulsed through the wound, passing between his fingers. Above him, Erin was going in and out of focus. Blond hair and then brown again. He saw her on their honeymoon, wearing a bikini, before she'd forgotten her sunglasses, and she was so beautiful that he couldn't understand why she'd wanted to marry him.

Beautiful. She was always so beautiful, he thought, and then he was tired again. His breaths became ragged and then he started to feel cold, so cold, and he began to shake. He exhaled once more, the sound like air being released from a tire. His chest stopped moving. His eyes were wide open, uncomprehending.

Katie stood over him, shaking as she stared down at him. *No,* she thought. *I'll never go with you. I never wanted to go back.*

But Kevin didn't know what she was thinking, because Kevin was gone, and she realized then that it was finally, truly, over.

41

The hospital kept Katie under observation for most of the night before finally releasing her. Afterward, Katie remained in the hospital waiting room, unwilling to leave until she knew Alex would be okay.

Kevin's blow had nearly cracked Alex's skull, and he was still unconscious. Morning light illuminated the narrow rectangular windows of the waiting room. Nurses and doctors changed shifts, and the room began to fill with people: a child with a fever, a man having trouble breathing. A pregnant woman and her panicked husband pushed through the swinging doors. Every time she heard a doctor's voice, she looked up, hoping she would be allowed to see Alex.

Bruises mottled her face and arms, and her knee was swollen to almost twice its usual size, but after the requisite X-rays and exams, the doctor on call had merely given her ice packs for her bruises and Tylenol for the pain. He was the same doctor who was treating Alex, but he couldn't tell her when Alex would wake and said that the CAT scans were inconclusive. "Head wounds can be serious," he'd told her. "Hopefully, we'll know more in a few hours."

She couldn't think, couldn't eat, couldn't sleep, couldn't stop worrying. Joyce had taken the kids home from the hospital and Katie hoped they hadn't had nightmares. Hoped they wouldn't have nightmares forever. Hoped Alex was going to recover fully. Prayed for that.

She was afraid to close her eyes because every time she did, Kevin reappeared. She saw the smears of blood on his face and shirt, his wild eyes. Somehow, he'd tracked her down; somehow, he'd found her. He'd come to Southport to take her home or kill her, and he'd almost succeeded. In one night, he had destroyed the fragile illusion of security she had managed to construct since she'd arrived in town.

The terrifying visions of Kevin kept coming back, recurring endlessly with variations, sometimes changing entirely; there were moments she saw herself bleeding and dying on the porch, staring up at the man she hated. When that happened, she instinctively groped at her stomach, searching for wounds that didn't exist, but then she was back in the hospital, sitting and waiting under fluorescent lights.

She worried about Kristen and Josh. They'd be here soon; Joyce would bring them in to see their father. She wondered if they would hate her because of everything that happened, and the thought made tears sting her eyes. She covered her face with her hands, wishing she could burrow into a hole so deep that no one would ever find her. So that Kevin would never find her, she thought, and then remembered again that she'd watched him die on the porch. The words *He's dead* echoed like a mantra she couldn't escape.

"Katie?"

She looked up and saw the doctor who was now treating Alex.

"I can bring you back now," he said. "He woke up about ten minutes ago. He's still in ICU, so you can't stay long, but he wants to see you."

"Is he okay?"

"Right now, he's about as good as can be expected. He took a nasty blow."

Limping slightly, she followed the doctor as they made their way to Alex's room. She took a deep breath and straightened her posture before she entered, telling herself that she wasn't going to cry.

The ICU was filled with machines and blinking lights. Alex was in a bed in the corner, a bandage wrapped around his head. He turned toward her, his eyes only half open. A monitor beeped steadily beside him. She moved to his bedside and reached for his hand.

"How are the kids?" he whispered. The words came out slowly. Labored.

"They're fine. They're with Joyce. She took them home."

A faint, almost imperceptible smile crossed his lips.

"You?"

"I'm okay." She nodded.

"Love you," he said.

It was all she could do not to break down again. "I love you, too, Alex."

His eyelids drooped, his gaze unfocused. "What happened?"

*   *   *

She gave him an abbreviated account of the past twelve hours, but midstory she saw his eyes close. When he woke again later that morning, he'd forgotten parts of what she had recounted, so she told him again, trying to sound calm and matter-of-fact.

Joyce brought Josh and Kristen by, and though children weren't ordinarily allowed in the ICU, the doctor let them visit with their dad for a couple of minutes. Kristen had drawn him a picture of a man lying in a hospital bed, complete with a crayon-scrawled GET WELL, DADDY; Josh gave him a fishing magazine.

As the day wore on, Alex became more coherent. By the afternoon, he was no longer nodding in and out, and although he complained of a monstrous headache, his memory had more or less returned. His voice was stronger and when he told the nurse he was hungry, Katie gave a smile of relief, finally sure that he was going to be okay.

Alex was released the next day, and the sheriff visited them at Joyce's to get their formal statements. He told them that the alcohol content in Kevin's blood was so high that he'd effectively poisoned himself. Combined with the blood loss he'd suffered, it was a wonder he had been conscious, much less coherent to any degree. Katie said nothing, but all she could think was that they didn't know Kevin or understand the demons that drove him.

After the sheriff left, Katie went outside and stood in the sunlight, trying to make sense of her feelings. Though she'd told the sheriff about the events of that night, she hadn't told him everything. Nor had she told Alex everything—how could she, when it barely made sense to her? She didn't tell them that in the moments after Kevin had died and she'd rushed to Alex's side, she'd wept for them both. It seemed impossible that even as she relived the terror of those last hours with Kevin, she also remembered their rare happy moments together—how they'd laughed at private jokes or lounged peacefully on the couch together.

She didn't know how to reconcile these conflicting pieces of her past and the horror of what she'd just lived through. But there was something more, too, something else she didn't understand: she'd stayed at Joyce's because she was afraid to go back home.

Later that day, Alex and Katie stood in the parking lot, staring at the charred remains of what had once been the store. Here and there she could see items she recognized: the couch, half burned, tilted on the rubble; a shelf that once housed groceries; a bathtub scorched black.

A couple of firemen were rooting through the remains. Alex had asked them to look for the safe he'd kept in his closet. He'd removed the bandage and Katie could see the spot where they'd shaved his head to apply stitches, the area black and blue and swollen.

"I'm sorry," Katie murmured. "For everything."

Alex shook his head. "It's not your fault. You didn't do it."

"But Kevin came for me . . ."

"I know," he said. He was quiet for a moment. "Kristen and Josh told me how you helped them get out of the house. Josh said that after you grabbed Kevin, you told them to run. He said you distracted him. I just wanted to say thank you."

Katie closed her eyes. "You can't thank me for that. If anything had happened to them, I don't know that I could have lived with myself."

He nodded but couldn't seem to look at her. Katie kicked at a small pile of ash that had blown into the parking lot. "What are you going to do? About the store?"

"Rebuild, I guess."

"Where will you live?"

"I don't know yet. We'll stay at Joyce's for a bit, but I'll try to find someplace quiet, someplace with a view. Since I can't work, I might as well try to enjoy the free time."

She felt sick to her stomach. "I can't even imagine how you feel right now."

"Numb. Sad for the kids. Shocked."

"And angry?"

"No," he said. "I'm not angry."

"But you lost everything."

"Not everything," he said. "Not the important things. My kids are safe. You're safe. That's all I really care about. This"—he said motioning—"is just stuff. Most of it can be replaced. It just takes time." When he finished, he squinted at something in the rubble. "Hold on for a second," he said.

He walked toward a pile of charred debris and pulled out a fishing pole that had been wedged between blackened planks of wood. It was grimy, but otherwise looked undamaged. For the first time since they'd arrived, he smiled.

"Josh will be happy about this," he said. "I just wish I could find one of Kristen's dolls."

Katie crossed her arms over her stomach, feeling tears in her eyes. "I'll buy her a new one."

"You don't have to. I'm insured."

"But I want to. None of this would have happened if it hadn't been for me."

He looked at her. "I knew what I was getting into when I first asked you out."

"But you couldn't have expected this."

"No," he admitted. "Not this. But it's going to be okay."

"How can you say that?"

"Because it's true. We survived and that's all that matters." He reached for her hand and she felt his fingers intertwine with hers. "I haven't had a chance to say that I'm sorry."

"Why would you be sorry?"

"For your loss."

She knew he was talking about Kevin and she wasn't sure what to say. He seemed to understand that she'd both loved and hated her husband. "I never wanted him to die," she began. "I just wanted to be left alone."

"I know."

She turned tentatively toward him. "Are we going to be okay? I mean, after all this?"

"I suppose that depends on you."

"Me?"

"My feelings haven't changed. I still love you, but you need to figure out whether your feelings have changed."

"They haven't."

"Then we'll find a way to work through all this together because I know I want to spend the rest of my life with you."

Before she could respond, one of the firemen called out to them and they turned in his direction. He was working to free something, and when he stood he was holding a small safe.

"Do you think it was damaged?" Katie said.

"It shouldn't be," Alex answered. "It's fireproof. That's why I bought it."

"What's in it?"

"Mainly records, but I'm going to need them. Some photo disks and negatives. Things I wanted to protect."

"I'm glad they found it."

"So am I," he said. He paused. "Because there's something in there for you, too."

42

---— 🌿 ———

After dropping Alex off at Joyce's, Katie finally drove back home, not wanting to return but knowing she couldn't put off the inevitable forever. Even if she didn't intend to stay there, she needed to pack up some of her belongings.

Dust rose from the gravel and she bounced through the potholes before pulling to a stop out front. She sat in the jeep—dented and scraped, but still running fine—and stared at the door, remembering how Kevin had bled to death on her porch, his gaze fixed on her face.

She didn't want to see the bloodstains. She was afraid that opening the door would remind her of the way Alex had looked after Kevin struck him. She could practically hear the sounds of Kristen and Josh crying hysterically as they clung to their father. She wasn't prepared to relive all of that.

Instead, she started toward Jo's. In her hand was the letter that Alex had given her. When she'd asked him why he'd written to her, he'd shaken his head. "It's not from me," he'd said. She'd stared at him, confused. "You'll understand once you read it," he'd told her.

As she approached Jo's, she felt the trace of a memory stir to life. Something that happened on the night of the fire. Something she'd seen but she couldn't quite place. Just as she felt her mind closing in on it, the memory slipped away. She slowed as she drew nearer to Jo's house, a frown of confusion creasing her face.

There were cobwebs on the window, and a shutter had fallen to the ground where it lay shattered in the grass. The porch railing was broken and she could see weeds sprouting between the planks. Her eyes took in everything, but she was unable to process the scene before her: a rusted doorknob, half dangling from the door, grime on the windows as if they hadn't been cleaned in years.

No curtains...

No entry mat...

No wind chime...

She hesitated, trying to make sense of what she was seeing. She felt odd and curiously weightless, as if she were in a waking dream. The closer she got, the more the house seemed to decay before her.

She blinked and noticed that the door was cracked down the middle with a two-by-four hammered across it, bracing it to the crumbling casing.

She blinked again and saw that part of the wall, up in the corner, had rotted away, leaving a jagged hole.

She blinked a third time and realized that the lower half of the window was cracked and broken; pieces of glass littered the porch.

Katie climbed onto the porch, unable to stop herself.

Leaning in, she peered through the windows into the darkened cottage.

Dust and dirt, broken furniture, piles of garbage. Nothing painted, nothing cleaned. All at once, Katie stepped back on the porch, almost stumbling off the broken step. *No.* It wasn't possible, it just wasn't. What had happened to Jo, and what about all the improvements she'd made on the small cottage? Katie had seen Jo hang the wind chime. Jo had been over to her house, complaining about having to paint and clean. They'd had coffee and wine and cheese and Jo had teased Katie about the bicycle. Jo had met her after work and they'd gone to a bar. The waitress had seen them both. Katie had ordered both of them wine...

But Jo's glass had been untouched, she recalled.

Katie massaged her temples, her mind racing, searching for answers. She remembered that Jo had been sitting on the steps when Alex dropped her off. Even Alex had seen her...

Or had he?

Katie backed away from the decaying home. Jo was real. There was no way she'd been a figment of her imagination. She hadn't made her up.

But Jo liked everything you did: she drank her coffee the same way, she liked the clothes you bought, her thoughts about the employees at Ivan's mirrored your own.

A dozen random details suddenly began crowding her mind and voices dueled in her head...

She lived here!

But why is it such a dump?

We looked at the stars together!

You looked at the stars alone, which is why you still don't know their names.

We drank wine at my house!

You drank the bottle by yourself, which was why you were so dizzy.

She told me about Alex! She wanted us to be together!

She never mentioned his name until you already knew it, and you were interested in him all along.

She was the kids' counselor!

Which was the excuse you used as a reason to never tell Alex about her.

But...

    But...

        But...

One by one, the answers came as quickly as she could think of them: the reason she'd never learned Jo's last name or saw her drive a car...the reason Jo never invited her over or accepted her offer to help her paint...how Jo had been able to magically appear at Katie's side in jogging clothes...

Katie felt something give way inside her as everything clicked into place.

Jo, she suddenly realized, had never been there at all.

43

Still feeling as if she were in a dream, Katie stumbled back to her house. She took a seat in the rocker and stared at Jo's house, wondering if she'd gone utterly mad.

She knew that the creation of imaginary friends was common among children, but she wasn't a child. And yes, she'd been under a great deal of stress when she arrived in Southport. Alone and friendless, on the run and looking over her shoulder, terrified that Kevin was closing in— who wouldn't be anxious? But was that enough to have prompted the creation of an alter ego? Maybe some psychiatrists would say yes, but she wasn't so sure.

The problem was that she didn't want to believe it. She couldn't believe it because it had felt so...*real*. She remembered those conversations, could still see Jo's expressions, still hear the sound of her laughter. Her memories of Jo felt as real as her memories of Alex did. Of course, he probably wasn't real, either. Probably made him up, too. And Kristen and Josh. She was probably strapped to a bed in an asylum somewhere, lost in an entire world of her own creation. She shook her head, frustrated and confused and yet...

There was something else nagging at her, though, something she couldn't quite put her finger on. She was forgetting about something. Something important.

As much as she tried, she couldn't seem to place it. The events of the past few days had left her feeling drained and jittery. She looked up. Dusk was beginning to spread across the sky and the temperature was falling. Near the trees, a mist was starting to roll in.

Looking away from Jo's house—which was how she'd always refer to it, regardless of the state of mind it implied—Katie reached for the letter and examined it. The outer envelope was blank.

There was something frightening about the unopened letter, even though she wasn't sure why. It might have been Alex's expression as he'd handed it over... somehow she knew it was not only serious, but also important to him, and she wondered why he hadn't told her anything about it.

She didn't know, but it would be getting dark soon and she knew she was running out of time. Turning the envelope over, she lifted the seal. In the waning light, she ran her finger over the yellow legal paper before unfolding the pages. Finally, she began to read.

To the woman my husband loves,

If it seems odd for you to read these words, please believe me when I tell you that it feels just as odd to write them. Then again, nothing about this letter feels normal. There's so much I want to say, so much I want to tell you, and when I first put pen to paper, everything was clear in my mind. Now, however, I find myself struggling and I'm not sure where to begin.

I can start by saying this: I've come to believe that in everyone's life, there's one undeniable moment of change, a set of circumstances that suddenly alters everything. For me, that moment was meeting Alex. Though I don't know when or where you're reading this, I know it means he loves you. It also means he wants to share his life with you, and if nothing else, we will always have that in common.

My name, as you probably know, is Carly, but for most of my life, my friends called me Jo...

Katie stopped reading and looked at the letter in her hands, unable to absorb its words. Taking a deep breath, she reread those words: *for most of my life, my friends called me Jo...*

She gripped the pages, feeling the memory she'd been struggling to retrieve come into focus at last. Suddenly, she was back in the master bedroom on the night of the fire. She felt the strain in her arms and back as she heaved the rocking chair through the window, felt the surge of panic as she wrapped Josh and Kristen in the comforter, only to hear the loud splintering sound behind her. With sudden clarity, she remembered whirling around and seeing the portrait hanging on the wall, the portrait of Alex's wife. At the time, she'd been confused, her nerves short-circuiting in the hell of smoke and fear.

But she'd seen the face. Yes, she'd even taken a step closer to get a better look.

That looks a lot like Jo, she remembered thinking, even

if her mind hadn't been able to process it. But now, as she sat on the porch beneath a slowly darkening sky, she knew with certainty that she was wrong. Wrong about everything. She raised her eyes to gaze at Jo's cottage again.

It looked like Jo, she suddenly realized, because it *was* Jo. Unbidden, she felt another memory float free, from the first morning that Jo had come over.

My friends call me Jo, she had said by way of introduction.

Oh, my God.

Katie paled.

...Jo...

She hadn't imagined Jo, she suddenly knew. She hadn't made her up.

Jo *had* been here, and she felt her throat begin to tighten. Not because she didn't believe it, but because she suddenly understood that her friend Jo—her only real friend, her wise adviser, her supporter and confidante— would never come back.

They would never have coffee, they would never share another bottle of wine, they would never visit on the porch out front. She'd never hear the sound of Jo's laughter or watch the way she arched her eyebrow. She would never hear Jo complain about having to do manual labor, and she began to cry, mourning the wonderful friend she'd never had the chance to meet in life.

She wasn't sure how much time passed before she was able to begin reading again. It was getting dark, and with a sigh, she stood and unlocked the front door. Inside, she took a seat at the kitchen table. Jo, she remembered, had once sat in the opposite chair, and for a reason she couldn't explain, Katie felt herself begin to relax.

Okay, she thought to herself. I'm ready to hear what you have to say.

...but for most of my life, my friends called me Jo. Please feel free to call me either, and just so you know, I already consider you a friend. I hope by the end of this letter, you'll feel the same about me.

Dying is a strange business, and I'm not going to bore you with the details. I might have weeks or I might have months and though it's a cliché, it's true that so many of the things I once believed to be important no longer are. I don't read the newspaper anymore, or care about the stock market, or worry whether it's going to rain while I'm on vacation. Instead, I find myself reflecting on the essential moments of my life. I think about Alex and how handsome he looked on the day we were married. I remember my exhausted elation when I first held Josh and Kristen in my arms. They were wonderful babies, and I used to lay them in my lap and stare at them while they slept. I could do that for hours, trying to figure out whether they had my nose or Alex's, his eyes or mine. Sometimes, while they were dreaming, their little fists would curl around my finger, and I can remember thinking that I'd never experienced a purer form of joy.

It wasn't until I had children that I really understood what love meant. Don't get me wrong. I love Alex deeply, but it's different from the love I feel for Josh and Kristen. I don't know how to explain it and I don't know that I need to. All I know is that despite my illness, I nonetheless feel blessed, because I've been able to experience both. I've lived a full, happy life and experienced the kind of love that many people will never know.

But my prognosis scares me. I try to be brave around Alex, and the kids are still too young to understand what's really happening, but in quiet moments when I'm alone, the tears come readily, and sometimes I wonder if they're ever going to stop. Though I know I shouldn't, I'll find myself dwelling on the fact that I'm never going to walk my children to school or that I'll never get another chance to witness their excitement on Christmas morning. I'll never help Kristen shop for a prom dress or watch Josh play baseball. There is so much I will never see and do with them, and sometimes I despair that I'll be nothing but a distant memory by the time they get married.

How can I tell them that I love them if I'm no longer there?

And Alex. He's my dream and my companion, my lover and my friend. He's a devoted father, but more than that, he's my ideal husband. I can't describe the comfort I feel when he takes me in his arms, or how I look forward to lying down beside him at night. There's an unshakable humanity about him, a faith in the goodness of life, and it breaks my heart to imagine him alone. That's why I've asked him to give you this letter; I thought of it as a way of making him keep his promise that he would find someone special again—someone who loves him, and someone he could love. He needs that.

I was blessed to be married to him for five years

and I've mothered my children for less time than that. Now, my life is almost over and you are going to take my place. You'll become the wife who grows old with Alex, and you'll become the only mother my children will ever know. You can't imagine how terrible it is to lie in bed, staring at my family and knowing these things, and realizing there's nothing I can do to change them. Sometimes, I dream that I'll find a way to come back, that I can find a way to ensure they're going to be all right. I like to believe that I'll watch over them from heaven, or that I can visit them in their dreams. I want to pretend that my journey isn't over and I pray that the boundless love I feel for them will somehow make it possible.

This is where you come in. I want you to do something for me.

If you love Alex now, then love him forever. Make him laugh again, and cherish the time you spend together. Take walks and ride your bikes, curl up on the couch and watch movies beneath a blanket. Make him breakfast, but don't spoil him. Let him make breakfast for you as well, so he can show you he thinks you're special. Kiss him and make love to him, and consider yourself lucky for having met him, for he's the kind of man who'll prove you right.

I also want you to love my children in the same way I do. Help them with their homework and kiss their scraped elbows and knees when they fall. Run your hand through their hair and assure them they can do anything they put their mind to. Tuck them in at night and help them say their prayers. Make their lunches; support them in their friendships. Adore

*them, laugh with them, help them grow into kind,
independent adults. What you give them in love,
they'll return tenfold in time, if only because Alex
is their father.*

*Please. I beg you, do these things for me. After
all, they are your family now, not mine.*

*I'm not jealous or angry that I've been replaced
by you; as I mentioned already, I consider you a
friend. You've made my husband and children
happy, and I wish I were around to be able to thank
you in person. Instead, all I can do is assure you
that you have my everlasting gratitude.*

*If Alex has chosen you, then I want you to believe
that I have chosen you as well.*

*Your friend in spirit,
Carly Jo*

When Katie finished reading the letter, she wiped her
tears and ran her finger over the pages before slipping
them back into the envelope. She sat quietly, thinking
about the words that Jo had written, already knowing she
would do exactly as Jo had asked.

Not because of the letter, she thought, but because she
knew that in some inexplicable way, Jo was the one who'd
gently urged her to give Alex a chance in the first place.

She smiled. "Thank you for trusting me," she whispered, and she knew that Jo had been right all along. She'd
fallen in love with Alex and she'd fallen in love with the
children and she already knew that she couldn't imagine a
future without them. It was time to go home, she thought,
it was time to see her family.

Outside, the moon was a brilliant white disk that guided her as she made her way toward the jeep. But before climbing in, she glanced over her shoulder in the direction of Jo's.

The lights were on and the windows of the cottage were glowing yellow. In the painted kitchen, she saw Jo standing near the window. Though she was too far away to make out much more than that, Katie had the sense she was smiling. Jo raised a hand in a friendly farewell, and Katie was reminded again that love can sometimes achieve the impossible.

When Katie blinked, however, the cottage was dark again. No lights were on and Jo had vanished, but she thought she could hear the words in the letter being carried on the gentle breeze.

If Alex has chosen you, then I want you to believe that I have chosen you as well.

Katie smiled and turned away, knowing it wasn't an illusion or a figment of her imagination. She knew what she saw.

She knew what she believed.

Reading Group Guide

Discussion Questions

1. When Alex first meets Katie, he senses that she is in trouble. How does he figure out what has happened to her?

2. What is the nature of Jo and Katie's relationship? How does Jo's profession play into their friendship? How does Jo help Katie adjust to her life in Southport?

3. What role do Alex's children play in the development of his relationship with Katie?

4. Katie and Alex fall in love very quickly. What draws them together? Have you ever fallen in love so quickly? If not, do you think it's possible?

5. On their first date, Alex says to Katie, "Everyone has a past, but that's just it—it's in the past. You can learn from it, but you can't change it." Do you agree

with him? Is it possible to truly put the past behind
you?

6. Alex is a widower who has had to raise two children
   on his own. How has he dealt with his grief in the
   years since his wife passed away? How has his need
   to respond to his young children's grief affected this?
   Have you experienced grief of this magnitude in your
   own life? How did you handle it?

7. When Katie tells Alex about Kevin, she says, "I hate
   him, but I hate myself, too." Why does she feel this
   way? How does Katie change as she spends more and
   more time in Southport? How is she different by the
   end of the book?

8. Despite his violent behavior and his incessant drinking, Kevin quotes the Bible constantly and takes the
   Ten Commandments seriously. How do you understand his behavior?

9. Katie's past puts Alex and his family in potential
   danger. Do you think it was irresponsible of Alex to
   involve himself with a woman he knew could endan-
   ger him and his children?

10. Why do you think the author chose to write a portion
    of the book from Kevin's perspective? Do you have
    any sympathy for Kevin? Why or why not?

11. Did reading this book give you a new or better under-
    standing of domestic abuse?

12. At the end of the novel, Alex tells Katie he is sorry for her loss. What does he mean by this? How does Katie react?

13. What do you make of Katie's discovery at the end of the novel? Do you find the book's ending believable?

14. This novel is in large part about safety and trust and how we often take these two things for granted. Did this book make you think differently about your own life and the things you value?

CHAPTER I

And Baby Makes Three

Wow!" I can remember saying as soon as Vivian stepped out of the bathroom and showed me the positive result of the pregnancy test. "That's great!"

In truth, my feelings were closer to...Really? Already?

It was more shock than anything, with a bit of terror mixed in. We'd been married for a little more than two years, and Vivian had already told me that she intended to stay home for the first few years after we had a baby. I'd always agreed when she'd said it—I wanted the same thing—but in that moment, I also realized that our life as a couple with two incomes would soon be coming to an end. Moreover, I wasn't sure in that moment whether I was even ready to become a father, but what could I do? It wasn't as though she'd tricked me, nor had she concealed the fact that she wanted to have a baby, and she'd let me know when she stopped taking the pill. I wanted children as well, of course, but Vivian had stopped the pill only three weeks earlier. I can remember thinking that I probably had a few months at least before her body readjusted to its normal, baby-making state. For all I knew, it could be hard for her to become pregnant, which meant it might even be a year or two.

But not my Vivian. Her body had adjusted right away. My Vivian was fertile.

I slipped my arms around her, studying her to see if she was already glowing. But it was too soon for that, right? What exactly is glowing, anyway? Is it just another way of saying someone looks hot and sweaty? How were our lives going to change? For better or for worse?

Questions tumbled over each other in my mind. And in that moment, as I held my wife, I, Russell Green, had answers to none of them.

Months later, the big IT happened, though I admit much of the day remains a blur.

Looking back, I probably should have written it all down while it was still fresh in my mind. A day like the big IT should be remembered in vivid detail—not the fuzzy snapshots I tend to recall. The only reason I remember as much as I do is because of Vivian. Every detail seemed etched into her consciousness, but then she was the one in labor and pain has a way of sometimes sharpening the mind. Or so they say.

What I do know is this: sometimes, in recalling events of that day, she and I are of slightly differing opinions. For instance, I considered my actions completely understandable under the circumstances, whereas Vivian would declare alternately that I was selfish, or simply a complete idiot. When she told the story to friends—and she has done so many times—people inevitably laughed, or shook their heads and offered her pitying glances.

In all fairness, I don't think I was either selfish or a complete idiot; after all, it was our first child, and neither of us knew exactly what to expect when she went into labor. Does anyone really feel prepared for what's coming? Labor, I was told, is unpredictable; during her pregnancy, Vivian reminded me more than once that the process from initial contractions to actual birth could take more than a day—especially for the first child—and labors of twelve hours or more were not uncommon. Like most young fathers-to-be, I considered my wife the expert and took her at her word. After all, she was the one who'd read all the books.

It should also be noted that I wasn't entirely deficient on the morning in question. I had taken my responsibilities seriously. Both her overnight bag and the baby's bag were packed, and the contents of both had been checked and double-checked. The camera and video camera were charged and ready, and the baby's room was fully stocked with everything our child would need for at least a month, including a bunch of things I didn't even know existed. I knew the quickest route to the hospital and had planned alternate routes, if there happened to be an accident on the highway. I had also known the baby would be coming soon; in the days leading up to the actual birth, there'd been numerous false alarms, but even I knew the countdown had officially started.

In other words, I wasn't entirely surprised when my wife shook me awake at half past four on Saturday, August 16, 2008, announcing that the contractions were about four minutes apart and that it was time to go to the hospital. I didn't doubt her; she knew the difference between Braxton Hicks and the *real thing*, and yet, in that moment, I also have to admit that as much as I'd been preparing myself, my first thoughts weren't about throwing on my clothes and loading up the car; in fact, they weren't about my wife and soon-to-be-born child at all. Rather, my thoughts went something like this: *Today's the big IT, and people are going to be taking a lot of photographs. Other people will be looking at these photographs forever, and—considering it's for posterity—I should probably hop in the shower before we go, since my hair looks as though I'd spent the night in a wind tunnel.*

It's not that I'm vain; I simply thought I had *plenty of time*, so I told Vivian I'd be ready to go in a few minutes. As a general rule, I shower quickly—no more than ten minutes on a normal day, including shaving—but just after I'd applied the shaving cream, I thought I heard my wife cry out from the living room. I listened again, hearing nothing, but sped up nonetheless. By the time I was rinsing off, I heard her shouting, though strangely it seemed as though she was shouting *about* me, not *at* me.

I wrapped a towel around me and stepped into the darkened hallway, still dripping wet. As God is my witness, I was in the shower for less than five minutes.

Vivian cried out again and it took me a moment to process that Vivian was on all fours and shouting into her cell phone that I was *IN THE DAMN SHOWER!* and demanding *WHAT IN THE HELL CAN THAT IDIOT BE THINKING?!?!?!? Idiot,* by the way, was the nicest term she used to describe me in that same conversation; her language was actually quite a bit more colorful. What I didn't know was that the contractions that had been four minutes apart were now—in the blink of an eye—only two minutes apart, and that she was also in back labor. Back labor, by the way, is excruciating, and Vivian suddenly let out a scream so powerful that it became its own living entity, one that may still be hovering above our neighborhood in Charlotte, North Carolina, an otherwise peaceful place.

Rest assured, I moved into even higher gear after that, slapping on clothes without completely toweling off, and loading the car. I supported Vivian as she continued to grimace, buckling her into the front seat and trying not to comment on the fact that she was digging her fingernails into my forearm. A moment later, I was behind the wheel, and once on the road, I called the obstetrician, who promised to meet us at the hospital.

The contractions were still a couple of minutes apart when we arrived, but Vivian's continuing anguish meant that she was taken straight to labor and delivery. I held her hand and tried to guide her through her breathing—during which she again offered various colorful sentiments about me and where I could *stick the damn breathing!*—until the anesthesiologist arrived for the epidural. Early in the pregnancy, Vivian had debated whether or not to get one before reluctantly deciding in favor, and now it appeared to be a blessing. As soon as the medication kicked in her agony vanished entirely, and I saw my wife smile for the first time since she'd shaken me awake that morning. Her obstetrician—in his sixties, with neat gray hair and a friendly face—wandered into the room every twenty to thirty minutes to see how dilated she was, and in between those visits I called both sets of parents, as well as my sister.

Then, it was time. Nurses were summoned and they readied the equipment with calm professionalism. Then, all at once, the doctor told my wife to push.

Vivian had pushed through three contractions when the doctor announced that one more should do it. Vivian was less exhausted than I'd imagined she might be—to that point, she'd been in labor only three hours—and when she pushed, the doctor began rotating his wrists and hands like a magician pulling a rabbit from his hat. The next thing I knew, I was a father.

Just like that.

The pediatrician took our baby, and though she

was slightly anemic, she had ten fingers, ten toes, a healthy heart, and a set of obviously functioning lungs. I asked about the anemia—the pediatrician said it was nothing to worry about—and after the pediatrician squirted a bunch of goop in our baby's eyes, she was cleaned and swaddled and placed in my wife's arms.

Just as I'd predicted, photos were taken all day long. But the funny thing is, when people glanced at those same photos later, no one seemed to care how I looked at all.

It's been said that babies are born looking like either Winston Churchill or Mahatma Gandhi, but because the anemia lent a grayish pallor to my daughter's skin, my first thought was that she looked a little bit like Yoda, without the ears of course. A *beautiful* Yoda, mind you, a *breathtaking* Yoda, a Yoda so *miraculous* that when she gripped my finger, my heart nearly burst. My parents arrived a few minutes later, and in my nervousness and excitement, I met them in the hallway and blurted out the first words that came to mind.

"We have a gray baby!"

My mother looked at me as though I'd gone insane while my father dug his finger into his ear as if wondering if the waxy buildup had clouded his ability to hear correctly. Ignoring my comment, they entered the room and saw Vivian cradling our daughter in her arms, her expression serene.

My eyes followed theirs, and when I looked upon my wife and daughter, I thought to myself that this baby had to be the single most precious little girl in the history of the world. While I'm sure all new fathers think the same thing about their own children, the simple fact is that there can only be one child who is actually the *most precious*, and part of me marveled that others in the hospital weren't stopping by our room, simply to witness history in the making.

My mom stepped toward the bed, craning her neck to peer even closer.

"Did you decide on a name?" she asked.

"London," my wife answered, without looking up, her attention completely devoted to our child. "We've decided to name her London."

My parents eventually left, then returned later that afternoon. In between, Vivian's parents visited as well. They'd flown in from Alexandria, Virginia, where Vivian had been raised, and while Vivian was thrilled, I immediately felt the tension in the room begin to rise. I'd always sensed that they believed their daughter had *settled* when deciding to marry me, and who knows? If the future was any indication, maybe they were right. Nor did they seem to like my parents, and the feeling was mutual. While the four of them were always cordial, it was nonetheless obvious that they preferred to avoid each other's company.

My older sister, Marge, also came by with her partner, Liz, bearing gifts. Marge and Liz had been together longer than Vivian and I had—they were going on seven years at the time. Not only did I think Liz was a terrific partner for my sister, but I knew that Marge was the greatest older sibling a guy could have. With both my parents working—Dad was a plumber and Mom worked as a receptionist at a dentist's office until her retirement a few years back—Marge had not only served as a substitute parent at times, but as a sibling confidante who helped me wade through the angst of adolescence. Neither Liz nor Marge liked Vivian's parents either, by the way, a feeling that had coalesced at my wedding, when Vivian's parents refused to let Marge and Liz sit together at the main table. Granted, Marge had been in the wedding party and Liz had not—and Liz had opted to wear a tuxedo—but it was the kind of slight that neither of them had been able to forgive, since other couples, all heterosexual, had been allowed the privilege. Frankly, I don't blame Marge or Liz for being upset about it, because I was bothered, too. She and Liz get along better than most of the married couples I know.

While our visitors came and went, I stayed in the room with my wife for the rest of the day, alternately sitting in the rocking chair near the window or on the bed beside her, both of us repeatedly whispering in amazement that *we had a daughter*. I would stare at Vivian and stare at London, knowing with certainty that I belonged with these two and that the three of us would forever be connected. The feeling was overwhelming—like everything else that day—and

I found myself speculating what London would look like as a teenager, or what she would dream about, or what she would do with her life. Whenever London cried, Vivian would automatically move her to her breast, and I would witness yet another miracle.

How does London know how to do that? I wondered to myself. *How on earth does she know?*

There is another moment, however, that is all mine, a precious memory and the only one I can still recall with pristine clarity.

It occurred on that first night in the hospital, long after our final visitors had left. Vivian was asleep and I was dozing in the rocking chair when I heard my daughter begin to fuss. I knew that I'd have to wake my wife in a few moments—my breasts didn't have what London needed—but I gently scooped my daughter into my arms. Before that day, I'd never actually held a newborn, and terrified that I might break her, I immediately pulled her close to my body.

I thought that London would begin to cry, and I was ready to hand her to Vivian, but instead, I saw my daughter staring up at me with unfocused eyes. She blinked twice and began to settle, finally closing her eyes again. I inched back to the rocking chair, and for the next twenty minutes, all I could do was marvel at the feelings she induced in me. That I adored her, I already knew; what I hadn't realized was that the thought of life without her seemed suddenly inconceivable, and I remember whispering to her that as her father, I would always be there for her, no matter what the future might bring. As if knowing exactly what I was saying, London pooped and squirmed and then began to cry. In the end, I handed her back to Vivian.

CHAPTER 2

In the Beginning

I told them today," Vivian announced.

It was a little past ten on a Friday night, and for the first time in what seemed like forever, we'd been able to share some alone time. We'd sat on the couch with the television on—harkening back to the pre-London days. As Vivian thumbed through a magazine, I realized how much I'd missed these simple moments.

Later, when we were in the bedroom, Vivian had slipped into her pajamas and crawled into bed. London had been asleep for three hours; at six weeks, she was sleeping almost four hours at a stretch, giving us hope that she might hit five or six hours sooner rather than later. Vivian hadn't had a full night's sleep since the night before the birth, and though she hadn't complained, she looked tired. Beautiful, but definitely tired.

"Told who what?" I asked.

"Rob," she answered, meaning her boss at the media company where she worked. "I officially let him know that after my maternity leave was up, I wouldn't be coming back."

"Oh," I said, feeling the same pang of terror I'd felt when I'd seen the positive pregnancy result. Since that time, I'd tried my best not to think about it. Vivian earned nearly as much as I did, and I think part of me hoped that she'd change her mind, even if the other part also wanted her to stay at home.

"He said the door was always open if I changed my mind," she added. "But I told him that London was not going to be raised by strangers. Otherwise, why have a child in the first place? If you don't want to be there, I mean?"

"You don't have to convince me," I said, doing my best to hide my feelings. "I'm on your side." Well, part of me was, anyway.

"Good. Otherwise, you shouldn't have married me in the first place."

I forced a smile. "You know that means we can't go out to dinner as much and we'll have to cut back on discretionary spending, right?"

"I know."

"And you're okay with not shopping as much?"

"You say it like I waste money. I never do that."

The credit card bills sometimes seemed to indicate otherwise—as did her closet, which bulged with clothes and shoes and bags—but I could hear the irritation in her tone, and the last thing I wanted to do was argue with her. Instead, I rolled toward her, pulling her close, something else on my mind. I nuzzled and kissed her neck, and she exhaled softly.

"Now?"

"It's been a long time."

"And my poor baby feels like he's about to blow up, doesn't he?"

"Frankly, I don't want to risk it."

She laughed, and as I began to unbutton her pajama top, a noise sounded on the baby monitor. In that instant, we both froze—as if London could hear us as well—and waited. Hoped.

Nothing.

Still nothing.

And just when I thought the coast was clear and I let out a breath I didn't even know I'd been holding, the noise from the baby monitor began again, this time at higher volume. With a sigh, I rolled onto my back and Vivian slipped from the bed, as disappointed as I was. By the time London finally calmed—which took a good half hour—Vivian wasn't in the mood for a second attempt and I didn't want to push her.

In the morning, Vivian and I had more luck. So much luck, in fact, that I cheerfully volunteered to take care of London when she woke so that Vivian could go back to sleep and get some much-needed rest. London, however, must have been just as tired as Vivian; it wasn't until I'd finished my second cup of coffee that I heard various noises but no cries emanating from the baby monitor.

In her room, the mobile above the crib was rotating,

and when I looked down at London, I saw a wiggly baby, full of energy, her legs shooting like pistons. I couldn't help but smile, and recognizing me, she suddenly smiled as well.

It wasn't gas; it wasn't a reflexive tic. This was a real smile, as true as the sunrise, and when she emitted an unexpected giggle, the already brilliant start to my day was suddenly a thousand times even better.

It's funny what life can teach a person, and the main thing I've learned is this: I'm not a wise man.

I'm not unintelligent, mind you. Or at least I don't like to think so. But wisdom means more than being intelligent, because it encompasses understanding, empathy, experience, inner peace, and intuition, and in retrospect, I obviously lack many of these traits.

Here's what else I've learned: age doesn't guarantee wisdom, any more than age guarantees intelligence. I know that's not a popular notion—don't we frequently regard our elders as wise partially because they're gray and wrinkled?—but lately I've come to believe that some people are born with the capacity to become wise while others aren't, and in some people, wisdom seems to be evident even at a young age.

My sister, Marge, for instance. She's wise, and she's only six years older than I am. Frankly, she's been wise as long as I've known her. My mom and dad are wise, too, and I've been thinking about it a lot these days because it's become clear to me that even though wisdom runs in the family, it bypassed me entirely.

If I were wise, after all, I would have listened to Marge ten years ago, when she drove me out to the cemetery where our grandparents were buried and asked me whether I was absolutely sure whether Vivian was right for me and if I really knew what I might be getting into.

If I were wise, I would have listened to my father when he asked me whether I was sure I should strike out on my own and start my own advertising company, when I was thirty-five years old.

If I were wise, I would have listened to my mom when she told me to spend as much time with London as I could, since children grow up so fast, and you can never get those years back.

But like I said, I'm not a wise man. And because of that, my life pretty much went into a tailspin, and even now, I wonder if I'll ever recover.

Where does one begin when trying to make sense of a story that makes little sense at all? At the beginning? And where is the beginning?

Who knows?

So let's start with this. When I was a child, I grew up believing that I'd feel like an adult by the time I was eighteen, and I was right. At eighteen, I was already making plans. My family had lived paycheck to paycheck, and I had no intention of doing the same. I had dreams of starting my own business, of being my own boss, even if I wasn't sure what I was actually going to do. Figuring that college would help steer me in the proper direction, I went to NC State but gradually came to the realization that I'd been fooling myself. The longer I was there, the younger I seemed to feel, and by the time I collected my degree, I couldn't shake the feeling that I was pretty much the same guy I'd been in high school.

Nor had college helped me decide on the kind of business I'd start. I had little in the way of real-world experience and even less capital, so deferring the idea of my own business, I took a job in advertising for a man named Jesse Peters. I wore suits to the office and worked a ton of hours, and yet, more often than not, I still felt *younger* than my actual age might indicate. On weekends, I'd frequent the same bars I did in college, and I imagined that I could start over as a freshman, fitting right in with whatever fraternity I happened to join. Over the next few years there would be even more changes; I'd get married and purchase a house and drive a hybrid, but even then I didn't necessarily always feel like the adult version of me. Peters, after all, had essentially taken the place of my parents— like my parents, he could tell me what to do *or else*— which made it seem as though I was still *pretending*. In quiet moments, I'd sometimes try to convince myself: *Okay, it's official. I'm now a grown-up.*

That realization came, of course, after London was born and Vivian quit her job. I was thirty years old, destined to remain an employee and be told what to do forever. While setting aside my dream was hard, it also fostered my maturity. The pressure I felt to provide for my family over the next few years required sacrifice on a scale that even I hadn't expected, and if that isn't being a grown-up, I don't know what is. After finishing at the agency—on days when I actually made it home at a reasonable hour—I'd walk through the door and hear London call out "Daddy!" and always wish that I could spend more time with her. She'd come running and I'd crouch to let her jump in my arms. She'd start talking a mile a minute about whatever she'd been doing, whether it was coloring or feeding the fish, or the bow that Mommy had put in her hair, and I'd remind myself that all the sacrifices had been worth it, if only because of the wonderful little girl I held in my arms.

I waded through my early thirties thinking I'd finally figured it all out. In the hectic rush of life, it was easy to convince myself that the important things—my wife and daughter, my job, my family— were going okay, even if I couldn't be my own boss. In rare moments when I imagined a future, I would find myself picturing a life that wasn't all that different than the one I was currently leading, and that was okay, too. On the surface, things seemed to be running rather smoothly, and looking back, that should have been a warning sign. Trust me when I say that I had *absolutely no idea* that within a couple of years— I'm thirty-seven now—I'd wake in the mornings feeling like one of those immigrants on Ellis Island who'd arrived in America with nothing in their possession but the clothes on their back, not speaking the language, and wondering, *What am I going to do now?*

When, exactly, did it all begin to go wrong? If you ask Marge, the answer is obvious: "It started going downhill as soon as you met Vivian," she's told me more than once. Of course, being Marge, she would automatically correct herself. "I take that back," she would add. "It started way before that, when you were still in grade school and hung that poster on your wall, the one with the girl in the skimpy bikini with the big bahoonas. I always liked that poster, by the way, but it warped your thinking." Then, after further consideration, she would shake her head, speculating, "Now that I think about it, you were always kind of screwed up, and coming from the person who's always been regarded as the family screwup, that's saying something. Maybe your real problem is that you've always been too damn nice for your own good. Being *too nice* always ends up biting you in the ass."

And that's the thing. When you start trying to figure out what went wrong—or, more specifically, where *you* went wrong—it's a bit like peeling an onion. There's always another layer, another mistake in the past or a painful memory that stands out, which then leads one back even further in time, and then even further, in search of the *ultimate truth*. All I really know is that I've reached the point where I've stopped caring where or when or why my life suddenly began to feel like I'd made a series of massive wrong turns: the only thing that really matters now is learning enough to avoid making the same mistakes again.

To understand why I feel the way I do, it's important to understand me. Which isn't easy, by the way. I've been me for more than a third of a century, and half the time, I still don't understand myself. So let me start with this. As I've grown older, I've come to believe that there are two types of men in the world: the marrying type, and the bachelor type. The marrying type is the kind of guy who pretty much sizes up every girl he dates, assessing whether or not she could be The One. It's the reason that women in their thirties and forties often say things like *All the good men are taken.* By that, women mean guys who are ready, willing, and able to commit to being part of a couple.

I've always been the marrying type. And I'm good with that. Lots of men—including my father, with whom I share virtually nothing else in common—are the marrying type, and their lives are better for it. To me, being part of a couple—being committed—just feels *right.* For whatever reason, I've always been more comfortable in the presence of women than men, even in friendship, and spending time with one woman *who also happened to be madly in love with me* struck me as the best of all possible worlds.

And it can be, I suppose. But that's where things get a bit trickier, because not all marrying types are the same. There are subgroups within the marrying types, guys who may also consider themselves to be *romantic*, for instance. Sounds nice, right? The kind of guy that most women insist they want? It probably is, and I must admit that I'm a card-carrying member of this particular subgroup. In rare instances, however, this particular subtype is also wired to be a *people pleaser*, and these three traits are, according to Marge, the root of all my problems. Because when taken together, these three things made me believe that anything was possible . . . that with just a bit more effort—if only I tried a little harder—then everything would turn out fine.

Marge is probably right, but lately I've begun to wonder how that happened. What was it that made me that way? Was it simply my nature? Was I influenced by family dynamics? Or did I simply watch too many romantic movies at an impressionable age? Or all of the above?

I have no idea, but I state without hesitation that the *watching too many romantic movies* thing was entirely Marge's fault. She loved the classics, like *An Affair to Remember* and *Casablanca*, but *Ghost* and *Dirty Dancing* were up there, too, and we must have watched *Pretty Woman* at least twenty times. That movie was her all-time favorite. What I didn't know, of course, was that Marge and I enjoyed watching it because we both had massive crushes on Julia Roberts at the time, but that's beside the point. The film will probably live on forever because it *works*. The characters played by Richard Gere and Julia Roberts had . . . *chemistry*. They talked. They learned to trust each other, despite the odds. They fell in love. And how can one possibly forget the scene in which Richard Gere is waiting for Julia—he's planning to take her to the opera—and she emerges wearing a gown that utterly transforms her? The audience sees Richard's awestruck expression, and he eventually opens a velvet box, which holds the diamond necklace Julia will also be wearing that evening. As Julia reaches for it, Richard snaps the lid closed, and Julia's sudden joyful surprise...

It was all there, really, in just those few scenes. The romance, I mean—trust, anticipation, and joy combined with opera, dressing up, and jewelry all led to *love*. In my nine-year-old brain, it just clicked: a how-to manual of sorts to impress a girl. All I really had to do was remember that girls had to *like* the guy first and that romantic gestures would then lead to *love*. In the end, another romantic in the real world was created. I've been one ever since.

In sixth grade—after seeing *Pretty Woman* and the first year I started having serious crushes on the opposite sex—a new girl joined my class, Melissa Anderson. She'd moved from Minnesota during the previous summer, and with blond hair and blue eyes, she shared the look of her Swedish ancestors. When I saw her on the first day of school, I'm pretty sure I went slack-jawed, and I wasn't the only one. Every guy was mesmerized. There was little doubt in my mind that Melissa Anderson was far and away the prettiest girl who'd ever set foot in Mrs. Hartman's class at

Arthur E. Edmonds Elementary School, or any other class in any other school for that matter.

Every boy in class had a crush on her at one point or another that year, including me, but the difference was that I knew exactly what to do while they did not. I was planning to win her over—what is romance for, if not exactly that?—and though I wasn't Richard Gere with private jets and diamond necklaces, I did have a bicycle and I had learned how to macramé bracelets, complete with wooden beads. Those, however, would come later. First—just like Richard and Julia—we had to get to *like* each other. I began to find reasons to sit at the same table with her at lunch. While she talked, I listened and asked questions, lots of them over the next few weeks, and when she finally told me that she thought I was nice, I knew it was time to take the next step. I wrote her a poem—about her life in Minnesota and how pretty she was—and I slipped it to her on the bus one afternoon, along with a flower. I took my seat, knowing exactly what would happen: She would realize I was different, and with that would come an even greater epiphany; she'd turn toward me and meet my gaze before offering a smile, and when we got off the bus, she'd reach for my hand and ask me to walk her home.

Except it didn't work out that way. Instead of reading the poem, she gabbed with her friend April the whole way home, and the following day, she sat next to Tommy Harmon at lunch and didn't talk to me at all. Nor did she talk to me the following day, or the day after that. When Marge found me sulking in my bedroom later, she told me that I was trying too hard and that I should just be myself.

"But that's who I am."

"Then you'd better think twice about that," Marge snorted, "because it makes you seem desperate."

Problem was, I didn't think twice. Did Richard Gere think twice? He clearly knew more than my sister, and again, here's where wisdom and I were obviously traveling in opposite directions down the highway. Because *Pretty Woman* was a movie and I was living in the real world, the pattern I established with Melissa Anderson continued, with variations, until it eventually became a habit I couldn't break. I became the king of romantic gestures—flowers, notes, cards, and the like—and in college, I was even the "secret admirer" to a girl I happened to fancy. I opened doors and paid for dates, and I listened whenever a girl wanted to talk, even if it was about how much she still loved her ex-boyfriend. Most girls sincerely liked me. I mean that. To them, I was a *friend*, the kind of guy who'd get invited to hang out with a group of girlfriends whenever they went out, but I seldom succeeded in landing the girl I'd set my sights on. I can't tell you how many times I've heard, *"You're the nicest guy I know, and I'm sure you'll meet someone special. I have two or three friends I could probably set you up with..."*

It wasn't easy being the guy who was *perfect for someone else*. It often left me brokenhearted, but in my obstinacy, I remained the king of romantic gestures whenever someone captured my imagination. And through it all, I tried to understand why women told me that they wanted certain traits—romance and kindness, interest and the ability to listen—while not seeming to appreciate it when they were actually offered to them.

I wasn't altogether unlucky in love, of course. In high school, I had a girlfriend named Angela for most of my sophomore year; in college, Rachel and I were together most of my junior year. And during the summer after graduation from college, less than a week after I'd taken a job with the Peters Group, I met a woman named Emily, and that's where things got interesting.

Emily still lives in the area, and over the years, I'd see her out and about, either alone or with her husband and their son. She was the first woman I ever loved, and I've come to realize that *romance* and *nostalgia* are often intertwined. I still often miss her. Emily was sweet and kind, quick to laugh, intelligent and with a passion for painting, a woman who might have been perfect for me. My parents loved her; Marge loved her. When we were together, we were comfortable even when silent. Our relationship was easy and relaxed; more than lovers, we were friends. We trusted each other and could talk about anything. She delighted in the notes I'd place under her pillow or the flowers I'd have delivered to her workplace for no reason whatsoever. Emily loved me as much as she loved romantic gestures, and after dating her for a little more than a year, I made plans to propose, even putting a deposit down on an engagement ring.

And then, I screwed it up. Don't ask me why. I could blame the booze that night—I'd been drinking with friends at a bar—or maybe there was some part of me that was afraid that I was still too young to get tied down. For whatever reason, I struck up a conversation with a woman named Carly. She was beautiful and she knew how to flirt and she'd recently broken up with a long-term boyfriend. One drink led to another, which led to more flirting, and we eventually ended up in bed together. In the morning, Carly made it clear that what had happened was simply a fling, with no strings attached, and though she kissed me goodbye, she didn't bother giving me her phone number.

There are a couple of very simple Guy Rules in this sort of situation, and Rule Number One goes like this: *Never ever tell.* And if your sweetheart ever suspects anything and asks directly, go immediately to Rule Number Two: *Deny, deny, deny.*

All guys know these rules, but the thing was, I also felt guilty. Horribly guilty. I was ashamed every time I looked at Emily, and even after a month, I couldn't put the experience behind me, nor could I seem to forgive myself. Keeping it secret seemed inconceivable; I couldn't imagine building a future with Emily knowing it was constructed, at least in part, on a lie. I talked to Marge about it, and Marge was, as always, helpful in that sisterly way of hers.

"Keep your stupid trap shut, you dimwit. You made a mistake—a whopper—and you should feel guilty. That's a crappy thing you did. But if you're never going to do it again, then don't hurt Emily's feelings, too. Something like this will crush her."

I knew Marge was right, and yet...

I wanted Emily's forgiveness, because I wasn't sure I could forgive myself without it, and so in the end, I went to Emily and said the words that even now, I wish I could take back.

"There's something I have to tell you," I began, and proceeded to spill everything.

If forgiveness was the goal, it didn't work. If trying to build a long-term relationship on a foundation of truth was another goal, that didn't work either. Through angry tears, she told me to get out and that she needed some time to think.

I left her alone for a week, waiting for her to call while moping around my apartment, but the phone never rang. The following week, I left two messages—and apologized again both times—but she still wouldn't call. It wasn't until the following week that we finally had lunch, but it was strained, and when she left the restaurant, she told me not to walk her to her car. The writing was on the wall, and a week after that, she left a message saying it was over for good. A little while later, I learned through the grapevine that she'd gone on a date with someone from work and had plans to go out with him again. I don't know whatever happened to him, but a few years later, she met the guy she eventually did marry. It was the year before I married Vivian, and I can remember feeling glum for a few weeks.

The passage of time has lessened my guilt—time always does—and I try to console myself with the idea that at least for her, my indiscretion was a blessing in disguise. I heard from a friend of a friend a couple of years after our breakup that she'd married an Australian guy, and in those rare moments I caught a glimpse of her, it looked as though life was treating her well. I'd tell myself that I was happy for her. Emily, more than anyone, deserved a wonderful life, and Marge feels exactly the same way. Even after I'd married Vivian, my sister would sometimes turn to me in quiet moments and say, "That Emily sure was something. You really messed that up, didn't you?"

I was born in Charlotte, North Carolina, and aside from a single year in another city, I've lived there all my life. Even now, it strikes me as almost impossible that Vivian and I met in the place where we did, or even that we ever met at all. After all, she, like me, was from the south; like mine, her job required long hours, and she seldom went out. What are the odds, then, that I'd meet Vivian at a cocktail party in Manhattan?

At the time, I was working at the agency's satellite office in midtown, which probably sounds like a bigger deal than it really was. Jesse Peters was of the opinion that pretty much anyone who showed promise in the Charlotte office had to serve at least a little time up north, if only because a number of our clients are banks, and every bank has a major presence in New York City. You've probably seen some of the commercials I've worked on; I like to think of them as thoughtful and serious, projecting the soul of integrity. The first of those commercials, by the way, was conceived while I was living in a small studio on West 77th, between Columbus and Amsterdam, and trying to figure out whether my ATM accurately reflected my checking account, which showed a balance with just enough funds to purchase a meal deal at a nearby fast food place.

On a Saturday night in May, a CEO of one of the banks who *loved my vision* was hosting a charity event to benefit MoMA. The CEO was seriously into art—something I knew nothing about—and even though it was an exclusive, black-tie event, I hadn't wanted to attend. But his bank was a client and Peters was my *do-what-I-tell-you-or-else* boss, so what could I do?

I remember almost nothing about the first half hour, other than that I clearly didn't belong. Well over half the people in attendance were old enough to be my grandparents, and practically everyone was in a different stratosphere when it came to our respective levels of wealth. At one point, I found myself listening as two gray-haired gentlemen debated the merits of the G-IV when compared to the Falcon 2000. It took me a while to figure out that they were comparing their private jets.

When I turned away from the conversation, I saw

on the other side of the room a familiar-looking man who was, I soon discovered, Vivian's boss. I recognized him from late night television, and Vivian would later tell me that he considered himself an art collector. She'd wrinkled her nose when she said it, implying that he had money but no taste, which didn't surprise me at all. Despite famous guests, his show's trademark humor was best described as low-brow.

Vivian was standing behind him, hidden from my line of sight at first. Like everyone else in the room, I couldn't help watching the talk show host, even though I didn't particularly like him. A minute or so later, he took a few steps forward to greet someone, and all at once I saw her. I could only stare, suddenly wondering whether she was the reason that everyone had been gazing in their direction. Her dark hair, flawless skin, and cheekbones that supermodels dream about made me sure she was the most beautiful woman I'd ever seen.

At first I thought she was his date, but the longer I watched, the more confident I was that they weren't *together*, that she instead worked for him in some capacity. Nor was she wearing a ring, another good sign . . . but really, what chance did I have?

Yet the romantic within me was undeterred, and when she went to the bar to get a cocktail, I sidled up to the bar as well. Up close, she was even more gorgeous, and when she happened to turn in my direction, her sultry eyes drew me in.

"It's you," I said.

"Excuse me?"

"The one the Disney artists think about when they draw the eyes of their princesses."

Not great, I'll admit. Ham-handed, maybe even cheesy, and in the awkward pause that ensued, I knew I'd blown it. But here's the thing: she laughed.

"Now there's a pickup line I've never heard before."

"It wouldn't work on just anyone," I said. I offered my hand and smiled. "I'm Russell Green."

She hesitated before taking my hand, but her eyes still showed amusement.

"I'm Vivian Hamilton," she said, and I almost gasped.

Her name was *Vivian*.

Just like Julia Roberts's character in *Pretty Woman*.

How does one actually know when another is *right* for you? What kind of signals does that entail? To meet a person and think, *this is the one with whom I want to spend the rest of my life*. For example, how could Emily seem right, and Vivian seem right, when they were as different as night and day? When the relationships were as different as night and day?

I don't know, but when I think about Vivian, it's still easy to remember the heady thrill of our first few evenings together. While Emily and I were warm and comfortable, Vivian and I burned hot, almost from the very beginning. Every interaction, every conversation seemed to amplify my growing belief that we were fated for one another.

As the marrying type, I began to fantasize about the paths our life together would take, our passionate connection burning forever. Within a couple of months, I was certain I wanted Vivian to be my wife, even if I didn't say as much. Vivian took longer to feel the same way about me, but by the time we'd been seeing each other six months, Vivian and I were a *serious item*, testing the waters on how each felt about God, money, politics, families, neighborhoods, kids, and our core values. More often than not, we were in agreement. Taking a cue from yet another romantic movie, the week before I moved back to Charlotte, I proposed on the viewing deck of the Empire State Building.

I *thought* I knew what I was getting when I dropped to one knee. But looking back, Vivian *knew* with certainty—not only that I was the kind of man she wanted, but *needed*.

And then what, you may wonder? After we made our vows?

Like every married couple, we had our ups and downs, our challenges and opportunities, successes and failures. When all the dust had settled, I came to realize that marriage, at least in theory, is wonderful.

In practice, though, I think a more accurate word is *complicated*.

Marriage, after all, is never quite what one imagines it will be, and even now I'm not exactly sure what I expected. Part of me—the romantic part—no doubt imagined the entire venture as an extended commercial for Hallmark cards with roses and candles and everything in soft focus, a dimension in which love and trust could surmount any challenge. The more practical side of me knew that remaining a couple over the long term was work, and took effort on both sides. It requires commitment and compromise, communication and cooperation, especially as life tends to throw curveballs, often when we least expect them. Ideally, the curveball slides past the couple with little damage; at other times, facing those pitches together makes the couple more committed to each other.

But sometimes, the curveballs end up smacking us in the chest and close to the heart, leaving bruises that never seem to heal.